Perdita, the Herb-woman's daughter, didn't seem the least surprised to see us. "So you had to come again," she said, without ceremony. "I told my mother about last time, and she said I was to warn you once more. Leave well alone."

"*You* go in the Wilderness," said Lalage.

"I told you before. I know what I'm doing. You obviously don't. There are certain Powers that create Their own pathways, pathways that sometimes cross upon themselves, making the Power even stronger. This—" she gestured towards the Wilderness "—is such a place!"

"Are they good or bad? Are they dangerous?" Brian was goggle-eyed.

"They are neither good nor bad. They are just there. And no, They aren't dangerous, unless They are disturbed. Then They are capable of destroying anything in Their way." She paused for a moment. "Don't say I didn't warn you." Then she was gone, leaping down the hill till she went out of sight.

There was a short silence, broken by Lally. "Well, what a load of old rubbish!" she yawned delicately and stretched her arms above her head. "Shall we go, then. . . ?"

BAEN BOOKS BY MARY BROWN
The Unlikely Ones
Pigs Don't Fly
Master of Many Treasures
Strange Deliverance

STRANGE DELIVERANCE

MARY BROWN

STRANGE DELIVERANCE

Copyright © 1997 by Mary Brown

A Baen Books Original

Baen Publishing Enterprises
P.O. Box 1403
Riverdale, NY 10471

ISBN: 0-671-87795-X

Cover art by Larry Elmore

First printing, August 1997

Distributed by Simon & Schuster
1230 Avenue of the Americas
New York, NY 10020

Printed in the United States of America

This One For
All
Our Friends

Acknowledgments—

To my husband, Peter, the
acme of patience and perseverance.
To the Baen "family,"
especially Jim and Toni.
To Sam—for all sorts of
reasons, none of them
concerned with writing a book!

BOOK ONE

REFUGEES

CHAPTER ONE

The Crew - (i)

The information banks were nearly full and had already started their retransmissions for analysis over a million miles away, to be then forwarded on from a Nymph-Ship to the main Nest. Even with their own speed home, aided by the most convenient of time-warps, all their data would have been processed long before they finally docked.

The whole craft hummed quietly as it completed its penultimate orbit. The full crew was on alert for these last few hours, moving busily about their duties; manning the controls, feeding the information banks, recharging the power-rods, discharging waste, preparing the stock for their last milking. Time enough to rest, suspend animation, when the machine was set on course for home.

Earlier visual examination of the planet below had shown the extent of the devastation. Fires raged out of control, seas steamed and rivers boiled, vast areas of land were blackened and pitted, cities lay in ruins and the amount of smoke and cloud needed the strong auto-rays to pierce their density and show a clearer picture on the monitors. The pollution sensors were still busy analyzing the air quality beneath, separating the usual contaminants from the new chemical and biological killers. These latter were most important, for if normal forays were to be made in the future and land expeditions mounted, there must be sufficient guard against their own destruction.

Information continued to come in. It seemed there were still many areas beneath that appeared normal, green and flourishing, with indication of both human and animal life, but some of these would already be infected by man-made destruction even now being borne on the errant winds, and would within weeks be empty and barren. . . .

The spacecraft accelerated over the melting snows and ice of the Antarctic and started on its last orbit.

The Villagers - (i)

The Mayor called an Extraordinary General Meeting in the Town Hall. For days rumor and counter-rumor had flown faster than the birds between town, village and hamlet, and the occasional garbled news bulletins they received on radio—the TV stations, even the local ones, had long since packed up—only made matters worse.

Everyone was uneasy, nervous and tempers were short. In spite of the continued good weather the stock were neglected, allotments untended. Several of the youngsters had already left for the city to the east, and the trickle had become a flood. This was the last thing the village needed, for it was coming up to harvest, and although the first hay harvest had been good, the next was ready for cutting, and the weather wouldn't hold for ever. Besides, the corn was ripening and there was the sugar beet to consider. The orchards promised well, winter-roots looked good, the hens were laying, but with communications having broken down over the last few weeks they might well have to depend on what they could produce themselves this winter, and if all the labor force decamped where would they be?

Damn this war! Or wars ... Whatever it was, it had nothing to do with them. Their state had never quarreled with anyone else. Neutral they were, neutral they had ever been. And lucky, too, with all those pictures of floods and earthquakes and such in other parts of the globe. Until the last couple of weeks nothing had touched them either, but then had come the increasingly annoying cuts in electricity and the busy signal on most mains telephone calls. The mobiles still worked, of course, but even with them there were an ominous number of silences on the other end.

That was another thing; those mobiles needed batteries, and that was yet more hassle, because the last weekly consignment of goods from the city had been three weeks ago, and then short of what they had ordered. Instead of the usual canned goods, tobacco, soft drinks, chocolate, long-life bread, cosmetics, videos, batteries, pet foods and biscuits, they had sent salt, pepper, spices, cutlery—why cutlery, for God's sake!—seed-packets—who wanted lettuce, tomato and radish seeds when the actual vegetables were delivered fresh?—and sheets and sheets of useless paper.

Obviously the wholesalers had got their orders

mixed, and some idiot in the village had accepted the load without checking the manifest. What was worse, he had signed for it and paid for it. . . . Of course he had tried to get hold of the suppliers, but so far hadn't been able to get through.

Then there was the problem of fuel; neither the gas tanker nor the bottled Camp-Gas trailer had called for two months, and they were dangerously low on both. Mayor? Who'd be Mayor? More like a scapegoat shopkeeper, that's what he was. Reelection? Who wanted that kind of trouble!

The Mayor looked down at his audience. All there, even the children. Of course with the constant cuts in the electricity and no direct programs on the TV, everyone was bored silly with rewatching the same old videos. Even a meeting at the Town Hall was better than twiddling their thumbs, and not everyone had CD players or radios.

No, there were still some absentees. Old Nial, the stockman, was missing but then his wife had broken her ankle last week, so he would be home with her. And the Herb-Woman never showed her face in the village if she could help it. "Herb-Woman," indeed! More like witch, if you asked him. . . .

He cleared his throat. "Citizens: I have called you here to discuss the worsening situation. . . ."

The Passengers - (i)

The entrance hall of the station was packed solid with shouting and screaming would-be passengers, and still they poured in through the arched portico. Long ago someone had tried to shut the gates, but they had been shoved to one side. In front of the gates to platform nine stood a double line of the militia, rifles at the ready.

The public address system was screeching and whining at full blast, but what with the din below and the inevitable distortion, no words were intelligible.

All of a sudden, intentionally or not, the gates to platform nine swung open, and after a moment's astonished hesitation—after all most of them had been there since dawn at the rumor of a last train— there was a concerted rush. The soldiers were swept aside, people fought with fists, elbows, feet, to be first onto the platform.

The train was there, sure enough, all ten cars of it, one of the older Volley-Class monorails, but all the doors were firmly shut. The crowd, increasingly frustrated, banged on the sides of the cars and some even tried to smash in the windows with fists, shoes, sticks, whilst above the hubbub the address system kept on bellowing out incomprehensible rubbish.

Suddenly the doors of the foremost carriage slid open, and there was a charge as everyone within reach piled in. It had obviously been intended that the rush should be controlled, carriage by carriage, but someone had forgotten to close the connecting doors and more and more passengers piled in until the whole train was rocking from side to side. Once this was realized the driver opened all the doors, fearful for his machine, and people poured in from every direction.

People were literally trampled underfoot, luggage— one suitcase per person—was torn away and everywhere fighting broke out.

Then the militia opened fire.

The Crew - (ii)

They were halfway round their final orbit when disaster struck. They never discovered what had hit them, but it was immediately obvious that the damage was considerable. Within minutes the craft was effectively without main power, though the auxiliary motor kicked in automatically.

If it had only been the power that was affected they could have managed to complete their survey and limp home safely, but it was more than that. The steering gear had also been seriously damaged, the craft refusing to obey commands, yawing violently from side to side. As they were still within Earth's gravitational pull they would have to do something, fast.

The automatic damage-sensors confirmed their worst fears. Apart from the loss of main power and the crippling of the steering, one of the main boosters was inoperable and the landing gear was suspect.

There were two options open to them. Their orders had always been perfectly clear; if there was the slightest chance of either the crew or craft being "captured" (and that included even the smallest part of the craft that could be used for analysis) they were to self-destruct. If, however, they had to land to correct a malfunction, provided the craft could take off again within a reasonable time and without discovery, then they were permitted to make the decision themselves. Of course, if the damage was irreparable, then they would immediately abort.

The crew conferred, decided. Within seconds a message was on its way to their nearest contact, on a routine Mars scan. Now to find a landing site. The way they were slipping sideways towards the earth meant they had no time to choose beyond what lay just beneath. The scanners showed two possible sites that answered their needs: remoteness from civilization and freedom from contamination.

They chose and set the coordinates. Now all they could do was wait.

The Villagers - (ii)

". . . and so I want you all to realize that this mood of senseless panic is thoroughly counter-productive." The Mayor finished his speech, not entirely satisfied that he had convinced his audience. "Any questions?"

There was a general hubbub, but at last a young man stood up at the back.

"It's coming nearer all the time. My cousin called me yesterday and said they were evacuating all the cities to the west." He tapped the mobile phone in his top pocket. "Says the air is contaminated."

"There's no official confirmation of that," began the Mayor, but he was interrupted by a woman at the front.

"You trust these Government reports? All they want to do is keep us quiet—"

"That's right! They don't want us to know the truth!" shouted another voice.

The noise grew; people were standing up, shaking their fists.

The Mayor spread his hands placatingly. "Listen! Whatever what's-his-name's cousin says, we have no definite news. I propose we pull ourselves together and stay put. After all this village has been here for hundreds of years and—"

"Hundreds of years be damned!" yelled someone else. "This is here and now!"

The Mayor thumped the table. "All right! What do you suggest we do?"

For a while they debated, and a vote was taken. It was agreed that they would wait another twenty-four hours before deciding further, in the meanwhile trying their best to contact reliable sources for news.

The Mayor should have been satisfied with his temporary victory, but he knew in his heart that it would only take the smallest spark of unease to fire a panic-stricken mass exodus. . . .

The Passengers - (ii)

No one knew whether it was the bullets or the panic that left so many collapsed on the ground but they were past caring now, trampling over those who had fallen like so much trash. Fear and panic had overtaken them all, the train was packed as tight as a Holocaust cattle-truck and, as a second volley rang out and the shrieks and screams of the wounded and dying rose above the general hubbub, the train driver decided enough was enough. He pressed the button to close the doors and opened the throttle.

The wheels screamed in protest, trying to get a grip on the rail, juddering and shaking the whole train, while the doors slammed open and half-shut again and again, frustrated from full closure by the bodies that jammed them, still struggling to get aboard.

The train started to move, imperceptibly at first, then at walking-pace, accelerating all the time. At the last door of the last carriage of all, five students were trying to pull the sixth free of the still-slamming automatic doors.

"Come on, come on, Padraig!" they urged, pulling at whatever part of him they could hold.

"For Christ's sake! Can't you see I'm stuck. . . ."

Just at that moment a strong arm held the doors open a fraction longer than usual and, as Padraig fell into the arms of his friends, a small girl carrying a suitcase was shoved on behind him by a stout, bearded man.

"Take her, take her, I beg!" he cried "I can't—"

The rest of his words were lost as the doors finally slammed shut and the train, gathering speed, left him behind. As the train finally quit the station Padraig found himself clutching a sobbing child to his breast.

The train roared on into the gathering darkness and those on board sorted themselves out as best they could, which wasn't easy as the carriage was meant to hold sixty seated, thirty standing and was now crammed with some two hundred.

The six students had managed to clear a small space near the toilets, fiercely guarding the six-packs which, to them, had been their essential luggage. Padraig sat down in the corridor and gathered the little girl, still sniveling, onto his knee and gave her a reassuring cuddle.

"What's your name then, darlin'?"

The Crew - (iii)

Side-slipping in the gravity pull to slow their speed, nevertheless the Earth was coming closer at a frightening rate. Now they were only just above the cloud layer, although the auto-rays showed a clear path

down. Far away to the right and to the left was concrete
evidence of continued conflict: fires raging out of
control, intermittent explosions, though these latter
were far less frequent than they had been days earlier.

Now the topography beneath was clear; to the west
was a great area of man-planted forest, to the north
high mountains, to the east an area of blasted heath,
and to the south an area of plain. It was obvious that
contamination was still driving in from the east, but
their weather sensors confirmed that the wind would
change overnight and blow the poisons back whence
they had come.

Some two miles to the south of the chosen site
lay a cluster of buildings, but it should be simple
enough to frighten away the inhabitants, if they had
not left already. The crew set their communications
center to the appropriate Earth-Speak for the area
they were approaching, in case it was necessary to
contact the Earthlings.

Now all they could hope for was that there was
enough power and the landing gear would hold up
in order to avoid a crash-landing and the inevitable
self-destruction.

The time had come. The crew pressed the correct
buttons, ensured the cattle were in suspension and
that the information banks were still churning out
their data.

Now all they could do was wait. . . .

The Villagers - (iii)

The villagers started to trail out of the open doors
at the end of the hall into the Church Square, but

it seemed some were not done arguing their views.
About halfway down the aisle a woman, her back
turned to the platform, was busy haranguing anyone
who would stop and listen. The Mayor groaned;
she was the village's chief busybody, on every
committee that would have her. Not believing in
direct confrontation, she would wait until everything
was decided before undermining the same with
contrary argument, until her opponents really
believed they might have made a mistake.

She was in full flow. " . . . more than time we had
a new one, with a bit more go to him." Could she
mean me, wondered the Mayor, trapped on his
platform, as the aisle was now jammed. "I, for one,
have had enough! They may say this war has nothing
to do with us, so why the electricity cuts, the empty
shops, no gas bottles, and all these rumors flying
about? Forgotten about us, they have, stuck away
in this festering hole . . . I'll tell you this. Very first
thing in the morning I'm taking my husband and
my son and we're going to the city where there's
plenty of everything."

Some youngster made a remark the Mayor couldn't
hear, but she rounded on the boy immediately.

"You'll laugh the other side of your face when there's
no more fuel for that rattletrap of yours! Least it'll
keep you quiet: no more of that confounded racket
first thing in the morning." She returned to her theme.
"My sister's got more than enough room for us and
a lovely deep cellar in case any old bombs go astray.
I'm not standing for any more of this shilly-shallying
and I strongly advise you to follow my—our—
lead. . . ." How long she would have gone on nobody

would ever know, for at that moment a man burst through the doors at the back and shouted, his face full of horror, "Lights in the sky! We're being attacked. . . ."

The Passengers - (iii)

The girl slept uneasily, her tear-stained cheek resting against Padraig's shoulder. The six students had shared out what little food they had, but it seemed she didn't fancy garlic sausage and gherkins; instead she opened her suitcase and took out a pack of jam sandwiches and a small carton of milk, amusing them by the fastidious way she wiped her hands and mouth afterwards on a paper napkin.

She had been no bother at all, except to ask once, anxiously: "When will Papa come?"

They had glanced at one another. "On the next train," said Padraig soothingly, knowing full well this was the last one. When she had finally fallen asleep they discussed what to do with her when they reached their destination.

"The orphanage, perhaps?" said Arne, who was the eldest. "Or the police, to see if they can trace any relatives."

"They'll have their hands full already," said Erik. "And the orphanage is Catholic. She's Jewish, unless I'm mistaken."

"Orphanages will take any faith," said Rod, rummaging for another beer. "Leastways I think so. . . ."

Alan yawned. "I'm for a piss. I'll take the child for a bit when I come back, Paddy." He prepared to fight his way through the crush of bodies, followed by the sixth of the group, Stew.

Half an hour later the beer was finished and they settled down with their backs against the inner wall of the carriage, their legs stretched out in front of them. They had been traveling for two days and were near exhausted. Like all the others on the train they were refugees from a conflict they could not understand, a world suddenly gone mad. Caught unawares on a field trip, they had struggled back to the college, only to be told the town was in enemy hands, although it wasn't clear just who "the enemy" was at that stage. It was Arne who suggested they go north, where he had distant relatives, and they had been lucky enough to hear of the train going the way they wanted. Lucky, too, to have been able to fight their way on at the last minute. Now, like the other refugees they slept where there was an inch or two to spare, too sleepy even to curse at other passengers who wanted to pass one way or the other for the toilets, stumbling awkwardly over prone bodies, legs and feet.

They were perhaps two hours into the five-hour journey when suddenly all the lights went out—

The Crew - (iv)

The crew pressed another button, and immediately all guiding lights were on, beaming across the countryside. Normally these would not be necessary, but under their part-crippled situation it was essential they had as much illumination as possible. Of course they risked alerting the Earthlings, but that was a risk that had to be taken. In their experience fear played a greater part in human makeup than did curiosity, but just in case they would let off some of their fireballs at the last moment.

By Earth-time they were less than a couple of minutes from landing. Below them the landing-site was clearly visible, but on closer examination it looked less inviting than at first. It was much more overgrown than they had thought, and in fact there was only one oval space that was clear; it would take very fine judgment to bring them down safely.

It looked increasingly likely they might have to use the final option, but in any case it was time to release the fireballs. . . .

The Villagers - (iv)

No one could have stopped the panic.

Everyone ran like rabbits as the fireballs zoomed overhead, hovered over the roofs, zig-zagged down the streets, formed a complicated dancing pattern in the air over the church, whose bells were ringing madly in a jangled carillon, and appeared to chase anything that moved.

Doors slammed, women were screaming, children crying hysterically. In every house shutters were pulled tight and everyone cowered under beds, tables, wherever they felt safest, eyes tight shut, ears covered. Out in the fields the stock ran around like crazy, but there was nowhere for them to hide, crying their fear to the impervious moon.

Suddenly there was a gigantic boom that rattled the windows and partially deafened most of the villagers; tiles slid off roofs, the church bells fell silent, and the moon was extinguished behind a bank of cloud.

It was a long time before anyone ventured to peek through a shutter, let alone open a door, but when they did, and had convinced themselves there was no more immediate danger, the whole place erupted into frantic activity. Engines were checked and revved and every last drop of gas and oil was emptied from the small filling station, not only into tanks but also cans and even bottles. Meanwhile the women and children were busy emptying refrigerators and freezers into Thermo bags and boxes, rolling up sleeping-bags and blankets; sandwiches were made, pets collected up, valuables and money tucked into bags, best clothes packed, all portable electrical goods stowed in trunks and trailers until finally, after less than four hours, the whole village was packed up and ready to go. Now all they could do was sit and await the first light of dawn. . . .

The Passengers - (iv)

And as soon as the lights were extinguished, the train seemed to gather speed. People woke from uneasy sleep as the carriages started to rock from side to side, to find themselves in darkness with nothing to be glimpsed outside on this cloudy night. Standing passengers stumbled and fell, or bruised themselves against the walls, trying to keep their balance.

In the last carriage, someone screamed, and soon they were all shouting and calling out, panicking.

The child woke with a start from the two laps that were cushioning her and clutched the nearest shoulder, which happened to be Padraig's.

He held her tight. "Hold on, darlin'! Just a bit of a blackout. . . . The lights will be on again soon. Let's sing a little song, shall we? Do you know 'Early one morning'?"

None of the passengers were ever to know that the driver of the train had suffered a sudden stroke and had fallen across the controls as he passed out, both shutting off the lights and opening the throttle to "Full." Had they still been on the plain this last would have posed no problem for there were automatic brakes on the line to curb any excessive speed, but up here in the mountains there were no such checks. While they still continued to climb the sheer weight of the train and it's overload would keep the wheels on the rail, but once they leveled out to approach the Mile-High bridge they were in trouble unless they could slow down. . . .

The Crew - (v)

False dawn was slowly greying the night sky, but already the small creatures of the wood were astir. The bats had returned to their roosts, and the butterflies and other flying insects would await the rising of the sun, but a few moths still fluttered about and a sleepy hedgehog ambled across the clearing towards its nest, too blind to sense anything unusual. Every now and again there was a rustle in the branches above and the wakening twitter of birds, but the first creature to venture near the strange object that lay where yesterday had been a stretch of rough grass and small bushes, was a curious rabbit. It approached cautiously, ready to thump out an alarm signal at the slightest movement, but the thing was still. The rabbit stood up on its haunches, sniffing the air, but there was no alien scent. Satisfied it was not threatened, the rabbit dropped down again and began to crop the grass.

Before long the whole wood was awake with its usual hum of activity, but from the strange craft, tilted crazily to one side, there was no movement, no sound, nothing. . . .

Except silence.

The Villagers - (v)

At first light everyone was ready, yawning a little maybe from their disturbed night, but packed and fueled and anxious to be off. The Mayor had done his best to dissuade the villagers from leaving, but realizing he would be the only one left behind, he had used what little authority he had left and had maneuvered the mayoral vehicle to the head of the queue waiting to cross the bridge.

Every vehicle that boasted an engine had been brought into use, and so had most of the trailers. In spite of the way people kept glancing anxiously over their shoulders towards the place where they had heard last night's explosion, if that was what it had been, there was a sort of holiday atmosphere about the whole evacuation. They even listened patiently to a prolonged blessing from the priest.

The Mayor made a last check; yes, everyone had

locked up. No, no one had been left behind. (No one except old Nial and his wife who had refused to budge, so at least there would be someone to take care of the stock until they returned.) There was the Herb-Woman too, of course, but then she wasn't really part of the village. Yes, continued the chorus, they had brought enough to eat and drink until they reached the city, hopefully later today, tomorrow at the latest. No, they hadn't been able to contact any of their relatives, unfortunately.

The Mayor knew he couldn't delay any longer. With a long blast on the whistle he had thought to borrow from the school, he waved the cavalcade forward, a motorcycle scout at his side to ride back and forth along the train of vehicles to ensure they traveled at the pace of the slowest. It was just like one of those vintage movies of the Wild West, thought the Mayor, settling down to try to enjoy himself.

They had gone scarcely a mile however, when his scout roared up alongside to report that all the traffic had been too much for the rickety bridge. Just as the last vehicle had gotten across safely it had groaned and collapsed into the river beneath.

The Mayor crossed himself: a bad omen. They would be away longer than they had figured. . . .

The Herb-Woman stood in the old square and watched them go, her finger caressing the ring on her right hand. Nothing but bad could come of it, she was sure. She had been gathering herbs last night—for some were better culled by the light of the moon—and she had witnessed both the strange craft hovering just before it disappeared in the

direction of the Wild Wood with a terrific explosion,
and the fireballs whizzing around the village. She
had guessed what the outcome would be. As for
herself, she was not afraid: her ring would give her
warning of any imminent danger.

She sighed. Why were people so quick to panic?
Old Nial and his wife wouldn't have left though, she
was sure of that. She would just go and rebandage
the old woman's ankle, give her another of her
draughts, and then go and see if she could help Nial
milk the stock. Already the half-dozen cows were
clustered by their gate, bellowing anxiously.

Behind her the rising sun lit the tips of the
mountains to the west the color of blood. . . .

The Passengers - (v)

The child opened her eyes and blinked in the rays
of the rising sun. She closed them again at once
because her head hurt. Putting up her hand she
discovered some sort of rough bandage. Puzzled, she
sat up slowly, because other parts of her hurt, too—
her back, a knee, a shoulder—and opened her eyes
again. Apparently she had been lying on the ground
with someone's jacket covering her, but she still felt
cold and shivery. Also hungry and thirsty. But where
was she? Why weren't they on the train? Was this
some sort of station, then? And why was it so quiet,
except for someone groaning behind those trees. . . .

Arne looked up from where they were trying to
make some decency out of the dead, and nudged
Padraig. "Your little charge is awake. Keep her away
from the worst."

The dead had been laid out in the lee of a little wooded hillock, their faces covered. There was little else the survivors could do, the ground was too rocky to dig graves, even if they had had the tools to do it. Later, perhaps, they could shuffle them closer together and build a cairn, so that at least they would be spared the crows, which were already circling.

There were clouds of birds in the ravine as well. Last night when the train had jumped the rail just short of Mile-High Bridge, rearing into the air like a tortured centipede before twisting free of the last two carriages and plunging down onto the rocks and river below, the survivors of those two last carriages had counted themselves lucky, even though the carriages had rolled and bumped their way down the steep embankment before coming to rest on their sides.

They had had to work all through the moonlit night to extract the trapped, both dead and living, the latter's screams and groans indicating their whereabouts. At dawn they took a count; of the three hundred and ninety-five who had been traveling in those last two carriages, ninety were dead already, and twenty more so badly injured they were unlikely to last the day. Of the rest, some fifteen had severely broken bones and couldn't be moved, which left two hundred and seventy either whole or with minor injuries only.

At first light a small stocky man with cropped fair hair had turned himself into a sensible organizer. It was he who had discovered a doctor with a sprained ankle and two trainee nurses among the survivors, and between them they were able to tend to the worst of the wounded. Of course there were no painkillers, except for a few aspirin and such among the other passengers, but they had done the best they could. The organizer had also sent half a dozen of the youngest down into the ravine, firstly to ascertain if there were any other survivors, and secondly to fill all the containers they could muster with fresh water.

There were no other survivors; those not killed by the fall had been drowned. They reported some mutilated bodies on the banks of the rushing river, but the water was already carrying the wreck of the train farther downstream. Well over a thousand must have perished, and in those panic-stricken moments after the crash Padraig thought the little girl must be among them too. She had been torn from his arms as the carriages rolled down the embankment, and when he had finally located her she had lain so still he had feared the worst.

However she was still breathing, and when he saw the bump on her head he guessed it was no worse than slight concussion. He had found water still trickling in one of the toilets, dampened his scarf and bound it round her head, then laid her gently down and covered her with his jacket. Now she was trying to stand up, her eyes full of suspicion and fear.

"Hey there," he said, sitting down beside her and drawing her onto his lap. "You have a nice nap? I'll bet you're hungry. . . ." He drew out a packet of cookies he had found among the wreckage. "And here I have the coldest and freshest water in the world. I should know, I went and drew it fresh, just for you, Princess!" She smiled a little at this, as he had intended.

"What happened? Where are we? Where's the train?"

"Breakfast first, questions afterwards . . ." But as she chewed on the cookies, his own stomach contracting with hunger as he watched her, he gave her an edited version of what had happened. To his surprise she seemed to take the news phlegmatically.

"Is that why my head hurts? Did you put the bandage on?" He nodded. Her face crumpled. "I've got other places that hurt, too. . . ."

He made a quick examination; nothing broken or sprained, just bumps and bruises, but enough to make a little girl uncomfortable.

"In that case, I shall just have to make a magic. Close your eyes." As she did as she was told he extracted a couple of fresh tablets from a bottle he always carried for his student hangovers. "Open your eyes! There . . ."

"Those are just aspirin!"

"They'll do the trick, just you see! Got any water left in that bottle?"

She took the tablets obediently, and soon he saw the frown between her eyes smooth out.

"Better?" She nodded. "Well, you just lie down and rest. I've got to help with those who are worse than you."

"Okay. Thanks. . . . I want to go to the bathroom."

Wordlessly he pointed to some bushes, but when she didn't return in five minutes he went in search of her, only to find she was standing by the side of the newest dead, those they hadn't been able to make decent yet. He made to snatch her up and carry her away, but she skipped to one side.

"I just wanted to see if Papa was right. . . . Yes, it's just as he said." She squatted down beside one of the men, who had died more or less peacefully, so his face was quite smooth, although his eyes were still open.

"You see?"

"See what?" He was genuinely puzzled, most children would not want to examine a corpse so intently. Perhaps that knock on the head—

"Papa always said that when you were dead you didn't need your body any more. The soul has already gone. Just look at his eyes. . . ."

"I'd rather not." He pulled at her hand. Already the flies, those ubiquitous pests, were crawling round the man's mouth. "It's not nice . . ."

"It's not nasty. He's flown away, don't you see? He's free! All that's left is just garbage." And she looked at him with a smile so incredibly sweet that, in spite of the bandage that made her look like a mini-bandit, he felt his heart lurch. "I'm glad Papa was right. We can go now. . . ."

By midday everything had settled into some sort of order, thanks to the man they were now calling the Organizer, with a capital letter. The dead had been buried under a pile of stones, the wounded were in shelter beneath the nearest trees, more water was collected, foragers sent out for mushrooms or edible fungi, berries, nuts or wild roots. Another man, who had brought his hunting rifle with him, disappeared into the nearby woods to look for game. Wood was being collected for a fire later and extra coats and clothes sorted for the night chill. Any leftovers of food—cookies, fruit, chocolate—had been put on one side for distribution.

Padraig dozed off, utterly exhausted, to be awoken by Erik.

"It seems the Organizer wants to talk to all the able-bodied." He nodded towards a rocky outcrop some distance from the wounded.

"Why? What's up?"

Erik shrugged. "Search me. But he looks pretty determined."

The Organizer - (i)

Hans Harald Gross looked down at his audience. He was pretty sure he had them captive now. He was a good judge of people, even if he said it himself, and this lot boasted no intellectuals. So, plain facts, larded liberally with rhetoric, and strung round with strings of friendliness, but salted with clear indications of who was to be boss. All ready for the pot.

He had spelt out quite brutally the situation in which they found themselves: miles from anywhere with no hope of rescue. Numbers of injured, plenty of water, but no shelter, no food. Beat them down first, bring them to the brink of despair, then offer a lifeline, however tenuous. He realized he was enjoying himself, his mind racing around like a supercharged powerboat, mixing his metaphors like mad, but who among them would notice? Perhaps the schoolmaster and his wife, there at the back— he would need them—but no one else, not even the six agricultural students, perhaps the most essential to his plan.

But he mustn't make his ideas too plain at first; let them make the suggestions and be encouraged to make the right ones, so that he could take control at just the right moment, blaming it on them if anything went wrong. Not that it would; this was the chance he had been waiting for all his life, the chance to found—

"What about the wounded? My husband . . ."

Patience . . . "As I said, in order to help the wounded we must find them food and shelter. There is nothing here, so we must go farther afield."

"We can't just leave them!"

"Of course not. I suggest that some of you volunteer to stay behind—perhaps those less fit to travel and the near relatives of those hurt, while the rest of us seek some hamlet or other which will provide what we need until we can get on our feet again."

"But where are these hamlets? Which way do we go?"

"Who goes? How many?"

"And who will lead us?"

This was what he had been waiting for. He held up his hand. "You are all sensible folk. You tell me the ways we cannot go."

After a lot of prompting they came to the right answers. Not south, the way they had come, because that way was the war they were trying to escape. The west was impassable, with the mountains rearing to the sky. That left the north, the way the train was headed before it crashed, or the east. He encouraged them to work out for themselves just how far they would have to walk to the north before they reached civilization, pointing out that it was inhospitable country with no way-stations to signal any civilized communities. He then gestured to the east, where the land sloped down to a thickly wooded plain that stretched into the misty distance. "If I were leading you, that is the way I should go. I'm pretty sure there are signs of civilization over there. . . ." And he pointed to where there might just be a plume of smoke rising into the sky. He did not add that he had carefully studied what scanty maps he had brought with him before addressing the group, nor reveal that he had been this way once before. Then they had hauled him away with the cuffs on, but that had been eight years ago. He remembered the farm where he had hidden, and especially the girl. . . .

If he could lead them to at least one place where they received help, then they should follow him the rest of the way "And if we find one place," he continued, "then there will be others." He hoped he was right—no, he knew he was! "As for who goes and who stays—that is up to you to decide. Let's make up our minds later today—hopefully after we have had a bite to eat," for from his elevation he had seen the hunter returning, waving cheerfully.

He expected a deputation later on, he wouldn't press the point of leadership right now—and he was not disappointed. After they had dined sparsely and greedily on what the hunter and foragers could find— four rabbits and two game birds from the former, six fish from the river down in the ravine caught by a couple of the students, all spit-roast—and various mushrooms, fungi, roots, berries and nuts from the other searchers. Barely a mouthful for each. All the better, thought Gross, sitting a little apart from the rest. Let them understand what hunger means. . . . From one of the inner pockets of his capacious all-weather jacket he palmed a bar of "Extra" and nibbled at it appreciatively. They said that one a day could keep you going for a fortnight. Well, he would see. . . .

He rewrapped half of the bar and slipped it back as he saw a small group of men approaching. This was it then.

The Villagers - (vi)

The Mayor finished his sandwich. High noon, and this had been their first halt. So far everyone's vehicles had stood up well, they had made steady progress, but the city was still some six or seven hours distant. They had met no-one else on the road, which could be good news, could be bad. Whatever . . .

He could see those who had gotten out of their vehicles were lying down in the shade, some of them looking as though a nap was in order; this wouldn't do! Okay, so some of them were elderly, but they must just keep on going. He blew his whistle, sent one of the motorcyclists to the rear to chivvy them up, and managed to get them all ready to move in reasonable time, but still they had wasted a half-hour.

No more halts he decided, and that was why when they found a curious mist lying across their way, he drove straight into it, the others following. It would be clear on the other side.

Only there was no "other side," and none would ever return to the village. . . .

The Organizer - (ii)

The greyness of dawn, and a slight autumn mist rising from the ground; everyone conversing quietly, as if afraid of waking the day. They were bound to feel nervous, thought Gross, despising them even as he made excuses. Never mind, he would toughen them up.

Needing little sleep himself he had moved among those slumbering and awake last night, listening, assessing, encouraging. After the voting on his leadership, he had tried to ensure he took those he needed most. To his (hidden) fury the hunter and two of the students had decided to try the trail to the north and wouldn't be budged. With them would go another thirty or so, but no other specialists. Some, of course, had decided to remain with the wounded, and these could be written off as far as he was concerned. Of course he had promised they would send back food and assistance as soon as they found it, and that would be a way of getting rid of those who were superfluous.

That left him with two hundred and seven, mostly healthy and fit. Of course some wouldn't make it, but with the help of Claus and George, who would be his lieutenants, they could arrange things so that no one was a burden. It was the tale of the gold that would hold those two. Jail left its mark on people, and if they couldn't see it in him, he could in them. They had asked him why they needed the other passengers, if all they were doing was raiding an old man's house in a remote hamlet.

He had winked. "Why, boys, you don't think we're taking them all the way, do you?" And they hadn't the wit to carry it further.

His greatest coup had been to persuade the doctor it was in the interests of them all that he travel with them, and not stay behind with the wounded as he had intended. Of course he would have to be carried on a litter, but it would only take a day's journey until they could requisition a cart, if he remembered the farm accurately.

He glanced at his watch: it was almost time. He expected one or two last-minute waverers, but his "specialists" were all there; the four remaining students had a little girl with them, a sister perhaps. If she survived she would make good breeding-stock in a year or two's time. . . .

He blew his whistle.

"Let's go. . . ."

CHAPTER TWO

It took those who survived nearly three weeks.

By dint of Gross pushing them hard, they reached the farmhouse he remembered by the last light of the first day. It was a poor enough place, owned by strangers to him; they had some scrawny chickens, a couple of pigs (the porker had already been salted down, to save on feed), goats for milk and cheese and, best of all, several sacks of flour in the barn.

In order to preserve appearances, so near the beginning of his enterprise, Gross bargained generously for food and shelter, letting it be known through his lieutenants, Claus and George, that he was the one paying. They built a fire in the courtyard and spit-roasted half a dozen chickens, and set the farm-wife to making bread as fast as she could. With that, goat-cheese and a stew of vegetables, they all fed better than they had since leaving the city, three days previously.

The farmer and his wife seemed to know nothing of the wars raging around them, so it was with little difficulty that Gross wheedled them out of more provisions to see them on their way, plus two cooking pots and the "loan" of their two-wheeled wagon and decrepit horse. By way of getting rid of four prize grumblers in the party, he sent them back the next day with a half-sack of flour and some cheese to relieve the wounded, loaded the small wagon with supplies and the doctor, and set off for the next farm, for which the farmer had given him directions, assuring him that it was but "a day's journey east."

In fact it took them two, and they had used all their food and the old horse was knackered before they reached it. The farm, however, was more prosperous than the first, and they were able to bargain for better provisions and exchange the horse and wagon for a pony and cart, better used to the rough tracks they had to follow. Once again Gross sent food back for the wounded, ridding himself finally of all those he didn't need for the rest of the journey.

Directions to the next farm were vaguer, but when they reached it three days later, there was barely enough for a scanty meal, and they pushed on for another two days, their food now strictly rationed. The students especially did what they could, foraging for berries, nuts and fungi, but it was not enough. One thing they had forgotten was salt, and Gross cursed himself as he saw the refugees down with the cramps or muscle fatigue. From now on, salt was essential, whatever else they had to do without. On the third day they came to their first hamlet: three farms run on a cooperative basis.

Plenty of food, but a hostile reception.

It seemed this enclave was in touch with outside life, and they viewed the intruders with suspicion, refusing at first to trade. It took real gold from Gross's hidden money-belt to persuade the inhabitants of their good intentions, but eventually they were allowed to rest and recuperate for a couple of days, eating their fill and loading the cart with enough to keep them going for a couple more days.

To Gross's fury, they lost three more of their number during the stay. One man, a skilled engineer, had hidden the fact that he was a diabetic. He ran out of insulin and that was that. Two women had feet so sore and blistered that they could not possibly continue and had to be left behind. It was either carrying them or the food and, although they were perfectly fit otherwise and would probably have been good breeders, they had to go.

The following night, on the road again, he found another fatality, a heart attack, and four defectors: a married couple and a pair of lovers. It was pretty certain that they had returned to the prosperous hamlet.

That night he gave the rest a severe lecture. Why desert when they were so near to reaching their goal, was his theme, and to reward them he "found" some precious bars of chocolate. Of course, he did not tell them he had no idea where the next food was coming from.

They listened dutifully, but the next day he had nothing to offer them but a farm that had long been deserted. They sheltered in the ruins, found and killed a couple of wild goats, a scrawny enough mouthful for each, but the students found a couple of bees' nests, so at least they had a taste of honey to keep them going.

That night they heard the far-off cry of wolves and there was an autumnal chill to the air.

By now, the thirteenth day of their journey, most in the party were suffering from exhaustion, lack of food and the niggling discomforts that lack of sanitation brings; sores wouldn't heal, scratches festered, colds turned into hacking coughs. Human relationships were deteriorating, too. Dislikes grew into something far worse, the grumbling was deafening and, worst of all from Gross's point of view, the distances traveled each day grew shorter and shorter. In the morning he decided on a desperate step. Taking four of the toughest, fittest men, he pressed on towards the east, pretending a knowledge he did not have.

He was the first to acknowledge that he had the luck of the devil. That day they found a valley with two prosperous farms. He bargained for enough food to send back to the main party with three of the men, staying behind with one of his lieutenants to await their arrival on the morrow.

He never explained when they arrived how he had managed it, but they were greeted by a splendid stew, fresh-baked bread and a positive feast of apples and pears for dessert. The barn was ready for shelter, eggs had been collected for breakfast, there was a pen of sheep ready for slaughter, two crates of chickens to be carried on the wagon and four sacks of flour ready to be loaded.

Nobody appeared from the farmhouse, and Gross explained they had vacated it especially for them, staying in the smaller house across the valley. He had decided they would stay for the next day, taking it easy, but he warned them not to approach the other farmhouse, as there was a man living there who had not agreed to be as generous with supplies as the others, and he was likely to take a potshot at anyone who approached, a warning which was realized the following day as one of their party was fired upon.

The women of the camp, being women, declared it Wash Day, rather than Rest Day. Not only was everyone to have a strip-wash, but as much as possible was to be laundered. It seemed the little girl was the only one with a change of clothing, for her small case, which she had refused to be parted from throughout the journey, yielded a complete change, so she was given the honor of the first tub. Combing her hair dry in the sun, she had just got it replaited when Arne and Padraig joined her, looking sheepish in nothing but their jackets and a scrap of toweling.

"You've got very hairy legs," she said uncritically. "Where are the rest of your clothes?"

"Strung up on a line with everyone else's," said Arne. "At least there's a good breeze to dry them. We're eating at midday. Twice in one day: unbelievable!"

She jumped to her feet. "Come on, then!"

"Where are we going?"

"Looking for mushrooms. Those funny-colored ones, orange and green. Where are Erik and Rod?"

"They couldn't find any towels," said Padraig, "And their legs are hairier than ours."

They headed for the nearest stand of pines and were lucky enough to find enough mushrooms to be piled up and collected later. Ahead there was a small dip, and a strange buzzing noise. Overhead a couple of crows were circling, and Arne and Padraig glanced at one another.

"Are you thinking what I'm thinking?"

Padraig nodded, and said to the girl: "We'll just stay here and see if we can't dig up a few more of these mushrooms, while Arne—er—goes to the bathroom."

When he returned he was paler than usual, but suggested that Padraig might feel like relieving himself as well, frowning in the direction of the girl as he did so. Padraig returned wiping his mouth as though he had been sick, and the two conversed in low tones as the girl trotted happily ahead, the mushrooms parceled up in Padraig's jacket. After the midday meal Erik and Rod went back into the forest with Arne, and returned looking serious, so she guessed they hadn't found any more mushrooms.

The following day the clothes were dry, the cart was loaded down with as much food as it could carry, and Gross addressed them all confidently.

"Well, friends, here we are about to start on the last stage of our journey. In only a few days we should find a safe haven. My friends at the farm assured me that if we strike a little south of east through the plantation we should come once more to civilization. . . ."

In fact no one had told him anything of the sort. The farmer, his wife and their eldest son had proved extremely uncooperative, so he had been forced to do something about it. The younger son had escaped across to the smaller farm before he could be dealt with, armed with the only shotgun on the place, and it was he who had been popping away at anyone silly enough to approach.

As for knowing where they were headed, the only

clues he had found were in an old atlas in the farm
kitchen. He could see the railway they had left, the
big city to the east, and in between a vast area of
forest and plantation and several tiny dots that could
have been hamlets, but not in the places they should
have been. Not surprising: the book had been printed
at the end of the last century. But there was
something—a town, a village, he could not tell
which—just on the infuriatingly worn crease in the
middle of the page, with an indecipherable name
attached. That was the way they must go. He wouldn't
be beaten: success could only be a day or two
away. . . .

". . . so let us press forward with light hearts and
our best foot forward."

As they left the farm behind them someone started
to sing "She'll be coming round the mountain," and
nearly all joined in, causing the crows to rise in a
screaming mass from the three hidden corpses in
the forest.

Now that they were walking through the plantation
proper the going was easier. The broad "rides"
provided plenty of space for at least half a dozen to
walk abreast, and the ground was cushioned with pine
needles. Because of this, and because they were fed
and rested, they made a good twenty miles that day.
Not that the endless trees didn't have their downside,
too. After a while the unfaltering straight lines began
to pall and then play strange tricks on the eyes. There
was little breeze and it was oppressively hot in the
middle of the day, but once the sun started to decline
they could feel the chill. Then there was the all-
pervading smell of pine: those who had once sought

it out in their cleaning-fluids, now swore they would seek another aroma. Anything but pine . . .

That night they feasted well on the food they had brought from the farm, though Gross realized they would have to be careful with water. They had brought bottles with them, but during the day's journey they had found only one stream, and that was a mere trickle. So he refused requests for washing-water, advising everyone to dampen a cloth and just wipe away any grease.

They were well on their way the following day when they realized something was wrong. The air had a misty, sultry quality, and a couple of people swore they could smell smoke. Gross was worried; once they reached their midday stopping-off place he sent one of the students to climb the highest pine. He reported back that, far to the south, there was a plume of smoke like a crooked finger, that was beckoning the wind right their way.

For the rest of that day Gross had them on a forced march, and that night they slept restlessly. Every now and again someone would open their eyes to where, now it was dark, a red glow illuminated the sky and, borne by a freshening south-west wind, there was a definite smell of burning.

By morning the cloud of smoke had grown into a great mass that half-filled the sky, smuts were borne on the freshening wind, and flocks of birds fled northwards overhead.

Gross grew increasingly worried; if this wind kept its direction, they were right in the path of the fire. Worse, if it shifted a couple of points to the east, their way was blocked. So, he harried them on as fast as he dared, knowing that if he didn't keep their trust he would lose them all, the strongest breaking away in fear and leaving the weakest behind.

And he needed them all. . . .

By sundown the smuts and flakes were raining down quicker and quicker, and they snatched a brief period of rest before Gross had them up well before dawn, pushing east as fast as they could. Now they could hear the roar of the flames, and there was no pretense that the fire wasn't catching up with them, fast. Personal belongings were tossed aside, their walk became a trot, the trot a run. Instead of keeping together, people broke off to right and left. Arne picked up the little girl and slung her over his shoulder, together with the suitcase she would not be parted from.

The pony drawing the cart panicked as it smelt the smoke and careened off to one side, smashing the wagon against a tree. Trapped in its harness it struggled desperately to free itself, until Padraig and Erik ran back and cut it free, picking up the injured doctor and carrying him between them as the pony dashed off ahead, snorting with terror.

By midday the sky was black above the scattered group, the smoke was drifting in tendrils through the trees, the roar of the flames almost deafening and large lumps of burning debris from the trees that were literally exploding were dropping all around them and setting fire to the undergrowth. People were fighting for breath, a middle-aged man dropped like a stone: a sudden heart attack. After a cursory examination he was left where he fell. Now running all around them were small animals—rabbits, squirrels, foxes—trying to escape the flames, while a couple of terrified deer raced right through the middle of the refugees, causing them to stumble and fall.

Suddenly the fire was around, beside, behind. One small gap remained, and with one accord all who could raced towards it with the last remains of their strength, to find themselves tumbling head over heels down a rocky incline and into a swiftly-flowing stream.

As they gratefully drank, doused smoldering spots on their clothing, coughed the smoke from their lungs then bathed their smarting eyes, it became apparent they had found a natural break in the plantation. The stream had obviously once been a larger river, for the banks were built up high on either side, and to the east there was a couple of hundred yards of stony ground before the regular lines of the plantation marched away again as far as the eye could see.

But would the fire leap across the gap and cut off any further progress? Fearfully they huddled together, all previous disagreements and grumbles forgotten in the greater peril. The thin little priest who had been with them all the way suddenly lifted his voice in prayer, and even those to whom church had meant little in the past joined their voice to his when he intoned the "Our Father."

Miracles did still happen, it seemed. They watched in growing relief as the fire roared on harmlessly to the north, only sending a few sparks in their direction. Gross ate half of the last bar of his chocolate—the manufacturer's claim had been right, he thought: I must look for some more when we reach civilization—and drank deeply, then took a swift head-count.

Seventeen missing. Well, it could have been worse. He still had a reasonable nucleus for his Great Plan.

He led them a couple of miles into the plantation, a ragged group of scarecrows, and then insisted on a small fire, although there was nothing to cook. To guide any survivors, he explained, and for the rest of the evening he blew three sharp blasts on his whistle every quarter hour to signal their survival. Two people turned up before they drifted into restless sleep, another four at dawn, but although they continued signaling until midday, there was no sign of any other survivors.

If the rest of that day was miserable, the next was worse. No food, and fierce quarreling over what little they could forage. Very little water, and some of them reduced to sucking the moisture from damp moss. Gross reckoned they had covered less than ten miles since they had fled from the fire. At this rate he would have to leave them behind and seek his own survival.

The next morning he could barely rouse them. By now some of them could hardly hobble; many of them complained of headaches, their tongues were swollen through lack of water and some were still coughing from the earlier smoke inhalation. At midday the pony turned up, obviously missing human company. Erik eventually caught it, and advised Gross to let it lead them, as it had obviously not suffered from lack of water during the time it was missing. Luckily it seemed to be heading in the right direction for Gross, and was eager to press on, fighting against the improvised halter, though placing the still-hobbling doctor on its back slowed it down a little.

They moved like underpowered robots, one foot

in front of the other, not speaking, scarcely breathing, shadowlike among the even more shadowy avenues of trees. The sun was a red ball in the west behind them when the little girl, Esther, noticed something was different. She tugged at Padraig's hand.

"Look, Paddy, look!"

"What is it, darlin'?" His mouth was so dry he could scarcely speak and his eyes were half-closed.

"The trees. They're different . . ."

At the same moment the pony gave a sudden whinny, bucked the doctor off its back and trotted off at an ever-increasing pace. Arne gave a strangled whoop of joy.

"By God, the lass is right; it's the end of the plantation!"

Oak, ash, sycamore, elm, acer, maple, thorn, brush, elder, thorn: ahead there was light through the thinning trees where sheep, horses and cattle grazed; ahead some half-mile distant were the roofs and church spire of a village.

With one accord they began to run, Gross in the van.

Esther would never forget the taste of that first meal in her new home.

At first all was jostling and confusion, with adults falling over her and cursing, but eventually one of the boys perched her up on the church steps out of the way, and another brought her a packet of cookies and a bottle of pop. When she had eaten she fell asleep, waking up to find someone's jacket around her, a bonfire in the square and all sorts of wonderful cooking smells to be sniffed and identified. Her

stomach growled in anticipation, but first she wanted
to use the bathroom. One of the women pointed to
a hall beside the church, and by the light of a couple
of lanterns she found the toilets, though they were
very smelly and wouldn't flush.

Outside again in the square it was still all bustle
and rushing about, but somehow there was now a
certain order to things. The women were all around
the fire, stirring cooking pots or poking at the flames
and the men were toting more firewood and water.
Plates and bowls and mugs were stacked up in one
corner, together with cutlery, and something large
was turning on a spit over the hottest part of the
fire. The man called Gross appeared to be directing
operations, and everyone was looking much happier.

It was quite dark now and, glancing at her watch,
she was surprised to see it was well after midnight.
She must have slept for three or four hours. At last
Arne brought her a plate, a spoon and some paper
towels.

"Not exactly the Ritz, princess, but better than
nothing. Mug of milk to follow . . . As for the chop,
fingers were made before forks!"

Why had she always been so picky over baked
beans? These were manna from heaven! The chop,
though: surely that was pork? But she had bitten
into it before the thought was properly formed and
once the taste was in her mouth she couldn't stop.
But hadn't dear Papa always said: "Adapt to the
circumstances, us Jews learnt that lesson a long, long
time ago, and that is why we have survived. . . ." Right.
This must be a circumstance, so she would enjoy it.
And afterwards, when they had all crowded into the

church and the priest, who had found a clean white frock to put over his dusty robes and invited them to eat a sort of tasteless wafer and then said lots of prayers, she was too sleepy to wonder whether this was another of Papa's "circumstances."

What had been, had been. Now was now, for the rest of her life.

The church clock grunted, wheezed and struck three, and Gross paused in his writing of lists. It was cold in the sacristy, and the candles were burning low, but there was so much to plan and to do! But he had practiced this sort of thing in his mind for so many years, that it shouldn't prove too difficult.

He had already reconnoitered the village, met the ancient stockman and his wife who, together with a mysterious Herb-Woman, had kept the beasts fed and watered since the villagers had decamped over a week ago. He had been down to the river and noted the broken bridge: unlikely anyone would be back in the near future, if at all. So, to all intents and purposes, this would be his little kingdom.

But he couldn't just stroll in and take over. Tomorrow they would vote him Mayor, no doubt about that, but he must ensure they were fed, watered, kept warm and sheltered. Thus the lists. He would send the agricultural students out tomorrow to check out the numbers and condition of the stock, plus assessing what needed to be harvested and estimating stocks of feed for the winter. He would get George, his lieutenant, to "unlock" all the houses with the set of keys he already knew he possessed, and all the food, clothing, bedding, crockery, cutlery, brooms,

brushes, pots, pans, buckets, axes, tools, bottles etc.
must be piled into the church hall for reallocation.
Each house must be inspected and people given new
homes. Then he must organize woodchoppers,
carpenters and plumbers, for without electricity
heating and sanitation would be a problem. Men and
women both must help with whatever had to be
harvested. Eventually when they bred, there would
be schooling, but that was in the future. There was
only one child at the moment, and she could be
housed with the schoolmaster and his wife so she
could learn and teach in her turn. Luckily the doctor
and the two trainee nurses had survived, and perhaps
the former could double as vet until he found
someone to be trained. . . .

He found himself yawning, snuffed the candles
and put the lists to one side till morning. He didn't
need much sleep, he congratulated himself, just like
his hero, Napoleon. Unfortunately he had not always
enjoyed the luck of the great; that fiasco in the army,
when he had been court-martialled, and the disaster
in the diamond mine—hadn't he doubled the output?
That time in prison hadn't been his fault, either: didn't
one always have to take risks to reach one's objectives?
This time it would be different, he promised himself.
This place had just fallen into his lap, together with
the refugees: an answer to a prayer. Talking of prayers,
though, that damned priest had spoilt his plans to
rename the village. He had thought "Grossville" would
have been nice, but in his exhortations earlier the
God-follower had told them all this place was their
deliverance, and they had chanted the name until
there was no doubt it would be just that: Deliverance.

Oh, well, what was in a name? He made his way out into the square, where the last embers of the fire were sparking gently in the pre-dawn breeze. Here was where they would erect his statue, together with the names of all those who had survived the forced march, but he mustn't rush things. Patience was the name of the game. . . .

A small child played around the trailer where his improvident mother was entertaining her "Friends," his only toys the debris around the site: sticks, stones, twigs, empty Coke cans. From these he had built his special place, a town where everyone lived happily ever after, because he made it so. Only he had the right to say how many streets there would be, how many people, service-stations, drug-stores, McDonalds, drive-ins, playgrounds. He could create, and he could also destroy.

Later, when he ran away from reform school, he used to dream at night of the perfect village, and when he was in jail he "borrowed" pen and paper and planned it all out. . . .

Hans Harald Gross raised his fist in the air and gave himself a silent salute. He had come into his own. They could never say it hadn't been his leadership that had brought them safely through, and by the gods! he would make sure they never forgot it!

BOOK TWO

DELIVERANCE

It was one of those con.
when you are more or less in   .ens.
I was walking down an im.   . in an
imaginary town with a bright mo.   g overhead,
and right around the corner I wa. going to find—
But I hadn't decided that yet. A handsome prince?
A wicked witch, whom I would rout with a wave of
my magic wand? A talking dog?

Then suddenly the dream went out of control; the
weather changed, I could hear the hail striking down
on the roofs around me and I ran for shelter and
snuggled into my—

My bedclothes? Blinking, I opened my eyes. Grey
dawnlight showed me only the foot of my bed and
the shadowy chest-of-drawers under the unshuttered
window. Then I heard the hail again, commonsense
reasserted itself and I realized someone must have
been chucking gravel up at the window. I tumbled
out of bed, nearly tripping over the bundle of
bedclothes I trailed with me, and peered out,
shivering.

There, his hand upraised to throw another handful,
was the pale face of Tam. "Are you ready?"

I pulled my sleepy thoughts together. Of course!

...ildren's Day, and I had
...to it ever since the August one.
... Had I overslept, then? "What's

...ven, but I thought you might like an early call.
I couldn't sleep."

"Shut up! You'll wake them all. I'll be down in a
minute."

Although we had been conducting our conversation
in strained whispers, my Nan was a very light sleeper
and my father wouldn't thank me for waking him,
though being a Saturday he was only working a half-
day. But he had always been a slug-a-bed, Nan said.

I pulled on my clothes hastily—much-patched
shorts, sleeveless tank-top—and, tucking my jacket
and sandals under one arm, I crept down the stairs,
being careful to miss out the ninth and third from
the bottom, those being the ones that creaked
abominably. A quick visit to the bathroom then I
unbolted the back door. Tam was already waiting,
having climbed the gate to the back yard. Although
he was over a half-hour early we both knew the reason,
although we didn't discuss it, and as always I invited
him to a bowl of muesli.

"If you can spare it. . . ."

Ten to one there had been nothing left out for his
breakfast again. His parents were lazy and selfish,
lavishing all their care and attention on his three elder
sisters, all now of more than marriageable age. Tam—
or Tamerlane to give his proper name—had been
an afterthought (rather the pursuit of no thought at
all, as Nan would have it), his mother had had a hard
time giving birth, and from then on he had been

neglected. He was a year older than I, but we had had our schooling together right from Pre-School, and Nan had gotten into the habit of giving me an extra sandwich for his breakfast, to be smuggled to him surreptitiously during the first lesson.

We had always gotten on well together, partly because we were of different temperaments—I was the more outgoing one—and partly because we asked little of each other. None of these demanding friendships, never out of each other's pockets, all giggles in the corner, just an easy-going relationship as comfortable as sheepskin slippers.

Last year had been a good one for the dried berries, apples and nuts so we added lots to the cereal, liberally topped up with goat's milk; and we both had seconds, before rinsing out the bowls from the jug of water in the sink, for of course the water wouldn't be on till midday. As Tam rinsed his hands, I couldn't help noticing how ill his rather tatty jacket fitted him now: perhaps Nan would help me make him another one for Christmas. He slicked back his dark hair—that was a way he differed from his plump sisters: his hair was dark and straight and he had brown eyes, whereas they had reddish hair and light blue eyes.

I fetched my wicker pannier from the larder and packed up the eggs I had hard-boiled the night before, handing Tam the apples that were to be his share of the feast. Each child in the village got paid in tokens just like the adults, ours for the extra work we did after school or in the evenings, and we were expected to provide our own food for these expeditions. We had chickens in the back yard so the eggs were easy, leaving me enough to buy the apples for Tam.

Everyone brought something different, and we shared
it out equally.

Tam handed me three tokens. "Sorry there's not
more; Grizzle pinched a couple for ribbons." Grizzle—
Griselda—was his eldest sister.

I shrugged. "Who's counting? C'mon, let's go. . . ."

It was a chilly morning and our breath plumed
out as we made our way to the Church Square, where
we had agreed to meet the others. Once the sun was
up it would be hot enough, but with the approach
of fall nights sometimes took on the sharper tongue
of frost.

Bill and Ben were already waiting for us under
the statue of Mayor Gross and they lurched to meet
us like a pair of clumsy colts, flinging their arms about
us and hugging till I thought my ribs would crack.

"That's enough. . . ."

" 'Lo Tam! 'Lo Pretty!" They capered around us,
arms linked.

"Sssh!" I put my fingers to my lips. "You'll wake
the grown-ups!"

They subsided at once and sat down on the steps
at the bottom of the statue. That at least was one
thing: they were biddable. Of course they were
fourteen now and should have been associating with
the Thirds instead of us Seconds, but their brains
hadn't grown with the rest of their bodies. Of course
it was a rule in the village that all deformed and
mutant creatures, human or animal, didn't survive
birth—I wasn't sure how this was managed, though
I guessed it must be something to do with being too
weak to survive. But Bill and Ben had slipped through
the net; they were beautiful, bouncing babies, on

whom their parents doted, and it wasn't until they were about three years old that it was agreed they were backward. By then it was too late for them just to disappear, and they grew up into handsome, inseparable children, with approximately one brain between the two. Tall, with brown curly hair, ruddy cheeks and bright blue eyes it was perhaps only their mouths that would give them away to an outsider; these were just too red, too loose, for normality.

They couldn't help it of course, but they had stayed in the lowest classes at school until, out of pity perhaps (and their still-doting parents insistence) they had been moved up into the Seconds, the nine to twelve-year-olds, and there they would probably stay. They just couldn't learn, or if they had it off pat one day, they had forgotten it the next. But they could draw, and were experts at taking things apart and putting them together again, breathing heavily as they did so. Speech they found difficult too, talking in extremely short sentences, and they tended to shorten words with more than two syllables, or twist them round; thus all our names had been abbreviated, and Tamerlane was Tam, I was Pretty. They were not William and Benjamin but Bill and Ben.

The church clock chimed a quarter of eight. Soon the streets would be busy, and the others were late. The sun was just up, casting long shadows across the square, touching with golden light the carved names on the plinth that supported the bird-limed statue of our Mayor. The names were those of all the survivors of that epic march Hans Harald Gross had led away from the wreck of the train, some forty-five years ago. There was my Nan's name, Esther

Goldstein, the youngest survivor, who became the wife of one Padraig Molloy some six years later.

I had never known my grandfather, who had died before I was born, and their daughter, my mother, was only a dim memory. Nan, as I called her, had brought me up from three years old; my father had little interest in me, for a long time wearing his grief for my mother like a kind of armor that I couldn't penetrate. He had been a widower now for seven years and, according to the rules Mayor Gross had passed, five years ought to be the limit for mourning. After that—or before, if it suited—a man was expected to find another woman of child-bearing age and wed her. Most families had two or three children at the least: ours was the exception. So, they would soon be "suggesting" he found a new mate. I didn't fancy a stepmother: the thought of someone taking over from Nan was not to be borne.

Rosellen and her brother Brian came panting up from the lower end of the village, trailing a yawning Alex.

"Sorry we're late," said Ros. "We went round to Alice's, but her Mam wouldn't let her come; says her cold's still bad."

I sighed: one short. Three if the other two ducked out; Lalage was famous for wanting her beauty sleep. At school one of our teachers referred to her, not very kindly, as our "Sleeping Beauty."

Actually there were six more "Seconds" eligible for our expeditions but their parents thought them too young (nine)—or too precious to join us, and they went down to the playground with a picnic for their day off. So we were normally ten, counting

Bill and Ben, which was quite enough to organize.

The twins leapt to their feet and lolloped away to the corner of the square which led away down past the park: that meant at least one of the two missing ones was coming. Good: both of them were there. Bill and Ben were actually impeding their progress, greeting them time and time again, but then everyone knew they were besotted by Lalage, or Lally as they called her. But then wasn't the whole village tolerant and proud of the most beautiful girl anyone could remember?

"Leave me alone!" said Lally pettishly, pushing the twins aside.

"Sorry we're late," mumbled Sven. He was a nice boy, if a bit shy. His grandfather, Arne, had been my grandfather's friend, and Nan used to say she had been pushed at first to choose between him and my grandfather when it came to marrying. But she always added that she had made the right choice. Arne and his son were shepherds, and Sven would be accepted once his schooling was finished; already he spent most of his spare time (when he wasn't waiting on Lally) with his father up in the pastures.

"Well," said Lally, "I'm ready. Where's it to be then?" She looked as if she was ready for anything but a tough hike. The ubiquitous uniform for us Seconders in the summer, boys or girls, was the briefest of shorts and tops: Lalage always managed to look as though she was one of the beautifully dressed dolls in the window of her parents' Gift Shop. Today she wore a pretty patchwork skirt with a frill at the hem and a sleeveless cotton top. Where in the world had she managed to get cotton, I wondered: someone had obviously been hoarding, for this was a material as scarce as a necklace of hens-teeth.

Not that she wouldn't end up as neat at the end as at the beginning, what with Sven and the twins to carry her pannier, disentangle her from thorns or burrs and lift her over any rough or muddy patches. Besides which, she was one of those fortunate people who always looked immaculate, whereas I only had to step outside the door to look as though I had been dragged through a hedge backwards.

It was Tam's choice of venue. We took turns to decide our destinations throughout the year—all except the twins, of course. He frowned as if considering, but I could tell by the slight shake in his hands that he already had a suggestion, but was afraid to voice it. If so, it must be somewhere we had never been before.

"Let's go somewhere different," I said, trying to help. "Surely you must have some ideas?"

He flashed me a grateful glance. "Well, yes . . . I had thought, just for a change, you know, we might go up to the Wilderness. . . . Just for a look round the outside," he added, sensing the disbelief in the air.

I thought about all I had heard, read and been told about the place at the top of the pastures, at the foot of the mountains. It was a strange blot of a place, like a tangled mass of trees with no end and no beginning. No one I knew had been anywhere near, because people like Sven said it was an impenetrable forest; at school we heard whispered tales of it being haunted.

My Nan had told me that two of the villagers

disappeared sometime after they arrived all that time ago, last seen going up in that direction. Our teacher had told us there was a scrap of legend in the village history, kept in the Town Hall, that related that once, in the dim and distant past, the site of the Wilderness had housed a place of worship, with a temple and a great ring of stones. Myth had it that when the village was founded they found the site deserted, and had pinched most of the stones to build their cottages. Retribution had been swift and sure; there had been a plague, a pestilence, a murrain of cattle and deformities among the children until they had returned what stones had not been broken up to their original site.

Arne told me that an old stockman called Nial, who had been left behind in the village when the refugees arrived, had told of strange lights in the sky and a great noise over by the Wilderness, which was what had originally driven the former inhabitants away. . . .

So the reaction to Tam's suggestion was not unexpected.

"We can't go there!" protested Rosellen. "It's haunted!"

"I'm not going," said Alex stubbornly.

"Ba-a-ad place!" chorused the twins. "Not 'llowed!"

Now if they hadn't been so quick to veto the idea, perhaps Lally would have been the first to agree. But she was the sort of person who wanted to be noticed, if for no other reason than being different. So this time she looked all around us and said slowly; "Not a bad idea at all, Tam. In fact I think it's a really *good* idea. Why did we never think of it before? We

could go up as far as the edge, have something to
eat and then take a quick peek. . . . You agree, don't
you, Sven?"

Of course: when did he ever disagree with her?
The twins were looking puzzled, as well they might.
Brian tugged at his sister's sleeve.

"Can we?" He was always game for anything: a
tough little lad.

I decided to support Tam, even if I had my doubts.
"I agree with Lally, I think it's a great idea. We don't
have to actually go inside. Just take a look around."

"Right!" said our princess, clapping her hands. "Are
we all agreed, then?" She looked at the twins, who
were wriggling around as though they wanted to go
to the bathroom. "Now then, my Billy, my Benjy,
you don't want to be left behind when your Lally
goes walkabout, do you? You *know* she can't do
without her faithful courtiers, don't you?"

They looked at one another doubtfully. "Big
smacks," said Bill (or Ben).

"Nonsense! No one's going to smack you!" She
puffed out her chest and I noticed she was beginning
to show little bumps of bosom. Well, she was a year
older. "Besides, you want to hear one of Pretty's
stories, don't you? If you're *very* good, she might
read you two." She turned to me. "You have brought
the book, haven't you? They do *so* like the pictures!"

Of course I had. It was a book of lavishly illustrated
fairy stories my Nan had brought with her in her
suitcase all the way from the train-wreck, the last
present her Papa had given her. It was very old and
very beautiful, and Nan had taught me to read from
it. I was allowed to borrow it for special occasions,

like today, and as I was the only girl in the village with a book like that, I was always in demand to read one of the fabulous tales.

The church clock struck eight.

"C'mon," said Tam. "Everyone will be up in a minute, and we don't want anyone to see which way we're going, otherwise they'll stop us for sure. . . ."

CHAPTER FOUR

Leaving the closed gates of the park to our left we walked down Denmark Street, where already doors and shutters were opening, steps were being swept and busy housewives chivvying the rest of the family up and out. Today was market day, and everyone would be crowding the cobbled Market Square in search of a treat or a bargain. It was amazing how someone else's rubbish became another's treasure. A rickety stool, children's bricks, a tin box, an outworn dress: these could be just what someone else needed.

At the top of Denmark Street we turned left along France Street—all thoroughfares were named after the different nations represented by the refugees— and now we were safe from prying eyes. Here were the dyeing and weaving sheds, the cobbler, the woodcarvers, all of course now deserted, and the back yards of the houses facing Main Street. The last building on our right was the school, and with a sigh of relief, we rounded it, crossed the play-yard, climbed the back wall, and found ourselves in the fields.

Now we could relax, stop looking over our shoulders in case we were questioned as to where we were going. These were the fields for sugar-beet, and we skirted them by the stone-walling and crossed into the next, one of those kept fallow this year. Next the hayfield, its second crop already cut and rolled out like an extended French hair-plait, turned and rolled anew every couple of days till it was thoroughly dry. It should be ready to bring in this coming week, which would mean extra tokens for us if we helped after school.

The joy of escape now got into our veins, helped perhaps by the haunting summer-scent of grass and flowers, nose-tickly and sneezy, and we started kicking the hay high into the air, rolling in it, bundling into our arms and hugging it, like cats crazy on cat-nip. The air was a kaleidoscope of color, for mixed with the hay were dried speckles of red, blue, yellow and white poppy; field-scabious, buttercup, marguerite.

Temporarily exhausted, we climbed into the most westerly of the sheep-pastures, where the yellow-eyed sheep scampered away, indignant at being disturbed. Sven frowned. "That ewe is still lame. Foot-rot. We've tried to treat it, but at this rate she won't survive to come down for lambing. Pity: she was usually a twinner."

Lally flapped her hands at him. "Oh, *do* stop talking shop, sweetie. . . ."

The pasture seemed endless. Here the rocks lay nearer the surface and we were continually stumbling and stubbing our toes in the open-toed sandals, except for Sven, who was as surefooted as one of his charges. To our left the dark and sullen line of the plantation retreated, and the land was open and free, only the sharp foothills of the mountains threatening our left flank.

Lalage suddenly stopped just in front of me, so I bumped into her.

"What's the time? I'm tired. . . ." She tired easily.

Tam looked up at the sun. "Nine-thirty?" As if in confirmation, faint and faraway beneath us we heard the church clock. Very few of the villagers had any wind-up watches or clocks that still worked, batteries being out of the question, so we learned the time by the sun, listening to the church clock, or trained our own internal time-pieces.

"Well, I want a rest," said Lally. "I vote we sit down right here and have a snack before we go on."

That was another thing. She always ate more than the rest of us put together, or so it seemed, but never put on a superfluous ounce.

I thought about it. "Well, we could go into the shelter of that far wall" —there was a sneaky wind, blowing first hot then cold— "and have a snack, I suppose." Tell the truth, I was ravenous as well. Muesli or no muesli, there was something hunger-enhancing about being outdoors. "What did you bring?"

She shrugged and jerked a shoulder to where Sven was carrying her pannier as well as his own. "The usual. Honey-cakes, nut-bread, cheese-fingers, some bon-bons. . . ." Why didn't she put on weight?

Ros and Brian had brought chicken and coleslaw so I turned to the twins.

"And you?"

Disentangling their words wasn't easy, but it sounded like meat and potato pies and sausages, which was great; their parents had the butcher's shop, and their pies and sausages were delicious—and worth many tokens. We could only afford one of the larger pies once a week.

Alex had brought fresh-baked rolls, and I suggested

we had a couple of sausages, a bread roll and a drink before we went any further. "If we have any more than that it will spoil the picnic proper."

Even though the sausages were cold they were full of a delicious herby mix, and the twins' mother had included two pots of her famous dips, one spicy, one tomatoey.

It must have been well after ten that we stirred ourselves and set off again, Lally the most difficult to move. First she complained of stones in her shoes, then an insect bite; it took an offer from Bill and Ben to give her a chair-lift to get her moving at all.

We climbed steadily for about an hour; the only one used to the terrain was Sven, accustomed to checking on the sheep with his father, but more than once as I stopped to regain my breath, I wondered why we had agreed to come this far. Not of course that we had realized it would take so long: still, the way down should be easier and quicker.

For a while we had lost sight of our objective, as the ground became more and more hilly, but finally as we topped the last rise, there it was before us; the Wilderness.

Then the sun went behind a cloud.

I think we all shrank back a little. The loss of sunlight made the wood look eerie and menacing, like a huge beast crouched ready to spring. I hadn't realized, either, how close we were to the mountains that reared up behind the wood, dark and lowering, sending down from their hidden tops a sudden chill wind, like the first breath of Fall.

Then the sun came out again and it was all different. There was just a large wood, looking too dense to

be penetrated, but its hedges, we could see even
from where we stood, were thickly clustered with
nuts and berries. Behind, the sunlit hills smiled
benignly.

We had landed up roughly midway along the
southern edge of the wood; from a map I had seen
in school of the village and its surrounds, the
Wilderness was roughly circular in shape and about
a mile across. Although after our long climb we all
felt like just flopping down and having a rest, I knew
if that happened the idea of collecting fruit or nuts
would go out of the window, so with a little gentle
bullying I divided us into two groups; I would take
Tam, Lally and the twins, the latter being tall and
strong enough to pull down the highest branches
we couldn't reach, and Sven with his crook which
served the same purpose, would take Alex, Rosellen
and her brother. At least those four would pull their
weight: as far as we were concerned Lally was more
decoration than use.

The sun moved on in the sky, we worked our way
busily along the fringe of the wood, and before long
the two wicker baskets we had with us were full of
cobs and blackberries. We had given ourselves a time
limit of an hour and at the end of that time, as we
judged it, we made our way back to meet the others
where we had left our food-panniers.

We were all now hot, sticky and genuinely tired,
even Lally, but we five all stopped in our tracks when
a figure suddenly appeared from the woods to our
left, the twins dropping the baskets in fright.

It was a girl, dressed in trews and a short-sleeved
jacket, her long brown hair plaited down her back.

Over her shoulder was a pannier full of what looked like mushrooms and fungi. She wasn't in the least fazed to see us.

"You make enough noise," she said. "Frightened the squirrels, and I had a rabbit eating out of my hand. Didn't you hear the blackbirds chinking away? And the jay?"

It was the mysterious Herb-Woman's daughter. About the same age as me, we only saw her seldom, on market-day for instance, selling honey or quail eggs, handcream or herbs, and usually doing a brisk business. She always wore a clean nettlepaper apron and a pair of mitts, more aware of cleanliness than most. They—being Mayor Gross and his council—had tried to insist that she attend school with the rest of us, but she had submitted to a test and had shown that she was way beyond most of us in reading, writing and math. After that they had left her alone.

Looking at her more closely now, I realized she wasn't wearing trews after all; she had pulled her brown wool skirt up between her legs and tucked it into her belt at the front. Her feet were bare, but she still wore a mitt on her left hand.

"Sorry," said Tam. "We weren't listening for birds. What have you been collecting, anyway?"

She jerked her thumb back at her pannier. "Mushrooms and herbs. You?"

"Nuts and berries. You been here before?"

"Plenty of times. I guess this is your first visit up here?"

"Yes. Everything seems much—bigger and better."

"Well just be careful; don't go into the wood—"

"You did!"

"But I know what I'm doing, and just how far to go!"

"Have you eaten?" I asked suddenly. I don't know where the question came from, all I knew was that I wanted her to stay for a while, get to know her better.

She shrugged. "I had breakfast."

"Join us," I urged. "We've plenty."

Lalage hadn't contributed anything to the conversation so far, but she suddenly asked:

"Do you read palms?"

"I can. A little. If the ambiance is right."

"The what?"

"Mood," I said.

"Oh. Okay, then. Tell you what: tell my fortune and we'll feed you. Meat and potato pies, sausages, honey-cakes, hard-boiled eggs, apples. . . . What else, Pretty?"

"It doesn't matter; that sounds great. But I don't tell fortunes for a bribe. I thank you for the invitation and will join you gladly. In return I will look at your hands and tell you just one thing each in return for your kindness. Is it agreed?" She had looked very solemn up to now, but suddenly she laughed, a gay, bubbling sound that had us all, even the suspicious twins, smiling in return. "I must confess I'm starved."

"How did you guess she read palms?" I whispered to Lally, as we walked round to join the others.

"Simple. Her mother does. And the cards. And the crystal ball. My mother visits her regularly, so do her friends. Come on, I'm starving too!" and she scampered ahead, leaving me wondering how many other people actually visited the Herb-Woman. No one else I knew would say they did, except for our cheery little doctor, who freely admitted he went to her for the special herbs he used in his medicines.

Mayor Gross had let it be known that he disapproved of any "charlatanry" as he called it: perhaps that was why all this visiting went on in secret.

We ate until we were well and truly full, saving only the last of the sausages and the apples for a snack before we made the long journey home. By the time we finished it was well over an hour after midday. We wiped our hands on the damp cloths we had brought in the panniers, then glanced at each other, unwilling to remind the Herb-Woman's daughter of her promise. She had not forgotten, however.

"Now then, who's first? Remember, just one prediction each. . . ."

The usually forward Lally, whose suggestion it had been, seemed unwilling to be first. She grabbed at Sven. "Go on . . ."

He held out his palm grudgingly. "Don't believe in all this stuff. . . ."

The girl glanced at his palm. "You will lose all you hold most dear, but your life will be the better for it."

"I don't understand. . . ."

"You will. Next?"

Brian pushed forward a grubby paw. "Ah! You will become a great trader!" He went pink with pleasure. Perhaps encouraged by his success, his sister, Rosellen, thrust forward her hand, only to snatch it back again, redder than her brother, when she heard she was to have six children. . . .

Alex's future lay in writing a book, apparently, but Tam's was a real puzzle. "Two choices you have; you make a right one and a wrong one. . . ."

The twins had been pushing and jostling to get to the front all this time, muttering: "Game, game! Want to play game!" and at last she took a hand in both of hers, smiling at them. With a strange sense of unease I noticed she didn't look at the lines on their hands, but just gazed at them.

"You will not be left behind," she said. "And you will always be together."

They looked at one another and laughed noisily. " 'Gether! 'Ways 'gether!"

She turned to me. "Don't you want to?"

I did and I didn't. Firstly, I didn't know whether to take it seriously or not; secondly, if it was true, did I really want to know? It had all been very mysterious, could mean almost anything—except for Rosellen's six children—and if she told me something, did that mean that it had to happen? Did I have no choice in the matter?

But while I had been trying to decide she had taken my hand firmly in hers. It was surprisingly cool for such a warm day.

"You will be a Journeyer, and you will never be alone. . . ."

While I was still trying to work this out—no one left the village to go on journeys, did they?—Lally presented her hand.

"My turn, I believe?" The answer came swift as a dart. "Not yet, but it will come." Once again she wasn't looking at the proffered hand, but somewhere into the distance, and again I felt that chill of disquiet. "One day you will be the most desired woman in the world, and they will fight over your possession. . . ."

Lalage took her hand away, glanced at it for a second, then waved it in the air. "You hear that, everybody? The most desired woman in the world!" She was only eleven years old, but at that moment she looked like an adult. She thrust her hand forward again, "Tell me more! How soon? When? Where . . .?"

But the girl stood up, brushing herself down and picking up her pannier. "I must go. . . . Thank you again." And in a moment she was running away down the hill, leaping from tussock to tussock like a young goat.

"Wait!" I called, rising to my feet and waving frantically. "You haven't even told us your name!" It seems silly, but she was always referred to as "Herb-Woman's daughter."

I thought she was out of earshot but she paused, turned, put her free hand to her mouth and called back: "It's Perdita. Perdita . . ." And then she was lost to sight.

Her absence left everything feeling flat and dull. I'm sure we were all thinking about her predictions, and wondering what they meant, but no one said anything. I myself was still puzzling over the word "Journeyer." I had often wondered what lay beyond our village, but apparently Mayor Gross had mounted two expeditions for that purpose, years before I was born. One party backtracked along the route the refugees had taken, but they found no sign of life.

The other party had crossed the river which was our eastern boundary by a temporary rope bridge, but had returned to say that the land was literally scorched brown and lifeless. After that no one had ventured farther, but the Chronicles, kept in the Town Hall, recorded three visitors from the outside. A week after they had reached the village a man had staggered in, horribly disfigured with burns, and had died within twenty-four hours. Later a man and a woman had appeared, been quarantined, and had died from some unnamed disease two weeks later.

There had been only two evictions from the village itself. One man had raped and killed a young girl, the other had murdered his brother. Town opinion had been strongly against any form of death penalty, so the two men had been slung across the river and disappeared into the Burnt Land, as it was called. As good as a death sentence, I reckoned.

Other crimes were only minor: a few cases of drunkenness, a couple of wife-beatings, small thefts. These were usually corrected by a spell in the tiny two-cell jail. At school our usual punishment was detention and extra community work—

"I'm bored!" announced Lally.

"Bored!" echoed Bill and Ben, breaking off their wrestling match.

"I've been thinking," said Tam. "If that girl—what's her name?—Perdita, came out of the Wilderness, how or where did she get in?"

I shrugged "She just sort of appeared. Why?"

Sven nodded. "I know what Tam means. Have you tried to get past that hedge? It like, sort of, pushes you back again. Try it." He got up and demonstrated, and sure enough, as he approached the hedge it seemed to repel him, although it had been quite content to let us pick its berries and nuts.

We all tried, and Sven was right; it was like bouncing off an invisible cushion, with an unpleasant, sick feeling if you tried too often. But Bill and Ben refused to be beaten; in spite of warnings they linked arms and charged the hedge like a pair of enraged bulls, only to land flat on their backs some feet away, an astonished look on their faces.

"Bites," said one. "Hurts," said the other.

For no reason I shivered, while the twins started to blubber. It took five minutes and some of Lally's bon-bons to calm them down, and by then I was willing to fall in with Tam's suggestion that we backtrack to where Perdita had appeared and see if there was a way into the wood.

It took some looking for, but at last we found it. At some time in the past a small stream had carved its way out of the Wilderness; long since dried up it had nevertheless left a channel about two feet across and three deep carved out of the earth. Disguised by a few fronds of bramble, it was nevertheless the way in. We touched the hedge above it and to both sides and met the same resistance as before, but down at ground level it appeared to be free of restraint.

I knelt down, pushed aside the briar, and looked in. A tunnel, about the same dimensions as the dried-up stream, seemed to lead into the forest; it looked about five feet long. . . .

"Well?" said Lally impatiently. "Does it go anywhere?"

"I guess . . ."

"If you want me to . . .?"

"Thanks, Tam, but no. I'll try it." And pulling my pannier round to my front, mentally crossing myself and with my eyes tight shut, I wriggled my way to the end of the tunnel and stood up.

CHAPTER FIVE

I felt as though I had stepped into another world. Trees arched high over my head, making a deep, green shade, the grass was knee-high and bushes everywhere offered harvests of the largest berries and nuts I had ever seen. Somewhere a blackbird was singing, squirrels raced the branches above, a family of long-tailed tits were cheeping softly as they searched for insects, and little paths and tunnels in the grass showed where rabbits, hedgehogs and mice had their thoroughfares. A couple of orange and black butterflies kissed above my head, then fluttered away to feed on a stand of angelica as tall as a man.

And it was warm, warm as a June day. Everything looked slightly hazy at the edges, like the blurring of distant mountains in summer, but nothing could blur the bright colors. Under a stand of pines to my left I could see the orange and green seta mushrooms the girl Perdita had been gathering, and the trunks of other trees sported red, yellow, brown and spotted fungi as big as dinner plates. A purple trumpet flower, like a giant morning-glory, trailed through the branches of a copper beech, and dark-green ivy, its leaves marked with cream death's heads, twined round the bole of a huge oak. It was wonderful, but there was also something odd going on. . . .

Everything was larger and brighter than life, that was it! I remembered a story my Nan had told me about a little girl called Alice who had fallen down a rabbit-hole and had wonderful adventures, including drinking magic draughts which made her larger or smaller.

Right now I felt like that Alice, the small one. . . .

I became aware of a noise, as far away as the buzz of a fly on a window pane, but somehow becoming louder and more insistent. With a start I realized someone was calling my name.

"Pretty! Pretty—where are you? Are you okay?" It was Tam.

I stopped being Alice and pulled myself together. Of course the others were still on the other side of the hedge, and would have expected me to either return or tell them to follow through the tunnel.

"Come on! You wouldn't *believe* this place!"

It took some time for them all to wriggle through, largely because Bill and Ben decided to try and come through in tandem, which was impossible, so they got stuck and panicked. By the time we had got that sorted out it must have been getting on for three o'clock, but a strange kind of lethargy seemed to have settled on everyone, and we wandered through the enchanted wood in a dreamy daze, marveling at the size and variety of the plants and the tameness of the animals.

By and by we found ourselves in a clearing, a large glade which must have been in the center of the Wilderness. Roughly circular in shape, it was scattered at its edge with some gray stones, some large, some small, but the most remarkable part was the grass in the middle, cropped short right down to the earth, just as if a flock of sheep had been busy. But there were no sheep, and no droppings.

Lally sank down on the grass, heaving a great sigh. "I'm exhausted! Story time, Pretty!"

Bill and Ben capered about in front of me, shouting "Wanna story, wanna story!" till I was like to be deafened. The others gathered round in a circle as I unwrapped the book from its soft leather covering and put it on my knee, smoothing the deeply-incised front with its faded gilt lettering.

Fifty-two Fairy-tales for Children from around the World was the title and as I opened the first gilt-edged page my mind went back . . .

. . . My Nan had told me it was a last present from her Papa and, as the ten-year-old Esther she then was, she had carried it with her in her suitcase all the long way the refugees had had to travel, only relinquishing the case to one of the students when she was too tired to carry it further. Ever since I was a child she had read me one story a week, then started again at the beginning the next year. Every Saturday night I had gone to sleep with vivid pictures behind my closed eyelids: princes and princesses, knights and dragons, wicked witches and clumsy giants, cats in red velvet boots and dogs with eyes as big as saucers, queens with hearts of ice, kings with the touch of gold. . . .

But when I came to decipher the stories for myself as I started to read, I found the stories I had heard were not the same as those on the printed page. The stories themselves were perhaps each only four or five pages long, interspersed with beautiful illustrations by artists with exotic names like Blampied and Dulac, and ordinary ones like Rackham and Robinson, but when Nan told the stories there were whole conversations and descriptions that just weren't there in the book. When, disappointed, I had asked her about these when she came to kiss me goodnight she had smiled.

"When I told you the stories, didn't you see in your mind more than the words I said? And now, when you start to read, don't you imagine more than just the words on the page? If you see the word 'castle,' for instance, haven't you already formed a picture of it in your mind? It's not just six letters, it's a place you have created."

She seemed to change the subject. "When I make a soup, what do I start with? A cup of concentrated stock. But that liquid on its own wouldn't be enough for three, so I add some water. Now there is enough to go round, but it would be pretty dull without the meat and vegetables to give it substance. Potatoes to thicken it perhaps, some herbs to give it special flavor. And last but not least, a pinch or two of precious salt. . . ."

She pointed to the page in front of me. "Some of those stories are very short, like my stock, so I made up words to stretch them out. Now there were enough words to go round, but I needed color, flavor, texture to flesh them out. That way they will be special to all, like my soup!"

"But—does everyone's imagination—" I stumbled over the word "—see the same picture?"

"Of course not! Let me think . . . Right. If I give you the word 'tree,' you will have one in mind. It could be the maple in our back yard, a cherry tree in blossom, a lone pine. And if I asked you what you saw, then asked your friends Tamerlane or Lalage, would their answer be the same? I'm willing to bet not. Try it sometime. . . . Our imaginations are all different: yours, mine, theirs. So, when you are telling a story and you want your listeners to see it the way you do, then you must fill it out with your own descriptions of how a person looks, what they are wearing, what their surroundings look like, even the way they talk to each other. 'Make your story come alive, then you will be a true storyteller!' "

She laughed and tucked me up. "I didn't tell you the stories how I saw it. What color was Cinderella's hair?"

"Black."

"And I always saw it as red. . . ." She blew out the candle. "Point taken?"

. . . "Which one do you want?" I asked.

"Rhyme first," said Bill (or Ben).

That was another treat Nan had given me. When she was younger she had written down all the nursery rhymes she could remember for the child who had been my mother, and had then gone round the village, coaxing more out of those residents who could remember, together with saws, maxims and sayings peculiar to their own background, and I now had a fat exercise book full of a rag-bag of delights. My memory was full of children's verse, useful to amuse those like Bill and Ben, and perhaps my own children one day.

"Okay. Which one?"

"Doctor one, Doctor one!"

This was their favorite and also mercifully short, as they always demanded an encore, and spent five minutes falling about giggling when the physician fell into his puddle.

"Right. Which story?"

" 'Stone Soup'?" suggested Tam. He knew that it was my favorite, just as his was "The Teeny-Tiny Woman."

"*Boring!*" said Lally. "You can't act to that!"

This was an extra which had grown out of the telling of the tales. I cannot remember exactly how or when it all started, but now, if we had room we acted out the stories as I told them, miming the action bit by bit. It was good practice for the little school playlets we put on at Christmas; as then, Sven usually played the handsome prince or hero, I played the wicked stepmother or a witch and Lally always played the part of the heroine or a princess, which was why her next remark wasn't exactly surprising.

"Sleeping Beauty would be nice. . . ."

"Beeping Sleauty! Beeping Sleauty!" chorused the twins, capering about. By now they could remember their parts as devoted courtiers to the princess, as all it meant was following Lally about as they usually did, given the chance.

I saw there was to be no dissent, so I opened the book at the right page (ninety-six) and looked with pleasure, as always, at the heavily scrolled words that started the well known tale: "Once upon a time . . ."

I read (or told my own version) of the fateful christening, then they acted it out, Tam playing the wicked Carabosse, his rolled-up jacket being the "baby." Then came Lally's entrance as the sixteen-

year-old princess pricking her finger on the spindle
(a dead twig) and falling into her hundred-year sleep.

As the others carried Lally to the mossy bank for
her to sleep, and the twins picked some very short-
stalked daisies to strew at her feet, I looked once
more at the illustration in the book, beautifully
colored, of the princess in her "sleep," and was as
always struck by the fact that it might have been a
real-life portrait of Lally herself.

I turned the page, looking over to where the others
had all disposed themselves as the sleeping King and
Queen (Alex and Rosellen), soldiers (Tam and Brian)
and courtiers (Bill and Ben). Sven was already walking
off into the wood, to reappear as the Prince. I looked
down at the book; irritatingly the wind had blown
the page back to the illustration of the sleeping
Princess. But there was no wind, and once more I
was sure I had turned the page. . . .

I turned it again, looked up once more at the
actors—all in place. As usual Bill and Ben couldn't
keep still and were wriggling about as if they had
ants in their pants. No one was very far away, so if I
raised my voice a little they would all hear me and
act out the last bit as I read.

I glanced down at the book: a reflex action as I
knew it by heart—and there was the picture of Lally/
Princess again! Even I was getting muddled over
which was which, and I must have turned the page
back myself. I must just get on with it, otherwise
we would never be home before midnight.

I turned the page again, put my hand down firmly
on it and cleared my throat. Everything was absolutely
still: no birds, no wind, no rustling in the undergrowth,

even the twins were quiet. "And so the Princess lay in her sleep for a hundred years, while all around her the forest grew thicker and thicker. During that time many would-be suitors tried to fight their way through the forest, but . . ."

And that was when I lost it all.

CHAPTER SIX

". . . and so they lived happily ever after." I looked once more at the picture of the Sleeping Princess/ Lalage, closed the book, folded it in its soft leather cover and put it back in my pannier. Then I yawned hugely and knuckled my sleepy eyes, a thing I had been told so often not to do because of dirt and germs. Opening them again I automatically checked the sky for sun-time. Only it wasn't there—

I sprang to my feet, my heart hammering against my ribs. Last time we had checked the sun it had been nearing four after noon: a half hour or so for the story, a quarter for packing up and finding our way out again, and then a leisurely couple of hours to get home in plenty of time before dark—but now the sun wasn't there: I could see it must be sinking away to the southwest by the reddening of the sky.

"Tam! Lally! Sven!" I called urgently. "It's late! Come on, we're going to be in awful trouble. Wake up, you idiots: stop shamming!"

But none of them was play-acting; every single one of them was fast asleep, exactly where they had been when I started the last part of the tale. I had to run across to where they sat or lay and shake each one awake. And when I did they all behaved as if I had woken them in the middle of some fantastic dream, trying to snuggle back to their original positions, close their eyes and recapture their escape. The easiest were Bill and Ben, who looked as if their dreams had turned nasty all of a sudden, and the most difficult was Lally. Sleep clouded her eyes, she moved like a zombie, just as if she had suddenly become the character she had been playing.

By the time we had worked out that we had less than an hour to get back home before night set in, we were all in a panic, though we did manage to agree it would be quicker and less dangerous to life and limb if we went back by the river-path, a reasonably well-trodden way that led straight to the Market Square end of the village. Of course there was more chance of somebody catching sight of us near the Wilderness, but it had to be risked. We were going to get punished anyway, because we couldn't possibly return in time. Of course Lally and the twins would get away with it; the former because she was never punished for anything, and the latter because we were in charge of them.

I don't remember anyone questioning why we had suddenly lost over two hours, nor do I recall much of that helter-skelter race back downhill, though in the morning I woke with bumps and bruises I hadn't noticed before. I do remember we met Sven's father halfway down, coming up to check on the sheep, the two collies fawning at his heels, but all he said was for Sven to remind his mother that he would be in late for his supper. He didn't seem surprised to see us in the gathering gloom, but went his way, whistling the dogs to heel.

It was full dark by the time we reached our homes, all at the top of the village, within sound of the church clock. Luckily we had seen no one else who mattered, although the tallow lamps were burning dimly at all the intersections.

I leant against the front door for a moment to catch my breath, looking towards the church clock, its face hidden by darkness. It must be long past eight now. . . . Taking a deep breath in anticipation of, at least, a rare scolding and probably the cancellation of next month's expedition, I lifted the latch and opened the door just as the church clock chimed out the hour. It sounded louder than usual tonight, but then it would, wouldn't it, when tonight of all nights I wanted it to shut up! With a sinking heart I counted the strokes.

Seven.

Frowning, I waited for the eighth stroke. It didn't come. It was the first time I had ever known the clock to be wrong. I shut the door and crept down the passage to the kitchen, where I could hear Nan humming softly to herself. I peeped through the half-open door. The shades were already down, a brisk fire burnt in the grate and the flues were in the "Oven on" position, which meant she had probably made pastry. She looked up from the table, where she had been darning one of my father's socks, by the light of the oil lamp.

"Hello there, sweetheart! Have a good day? Did you find some fruit?"

Nothing about being late. I went over and gave her a kiss, then opened my pannier, ready to apologize for the berries, which must have been jounced to a pulp on my back in that reckless run down to the village, expecting to explain its ruin and my tardiness some way or other. But no, as I opened the two covered wicker boxes the berries tumbled out onto the table, looking as if they had just been picked, large, firm and juicy. The same with the big, glossy hazel-nuts.

She exclaimed over the size of my offerings. "My! I've never seen fruit that size! If it tastes as good as it looks . . . Mmmm! It does too! We'll bottle these, I think, too good to waste in a pie. The nuts we'll keep for the Christmas cake. They should store fine in the pantry. But you haven't said where you found them."

Suddenly I couldn't quite remember. It sounds stupid, but I had genuinely forgotten the exact place. We had climbed past the Top Pasture, that I recalled, we had found a hedge—somewhere—and picked the fruit, we had come back down the river path. All that was quite clear. The bit in between wasn't. I pulled the book out of the pannier. I had taken it with me, so presumably at some time I had read the others a story, but I couldn't seem to remember which. . . . Oh well, I suppose it didn't really matter. I yawned, suddenly very tired.

"We went up past the Top Pasture," I said, "and found a super place, a sort of—thicket—I suppose you'd call it. Oh, and we met the Herb-Woman's daughter up there. Perdita." Yes, I suddenly remembered that.

Nan shot me a sharp glance. "Did you talk to her?"

"Yes. She shared some of our food. She seems very nice."

"I'm sure she is. But perhaps you had better not

mention that to your father: you know he hasn't much time for herbs and superstitions and things like that."

Nor for things like fairy-stories either, I thought, remembering how he used to sniff in disapproval when he caught Nan reading to me.

"Now, child, get yourself washed—there's a pan of hot water on top of the stove—and I'll lay up. Take the book upstairs and change into your night-things. And if you yawn just once more without putting a hand in front of your mouth, I'll drop a stone down it! Go!"

As I stumbled up the stairs she was putting father's felt slippers by the hearth to warm, and when I descended again he had just come in from his chess-games down at the Games Club. I could tell from his manner he had won at least one game.

"Supper ready? It's past nine, you know. . . ."

Nan bustled about, putting a large casserole of pastry-covered stew on the table, together with a dish of baked potatoes, butter and chopped chives for garnish. She pulled out the plates from the warming drawer.

"My goodness: as late as that? It only seems five minutes since Pretty came back. She's picked some fruit for bottling and some fine nuts."

"Was she on time?" He often talked like that, as though I wasn't present. I had grown used to it.

"In plenty of time; the church clock was just striking seven as she came in."

So she hadn't realized I was late; I breathed a sigh of relief. Thank goodness I hadn't started apologizing. I hoped to goodness no-one would realize the clock was wrong when we went to church in the morning.

He turned to look at me; he had a disappointed sort of face and seldom smiled. "You've done well then; did you go far?"

"A fair way, Papa."

"Early bed then." He turned back to his dinner. Nothing I wanted more. At least in the morning I could ask the others where on earth we had *been*! And check the clock.

Apparently the church clock must have had a transitory hiccough at just the right moment for us, but the following morning it was back to normal. The bell started tolling at ten minutes to eleven and by five to the majority of people were already seated for the Family Service. I glanced round for the others, and one by one got reassuring glances; so we were all in the clear.

Nan nudged me. "You'll see them all later. Remember where you are. . . ."

This Family Service had grown out of the disparate religions the refugees had brought with them, forty-five years ago. Then, about a third had been Catholic, a third agnostic or atheist, and the rest divided between Baptists, Congregationalists, Mormons, Islamists, Buddhists, Seventh Day Adventists, Methodists, Presbyterians, Christian Scientists, Jehovah's Witnesses et al. There had been only one of the Jewish religion: my Nan.

There had also only been one priest: a Roman Catholic. Luckily he had been two things: an ex-army chaplain, used to communicating in all religions, and also a kind and wise man. It was he who had agreed with Mayor Gross to hold services in any denomination required, but who had also suggested he hold a multi-denominational service for everyone on Sundays, for all the religions present agreed there was only one God or Creator, and he could build on that.

Surprisingly, it had worked. The religions seemed to all blend into one, and the distinctions vanished with the years. Most of the agnostics and atheists fell in with Mayor Gross's strongly expressed wishes, and over the years became indistinguishable from the truly religious. It also helped the Mayor's plans that we were taught religious values as part of the school curriculum. My Nan had accepted the multi-denominational services happily, and now, like most of us, she just called herself a Believer.

It was always a cheerful service, with happy hymns. The main worship lasted a half-hour, then those who wished for Communion stayed behind for another quarter-hour. We children were always blessed and allowed to go and wait for the adults outside.

As we sang the usual "All things bright and beautiful," preparatory to being dismissed, I thought how much better the organ sounded since it had been overhauled and the bellows given new leather. It was still hand-operated, of course, since the lack of any "Electricity," a magic Nan still talked about, had meant it was now converted to manual handling. It was Tam's secret ambition to play this organ; he was the most proficient and dedicated amongst us as far as music was concerned, spending long hours on the recorders he painstakingly carved for himself in the Wood Workshop.

The hymn came to an end, the old priest—he was

over eighty now, and there was no one ordained to replace him: Mayor Gross would have to think his way past that when the old man dies, I thought— blessed us youngsters and we escaped to the Square, to relax until the rest of the congregation appeared for the usual ritual walk around the park. After a half-hour or so the women would excuse themselves to prepare the dinner, the men go down to the tavern for a cider or two, and us children would escape to the Rec. for an hour's play.

Tam, Sven and Lally were already sitting around the steps of the memorial as Rosellen, Brian and I joined them. Alex waved to us, but he was busy chatting to two of his mates, and of course Bill and Ben were still in church with their parents, having taken First Communion as Catholics last year. Mostly, I suspected, so their parents could keep an eye on them.

"Everyone get in okay last night?" I asked.

They gazed at me blankly.

"It was dark," I reminded them.

"I was in by seven," said Lally, and all the others agreed they had been also. Was it just me? But I noticed Tam was looking doubtful.

"I—I thought we were late, too," he said. "But the fruits were great. My sisters ate all the berries for supper."

"Our mother made them into a pie," said Brian. "It was ace!"

Rosellen frowned. "They asked us where we picked them, but I couldn't quite remember. . . ."

"Neither could I," said Sven. "I remembered to give my Mam the message from my Dad, but when she asked where we'd been . . ." he shrugged.

"We had a *super* day," said Lally determinedly. "I remember playing Sleeping Beauty."

"I remember having a nap—" said Rosellen.

"So do I," said Tam. "And crawling through a hedge somewhere. . . ."

"That gypsy girl told me I would be the most desirable woman in the world," said Lally complacently.

It hadn't been *exactly* like that, I thought. Each one of us seemed to recall some part of yesterday, but it just wouldn't get together into a whole in my mind.

Just as I was trying to puzzle out all this lapse of memory the church doors opened and the rest of the congregation streamed out. Bill and Ben left their parents and scampered over to Lally's side. I saw their parents exchange a quick word, then they joined us by the memorial. They were both tall and stout, with red faces and small eyes.

Their mother spoke. "Good morning, children." We gave the obligatory bob or curtsey, according to our sex, which was due to any non-family member in the community "Er . . ." she seemed nervous. "I want to thank you for looking after William and Benjamin yesterday on your day out. The fruits they brought back were quite—special." She fiddled with her seed necklace. "I just wanted to ask . . . Did anything *unusual* happen?"

We glanced at one another.

"Unusual?" said Lally. "No, I don't think so. We had a picnic, and Pretty read us the 'Sleeping Beauty,' and we were home on time. Why?"

"Beeping Sleauty," echoed the twins.

"The twins kept on waking up last night," said their

mother firmly. "They seemed to be having some kind of joint nightmare. . . ."

"Pillarcats," said (I think) Ben.

"Big stings," said the other. They stretched out their arms, and I could see where the skin was punctured and sore.

"I've got the same," said Lally indifferently, and proffered her arm which was likewise marked. So was Sven's.

"Lots of mosquitoes this time of year," he said. "But no caterpillars, as far as I know."

I looked at my arms, as did Tam, Brian and Rosellen. No marks.

"It must be something they ate," said Tam, "I was fine." The rest of us nodded.

The twins' father nudged their mother. "I told you so! They always have indigestion after eating sauerkraut."

Lally giggled. "Perhaps they'd better not have any more. . . ."

The twins stamped their feet in a joint tantrum. "Like krautsauer! Want more!" Now they were both shouting like a couple of idiots, their faces as red as their parents', the tears running down their cheeks in rivers.

I nudged Lally. "Come on: do your Royal Highness bit. Shut them up."

Lally favored the rest of us with a slow wink, then marched over to the twins and tapped them on the shoulder. "What is all this unseemly behavior, then? I will not tolerate anyone at my court who does not conform to the correct protocol! Anyone who does not behave is instantly banished!"

Miraculously the twins stopped their bawling immediately.

"*That's* better! Now, you may make your apologies!" and she mounted the lowest step of the memorial and thrust out her hand imperiously. Happily now carrying out a ritual they understood, the boys advanced and bowed, sweeping imaginary hats from their heads and then kneeling to kiss the offered hand.

"Pillion mardons, your Highly!" they chorused. "Now smack bottoms!" and they turned and stuck their rumps in the air.

The rest of us had seen all this before: their parents hadn't, neither had the rest of our families, who were drifting closer with obvious curiosity. The faces of the twins' parents were getting redder and redder with embarrassment and anger. They didn't realize how easily Lally could make the boys do anything, and to them this regimentation must have looked both cruel and degrading. I don't believe, looking back, that we meant to be cruel: Bill and Ben both loved play-acting and performed it with innocent enthusiasm, and we never took advantage of this. Well, hardly ever. We laughed at them sometimes admittedly, but they laughed too, and happily, not realizing they were the butt of our jokes.

Tam nudged me. "Duke of York," he whispered urgently.

I caught on at once. "The Grand old Duke of York/ He had ten thousand men/ He marched them up to the top of a hill/ And he marched them down again."

The twins changed their act at once. They snapped to attention and marched on the spot, their backs straight, imaginary rifles held steady. "Right turn!" I intoned. "Home. Quick march!"

And off they trotted, their bewildered parents in hot pursuit.

Lally collapsed in a paroxysm of giggles. "Did you see her face?"

It was strange the way we played soldiers, Indians and Cowboys, Pirates, I thought. We had never had any experience of these, except for the twenty-one volume encyclopedia we were allowed to examine in the Town Hall and the stories of the films our families had passed down to us. All of these were second, third, fourth hand, but we still copied the pictures and made eye-patches, wooden swords, headbands of pigeon's feathers and bows and arrows. . . .

It was a pity we only had a few books in the village. Apart from the encyclopedia, a huge atlas, several dry-as-dust law books, a ten-volume dictionary, a book of Business Studies, Shakespeare, Oscar Wilde, Bernard Shaw, Arthur Miller and a large Bible (all in the Town Hall), there were Bibles and Prayer-books in the church, some geography, history and science books at school, and the rest of our entertainment was gleaned from the so-called "Library," situated in a small shop that had once been an electrician's, next to the Town Hall. Here were stored all the fiction and fact collected from the empty houses when the refugees had taken over. It was a motley lot, varying from collections of Mark Twain and Dickens to paperback cowboys and "Hints for a Flower Border," by way of knitting patterns, Cook-Books, Guides to Travel Abroad and Hints on Baby-Care.

I had enjoyed much of the fiction; as we were only allowed to read in the Library itself, some of the books were still readable. I had read *Jane Eyre* twice, *The Lord of the Rings* three times and *The Way of the World* four, all of these in the half-hour snatches we were allowed. We were only let in there Mondays, Wednesdays and Fridays, after school and chores. Adults any time between two and four; closed Saturdays and Sundays—

"Hey, there! You're not listening. . . ." said Tam's voice in my ear.

"Sorry! What did you say?"

"Are you coming to play Hopscotch?"

And suddenly that was more important than books, lost hours and forgotten rendezvous.

"You bet! An apple to a pear I beat you square!"

CHAPTER SEVEN

The wind chased Tam and me up the road to Church Square, the leaves running ahead and whirling into spirals across the cobbles. It had been a great idea planting trees all along the Main Street, but an October morning like this gave extra work for the street-sweepers, as they tried to confine the dancing debris into heaps for burning.

One of my earliest memories of autumn was the evocative reek of bonfires heralding a night of nibbles by the fire, of storytelling, of woolens airing on the fireguard, a hot brick wrapped to take the chill off the bed. Thick soups, sticky toffee, wedges of fruit-and-nut cake: all treats in compensation for the inevitable runny noses and chilblains.

We arrived at the memorial at the same time as Rosellen and her brother, and just as the church clock chimed the quarter after eight. Strange how one never seemed to notice it getting lighter day by day in the spring, but winter darkness rushed in like the October gales. During the dark months people only worked in daylight, as there was no electricity, and candles and oil had to be conserved.

At the celebrations last month of Deliverance Day, as they called it, there had been a forum in the Church

Hall. A number of the original settlers had been invited up onto the platform to discuss what they most missed after forty-five years; every one of them put electricity at the top of their list. They cited the ease of pressing a switch to illuminate their houses, turn on their 'fridges, ice-boxes, mixers, blenders, radios, TVs, heaters, air-conditioning.

The second thing on their list was lack of transport: with no gas there were no cars or motorbikes (although I couldn't imagine where they thought they could go). Their other grumbles were mostly the lack of cotton goods and tastes they couldn't duplicate: chocolate, coffee, whisky, tobacco. They had herbal tobacco, of course, and carefully hoarded marijuana (strictly medicinal), but apparently it wasn't the same.

They were then asked by Mayor Gross what they most appreciated about their life now. I guess they had been conferring beforehand, because they all talked about Peace, Security and Good Management, all answers calculated to please the Mayor, sitting up there in his distinctive robes and chain, his bald head gleaming in the light from the stage reflector-lights. There were also mumbles about Equal Opportunity and Jobs for All, dull stuff Tam and I agreed, sitting at the back as we were, playing Cat's cradles. There had only been one remark worth remembering; a wizened old chap said how much he liked the fruit sorbets stored in the Ice-House, but couldn't they come a bit cheaper?

All in all, it seemed they missed more than they had now.

"Neither Alice nor Alex are coming," said Rosellen without preamble.

"But her cold's better," said Tam. "And Alex hasn't been off."

"I guess they've had a month to think about it," said Ros. "Or their parents have. I reckon they've been listening to the gossip about the twins having nightmares."

"Their loss," I said. "The others'll be here."

"Far as I know . . ."

And on cue, the twins came trotting across the square, their baskets bumping on their backs. With the cooler weather their mother had knitted them woolen caps, one blue and one green, with silly yellow bobbles on the end which kept hitting them on the face as they swung their heads from side to side. If it had been an attempt to tell one from the other, that had failed also, for in five minutes they had swapped and then back again and when they did that there were either two Bills or two Bens.

It was only ten minutes later, rather than the usual fifteen, that Sven and Lally turned up, excuses you could mutter under your breath as the latter said them, knowing just what was to come. Either her parents had overslept, forgotten to call her, or they had had to make up her basket of food. It never varied.

Having got that over, she said brightly: "Where's it to be then?"

"It's your turn to choose," I reminded her.

"Oh. You sure?" She wasn't usually so backward in coming forward. Suddenly she whipped off her embroidered headscarf. "How do you like my hair?"

"It's—it's very ethnic," said Tam at last.

"Exactly! It's meant to be. I had my Mam copy it

from one of those pictures of black people in the Encyclopedia."

"I think it looks very nice," said Sven, loyally. He would.

She turned to the twins. "Well, boys?"

At least you always got the truth from them; the word "tact" was absent from their vocabulary and their understanding.

They shook their heads, sadly. "Like doll," said one. "Not Beeping Sleauty," said the other.

"Well, *I* like it, and that's all that matters. . . . What do you say, Pretty?"

I chose my words carefully. "I think you're the only person I know who could get away with it," I said truthfully. "I should look like the pits!"

"Your hair isn't long enough anyway," said Rosellen, spoiling my compliment.

"Aren't we going anywhere?" interrupted her brother sullenly. "I'm bored!"

"Of course we are!" said Lally, but she still looked uncertain. Was all that business with her hair just a diversion while she tried to make up her mind? She glanced at us all, shrugged her shoulders, then said at last: "Same place as last time, I guess. It was a good day. . . ."

But where *was* last time? I could see the same puzzlement in all our faces, and was just about to open my mouth to say so when the problem was solved from an entirely unexpected direction.

"Same place, same place!" chorused the twins, and set off up Denmark and across France, so fast we had to run to catch up with them. By the time we had climbed into the first pasture and were headed

north-east I think we all remembered where we were
headed: the Wilderness. Of course—how stupid of
me to forget—but I could have sworn the others had
had the same lapse of memory, apart from the twins,
of course.

This time we didn't stop for a snack, didn't stop
for anything; even Lally kept up with the rest of us,
so it was just midday when we collapsed on the rough
grass in front of the tall hedge that surrounded the
forest.

"Wow! I'm whacked!" said Ros. "Why did we have
to travel so fast?"

"We were late last month," Tam reminded her. "At
least now we've plenty of time."

"Well, at any rate now we won't have to share with
that gypsy girl," said Lally. "What's everyone brought?"

And as we shared out cheese and onion pasties,
sausage rolls, bacon sandwiches, tomatoes, potato
salad, tacos, fruit dumplings and honey cake, the
fluffy white clouds raced overhead like a flock of
stampeding sheep, and a few late southerning
swallows scooped insects from only a few inches
above the ground.

This time, I told myself, we'd better keep a better
check on the hours, we'd remember where we'd been,
and we wouldn't go to sleep. . . .

Putting aside some ham sandwiches and hard-
boiled eggs for later, we packed up and made our
way round to where we recalled the tunnel in the
hedge, reckoning it was now a little after one, with
plenty of time to collect whatever was edibly available
and have a story, too.

The twins had raced ahead again, and they had

a surprise for us; they came jumping down the hill towards us with Perdita in tow, holding a hand of each. She didn't seem the least surprised to see us.

She dropped the twins' hands and set down her pannier, full this time of precious walnuts and some bell-like flowers I hadn't seen before. "So you had to come again," she said, without ceremony. "I told my mother about last time, and she said I was to warn you once more. Leave well alone!"

"*You* go in there," said Lalage. "Look at your baskets."

"I told you before. I know what I'm doing. You obviously don't."

"Of course we do!" said Sven. "Why should it be any different for you?"

"Because. Just because. I know what my mother knows, and she is a Wise Woman as well as a Healer." She crossed her arms across her chest and set her legs apart, looking the very picture of a miniature market woman, in her trews, short skirt and headscarf. "She told me to pass on this message. There are certain Powers in this world—and out of it—that they don't teach you about in school, or books either."

"Magic?"

She shook her head impatiently. "No, Rosellen Brown, not magic. That is something else again. I'm talking about Power, real Power. Power that can exist in the air around us, in the earth beneath our feet. Power that creates Its own pathways, pathways that sometimes cross upon themselves, making the Power even stronger. This—" she gestured towards the Wilderness: "—is such a place!"

"Are they good or bad? Are they dangerous?" Brian was goggle-eyed.

"They are neither good nor bad; They wouldn't understand such a distinction: They are just *there*. And no, They aren't dangerous, unless They are disturbed. Then they are capable of upsetting the balance, of destroying anything in Their way." She picked up her pannier. "There, I've had my say; don't say I didn't warn you."

"But just where are They in there?" asked Tam. "I didn't see anything unusual last time."

"You won't *see* anything; it's more—a sort of feeling. Just keep to the edges, don't venture into the center, then you should be all right." She paused for a moment. "Are you sure you saw nothing out of the ordinary before? Something you wouldn't expect to find in a wood?"

"Such as?" asked Brian.

She looked at us all. "If you didn't, well enough. Remember what I said!" and she was gone, leaping down the hill till she went into a dip in the pastureland and out of sight.

There was a short silence, broken by Lally.

"Well, what a load of old rubbish!" She yawned delicately and stretched her arms above her head. "Shall we go, then? Sven, you'll help me, won't you? And Bill and Ben, you can pick the fruit. . . ."

But the twins were holding hands, a clear indication that they were disturbed.

"Oh, come on, you 'fraidy cats! Look! Your Lally isn't scared!" And she knelt down and pushed her way into the tunnel, closely followed by Sven. The twins looked at each other, loosed their hands, and scrambled to follow, one at a time, thank goodness. Ros and Brian followed, and Tam and I were left looking at one another.

I shrugged. "We'd better go too."

Once again, it was like walking into another world. It seemed the Wilderness was weeks behind the rest of our world as far as weather was concerned. Here it wasn't October, it was still September. The leaves were just turning, the more colorful ones spiraling down gently onto the yellowing grass with a tiny sigh of regret. We found the walnut trees and I picked enough for Nan to pickle, then sought out the seta mushrooms for drying, and perhaps a couple for supper tonight.

We could hear the others calling to one another, laughing and making a great business of collecting their berries or whatever. We sat down under a maple tree, scarlet and red in its autumn dress, ate a few juicy blueberries, and watched the sunlight flickering through the trees, replete and content. A rabbit thumped the ground some way away, and a couple of roe deer, no bigger than dogs, raised their horned heads from where they had been grazing, their ears twitching back and forth, their black noses sniffing, their dark eyes questing. Then, as one, they bounded away into the undergrowth.

Tam sighed, his hands behind his head. "It's almost too good to be true. . . ."

"I know what you mean."

"Magic. Just like your fairy-tales."

"Not mine. Everybody's."

He repeated almost what I had said a moment earlier. "You know what I mean."

And that was the nice thing. We knew each other so well that nine times out of ten we were completely in tune. We seldom quarreled, hardly ever argued and we could discuss any subject under the sun without embarrassment. But his next words caught me off guard.

"Did you know your father is courting my sister?"

"You *what*?" I jerked up right. "He *can't*! Which one? *Why*?"

He put his hand on my arm. "Calm down! Or I'll wish I hadn't told you! My mother says he was given warning some time ago he should be looking for another wife, seeing it's seven years since your mother died. Apparently he didn't do anything about it, so he was told by Mayor Gross, official-like, that he had picked out two prospective brides, and if he didn't propose to one or the other soon he'd face a heavy fine."

I nodded: this was the law. "Which—which ones did the Mayor choose?" All the while I was squirming inside, both with the shock and the thought of my father bringing someone strange into the house to usurp my Nan's position. And mine . . .

"Number one was the widow Lestrange. . . ."

"Oh, no!" Her husband had been a woodman, crushed a couple of years ago under one of his trees. She was a shrewish woman, in her thirties, and they had three rumbunctious sons, ten, eight and six. "There just isn't room for that many in our house!"

"My sister would be worse!"

He had three sisters, Griselda, Georgina and Gabrielle, referred to by us—and most other people behind their backs—as Grizzle, Gorger and Gabby, which just about summed up their characters. I moaned. "Which one?"

"Any. They're all available. Twenty-nine, twenty-seven and twenty-four and never an offer between them. You can imagine the fuss my mother and father have made over his visits—"

"Visits? How many times has he been?"

"Only three; he seems to favor Grizzle."

How come my Nan and I didn't know anything about all this? But perhaps she did and hadn't wanted to upset me. But to think of Tam's sister becoming my stepmother! The idea wasn't to be borne!

"Oh, Tam, what can we do?" But even as I said it I realized that perhaps I couldn't expect him to be a willing ally in retaining his sister. For one thing if there was a marriage there would only be two of them to bully him instead of three, and for another it would mean he at last could have a bedroom of his own instead of having to sleep on a pallet in the kitchen.

He shrugged. "I don't know. If we could just say 'Abracadabra' or work on a magic spell. . . ." He shrugged again. "At least Grizzle is one degree better than Gabby. . . ."

But he had given me the germ of an idea. I wouldn't say anything to him right now, for fear of making a fool of myself. Besides, first I should have to save some tokens. . . .

Bill, or Ben, came charging through the long grass just at that moment, faces red, knees pumping high.

"Lally say . . . Time. Beeping Sleauty!"

The glade seemed lovelier than ever. The grass was still a vivid green, cropped close as before, but

now it was patterned with the brown, yellow and
red leaves which made it look like an exotic carpet.
Dew still sparkled on gossamer webs stretched
between bush and tree, and brimstone butterflies
fluttered on the fringes of the trees. A cloud of midges
danced for tomorrow's good weather and a group
of green and red finches chattered away among the
trees.

Everything was calm, beautiful, calculated to lull
us into a sense of well-being, but there was a core
of unease right deep down inside of me. Could some
things be too good to be true? I couldn't help
remembering the words Perdita had used. "Don't
venture into the center. . . ." And here we were,
exactly where she had told us not to be. But nothing
bad had happened to us last time, except that we
had been late starting off back home.

I glanced up at the sky, confirming the time with
Tam: about a half after two. Plenty of time. I opened
the book.

"Everybody ready?" There had been no discussion
on the story this time I thought as I found page ninety-
six, and no request for a nursery-rhyme from the
twins. Everyone was eager to get down to the story
and return home without any hassle.

This time it was so easy I didn't have to tell the
story: it told itself. All I had to do was sit back and
watch the procession for the baby Princess's christening,
the gold robes, the jewels, the fairies one after another
bringing their gifts. Then, after the wicked fairy flew
in on her broomstick and delivered her prediction,
there was a rapid switch to the attic room where the
Princess pricked her finger on the spindle, the wool

unwinding from the stick as she fell to the ground in a deep sleep.

Now came the sad procession as the Princess was carried on a golden bier to her canopied bed high in the castle, her hair carefully combed free of its ethnic plaits, and spread on the pillows, the gossamer curtains drawn around her slumbering body, and one by one, from the King and Queen on their golden thrones, down to the cook in the kitchen stirring the soup, and the Palace dogs and cats, they all fell asleep just where they found themselves.

The forest grew thick and fast about the castle of the Sleeping Princess, and suitor after suitor was foiled in their attempts to force their way through to the chamber where the Princess lay. But at last, after one hundred years, a Prince on a white charger found his way through the forest and—

"Hell and damnation!" yelled Sven. "I've been stung again!"

I jerked my eyes open: I didn't realize they had been shut. Poor Sven was staggering about at the edge of the wood, holding his wrist.

"Oh, come on, you lot! Wake up! Show a bit of sympathy!"

The others were all yawning and rubbing their eyes, all except Lally, who lay still as if in a coma. I glanced up at the sky, terrified that we would be late again, but no, the sun said it was only three-thirty at the latest. I heaved a sigh of relief.

"We'd better get this finished. It's getting late."

But it proved almost impossible to wake Lally into any sense at all, and when we did, she protested she felt too tired. Indeed she looked pale and drawn, and there were a number of small puncture marks of the soft skin on the inside of her wrists, and all she could do was bemoan the fact that someone had undone her new hairdo, and it looked terrible. . . .

We ate what food was left, and by this time she looked better and the puncture marks had faded, but she was glad enough to accept a chair-lift from the twins on the way down to the river-path.

As we were nearing the village I heard Brian ask his sister: "Who were all those other people?" I didn't hear her answer, but it set me to thinking.

I was puzzled; I too had thought there were others taking part in our mime, but had thought it was because I must have dozed off. I turned to Tam. "Did you see anyone else up there? You know, when we were acting out?"

He looked at me, surprised. "Yes. Courtiers, a sort of castle, other things. But I thought I was asleep and dreaming. You too?"

I nodded, although already the whole afternoon was fading into the forgotten, like a real dream.

And just before the whole thing slipped from my mind I had a disturbing thought: was it possible for eight people all to dream the same thing at the same time?

CHAPTER EIGHT

My father and Griselda were married in the first week in November.

He wore his leather trousers and jacket, with an embroidered vest over a woolen shirt; she wore a bleached woolen dress with a scooped neckline, and a headdress of white feathers and seed pearls. They both looked very nice, and also like a pair of complete strangers.

During the ceremony I glanced across the aisle several times to where Tam sat with his parents but he kept his head averted. His other sisters were bridesmaids; I hadn't been asked.

After the ceremony the happy couple went straight to Honeymoon House, the cottage that had once been used for quarantining. There they would stay for three days, undisturbed, food and drink provided free by the Council, as was the custom.

I still felt sick that I hadn't been able to prevent the marriage: it wasn't as though I hadn't tried. . . .

I tried my idea out on Tam one afternoon when we were alone in the Town Hall, doing minor repairs to the two models that always stood in pride of place in the entrance hall: Old Deliverance and New

Deliverance. Of course the village had had a different name before the refugees arrived, but that was long forgotten. It was always the custom during the September celebrations for Deliverance Day for everyone to file past the two models, to admire the changes made during their years of occupation, and every year Mayor Gross made sure there was something else to congratulate him upon.

This year it had been the building of the new road down to where the smithy and metal-working sheds would be resited next year. The villagers had complained for long enough about the noise made by the hammering of metal, and the half-mile or so of distance should make a welcome difference.

Looking at the two models now, as we straightened here, re-glued there, it really was extraordinary the improvements the Mayor had initiated, like the man or not. Older houses pulled down, roads repaired, the construction of the Park, a crèche, a children's playground with swings, a roundabout, climbing frames, hopscotch markers and basketball nets and a skipping area. There was a men's outdoor club too, with built-in chess and checkers boards, horse-shoe pitching, quoits and boule. For everyone were the laundry, the bathhouse, the fresh-fish pond, the icehouse, the bathing-pool, the playing field (football, baseball and athletics), and proper sanitation pits. As far as work was concerned there were the weaving sheds, the dyeing and tanning works, the woodcutting and fashioning shops, the refurbished mill for grinding the corn, the boiling sheds for the sugar beet, a huge storehouse for potatoes, corn flour, sugar and the dwindling supply of salt (a teaspoonful per person per month). Then there were the buildings for the candle-makers, furniture builders, the recycling of all materials—for more clothes, rag-rugs, cleaning cloths, dusters—the soap-makers and a large pottery. Not to mention the feather-pluckers, the toymakers, the music-makers, the paper mill, the ink and paint processors and the brewery.

I plonked a green wool tree down onto the Main Street, eyed it critically, applied glue and stuck it down, my tongue poking out with concentration.

"Well, what do you think of it?"

Tam looked up from where he was re-aligning a fence. "It's a bit crooked. . . ."

"Not the tree, idiot! My *Plan* . . ." I tilted the tree a fraction to the left. Better.

"It wouldn't work! I don't believe in all that stuff anyway."

"All you want is to get rid of her!"

"Yes. But—oh, listen Pretty! If I thought for a moment it would help . . . Heck, I want you to be happy, too!"

"Why shouldn't it work?"

"Just think about it. You intend asking the Herb-Woman for a magic charm to stop my sister marrying your Dad. One, we don't know whether she will or can, and two, how on earth do you pay for a thing like that?"

And three, you don't believe in magic anyway, I thought. "It's worth a try. I've asked, and got, a meeting with her. . . ."

I had spoken to Perdita at the market on Saturday, where she was bargaining for thread with a basket of duck eggs. Her eyes widened when I told her what

I wanted, but she hadn't laughed or anything.

"I can't answer for what my mother can or cannot do," she said "But I will ask her to see you."

"When?"

"A lunch-time? Monday, say?"

"Make it Tuesday. There's someone I need to see first. . . ." I wanted Tam to come with me. "How much will it cost?" I required time to work for some extra tokens, too.

"You'll have to ask her."

And with that I had to be content.

"So, you will come with me?" I glanced across at Tam.

He shrugged. "What use would I be?"

"You'd be *there*! I feel—a bit scared, perhaps. You know we're not supposed to visit her. Come on. All we have to do is say we are having lunch at each other's house and we've both got alibis. Go on, be a pal!"

He gave me a sudden grin. "If you're game, so am I. . . . Got any more of those trees? These two have come unraveled."

On Tuesday night I saved a couple of rolls and smuggled them out in my satchel in the morning. They were a bit stale, but the only luncheon we were likely to get. Making sure we were the last to leave school at twelve-thirty we strolled behind everyone else and, once they were out of sight ahead we made a quick dive into the cemetery behind the church, crossed into the orchards that sloped south from the village, coming out on the south-west corner. Skirting the tree-nursery we found a track that led to a small copse, behind which a thin trail of smoke rose straight into the air.

That must come from the Herb-Woman's cottage and, sure enough, there was Perdita waiting for us at the edge of the trees.

"Thought you might have changed your mind."

"No way," I said, although the thought had crossed my mind more than once since Saturday.

"How long do you have?"

"We have to be back at school at two, for math and PT," said Tam.

School hours were a moveable feast, depending on the time of the year and the requirements of planting, sowing, haymaking and harvest. Candles and oil were too expensive for illumination, so all hours of daylight were utilized during the winter, and the school was closed when we were needed in the fields or orchards, the crèche opening every day for those too young to participate. All part of Mayor Gross's Communal Plan.

"Time enough, then," she said. "Follow me."

There, behind the copse—birch, hornbeam, Spanish chestnut, beech, larch, mulberry, cedar, walnut, maple and oak—was the most ancient cottage I had ever seen. Long and low, with a thatch of reeds, it seemed to have made a bed for itself in the turf, like a wild animal scooping out a bed-hollow. To one side was a covered wood-store, on the other a large pen holding chickens and ducks. In front, where the land sloped away to the south, was a small orchard and a well-tended vegetable-garden, to the left of the orchard were bee-skeps, by the vegetable-garden the well. In front of the cottage was a pleasant confusion of herbs and flowers, most of these now tied and bagged for drying and seeds, although the

bay, rosemary, sage and thyme were still green and
fresh.

Perdita led us up a pebbled path to the open front
door.

"They're here, mother," she said, and turned back
to us. "Take care: two steps down."

"Come in, come in and welcome," said a low, rich-
textured voice.

At first it was too dark to see anything clearly, but
as my eyes grew used to the lantern-light above the
table, with its real glass mirror reflectors instead of
the usual metal ones, I began to distinguish one object
after the other.

But it was my nose that did the first exploration.
If you walk into anyone's house for the first time
the essence of the home comes rushing to greet you
before anything else, and if you are away from your
own home for even a day or two, you can be surprised
at its odor when you return.

Houses can smell of almost anything, but usually
the scent that lies over all is a reflection of its interests.
Food, good or bad, soap and polish or dust and grime;
bodies, clean or unwashed, clothes, ditto; wood fires
or the more expensive charcoal; tallow, oil or
candlewax. Fresh, stale, sweet, sour, sharp, bland—
I thought I had smelt them all. This cottage was
different. For a start all the smells were clean ones,
but there was the sort of mixture that you felt might
change from day to day and not be impregnated into
the walls and ceiling forever as in so many houses,
even with a change of tenant and habits.

Here one smelt the pungent smoke of apple-wood,
a rich stew, fresh-baked bread, airing clothes, drying

herbs, stored apples, beeswax, cheeses, feathers, fresh milk, a spicy smell I couldn't identify and a sort of warm, furry aroma.

Then the Herb-Woman came out from the shadows and I found that Tam and I had stepped back a pace and were clutching hands. It wasn't as though we had not seen her before, although only at a distance. We both knew she was tall and dark-skinned, but here in the shadows and confines of her own home she suddenly looked twice as tall and much darker. Looking back now I suppose she must have been about six feet tall and broad with it, but to us she seemed like a giantess in the confined area of the cottage. But only for a moment; she smiled, and suddenly seemed a reasonable size again. Her teeth were very white against her nut-brown skin. I had never seen anyone with such a dark skin before, except in pictures; Nan had told me there were three colored people among the original refugees: a nurse, a medical orderly and a cook. They had handed their skills on to others, but had not married, nor had there been any children.

I forgot it was rude to stare. She had a hawky nose, black eyes, a wide mouth and greying crinkly dark hair plaited around her head—

"You'll know me next time, child." But the words weren't unkindly spoken.

I went bright red, I could feel the heat rising into my face. Remembering my manners too late, I bobbed her a curtsey.

"Beg pardon, ma'am: no offense intended."

"And none taken. Well, what do you think? Would I look better with a lighter skin?"

How had she read my mind? I blushed again, but she was the sort of person to whom you told the truth, so I looked at her again. Everything looked just right; I tried to imagine her with skin as fair as Lally's, but with her own features . . . No.

"It suits you," I said. "You'd look silly any other color."

She clapped her hands. "Well, child, that's just about the best compliment I've had in an age!" She beamed at us both. "Now I understand you have a problem, so why don't you take the weight off your feet, pull out a couple of stools—that's right—and just sit down and share a bowl of stew with Perdita. You won't have eaten yet? No, I thought not." She reached into a cupboard and brought out three bowls, real china ones, blue and white, not the coarse pottery we had in the village, and three soup spoons from a drawer and put a fresh roll in front of each of us. Perdita came in with a jug of water and sat down as well.

"We do have some bread, ma'am," said Tam, bringing out the rolls I had saved.

"And as stale as yesterday's news; mine's baked fresh. You just do me a swap, and you'll be doing my chickens a favor." She swung a small cauldron on a trivet away from the fire and, without spilling a scrap, transferred a generous ladleful of thick stew into each of our bowls. "Now, eat hearty; talk comes easier on a full stomach."

It was delicious, rich with thick chunks of vegetables; I identified potato, carrot, turnip, swede, onion, leek, celery, cabbage, beans, tomato, the whole touched with a hint of garlic and parsley. I complimented our hostess as I pushed back my bowl with a sigh of contentment.

"Glad you liked it. I always keep a pot simmering during the winter, just add a bit of this and that as we get it. That way I always have something to offer my guests."

Guests: I liked that. It made me feel more special, as if she would listen to us without laughing, or dismissing us out of hand.

She poured a little red liquid into three glasses— yes, real glasses: we only had two precious ones at home—and topped it up with well-water.

"My special distillation: do you like it? Blackberry, sloe and elder."

I nodded. Tam said: "Better than that cordial they make in the village!"

She took a chair at the head of the table, Perdita brushed crumbs into a tray, wiped the table with a small cloth, put the bowls and spoons into a bucket and carried them outside, presumably to wash up.

Her mother turned to us. "Now then, children: what can I do for you?"

This was going to be difficult. Tam and I looked at each other, "Well, I—that is we . . . No, it's really my idea. I wanted to know if it is possible to . . ." My voice trailed away.

"Let's see if I can make this a little easier for you. I'll make a guess that this has something to do with a certain wedding, and that you want to know if there is anything I can do to prevent it taking place? Am I right?"

"How on earth did you know?"

She smiled at Tam. "Not much is missed out here.

I do have other visitors, you know, and people love to speculate."

I wondered for one wild moment whether Griselda herself had come to visit, asking for a love-potion to entrap my father, but decided that this was too far-fetched. After all, she had been unmarried for so long that she would have visited long before if she had believed in it all. . . .

"And what's in this visit for you, Tamerlane-the-Great? By this marriage you have much to gain and little to lose."

He glanced at me. "Pretty is my *friend*! I think I would even rather keep Grizzle if it means she and her Nan will be unhappy."

"I wouldn't ask that of him," I put in. "I *want* him to have his own room instead of the sofa or a pallet in the kitchen."

"Then what do you want me to do?"

I was silent. It had all seemed so simple yesterday, even this morning, now it wasn't. Any one of Tam's sisters were equally awful, but wouldn't that widow with three sons be worse? And that would mean, too, that Tam wouldn't get his own room; and supposing that Mayor Gross came up with an even worse alternative?

"I don't know . . . I just want life to be as it always has been, that's all."

"Life does change, you know, even as you do. What was—or is—so special about your life that this marriage would change?"

I thought for a moment. In the initial rejection of the thought of Griselda being in the house as my stepmother I had just known everything would be horribly different. Now I thought more carefully of what was most precious to me, and my words came more slowly.

"Well, first of all it's going to be bad for Nan. I help her with the housework, of course, but it's her house: she's in charge, she doesn't have to answer to anyone. It's nicest of all in the evenings after supper when my father goes down to the club, and we sit by the fire and tell stories or just talk. . . ."

"Anything else?"

I thought again; was there anything? I remembered another of Tam's trials.

"She hits Tam quite hard sometimes. I wouldn't want that. I'd run away!"

"Where to?" asked Tam, with interest.

"I don't know! Somewhere, anywhere . . . Oh, you know what I mean!"

"Well we certainly don't want that!" said the Herb-Woman briskly. "So, let's see if I've got this clear. You wouldn't find the thought of this marriage quite so reprehensible if there was no usurping of your Nan's position and you and she still had your time together in the evening. . . . Oh, and no smacking. Right?"

"Er . . . Yes. I guess so."

"You have been thinking about your Nan first, and all credit to you. But she isn't getting any younger. Don't you think it would help if she had another woman to help in the house? I know you do your best, but you're not always there."

"Grizzle's hopeless at housework and she hates cooking," said Tam gloomily.

"Then perhaps she would be grateful for your Nan

to keep her cooking unchallenged, and Griselda would look after the bedroom and be allowed to reorganize and keep clean the parlor, so she could entertain her friends, seeing you don't use it very often. . . ."

No, we didn't; Nan usually entertained her friends cozily in the kitchen, which was a far nicer room. But how did she know?

"You'd be surprised at how people change when they can take a pride in a room or two of their own," said the Herb-Woman. "If she thought she could have her family and friends to visit in a place of her own, she would keep it immaculate, I'm sure."

It all seemed a bit simpler now.

"So," she continued, "we've solved one or two problems. Tam will get his own room, Griselda has her husband, your Nan will get some help, but she will still be in charge. But there is one person we haven't considered in all this. Your father."

"My father?"

"It's his wedding too, remember? How's he taking it?"

He seemed embarrassed by all the fuss, but I had caught him whistling the other day, a thing he seldom did, and he was cheerful enough.

"He—seems to be looking forward to it," I said, surprised that I hadn't thought about it before.

"Exactly. I know he missed your mother as a person desperately, and he's not a naturally open-hearted man, but after a while don't you think he must also have missed the comfort of a partner to share his bed and his innermost thoughts and feelings? Why do you think he goes out every night to the Club? Why do you think he hasn't wed again before this?

Could it be that although he is a lonely man, he knows inside just how much your Nan might resent someone taking her dead daughter's place in his affections and that you might feel the same? Have you ever stopped to think he might not feel welcome in his own home?"

I was devastated. How could she criticize us like this! And yet . . . But before I could say anything she was off on another tack.

"Do you have any games at home? Chess, checkers, dominoes?"

I thought. "Dominoes, yes, and I think there's a chess board that doubles for checkers somewhere, but I think there are some pieces missing. No cards, though . . ."

"My sister loves games," said Tam unexpectedly. "Specially ludo."

The Herb-Woman smiled broadly. "I think I can see all your problems vanishing through the window. Tamerlane, you're clever with your fingers; your present to the bride and groom can be some new chess and checker pieces. When's the wedding?"

"A week on Friday," we said in unison.

"Well, I can tell you now that this marriage has too much potential happiness in it for me to help you stop it. What I can and will do is to try and smooth out some of the rough corners."

"Aren't you going to cast any spells?" asked Tam, looking disappointed.

"Spells are for witches, black or white, and I'm not one of those," she said firmly "But I am going to do some thinking and some talking around. And now you must be off, otherwise you will be late."

She turned to me. "Come back here on your own, the same time next week."

I paused in the doorway. "Er . . . how much will it be?"

She didn't hesitate. "A four-kilo bag of cornflour."

That would be twelve tokens; I had seven. Tam nudged me.

"I've got two."

I could probably earn three more before the wedding, or borrow from Nan. "When do you want it?"

"Bring it with you next week. Now go, and my blessings be with you. . . ."

When I arrived the following Tuesday Perdita wasn't there; her mother explained she was out gathering roots, so I sat down alone to a slice of cheese and onion pie, an apple and a glass of goat's milk. As I ate, I had a chance to take in a bit more of my surroundings. The room was long and low and one end was curtained off, probably leading to the sleeping quarters. At the other end was a recess, with a bead curtain enclosing a pantry or larder. The fireplace was opposite the door, flanked by a slow and a fast oven, and above hung a dryer for clothes on a pulley. Bunches of herbs hung to dry from the ceiling, the floor was of old, cracked, uneven black and red stone tiles and the walls were ceiling-high with cupboards, chests and shelves. The two small, sunken windows let in a little light, but the lantern was adequate to see what I was eating. As I finished I heard a strange sound.

"You've got a cat!"

The Herb-Woman smiled. "Of course! Would you like to see her? She and her kitten are in a basket by the fire. Slowly and gently now . . ."

In a wicker basket lay a sleek black cat, yellow eyes blinking sleepily, and by her side, sucking greedily, was a smaller version of herself. Wonderingly I stretched out a finger and stroked the small stomach, tight as a drum with milk, and for a reward got a definite crackly purr, although the mother cat shifted her body with a warning chirrup, trying to shield her babe from a stranger. The Herb-Woman spoke to her soothingly and she relaxed, allowing me to stroke her as well.

The feel of the fur under my hand was magic; stimulating and soothing at the same time. I had never touched a cat before. We were not allowed to keep pets of any kind in Deliverance, Mayor Gross decreeing that they were unnecessary and a drain on resources. Dogs were bred for shepherding or as guards; cats were tolerated as mousers or ratters in the warehouses. Any superfluous pups or kittens were disposed of at birth, like mutant stock or babies. As I stroked the cat's fur, the first tiny seed of rebellion against this slaughter stirred in my mind.

"Just one kitten?" I asked. "Did you drown the other ones like they do in the village?"

For the first time I saw her angry. "Certainly not! All God's creatures have a right to live! I rescued this cat when she was a kitten. Her mother had hidden her from the destroyers-of-life and showed me where to find her, knowing she was deformed. She has a club tail, and her insides are not meant for breeding, that is why she will probably only have the one kit. But her daughter will breed well. She is perfect."

"I wish I had a cat." It was out before I even thought about it.

"In that case I promise you will have one. Sometime soon." She sounded very sure. "And now we must settle a couple of the problems still outstanding: how to make Griselda accept her new position happily, how to ensure you all enjoy each other's company, how to guarantee you and your Nan get your usual time together. Come and sit down, and I will tell you what you must do. . . ."

A half-hour later I rose from the table, dazed by the tasks ahead of me, wondering, not for the first time, whether it was all worth it.

"It will be," said the Herb-Woman, smilingly reading my thoughts. "But remember: everything must be done just as I say, otherwise it will all go wrong. Here is the final charm, to be fastened above the bedhead," and she handed me a packet of dried flowers and herbs and what I could only describe as a dented, much-used sprinkler rose.

"But it looks just like—"

"Never mind what it looks like: that's just to deceive the unbelievers."

"But what do I—"

"You stick the dried flowers and herbs into the rose until it is covered, into whatever pattern you think most appropriate and fasten it onto the bedhead. It will form a magic rosette, the more potent, the better the pattern."

"But how will I know what pattern to choose?"

"Just think about it. Griselda's favorite color is

yellow: you have yellow flowers there and blue: blue is a male color."

I stumbled out into the sunlight, eye and mind blinded, and it was only as I reached the edge of the copse that I realized there was one question unresolved. I turned back but she was right behind me.

"And if you ever fear she will lift a hand to you, just stare her straight in the eye and yell: 'Brandy-snaps!' "

During the three days my father and Griselda spent in Honeymoon House, Nan and I worked as we had never done before. We distempered the bedroom and parlor, moved the furniture around as the Herb-Woman directed—in the bedroom the bed moved to face the window, the dressing-table under the latter—and removed any trace of my mother's occupation, right down to a couple of vests and a shawl, sent to the Recycling Shop. The mattress and pillows were stuffed with fresh feathers, curtains and rag-rugs moved around so that all those with the slightest hint of yellow were in the bedroom.

Nan told me Grizzle had seen the bedroom on a visit before the marriage and had come back downstairs looking like a frog having a problem with a wasp. I bet that now she wouldn't recognize it.

I had thought hard about the rosette, but finally come up with what I hoped was a good idea. Remembering what the Herb-Woman had told me about the colors I wove a large "I" for Ivor, my father's name in blue flowers, encircled by a "G" for Griselda in yellow ones, surrounding them with the other green and white herbs and flowers, and this proved to be the highlight of their return, my stepmother refusing to have it moved.

We had put their wedding presents—leather waistcoat, fishing gear, socks, gloves and a scarf for him, plus the statutory dowry of two hundred and fifty tokens; ribbons, mats, necklaces, pokerwork ("There's no place like Home" and "East, West: Home's Best") and a couple of throws for Grizzle. Tam had carved some very creditable chess-men and checker-pieces, and I gave them something that Perdita had passed to me at the market on Saturday.

"My mother found these yesterday. . . ."

It was a pack of hardly-used playing cards. My father handled them as reverently as if they were communion wafers, doing a fumbled fan of the cards.

"Long time since I've done that. . . . Where did you get them?" but luckily he didn't wait for an answer.

Everything else worked out surprisingly well, just as the Herb-Woman had predicted. Grizzle—I learned to call her "Griselda," for as she coyly remarked, there weren't that many years between us—(nineteen??)—praised Nan's cooking, and kept parlor and bedroom spotless, entertaining both family and friends often.

Once Nan and I had learnt the new games (Grizzle had brought her own ludo and snakes and ladders) we all enjoyed an hour or two of games after supper at six, my father teaching us bridge, whist, rummy, "Continentale," poker, "vingt-et-un," "Racing Demon" and even "Snap."

And prompt at eight o'clock every night in the

winter my father and Griselda retired to their
bedroom, true to the charm of the rosette, and Nan
and I had our time together.

And never once did I have to invoke the dreaded
"Brandy-Snaps!"

CHAPTER NINE

Partly due to the weather and partly due to Mayor Gross's propensity for scheduling Children's Day each month on a day which was a holiday anyway—Christmas and Easter, for example—it was the following May before we could have a kids-only day out again. True it had rained on the day designated in November, the snow was too thick in January, but it seemed that the usual dry weather in February was ideal for a day of stone-picking before the plowing and sowing in March, us following the horse-drawn plow with seeds or potatoes.

Ten to one it would be haymaking in June, weeding and shearing in July and the beginning of harvest in August, so even the Mayor couldn't deny us a free day in May, though it must have been a temptation to marry it to May-Day, on the first as always.

It would be a fourteen-hour day for us—seven in the morning till nine at night, all being well—and our families had packed extra provisions, so we wouldn't need to expect supper when we returned. It appeared that Alex and Alice had decided to be part of the other group again, so it was Lally, Sven, the twins, Rosellen and her brother and Tam and I that assembled by the Memorial as usual.

Nobody could remember whose turn it was to choose, so we had an amicable quarrel as to where we would go, only agreeing that we wouldn't go south of the village, where the other group were going. It seemed everyone wanted to do something different. Bill and Ben wanted to see "Baa-Baas," while Sven, after all the traumas of lambing, wanted to get as far away as he could from any sheep. Lally wished to pick some flowers, Brian to do some exploring, Tam wanted to find some suitable wood for carving, Rosellen wished to see whether the swimming pool was ready and I felt like agreeing with everyone for once.

So, Sven and I were easy, and it was the ever-practical Tam who suggested that we could satisfy most of the ideas put forward if we followed the river road north, starting with examining the possibilities of the pool.

This was only a quarter-mile from the village, at the site of what must once have been a sports complex planned by the previous villagers. Only the roofed and open-sided pool had been completed, but with the lack of electricity it had been adapted over the years to take a direct intake of water from the river into the upper end, and an outlet at the bottom of the lower end went straight back into the river, so all through the summer it was clean, clear and ice-cold, as the river was snow-fed from the mountains.

Disappointingly, it was obvious as we approached that workmen were still clearing it of winter-debris and preparing to scrub it out.

"When will it be ready?" asked Rosellen, peering over the edge.

"Couple of days, miss," said one of the two men, resting from his work. It was certainly warm under the roof with no breeze today. "Going far?"

"As far as it takes," said Brian, the standard answer.

The other man grinned. "Well it better not take you too far; looks as if the weather's changing. Could be in for a storm. . . ."

We looked at Sven, like all those who worked mainly out of doors, he had a keener sense of changes in the weather.

He shook his head. "Don't know. See what the sheep are doing. . . ."

This was our next stop, for Bill and Ben to watch their "Baa-Baas," and while they hung over the nearest fence watching the lambs gamboling in one of the meadows, we parceled out our first snack. The lambs were now all-but weaned, more teenagers than babies, but they were having a grand old time chasing each other, play-butting, jumping like chamois from rock to rock, while their mothers nibbled the still long grass, probably glad to be rid of them for a while. During the last five years Sven's father and grandfather had been experimenting with the tups and ewes to produce twin lambs, and this year had had a ninety per cent success.

I glanced up at the sky: no sign of bad weather. The sky was chicory-blue with tiny fluffy white clouds, almost a copy of the skipping lambs beneath.

"Where next?" asked Rosellen, wiping crumbs from her skirt.

"I haven't seen any decent flowers yet," moaned Lally.

"Might be some farther up," said Brian. "That way

we could have a bit of exploration as well."

"Why not," said Sven. "I'm game."

At first the going was easy, but fewer people came by this way as the last of the pastures were now beneath us, so the river path finally petered out, and we were scrambling over stony ground, skirting the rocks that heralded the steep foothills of the mountains. Far, far away the tallest of these were still capped with snow, but these nearer hills were only a few thousand feet high. By now we had climbed about five hundred feet and Lally was already lagging behind, complaining that her feet hurt, so we sat down for a rest. It was near midday by now so by unspoken consent the rest turned into a protracted lunch.

From this height we had a splendid view, as we munched our way through meat and vegetable pasties, spring rolls and shortbread. The sheep in the pastures looked like tiny dots and the houses in the village like toy homes, all cozy and neat. Up here though it was a bare and barren place, with a few straggly bushes, thorns and scrub. Even the newly arrived swifts were no longer wheeling over our heads.

Suddenly I shivered, and at the same time Lally said: "I'm cold. . . ."

So it seemed was everyone else. From nowhere it seemed a chill breeze had sprung up, the cloud-cover had increased and the horizon looked somehow hazier.

"Let's go," someone said.

"Where to *now*!" snapped Lally. "Don't forget I want to find some flowers: everyone else has had what they wanted."

Suddenly the twins sprang to their feet and started to gabble excitedly. Following their pointing fingers we saw a patch of brilliant sunlight fixed on a splash of green almost directly beneath where we sat. A jumble of trees, a tangle of undergrowth—The Wilderness! I seemed to have forgotten it existed, but now as I craned my neck to look down I suddenly remembered what a wonderful place it was.

"Go see! Go see!" called out the twins, capering about so energetically that I was frightened they would slip on the rocks.

"Of course," said Lally. "There are bound to be loads of flowers down there. *Why* didn't we think of it before?"

"Nice place," said Sven, nodding, and Rosellen and Brian were also enthusiastic. I recalled that we had been there before—once, or twice was it?—and looked at Tam, to see if he remembered, but all I got was a rather puzzled smile.

I recalled a place where everything was bigger and brighter than the world outside and in the fairy-tales Beauty played with the Beasts—no, that was wrong: a slip of thought. It was Beauty and—

"Beeping Sleauty! Beeping Sleauty!" cried out Bill and Ben. "They be waiting . . ."

Sleeping Beauty. That was it. My memory was playing tricks. I had been going to read a story up here after we finished lunch, but now of course the venue had been changed; I patted the book of fairy-tales in my pack, newly covered by my Nan with a piece of oiled silk she had bargained for to preserve the leather.

We made our way down diagonally across the rocks

to the western border of the Wilderness, to be faced by an eight-foot-high impenetrable hedge.

"Where's the way in?" wailed Lally. "I want my *flowers*. . . ."Suddenly Tam seemed to come to life. "Farther down," he said and, pulling a recorder from his pocket, began to play a tune I recognized as "Over the Hills and Far Away." "Come on! I'm the Pied Piper!"

"Dyed Riper! Dyed Riper!" sang the twins, as I recited the poem to anyone who would listen. Of course now we remembered where the tunnel was, although we had to peel away the new growth, mostly bramble, before we could scramble through one after the other.

I think everyone said "Wow!" one after the other, and that just about summed it up. The Wilderness had been spectacular enough in the autumn, as I remembered it, but in spring it was something else. Then the colors had been dark and vibrant, now they were bright and sparkling. There were a hundred different fresh greens, or so it seemed, and where the dark fruits had sported their ripeness were now the flowers that created them. It seemed that March, April, May and June had met together in a riot of spring and early summer flowers; the sweet-smelling creamy jonquils and yellow and blue mini-iris belonged to March; April was responsible for the pinks and ivories of wild service and sloe, the bright yellow daffodils; May had carpeted the floor of the forest with an azure drift of bluebells and hanging bunches of pale blue lilac; only in June would you expect to see the brighter scarlet of corn-poppy, the candy-stripes of clematis and the pink

and red of dog-roses. Over all was the thick, honey-
sweet suffocation of may-blossom, both red and
white.

There was a cacophony of sound. Not only the
birds—blackbird, thrush, robin, wren, tit and siskin,
and the faraway drum of a woodpecker, but also the
sonorous drone of insects, bees and bumbles, beetles
and crickets.

Even the air was different; laden with scent and
sound, it had a heartier, thicker quality, warmer than
outside in the ordinary world. Even looking up at
the sky above we could see the sun still shining, just
a few baby clouds scudding above. The whole
atmosphere was extremely enervating, so much so
that Lally's flower-gathering took less time than I
expected, before we seemed to drift by common
consent towards the center of the Wilderness, multi-
colored butterflies dancing about our heads, even
alighting on exposed flesh to seek the salt on our
skin.

Such loveliness all around made the heart ache
with childish longings that anticipated the changes
into teenhood; you knew you wanted something,
yearned for it, but weren't quite sure what it was.

But there was something I was supposed to
remember and as we came to the glade and into the
sunshine my memory jumped in and out of the edge
of consciousness. Strange, in here the Outside had
a sort of foggy insubstantiality, just as in the village
this place was like a dream impossible to recall clearly.
What was it I had to be careful of? It was important—
something about strength . . . No, Power. Yes, that
was it: Power. But what sort?

Suddenly I couldn't be bothered to think any more. I sat down by one of the old grey stones that littered the edge of the glade and closed my eyes, the sun red against my lids. A little breeze patted my face, ruffled my hair, and I could hear the others enjoying themselves. Bill and Ben were chanting something silly and jumping over one of the stones, Tam practicing runs on his recorder, Lally was sorting her flowers with Sven at her side and Ros and Brian were chasing each other in and out of the trees. Deliciously dozy, I leant back against the stone—

A sharp tingle ran up my spine, I opened my eyes and for the first time noticed how evenly the grey stones were spaced around the glade, curving away on either side of me in an almost perfect circle. Some were big, some small, but there seemed to be a certain pattern in their placing, as if—

"Come on, Pretty! Story-time . . ." Lally was shaking me awake. With a sigh I sat up, leant forward and drew the book from its covers, for once curiously reluctant to open the pages. Not that I needed to: they fell open at the right place, as if eager invisible fingers were ahead of me.

"Once upon a time . . ."

How nice it was, I thought, as I heard my voice telling the so-familiar tale, to have enough people to play all the parts. King, Queen, Prince, courtiers, servants, godparents, soldiers, the wicked Carabosse, and of course the beautiful Princess herself. The costumes were wonderful too, and the scene-changes excellent, from christening-cot to spinning-wheel to flower-strewn bower. I looked down at my book. Yes, everything was an exact copy even down to the wart on the chin of the witch.

I leant back against the stone—

Wait! This was all wrong! We didn't have that many people, we didn't have any costumes, we didn't have any scenery!

Dropping the book, I jumped to my feet, staggering for a moment as the ground seemed to shift beneath my feet and the silvery towers of the castle swayed before my eyes like the scenery in the Church hall did when hit by a draught—What castle? Where the hell had it come from, with its colored pennons flying, the broad drawbridge leading into the Great Hall where the Princess lay on a—on a . . . This wasn't a palace, this was a castle where the ogre lived in Jack and the Beanstalk!

I must be dreaming! I glanced down at the book at my feet and it was spinning slowly in a circle, the pages flapping wildly from story to story, picture to picture: Cinderella, forests, Tin Soldier, fairies, Rumpelstiltskin, witches, Aladdin, giants, Goldilocks, talking dogs with eyes like saucers! And while all this flickered in front of my eyes, the same pictures were happening in the background, like giant shadows a second or two behind their originators, and I thought I saw—no, it was horrible!

I shrank back against the stone, hiding my eyes, but someone had given me a sharp shove in the back, so that I fell forward on my hands and knees, the book almost slamming shut under my right hand. Scrambling up, I blinked in disbelief, for there were my friends calmly acting out the rest of the story, Lally lying on her back with a posy in her hand, Sven striding out of the wood to claim his bride, and the others feigning sleep—but where was Tam?

There, lying by one of the stones. I ran over and helped him up. "You all right?"

"H-have *They* gone?"

"Who?"

He looked around, rubbed his eyes, shook his head. "Don't remember . . . Bad dream, I guess."

I looked across again at the others: the play was over. Lally stretched and yawned. "I had a wonderful dream. . . ."

Tam pointed to the soft skin on the inside of her elbow. "You've been bitten again!"

"Can't feel it . . .!" Indeed the redness was fading.

"I've been bitten too!" Sven looked at his wrist. "Mosquito probably."

The others looked at their arms and wrists. All had been bitten apart from Tam and myself.

Brian sucked at his bite. "Not bad: tastes like rusty metal."

"You're revolting!" said Lally.

"Don't you suck a bloody finger and pick your scabs?" he asked. "I do. And so does she," he nodded at his sister. "Although she probably won't admit it."

"Oh, come on!" said Lally impatiently. "I'm *hungry*! What time is it?"

We looked up at the sky. It seemed to be clouding over.

"Getting on for five," hazarded Sven.

"*Told* you I was hungry," grumbled Lally, yawning again. "But at least now we can have tea and supper together."

How time flew! I could have sworn we had been

in here an hour, an hour and a half at most, but it must be nearer three or four. The passage of the hours didn't seem to matter in here.

As we approached the tunnel in the hedge to the Outside, we could hear a strange noise, as though a herd of ponies was thundering past. We looked at one another, frowning, but the twins were eager to eat and pushed through first, followed by Lally. I could hear vague shouts and cries as Ros, Tam and Brian followed, which left Sven and myself. For a moment I hesitated, looking back at the sunlit, dreaming wood, then pushed through to the other side, Sven right behind me.

Everything was different.

For a start it was raining. Not only raining, it was literally pouring down, bouncing back off the ground almost knee high; that was the thundering noise we had heard. In a moment we were completely soaked, even the beautiful Lally looking like a drowned rat.

I had never known a storm blow up so quickly.

Back in the Wilderness it had been warm and sunny, out here great thunderheads reared up above our heads, spilling water like a waterfall. And it was bitter cold with it, too, so that we were not only wet through, we were shivering. I could feel my teeth chattering.

But worse than the rain was to come. We were discovered!

There, only ten yards away, stood the dripping figures of Sven's father and grandfather, clad in oilskins, crooks in hands, dogs at their heels, obviously checking on stray lambs. There was no way they hadn't seen us, and it was obvious they were as mad as hell.

Sven's father shouted something to his son, furiously beckoning with his crook.

"Aw, *shit!*" said Sven.

The rest of us turned and ran.

I remember very little of that mad dash for home. I can remember running as if the Devil himself was at my heels, of falling once or twice; remember Lally screaming at us to wait for her, Tam's scared face, the twins howling like banshees, Brian dragging Ros after him, and then we all got separated.

Nan told me afterwards that I staggered in looking like something out of a horror story, blood running from a graze on my knee, soaked to the skin and so out of breath I couldn't say anything. Having seen the rain she had thought we were sheltering somewhere, but had put water on to heat in case. She took one look at me, got out the tin bath, stripped me, bathed me and toweled me dry, then put me to bed with a hot toddy and a couple of warm wrapped bricks.

Outside the lightning flashed, the thunder crashed, the rain ruined the cherry blossom down in the orchards, but in five minutes I was asleep, the last thing I heard being Nan telling me the book of fairy stories had survived the rain intact. . . .

The following morning I woke with a sore throat and a headache, aching all over, and by lunchtime I was running a fever. The doctor came, shook his head and prescribed warmth, rest and lots of liquids, but the following morning I was much worse, ranting and raving of I knew not what. My father thought that I should go to the Infirmary for all-round nursing but luckily I was saved by the Herb-Woman; she had heard of my illness, recognized the symptoms and sent round Perdita with two small phials of medicine, luckily when Nan was on her own.

From then on I recovered rapidly, and two days later was allowed downstairs to receive my first visitor, Tam. He had brought me a posy of wild flowers.

I sniffed them appreciatively. "Thanks. What's been happening?"

Nan tactfully left the room. I had told her my version of what had happened, as far as I could remember it. We had found our way into the Wilderness to pick some flowers and had not realized that a storm was brewing. I was sure there was more to it than that, but I couldn't recall exactly what. Curiously, when all the parents compared notes, none of the others could remember anything more than I did.

Sven and Tam had received a beating—"Mine wasn't too bad," said Tam, "but Sven still finds it difficult to sit down."—Ros and Brian had been forbidden all privileges for a month, Bill and Ben (as usual) were excused because it was all our faults that they were there, and the crushed flowers in Lally's pannier bore out our stories. Her parents were so touched by her disheveled appearance that they went out and bought her a new dress. . . .

But that hadn't been the end of it. Mayor Gross had heard of our disobedience and they had all (except for me, confined to bed) been summoned to his awesome office, all heavy oak and red leather. There they had been lined up in front of his desk, girls with their hands clasped in front, boys behind, as usual when listening to an adult.

"And he proceeded to give us a right rollicking," said Tam. "He was thumping his fist on the desk, shouting at us till the spit started to fly! Apparently we were a group of graceless, impudent, disobedient children, a disgrace to Deliverance after all he had done to build up the community, that rules were made to be obeyed—you know the sort of thing."

I almost wished I hadn't missed it.

"He went on and on, finally getting up and strutting around the room with his face all red, until he'd reduced the twins and Lally to tears, and the rest of us were trying not to laugh. . . . You would have giggled, I know you would. He looked so silly spouting all that self-righteous rubbish and marching about like a little dictator—what's that one in the encyclopedias?"

"Castro?"

"No, the other one."

"Napoleon?"

"No, more recent. A hundred years or so ago . . . The one with the little moustache who always had his hand in the air as if he was asking to be excused so he could go to the bathroom."

"Oh, Adolf Hitler."

"That's the one! He behaved just like a right little Hitler."

But dictator or no, Mayor Gross had extracted a promise from them all that never, ever, as long as they lived, would they visit the Wilderness again. . . .

BOOK THREE

POWERS

CHAPTER TEN

Graduation Day, Jubilee year, and it was stifling hot in the Church Hall.

After they built the Community Center (crèche, games room, Bingo Hall, library, cafeteria) they had tried to christen this place "The Little Theater," and indeed that was the name on the placard over the double doors at the front, but old habits die hard.

Us Thirds who had qualified for our diplomas sat at the front, stiff and uncomfortable in, for the boys their best clothes, and for the girls cotton kaftans passed down from years past, probably originally made from sheets. They had been mended a dozen times, shortened and lengthened according to the wearer and were singularly unflattering, making us all (apart from Lalage of course) look at least six months pregnant. Pinned to the breast, and to the jackets of the boys, was an embroidered replica of the town shield, designed by the mayor. The shield was quartered; top left and right: white moon and stars on dark blue, sun on light blue; bottom: left, stick figures on a green background, man, woman, two children. Right-hand side, representational white house and green tree on a yellow background. On top of the shield was scrolled "Deliverance"—mine

145

was spelt wrong. "Deleverance." So much for schooling all those years ago. Underneath was the town motto: "Work Makes Freedom."

I wasn't too sure about that; the more one did, the more there seemed to be. The words themselves, too, seemed oddly familiar: I was sure I had read them before, in a different context.

Behind us our parents and friends whispered and gossiped amongst themselves but we had to be still, behave ourselves and try not to sweat too much. At my side Ros surreptitiously wiped her forehead on the hem of her garment and I could see Tam was uncomfortable in his best suit, shifting restlessly in his seat.

Through the open skylight above us I could hear the creaks and groans as the church clock prepared to strike the hour. Good: Mayor Gross was never late. As the hall could only be lit by reflector candles or lanterns this skylight was a great boon—in daylight, in summer and if it didn't rain! It extended right across the stage; sometimes we had trouble with birds flying in, so now there was a net permanently stretched below it.

There was a rustle in the audience behind us, a toot on the ceremonial trumpet, the church clock started to strike, and Mayor Gross, in full ceremonial regalia and carrying his wand of office, marched up the aisle to the platform, climbed up the steps and sat down in his special chair (handcarved oak and red leather) flanked on either side by the head and deputy head of the school.

By now the Mayor was a living legend. No one knew quite how old he was but the best guess was that he must be in his late seventies. His hair, worn long, was white, but his back was straight, his step and voice as fit as if he were thirty years. We sat up straighter.

First the speeches. The head teacher, Mr. Palmer, rambled through a list of how well we had done, how we were a credit to the village, how the future could be safely left in our hands, etc. etc. Same old speech every year. We all dutifully clapped in the right places, but I became distracted by a large wasp that must have flown in through the skylight, and was now circling slowly around the Mayor's head.

The wasp was joined by another, and another.

"It must be his hair-oil," whispered Ros, and someone, somewhere gave a smothered giggle just as Gross rose to his feet to make his customary speech on this sort of occasion. Now a giggle can be more infectious than the measles, and there we were trapped in uncomfortable clothes between our parents and the mayor and we knew it was supposed to be a solemn occasion, but that made it all the worse. I tried to stifle my rising hysteria by disguising it with a fit of coughing, but then everyone seemed to have the same idea, and Mayor Gross's fine words were lost in a cacophony of hackings, clearings of the throat and pretend sneezes.

He stopped, glared at us, and suddenly we were quiet. There was something about him that always made me feel uneasy. Perhaps this was because when we were young he was an effusive parent-threat. "Behave yourselves, otherwise Mayor Gross will get you!" These sort of things have a tendency to stay with you, even though you realize they don't mean a thing as you grow older.

It was time for the ceremony proper.

One by one we stepped forward and were presented with the wax seals—our names and the date on one side, the village shield on the other—ready strung to hang around our necks. We all shook hands with the Mayor (he was wearing white gloves, no sweaty palms for him) and then it was time for the form prizes, a small bag of tokens for each excellence. There were twelve different classes for the Thirds: Math, Science, Biology, Physical Geography, Agriculture, Literature, Grammar, History, Music, Handicrafts, Visual Expression (which included dance, art, architecture, acting, reciting, mime) and P.T. Optional extras included The Bible and Meteorology. Two other prizes were awarded for Good Conduct and All Round Excellence.

There were sixteen of us graduating, not counting Bill and Ben, who had been included because they were at least three years older than the rest of us and were ineducable anyway, so there was, surprise, surprise! a bag of tokens for everyone. Tam got one for Music, Ros for Handicrafts (her brother Brian wouldn't graduate until next year), Sven Meteorology, Alex All Round Excellence, Lally Good Conduct and for me the Literature prize. We were all dying to count our tokens, but it was time for the closing song.

This was addressed to the Mayor: "Sir, dismiss us with your blessing, ne'er again to gather here . . ." My Nan told me that this song, which had a sad, beautiful tune was based on an old hymn: "Lord

Dismiss us with Thy Blessing . . ." and I could tell she didn't approve of the transposition.

Our head teacher gave us the carefully pitched note and we were away, but we were only just into the second verse when the worst happened.

We had all been trying to ignore the cloud of wasps, and now flies also, that were dive-bombing Mayor Gross's head, but the two nearest him on the platform couldn't stand it a moment longer and leapt forward, clapping their hands like Spanish dancers, trying to kill as many of the insects as they could.

The trouble was, it was Bill and Ben who were the nearest.

They were about six-foot-three now, and about as graceful and effective as the work-ponies that drew the wagons. Mayor Gross was batted from side to side between the clumsy pair like a rag doll, his robes flapping around his ears, his chain bouncing up and down on his chest. We were all laughing, clapping and cheering now, and the audience were on their feet applauding when suddenly everything changed.

Mayor Gross turned comedy into drama, shock replacing humor.

He suddenly stepped back from the two boys, who collided with each other and collapsed on the stage. His face thunderous, the Mayor snatched up his wand of office and quite literally broke it over their heads, leaving blood trickling down their foreheads and ears.

There was instant silence, but the Mayor, his face still distorted with fury, muttered "Don't forget that I who made you can also destroy you. . . ." Then he turned and walked off the platform, the audience too shocked to do anything but let him through in silence.

Once he had gone however the place was pandemonium, the twins' parents rushing up to the platform to comfort their darlings, who were now howling with pain and shock.

Tam grabbed my hand: "Let's go!"

We jumped off the platform and ran down one of the now-empty side-aisles and out into the sunshine.

"Phew!" said Tam.

"Do you think they were badly hurt?"

He shook his head. "Their heads are pretty thick. Fancy a swim?"

"I'll get out of this rubbish and meet you there."

By tacit consent we didn't discuss what had happened, especially as we were soon joined by the others, who had enough speculation for the whole village. Apparently the twins had been pacified by lollipops from the ice-house, and a clean-up and bandaging at the Infirmary. No lasting damage, and they were now strutting about with white turbans on their heads as if they wore trophies from some strange encounter.

The Mayor had sent their parents a short apology implying that he had believed that he was being attacked, the twins' behavior being, at best, erratic.

Cooled off almost to the shivery stage, Tam walked me back to our house where I invited him in, knowing that Nan would have the kettle on. She made a pot of chamomile tea, pouring it into the wide, shallow mugs that meant it would cool down more quickly, and brought out some slices of tortilla. We munched in silence, nobody wanting to be first to speak about what had happened, I guess.

It was Tam who broke this, while accepting his second mug of tea. It seemed a curious question, given the circumstances.

"How many kinds of power are there?"

"Power?" echoed Nan, obviously ready to accept the way the conversation was going. "When I was a kid there were all sorts no longer in use. Atomic, solar, electricity, gas. . . . Why?"

"What's left now?"

She thought for a moment. "The power of God?"

He nodded.

"Volcanoes, floods, thunder and lightning; all the powers of Nature," I contributed.

He nodded again. "And?"

What else was there? I was suddenly reminded of the Herb-Woman's words, and I repeated them, stuttering slightly. "She—she said there were Powers th-that we knew nothing of. Ancient Powers . . ."

Nan nodded. "She is probably right. . . . What's this leading up to, Tam?"

He considered for a moment. "All the examples you have given me are correct in their own way, but none of them depend for their origin on human behavior; control, yes, but not wholly human through and through, with no natural or artificial assistance."

Nan sighed. "You're talking about the Mayor. . . ."

"It was unforgivable what he did to the twins!" I burst out. "Mayors just don't behave like that! Especially him! Why, he's always extolling the value of controlled behavior, of stoicism. . . ." To me his behavior was just as shocking as if his statue on the memorial had suddenly come to life and marched down the street, shattering windows with stones. "Weren't you shocked, Nan?"

"Shocked, yes, but not surprised. Surprised only that he has managed to hide that side of his nature for so long." She paused, considering. "You see, I could sense there was a hidden fire inside him fifty years ago, when he led us here. Without his leadership we none of us would have made it. He was single-minded, ruthless, but he had *strength*! Even though most of the time we were weary, hungry, thirsty and would have given up less than half-way here, he made us keep going. We weren't allowed to stop for anything, even for those who fell behind or—disappeared." She frowned as if at a sudden memory.

"He made *his* strength *our* strength," she continued after a moment. "But even then it was hidden. He never stormed or shouted: all his power was contained within. And anyone who has that sort of power bottled up inside him must let it out sometime, even if he doesn't realize it. He has had it good over the last fifty years, everything working right for him, slowly but surely: But there's been no *action*, and a man like that needs it. So when the twins, with the best will in the world, tried to help, and only succeeded in making a man who has a high opinion of himself and the dignity of his position look like a clown in front of those he considers to be his own people, he snapped. That's all there is to it."

"But it could happen again," I said.

"Sure, but I don't think it will. Besides, he's getting on; he won't last for ever."

"His sons could be worse," said Tam. "Especially the eldest. He even looks like his father."

"Isn't he the one who's taken over the organization of the Youth Brigade? And didn't you say you weren't interested?"

"It's just an excuse to get extra, unpaid work out of us, Mrs. Malone," said Tam. "Besides, I don't like the idea of all that drilling and marching about. It reminds me of the Hitler Youth they taught us about in History."

She looked disbelieving. "That all happened ages and ages ago! All that was an encouragement to racial genocide, and resulted in what my Papa called the Holocaust."

"It could happen here. . . ."

"Never! What a thing to say, Pretty! We're all integrated here perfectly happily. There's no case of racial or religious bigotry. I am a Jewess and I married a Roman Catholic; old Arne was a Lutheran and married a Quaker—but don't we all worship at the same Church? Well, then . . ."

"Where are all the coloreds that must have been on the train?" asked Tam quietly. "And why do no deformed babies survive the day of their birth?"

She got up, a sudden high color in her cheeks. "I think that is enough!" she said. You children weren't here at the beginning. There were some coloreds, but they died. And deformed babies can't survive anyway; it would be cruel to let them try. Have you both finished? Then I'll just clear away—"

I put my hand on her arm. "Did you hear what Gross said just after he had hit the twins?" She shook her head. "You, Tam?"

He nodded. "He said: 'Don't forget that I who made you can also destroy you. . . .'"

Nan stood stock-still, tea-pot in one hand, plate in the other. "You must have misheard him."

"Both of us?" I said.

"Well . . ." she shrugged. "Destroy us? How could he do that? Build a bomb? Execute us single-handed? He's an old man, and maybe he has delusions of grandeur. The simplest thing is just to forget what you heard, but make sure none of you invite his wrath. Just keep out of his way. Promise?"

We promised. It didn't help that I could see Nan looked definitely worried by what we had said.

A month later, after hay-harvest, we ex-Thirds and our families met in the Town Hall to learn what our future held. The system was simple enough. There were a number of jobs, permanent ones, available each year, either through death, disablement, pregnancy or new opportunities. A list was decided upon by the Council, families and Thirds were canvassed separately to assess their preferences, then the Council decided who should get what.

It was a much more decorous meeting than the last. We were each seated with our families and Bill and Ben were well at the back. Mayor Gross, flanked by the Council, all six of them, rose to his feet, cleared his throat and after the usual greeting continued with what must have been a well-worn routine.

"None of our decisions has been taken lightly, and I believe that each of you youngsters will find yourself in a position which will suit your talents, give you job satisfaction, fulfill your ambitions and, most important of all, provide a needful service to the community." He paused, looked at each of us in turn.

"Of course if any of you feel, after a reasonable trial, that either you are not suited to your tasks, or would like to try something different, then you are free to come and discuss the matter with me, and I'm sure we can reach a compromise."

"I'll bet!" muttered someone behind me, though I couldn't see who it was.

"Any questions?" No questions. "Very well; I shall read the list alphabetically. . . ."

Afterwards, drinking the courtesy mugs of cider and eating potato chips, we discussed the results, some happy, others not. It had been about eighty per cent predictable, of course, but some of the postings came as a surprise.

Who would have thought, for instance, that Norbert, always so neat and tidy, would be apprenticed to the charcoal-burners, or that Elfrida, the clumsiest girl in the class, always dropping things, would be posted to the pottery sheds? Others were no surprise. Lally and Ros apprenticed to a seamstress, and the former would then take training with the hairdresser, while the latter worked with Lally's parents in the Gift Shop for a while. Sven would become the official under-shepherd, now that Arne's arthritis was making it impossible for him to continue, except in a consultative position.

The twins (no surprise) would continue to assist their parents in the butcher's shop, and Alex, the brainy one of our class, was to become an assistant teacher at school. That was the post I had wanted most, but had to be content with what Tam called the position of Miss Inky-Fingers, deputy-clerk in the Town Hall. It was a responsible post, for it meant attending Council meetings, taking notes and then entering them in the great, heavy ledgers that recorded the village's history. I would also record births, marriages and deaths, all under supervision at first of course.

It would be nice, to be writing on that beautiful, smooth surface of the old ledgers; paper in the village had always been a problem. There had been some left when the refugees arrived, mostly school exercise books and letter-paper, but these had been used up, and we now relied on the slow process of hand-laid paper, made from the most fibrous plants: nettle, cow-parsley, burdock, mallow, angelica. The best came from rags, especially cotton or linen, but these were like gold-dust. At school we were taught orally, or from the reconstituted blackboard, but it was frustrating for the teachers. I was lucky, because Nan had a mysterious supply of paper which she doled out on birthday and Christmas, so I could indulge my love of scribbling.

Nobody asked where it came from, but outside the family it was only Tam who knew about it.

He was over the moon, of course, having secured the post of deputy-organist and as well continuing to work in the Music section of the woodworking sheds, and also being entrusted with taking the Junior Recorder class.

He called round later to see if I wanted go to the Dance. These were held once a month, on a Saturday, the music being provided by volunteers, so you never knew who would turn up, often with improvised instruments. The country music section was fairly well organized, with pipes, drums, harmonica and a two-stringed plucking instrument, but some of the others were truly awful.

In reality for most of us those dances were only a chance to show off our new dress or whatever and chat up whoever we fancied. I had no new clothes and was quite happy with Tam, so I shook my head.

"I don't think so, thanks. It's too hot, anyway. Think I'll take a walk instead."

"Mind company?"

" 'Course not."

"Pick you up after supper then."

That was the nice thing about Tam; if I had said I wanted to be on my own he would have accepted it without question. Of course we had grown up together, been together at school from the respective ages of six and five, but it was more than that. Usually at that age it was same-sex friendships, but we had always gotten on better in a boy-girl relationship. Of course when we were young Tam had just been Tam, and I never noticed anything different in his appearance unless he had, say, lost a tooth or gotten a black eye, but as we both approached puberty I became far more conscious of his face and figure, his height and his deepening voice. It was as if I was gradually seeing him unfold. At times I wished we were still kids again, at others I just couldn't wait for the changes.

Once we had just been good mates, preferring working, playing, exploring together, and we could tell each other anything; now there was a sort of constraint as though suddenly the difference in our sexes had become the most important thing in the relationship. Of course we had both done our lessons on sex together, in a perfectly correct and unemotional way as part of our Biology course, but when I started my periods I suddenly realized that what had been learned objectively had suddenly become intensely personal as far as I was concerned.

Part of me wanted to shout to the world that I was now sexually mature, I could have babies, I was *grown-up*, but the other part resented the discomfort, the mess, my aching breasts, the increasing curve of my hips and the intrusive growth of hair on my body. I didn't know whether or not I wanted Tam to know, and hadn't the slightest idea how to tell him, anyway.

Fortunately, after all my anxiety, it was solved in the simplest way possible. Tam had come round to ask me to go swimming, it was the first day of my period and I hadn't known what to say. After I had faltered myself to a stop with lame excuses, he had suddenly grinned.

"Congratulations!"

"What for?" I had said, disconcerted.

"On growing up gracefully. Oh, come on Pretty, I've got three sisters, remember? They talk about these things all the time. . . ." He must have noticed my blushes, for he gave me an awkward hug. "Listen, if it makes you embarrassed, let's have our own private code, then no one but us will know what we're talking about. Let me think . . . I know: TOM."

"Tom? Who's Tom?"

"Not *Tom*, silly. Tee, Oh, Em. Time Of Month. Got it? Right. Like a game of chess?"

"Make it dominoes. . . ." Suddenly I felt much better.

"Okay. Best of seven?"

After that I didn't need to tell him when I was due; I thought either he had a sixth sense or he counted on his fingers. A long time afterwards he told me I was always grumpy just beforehand and kept falling over things and dropping them, but at the time I just thought he was one of the most sweet and understanding people I had ever known.

He was on time as usual, and we strolled through the village, enjoying the balmy air. It wasn't dark yet, and we exchanged greetings and smiles with those we met. Most of our contemporaries were going to the dance, and Ros had a new dress, towing a rebellious Brian as chaperon. Alex was escorting a thin girl called Sue and the twins were marching up the street with arms linked, but we didn't see Lally or Sven. I was glad we weren't going.

"Shall we walk up a bit?" said Tam.

We took the river road for a mile, then branched off to the left where a narrow walled lane, used for bringing feed up by pony-cart during the winter, divided the High from the Low pastures. The moon was a bright lantern and with the dusk the bats swooped above us and moths fluttered about my hair. Far away came the soft hoo-hoo of an owl. Tam held out his hand: I took it. It seemed a comfortable thing to do. He had never even kissed me but somehow I didn't want to rush things, to change our relationship again. Not just yet, anyway . . . Besides I was scared, both of not knowing what it would be like, but most of all uncertain whether he liked me as much as I liked him, and if—

"Ow!" He had squeezed my hand really hard.

"Sorry." He released it and turned me so I was looking due north. "Look!"

I couldn't see anything unusual. "What am I looking for?"

"Lights. There!" And now I could see them too. Lights flickering in the distance—a distance that could only mean one place: the forbidden Wilderness!

CHAPTER ELEVEN

"Who—or what—the hell is *that*?"

Who-or-what indeed. The Wilderness was not only forbidden to us but to adults as well, ever since some mysterious disappearances soon after the refugees arrived fifty years ago. Some people said that those lost were not worth keeping anyway, but that was not the point. The place was out-of-bounds to everyone. So, who could be risking themselves up there?

"It could be Sven and his father looking for an injured sheep?"

Tam shook his head. "We passed his father and grandfather in the village."

"We didn't see Sven—or Lally."

He turned to me. "They wouldn't be so *stupid* . . . Would they?"

"You know she can make him do anything."

As we watched the bobbing lanterns were lowered, became still for a moment, then disappeared.

"They've gone inside!"

"Let's go!"

I don't think we had any idea what we thought we were going to do, just go there and see if we could stop them, talk to them, whatever. Tam helped me over the stone wall and we ran up one of the sheep-tracks toward the dark bulk of the forest, some quarter-mile away. Long before we got there we were out of breath and I had a stitch, so when we reached the hedge we stopped for a moment to recover.

There wasn't a sound as we made our way round the hedge where—surprisingly—we remembered the tunnel to be; even the sheep were silent. When we got to the entrance we knelt down; as I had grown at least six inches in height and several in width since we were last here, five years ago, I expected the tunnel to be impossible to traverse, but no; if I was correct, it had been widened and deepened since then. Indeed I could smell freshly crushed leaves and grass, which meant that someone had been through here recently. We had no lantern, but the waxing moon was bright overhead as we looked at one another.

"Shall we?" I whispered.

"We shouldn't. . . ."

"Just to the end of the tunnel?"

"No further, then. I'll go first. . . ."

We stood up inside, brushing the debris of the tunnel from our clothes. If we had thought it was quiet outside, the silence inside was positively deafening. Outside there had been a pleasant little breeze, here the air was still. Not a leaf stirred, there were no rustles in the undergrowth, only the sound of our own breathing.

"I was sure they came in here. . . ." I could hear the beginning of doubt in his voice.

"They did." I found we were both whispering. I made up my mind. "I'm going to take a look further in."

"We can't. . . ."

"We've got this far. I've got to know for sure. Coming?"

I suppose he could have tried to stop me physically, but he didn't. In spite of his natural caution, I guess he was as curious as I was.

In front of us now, lit by moonlight, was the trail we had followed all those years ago to the glade where the story of the Sleeping Princess had come so vividly to life for us all. Strange how it was all coming back so clearly to my mind, the smell of trodden clover, daisy and dandelion fresh in our nostrils; then there had been sunshine, now it was moonshine but the path was as clear as if it were yesterday.

As we approached the glade another smell came to our nostrils, this time not a pleasant one. Ashes? Pig manure? Some kind of chemical . . . No, I couldn't identify it at all. We came to the edge of the glade, still having neither heard nor seen anyone, and I stopped so abruptly that Tam bumped into me.

"What is it?"

"It's . . . It's different."

I couldn't understand it. Was my memory playing me tricks? I remembered a little garden of delight, a ring of stones surrounding a patch of short cropped grass, the whole edged with shrubs and trees. Now it looked like a desert. The ring of stones was there, looking smaller than I remembered but maybe that was because it seemed the trees and shrubs had moved farther back. And the circle of grass just wasn't there any more; instead there was a sort of sea of churned mud, like the trampled mess left by cattle going to the drinking-trough. And the foul smell was stronger than ever—

Tam gripped my arm. "Listen!"

Then we both heard it: a giggle, a girlish voice. "Clumsy oaf! Can't you even *walk* straight?"

It was Lalage's voice, no doubt of it. And if she was here then Sven would be with her.

I moved forward, but the moon went behind a cloud at that very moment and I hesitated. After what seemed like a long minute, the moon slid out again, and the slushy circle came once more into view. And into that circle came Lally, dancing as though she heard music beyond our hearing, her dress floating around her with the grace of a ball-gown, her head turned to watch as Sven came stumbling after in a clumsy parody of her steps. He mumbled something as Tam drew me back into the shelter of the trees.

"Ah, sweet Prince, my name is . . . But nay, I protest; you must guess!"

Another mumble from Sven.

"No, it is not that. Another guess? No? Then would you ask your musicians for another air, that we may dance the hours away. . . . How about one of those *divine* waltzes? Yes, yes: that's it!" and she swung away in graceful circles, in the arms of some invisible partner, Sven following doggedly behind. Suddenly she stopped dancing, held her hand behind her ear in a pantomime of listening, and began to count. "List, I hear the chimes! Three, four, five, six . . . I must be away before the stroke of twelve. . . ."

"My God!" breathed Tam in my ear. "It's Cinderella now!"

But I could hear the chimes too. . . . It must be the wind bringing us the sound of the church clock in the village, I tried to convince myself. Except that there was no wind and it certainly wasn't midnight—

The moon slipped once more behind a cloud, there was the sound of running feet, then the moon emerged again and we were gazing out on an empty glade, empty that is except for the sound of mocking laughter, not pretty girlish laughter but merriment that had a gloating sound, like a miser chuckling over his gold, and it finished with a sibilant hiss, as if the same hoarder was rubbing his palms together in glee. . . . No, it wasn't like that either, it was as if the star had left the stage and an understudy was practicing a laugh she couldn't get quite right.

The hair rose on the back of my neck, and I had to stifle a scream as Tam put his hand on my arm; instantly the moon disappeared again and we were left in a breathy, humid darkness. Under my feet there was a faint tingling, as though I had the beginning of chilblains.

"What's the matter, Pretty?"

"Didn't you hear it? The clock chiming . . . That awful laugh!"

He shook his head. "I didn't hear either."

Was I going mad? "You must have!"

Again he shook his head. "But you've got sharper ears than I have. You sure it wasn't a nightjar you heard? They make a funny sort of churring noise. . . ."

Suddenly I wanted to forget that laugh. "The others have gone by now. Let's go!"

We hurried back and out through the tunnel again and it wasn't until we were outside that we saw two figures ahead of us, making their rather slow way down to the village. We followed, a cautious distance behind. "Why on earth were they playing that stupid Cinderella game?"

"Don't ask me! But you know what Lally is like: she's always wanted to play princess."

"Yes, but why come all the way up here?"

He shook his head. "She could act out her fantasies anywhere. That place was hardly a theater. Besides, only children still play at fairy-tales."

Only four or five years ago you were acting-out with the rest of us, I thought. But I didn't say so.

The moon was now clear of cloud-wrack and we could see the two ahead of us quite distinctly; we found we were walking slower and slower to keep a reasonable distance back from them. It looked as if one or the other was having difficulty in walking; they were clasped close together, but stumbling and swaying as if they had drunk too much cider.

All at once Lally fell down, dragging Sven with her.

"Come on," said Tam. "There's something wrong!"

It didn't take long to reach them, but by the time we arrived they were on their feet again.

"Are you okay?" I asked anxiously, retrieving one of their lanterns, which had gone out. Tam relit it, adjusting the shutter so it shone full on their faces.

"Of course we're okay," said Sven gruffly. "We just took a tumble, that's all. Where did you come from, anyway?"

"We saw your lanterns—sure you're all right?"

They didn't *look* all right. The lantern showed a deep scratch down Sven's left cheek and he had skinned knuckles, but Lally was in a much worse state. She was swaying from side to side, muttering unintelligibly, her eyes closed, her face chalk-white, her unpinned hair hanging in tangles down her back.

"Lally?" If I hadn't seen her dancing so vivaciously only a short while ago I would have thought her really sick.

"Leave me *alone!*" Abruptly she sat down, clutching her stomach.

I knelt beside her, brushed the hair back from her damp forehead. It was the closest I had been to her physically for years. Although we were in the same class, she had her friends, I had mine. The only time we had shared one another's company had been those magic moments in the Wilderness when she had been our beautiful Sleeping Princess—

"Leave me *alone!*" she said again, more vehemently, striking my hand aside and glaring at me. For once she was not even pretty. On her neck were what looked like a couple of love-bites, and a trickle of blood had leaked from one nostril. She smelled strange, too: not unwashed, but rather as though she had sprayed herself with a sort of burnt, chemical perfume. Her feet were muddy, too.

Scrambling to her feet, she took Sven's arm. "Take me home," she muttered.

Tam handed back the lantern. "May as well go down together," he said equably. "Just in case."

I took the other lantern, as Lally made no effort to pick it up. It wasn't a comfortable journey. We obviously weren't wanted, at least as far as Lally was concerned, and Sven seemed unusually subdued, even for him. They also stumbled again from time to time. When we reached the outskirts of the village however, Lally snatched the lantern from my hand and ran off in the direction of her house, still stumbling a little.

"Sorry," said Sven gruffly. "She's always like that—afterwards."

"After what?" I asked.

"After . . . after we go *There*."

"We saw you," said Tam. "Dancing. We thought you went there for something else. You know . . ."

"He means sex," I said bluntly.

Even by lantern-light I could see he was blushing. "Heavens, no!" he said hurriedly. "She has never let me near her. She's not like that, never was." Perhaps it was the night, perhaps the relief of being able to share at least what must have been an awkward secret, but he was becoming unusually expansive. "Lal is normally very prudish, whatever impression she gives to other people. You may not think it to look at her, but it's only there that she really lets herself go."

"You mean—that's not the first time you've been in the Wilderness since we were forbidden?" Tam sounded incredulous.

"Oh, no. Many times."

"But—but . . . What about the ban? What Mayor Gross said?"

"Lally said it didn't matter. She said she had her fingers crossed, so when she promised it didn't count. As long as we weren't caught."

"What's there that's so important?" I asked. "It looked pretty dismal to me."

"Oh, no!" His face looked different, enthusiastic. "It's great, it really is! You've no idea. . . ."

"Tell me."

"Well, it's kinda difficult to explain. Like—it's neat

when we're there, but sorta difficult to explain why afterwards." He sounded confused. "It's not like we actually do anything. It's—it's just nice. Happy."

"I heard chimes," I said. "And a strange kind of laughter."

"That'd be us," said Sven. "We laugh a lot. So do They, but They haven't got it quite right yet. Guess they aren't used to it."

"They?"

But now he looked confused. "They? What They?"

"You said—"

He shook his head. "I didn't say anything about anyone else. It's just us, is all." And he would say nothing more.

It wasn't until I was safely home that I remembered those livid marks on Lally's neck, and wondered how they had got there if what he said was true. That she wouldn't let him anywhere near her.

One month later I woke early with a feeling of anticipation, but for a moment couldn't remember why. Then I realized; it was Dating Day! Anticipation was immediately replaced by butterflies in my stomach.

Of course that wasn't its real name, only what we called it in secret. Officially it was Choosing Candidates for Summer Camp. It was the day in the year when Mayor Gross decided who was going to pair off with whom. Of course his decisions didn't come out of thin air; they were based on observation, parent's wishes, teacher's recommendations and a bit of discreet spying here and there.

By the time the girls reached sixteen and the boys

a year or two older it was reckoned we were ready for marriage—or at least what was called "Commitment." To prove that Mayor Gross had chosen right, those he considered eligible were sent on a ten-day camping trip, away from adult supervision, to "get to know one another better."

Sometimes these liaisons worked out, sometimes they didn't. Those that failed were usually recycled at a later date with a new partner, and eventually most people were matched correctly. There were very few bachelors and spinsters in Deliverance, a few widows and widowers, but they were encouraged to remarry, like my father.

All this partnering was highly embarrassing to us, mainly because it was usually a foregone conclusion as to who would be chosen. Of course we weren't named in pairs, but nevertheless everyone knew, for instance, that Lally and Sven would be matched and probably Tam and myself, because we had been together for so long. Ros had had so many beaux that I couldn't guess who she would be picked with, but some of our other mates were easier to predict.

I took my towel and soap and went downstairs to the yard, taking care not to wake Nan, who now shared the attic with me, Griselda's two babies having taken over her room. We didn't mind—at least I didn't. It was nice to share.

Nan had left me a covered pitcher and basin in the tented wash-area and I had a quick all-over. The water was warm, it had been such a balmy night. Hanging the towel on the line to dry, I tipped the washing-water onto the vegetable garden, and fed and watered the hens, removing three eggs from the nests.

In the kitchen I found Nan was already up, with a large bowl of muesli and a drink of goat's milk for my breakfast. As the Dating Day meeting wasn't until midday I carried out my usual chores—fetching water, putting out the garbage for collection (being careful to keep scraps for the piggery apart), sweeping and dusting our attic room and making the beds, peeling vegetables for lunch, going to the baker's and stacking wood for the oven which would be lighted in the evening.

At half-past eleven I went up to change into my best—multicolored skirt and sleeveless top—and at a quarter to the hour I set off with Nan, my father and Griselda (the latter heavily pregnant with her third) for the Church Hall, the babies having been left with a sitter (a token per child per hour, the standard rate).

It seemed most of the village was headed in the same direction as us—something to gossip about for days afterwards. And not only gossip: although gambling was expressly forbidden, many tokens would have been placed secretly with the unofficial bookie, a metal-worker called Ronnie Whelan, via one or other of his runners, the two convenient street-cleaners. If business was slack, Whelan would open a book on how many lambs would be born in any particular month, whether it would rain on St. Swithins, snow on Christmas Day, even whether Mrs. So-and-So's baby would be a boy or a girl or whether Mr. X would reach his ninetieth birthday. And of course behind closed doors the betting was fast and furious on some board games. Even in school we had gambled on beetle races in the playground, but only for an apple, a bon-bon, a piece of ribbon.

When we reached the Church Hall it was already three-quarters full, with five minutes to go, and by the time the church clock struck midday and the Mayor took his place on the platform, there were latecomers standing at the back.

First came the predictable speech about family values, responsibility to the community, the necessity to hand on to future generations those most fitted to "carry the torch," whatever that meant. Then came the bit about the pride the village had in its youngsters, the excellence of their upbringing, their high moral standards etc. etc.

Now for the naming of those chosen for Summer Camp. As expected there were adjustments from the previous year, with a switch of partners. The most surprising was a twenty-year-old girl, Selina, who had been twice before and had refused her parents' choice both times. She had been waiting for Hans, two years her junior, who had been one of our class, and at last she had got her wish. That was great, because I knew, via Ros, that he wanted her, too. Sven and Lally. Me and Tam, no surprises though I knew I was blushing and daren't look for him in the audience. Ros was paired with Alex, not her first choice, I was sure of that, but in the last few years she had been through all the eligible males like a dose of salts and was on her second lap.

Eventually all were named, ten pairs, and the Camp was scheduled to start on Monday. Ten days of freedom. . . .

All at once there was a bustle at the back. Two figures were marching down the aisle towards Mayor

Gross, another two in tow behind them. With mingled horror and amusement I saw it was Bill and Ben and their parents.

Their mother came to a halt. "What about our two? What about William and Benjamin? It's not fair to leave them out. Why can't they go to Summer Camp, too?" And she stuck her hands on her hips and glared at the Mayor, her husband behind her grunting his approval.

Behind them the twins started a little jig.

"Wanna go!" they chanted. "Wanna go . . ."

CHAPTER TWELVE

If they had planned it for months, the twins and their parents couldn't have hoped for a greater impact.

There was a moment of complete silence, then hubbub, those at the back standing up to get a better view of the confrontation.

"Well?" demanded the twins' mother. "Among that lot you've two pair as has been before, and for one girl it will be the third time. I can count, you know. . . ."

"Let them go!" said their father, hunching his shoulders and clenching his fists, as if he was about to thump the first person who opposed him. From behind some wag decided to stir it still further, and encouraged a chant of the same words: "Let them go! Let them go! Let them goooo . . ."

Mayor Gross was completely at a loss. But he tried. "Now then, boys: I realize you must be disappointed, but the participants have already been chosen. Perhaps we could arrange something for next year. . . ."

They burst into tears. Not just quiet sobs but great floods of tears running down their cheeks and dripping off their chins, accompanied by howls like a couple of caged wolves. The sight of the two blubbering boys was too much for some of the audience, who started to giggle. Everything was becoming pure farce; didn't their parents realize what this camp was all about, I wondered? How on earth could Bill and Ben play the dating game? They would never be allowed to marry anyway, in case they passed on their disabilities. Besides, they were quite happy with each other. And Lally, of course.

"It would not—not be suitable for them to go," said the Mayor, in his most commanding voice. "This is a boy/girl camp, not a holiday for all who want to go. Besides, as you well know, William and Benjamin require constant supervision: they could not be allowed to go off on their own, as these other young people will. No, I'm afraid there is no question of them being allowed to go."

"One moment!" A clear, high, girlish voice: Lally? She came dancing down the aisle, dressed as usual to kill, in a blue dress threaded with white ribbon. She came right to the front and gazed up at Mayor Gross.

"Excuse me sir?"

"Yes?" He was scowling at yet another interruption.

"I believe I have a solution to the problem," and she smiled charmingly up at him. "My friend and I are used to the boys, and we should be only too glad to keep an eye on them at camp. They can have a tent next to ours and can go on expeditions with us. What do you say, sir?"

I couldn't believe my ears and, glancing across at Sven, neither could he. When we were kids Lally had quite enjoyed the twins' adoration, but in recent years she had declared herself more than once sick

of their slavish attitude, spurning all their advances
and throwing away their little offerings of tired flowers
and squashed bon-bons. Not that the twins were
deterred: they just accepted it, as they did most things,
as part of the puzzle of life.

"But my dear Lalage," said Mayor Gross: "The
whole point of this camp is to give you and your—
your friend, time to get to know each other better,
and—"

She gave him a demure bob-curtsey. "And I cannot
pretend that we were not looking forward to it, but
I should *hate* to think of them being deprived of a
holiday. So, you will let them come, won't you?"

"Well, if you're sure . . ." He didn't like it, we could
see that, but he couldn't very well refuse now.

The twins and their parents were beaming all over
their faces: the best cuts of meat for the Gift Shop
for a while to come, I thought cynically. But I was
sure that wasn't what Lally had in mind when she
sacrificed herself and poor Sven, who was still looking
bewildered. No, she was now looking like the
proverbial cat with the cream, and that was a bad
sign—for somebody. As we left the twins were
chanting: "Beeping Sleauty! Beeping Sleauty!" just
as they had all those years ago when life had been
so much easier to understand. . . .

The camping site was some five miles south of the
village, about a quarter-mile from a quiet stretch of
the river. Once, before the refugees came, it had
obviously been used for grazing or haymaking, for
there was an old barn standing on the forest side,
most of its timbers silvered with weathering, where

it hadn't been repaired. The land was flat here, ideal for putting up tents, with the barn as a backup in case the weather became impossible. It had been fitted out with two-tiered bunks, washing cubicles, a dining-area and storeroom, and an open range for cooking.

In the last twenty years, the age of this camp, there had been only two washouts, but this year the weather looked set fair for the ten days we should be away and we sang and whistled as we followed the cart piled high with provisions, bedding, fuel and personal possessions down the trail to the site. Dust and seed-pods flew away from our feet, we were all in a holiday mood and the sounds of "She'll be Coming Round the Mountain" and "Clementine" vied with the babble of larks above and the rush of the river below to our left.

Joe, who drove the cart, was the Chief Gardener; his wife Betty, a nurse, was already at the camp. They were a childless couple, but for years now had run the camp, obviously enjoying the company of young people. She would be preparing lunch, for she did all the cooking; he would already have dug the latrines downwind. They lived in the barn for the ten days, keeping out of the way, but always ready to help if the need arose, and taking care of the unadventurous who chose to stay on-site for the duration of the trip.

While we were actually at the camp we were expected to help with the chores; fetching water from the river, chopping wood, cleaning pots and pans, keeping the camp-site tidy. But once we were away . . .

We arrived in time for lunch—meat-pies, salad and fruit—to find the eleven tents already erected

at a discreet distance from each other, and something
delicious-smelling cooking on the slow-barbecue.
Screens were set up around the two latrines, and
after lunch we retrieved sleeping bags and washing
things from the cart and set off to look for a tent.
Lally and Sven had chosen a tent near the river, with
Bill and Ben next to them, and we took the one just
above. There was no pretense about girl sharing with
boy now, though those who didn't care to—like Ros
at the moment—were free to share with one of their
own sex.

After lunch Tam was inveigled into a game of
Bataille in the games area to the south, so I decided
to explore on my own. Climbing the steep slope
behind the camp I saw a faint strand of smoke from
the village, five miles to the north, and the haze of
far mountains beyond. To the west the sullen green
of the plantation encroached less than a mile away;
to the east, across the river, the land lay barren and
rock-strewn, not a tree or shrub or blade of grass to
break the monotony.

I looked down at the camp; I hadn't realized I had
climbed so high. The tents looked like toy ones, the
people like ants. The lads were still playing Bataille,
Bill and Ben were kicking a ball about, some of the
girls were stretched out sunbathing, others splashing
about in the shallows of the river.

I sat down and nibbled at a few blades of vinegar-
grass, relishing the sharp tang. It was all very peaceful:
perhaps for the first time in my life I had unlimited
space all around me, I was completely alone and
had no responsibilities. Of course I had been alone
before; in the fields, by the river, the library, my

bedroom, an empty house, but the occasions for this had been circumscribed; time had been short: more chores, school tomorrow, a hole in a stocking to mend, candles or lanterns to light, someone's birthday to remember ...

But now, alone in this emptiness of grass and sky, I was free. I could stand, sit, lie, rest, run, leap, sleep as and when I pleased, free of all constraints: free of time most of all, the one thing that tied us all with bonds we couldn't break, an invisible tyranny that ruled us all.

I felt as if something that had been weighing me down for years suddenly blew away on the soft summer breeze, and for some silly reason I felt like crying for the blessed loss of care.

I lay back on the grass and closed my eyes, stretching out my arms and legs into a star shape and letting the sunshine leach out all the innate weariness, stiffness and impurities from my body. The breeze, warm and grass-scented, touched my cheeks, my legs, my arms with tiny impersonal fingers, soothing and caressing in one. I could hear the drone of a bumble-bee, the song of larks, buzz of gnats and even, I fancied, the scurry of ants and the bending of grasses. . . .

I awoke with a start: The sun had left me and was curving down towards the plantation in the west, reddening the sky as it went. A fine day tomorrow. I must have turned onto my right side as I slept, for I could feel the crease of grass-marks on my cheek, and see them on my arm and leg. It must be near seven, and time for supper; a moment later, as if echoing my thought, there came a tinny clatter from below: the supper-bell.

Rising to my feet, I started to brush the grass and debris from my clothes. To my left the last of the swallows were snaring insects, skimming off the river with the bats; to my right fingers of shadow were creeping towards the camp—

What was that? A flash of a lighter color at the fringe of the trees as though someone was creeping out to take a better look at us— By the time I had blinked it had gone, whatever it was. Perhaps I had imagined it. Perhaps it was just another of the campers, exploring like me. If so, why wasn't whoever-it-was making their way towards supper?

Anyway, it was none of my business; I wasn't about to miss my food worrying about shadows. I ran down the hill.

"Where've you *been*?" asked Tam.

"Exploring. I went up the hill; everything looks great from up there."

"Surely that didn't take six *hours*?"

"I fell asleep—"

"Typical!"

"Typical nothing! Anyway you were quite happy to mike off and play Bataille!"

"So? At least I was using up a bit of energy . . ." He was laughing at me.

I bristled. "If you had come with me you might have seen—" I stopped. He was obviously in a teasing mood, and any suggestion that I had seen a stranger lurking on the fringes of the plantation would have been met with derision.

"Seen what?" He was helping himself again from

the bean-pot supper-dish. One thing about Tam: he could eat enough for two and still remain as thin as a lath. His sisters used to call him "Hollow Legs."

"Oh—lots of things. You can see for miles," I added lamely.

"Maybe I'll go up there tomorrow morning. I could get some ideas on where to go for our expedition." He didn't look at me as he said this, and for no reason I found myself blushing. It was the custom for those couples who so wished, to pack up food and sleeping bags the following day after lunch, and go off for a few days on their own, leaving behind those who were content to spend their nights (and days) in their laced-up tents and also those who were dissatisfied with the choice of partner.

So, he was happy that we should go off together. Somehow I hadn't thought this far, and felt embarrassed at the omission. What would he expect of me? Come to that, we were supposed to be sharing a tent tonight, but I thought he wasn't the sort of person to try to change our relationship in a tent not a million miles from the others.

When we returned to the village we would have to fill out a standard questionnaire on our experiences with our partner, and it was Mayor Gross who finally consented to Commitment or Marriage. I suppose it was as good a way as any to have an independent arbiter. I knew there had never been a so-called "divorce" in the village, although perhaps a half-dozen separations. These couples were not allowed to remarry. Any children of the marriage under ten years old stayed with their mother; at ten they were allowed to choose which parent to live with. As the Mayor himself stated: it was the "civilized" way to live.

After supper, and a share of the washing-up, a group of us played "Homopoly" inspired by a game of my Nan's childhood, and based on buying and selling property in a fictional town called "Erewhon." Alex won, after a busy couple of hours: he usually excelled at these sorts of games, being the junior chess champion as well.

There was no lights-out or curfew on holiday, and some of us had made reckless vows to stay up all night to celebrate, but when it came to it we were all ready for bed at much the usual time. I caught myself out in a couple of enormous yawns, decided enough was enough, went for a wash and visited the latrines, then took my lantern to the tent. As I passed, I could see over half the other tents were already illuminated with a warm glow.

There was no sign of Tam. I reckoned he was giving me time to get undressed and into my sleeping-bag. Once in I wriggled around for a bit, trying to get comfortable, although the straw palliasses we had been given ironed out the worst of the unevenness of the ground and some of its hardness. I was dozing when I felt the tent-flap pushed aside.

I opened my eyes sleepily. "Hi, there! Thought you'd got lost. . . ."

"Watching the stars . . . I'm shattered; go to sleep. Talk to you in the morning."

And although I was camping out for the first time, the ground was hard and I was sharing the tent with a stranger, I fell asleep almost at once, waking only briefly a couple of times to find the lantern doused, the tent-flap fastened back to admit a welcome breeze, and the sound of soft breathing. . . .

Someone was pinching my toes. "Wake up, sleepy-head! Breakfast . . ."

It was Lally, of all people. Blinking sleepily, I glanced across the tent, but Tam's pallet was empty.

"He's gone walkies, your partner," she said. "Up top, spying out the land." She paused. "Have a good night?"

I knew what she meant but preferred to take the question literally.

"Slept like a dormouse. You?"

"Oh, the same," she agreed. She glanced away. "Er . . . where are you two off to?"

"Haven't a clue," I said, discarding my shift and wriggling into my clothes. "I don't think Tam has decided yet."

"Don't you get a say?" She sounded incredulous.

"Just because Sven does whatever you say without question, it doesn't mean we work the same way. I'm quite happy for Tam to make the suggestions."

"I'll bet!"

"You know what I mean!" I could feel myself blushing again.

"Okay, *okay*, no offense: just joking. . . . What I really wanted to ask was a sort of favor."

"Such as?"

"Could we—Sven and the boys and I—go part of the way with you? Just a few miles, till we get away from the camp. And then meet you same place after lunch on the last day?"

Knowing Lally, there was more to this than met the eye. "I'll ask Tam," I compromised.

"Don't forget we're saddled with the morons."

"They're not morons: they're good boys, treated right." I brushed my hair vigorously.

"Exactly: boys, not men. Come on, you know they're not *normal*?"

"That doesn't give you the right to—"

"It gives me every right! Didn't we offer to give them a holiday, take care of them?"

"*You* did," I said, remembering. "I don't recall Sven having any say in the matter. Fact is, when I looked at him he seemed utterly flabbergasted. Why did you volunteer to take them, anyway?"

She smiled, a sickly-sweet Lally special. "Out of the goodness of my heart: why else?"

"I don't know, but I'll find out."

"There's nothing to find. . . . Come on, give us a break. You will let us travel partway with you?"

It was like the answer to a puzzle without the question. While I was eating breakfast I kept wondering what was motivating her.

I asked Tam whether he had enjoyed his walk.

"Great! You can see for miles. Of course there was a bit of mist this early, but it's given me an idea or two."

I told him of Lally's request.

"Did you tell her we hadn't decided?" "We" . . . I liked that.

"Of course. She said it didn't matter."

He shook his head. "I just can't figure out that girl. Why should she need us?" He sighed. "Okay by me, so long as you don't mind. But only for a few miles; I don't want her spoiling our holiday." "Our," I liked that even better.

On the way to tidy our tent I told her yes, but she

didn't seem particularly grateful. All she said was: "I knew you'd see it my way. . . ."

I wished I did.

Tam and I went for a swim, then he suggested we go to look at the maps in the barn, which showed possible routes to the north and south. But when we got there, map-reading was put right out of mind. A red-faced and obviously angry Betty stood in the door of the store-room, hands on hips, while her husband Joe scrabbled on his hands and knees at the rear. In his hands he held a piece of board; at his back was a neat gap in the wall.

"What's up?"

"Someone's been stealing the stores, and it's not the first time it's happened!" said Betty.

CHAPTER THIRTEEN

"What's missing?" I asked.

"You said this wasn't the first time?" added Tam.

"What's missing this time is, as far as I can see, a small sack of flour and a jar of corn-oil. And yes, this is the third time this has happened. Three years ago I thought it was our fault," said Betty. "That time it was a jar of honey and dried fruit. We replaced the goods at our own expense. The following year it was a sack of potatoes and a small cooking pot. This time we knew we weren't to blame, and it wasn't any of the campers."

"Tell them what we found last year, Bet," prompted her husband.

"Oh, yes, in place of the goods was a little bag of shells, those ones that curve in on themselves, that they taught us at school were once used for barter in some native place or other."

"Cowries," said Tam.

"That's them. Well, we took them to—" she looked at her husband: "to someone we know, and she gave us more than enough tokens to cover the loss." The Herb-Woman, I guessed. "She said that if ever more stuff was pinched then we were to bring her whatever was left in its place and she'd give us a good price.

Well, that's fair enough, but what I want to know is who in the village is pinching it!" She clasped her hands over her heart. "Fair gives me the shivers to think as someone's creeping in here at night and nicking stuff. Must be for the hell of it, 'cos no one starves in Deliverance, as you know. Teenagers doing it for a thrill, I guess—begging your pardon, Pretty, Tam—but you know what I mean. . . ."

I nodded, but all I could think of was the figure I had seen on the fringes of the plantation last night. Could that have been the thief? I wished now I had told someone else at the time. Even if they had laughed at me then, I would have been proved right by events.

Thinking about thievery, I recalled that for the last few years there had been a number of things that "went missing" around this time of year, a few eggs, a loaf or two, a string of sausages. No one reported the losses, because no one wanted to involve Mayor Gross in an investigation that would drag on into suspicion-filled months and would lead to the wrong person(s) being convicted (probably).

Tam interrupted my thoughts. "Did whoever it was leave anything this time?"

Joe scrabbled around at the back of the store. "Not looked. Nothing so far . . . Ah, yes!" He held up a string of beads. "What'll we do with these, then? They don't look much to me. . . ." He held up a necklace of alternating blue and white stones. Tam took it from him, and I could tell from the sudden stillness of his body that he had discovered something. But when he spoke his voice was casual enough.

"Bit tatty," he said. "What's the cost of the goods

that were taken? I mean how much would it cost to replace them?"

Husband and wife looked at one another. She shrugged. "Fifteen tokens, I reckon," said Betty. "Suppose I could take them to—to the same person."

Tam weighed them in his hand. "Well, they're not worth much, but they're quite pretty." He grinned. "I believe I could find a home for these. I think I've got that many tokens with me. Save you the trouble of going to someone else. . . . What do you say?"

They were obviously relieved. "That's kind of you, Master Tam," said Joe. "But what guarantee have we that whoever-it-is won't try the same thing next year?"

"None at all," said Tam. "But all you have to do is borrow one of the guard dogs. Say you've been having trouble with foxes. I'll go get those tokens. . . ."

While he was away, and I was wondering to whom the "tatty" beads were destined, several others wandered in to look at the large map on the wall.

This was a hand-drawn effort, a rough contour map showing land to the north, south and west of the village, the river forming the eastern boundary, with a neat red line drawn around the edge. To the north it stopped at the foothills, the Wilderness being excluded. To the west the red line bisected the Plantation about three miles in; to the south the boundary was twenty-five miles from the village. In between were marked some "Camping-sites." A note at the bottom said that the southern boundary was marked by three on-site boulders, marked with a cross. "The red line is the limit of any exploration," the note added. "No one is allowed beyond this line."

Most of the couples had decided where to go already, and were just memorizing their routes. Three couples were staying in camp: Selina and her Hans, Ros and Alex and a plump girl called Peggy and her partner Charlie. Ros had gone off Alex, Peggy off Charlie, so the two girls were sharing a tent for the time being. I was willing to bet Ros wouldn't last the week without a change. . . .

I wondered where we would go. There was a fair-sized wood about five miles away, and if we did a couple of treks we could take the tent and have a cozy home-from-home. Or there was the river way, but a few of the others were taking that trail. The plantation looked a bit gloomy, but—

"Can you organize Lally and Co. to be ready immediately after lunch?"

"I think so. . . . Where are we going exactly, Tam?" He was looking over my shoulder at the map.

"Well, we've got to drop off the others somewhere, so I thought that wood—" he pointed to the one I had been studying. "Then we can take off on our own."

"Are we taking the tent?"

He looked at me in astonishment. "What on earth for? We've got to travel as light as we can."

I was amazed. I was the one who usually made the decisions, and I was about to say so, when I thought better of it. All right, if it made him feel good I'd let him take the lead, at least for a while.

"I'll tell Lally," I said.

Surprisingly they were well advanced in their packing. Apparently they were taking both tents, for these were rolled up, together with four sleeping bags, all suspended from two metal carrying poles, remnants of the days when the villagers had had television aerials, which of course had no use now. Two loaded rucksacks stood by the side, and the twins were flexing their muscles, while Lally sat under a nettle-paper parasol chewing a bon-bon.

"Hi," she said. "Sven's gone for the food."

I watched Bill and Ben practice lifting the loaded poles, giggling, and was aware of at least one reason why Lally had agreed to look after them. In the encyclopedias I had studied there had been photographs of intrepid explorers trekking through forests, across deserts, up mountains, carrying at best a camera and a swagger stick. Behind them came their bearers, loaded down with all the baggage. Lally had found hers.

"Mrs. Livingstone, I presume?" I said.

"Huh?" She didn't read encyclopedias.

"Tam wants us all to be ready after lunch," I said. "But I see you're already packed."

"We're ready when you are."

"Have you decided what you're doing for the rest of the time?"

She put her finger to her lips. "Yes, but it's a *secret*, isn't it boys?"

"Secret, secret!" they chorused.

I reported back to Tam, indignant at the use to which she was putting the twins.

"You don't have to be sorry for them," he said. "They're big and strong and will be perfectly happy carrying the gear if it's for Lalage. Trouble is, you always put yourself in other people's positions. You can't think and feel for all of us, you know; everybody's different."

Tam was changing before my eyes. He wasn't usually so critical, or so outspoken. The fact that he was probably right about my fussing didn't help either.

I changed the subject. "What food are we taking?"

Surprising me again, he was ready with a list which he ticked off on his fingers. "Flour, salt, oil, muesli, bacon, pemmican, cured sausages, dried fruit, chamomile tea, honey; four large potatoes, onions, carrots, tomato paste, cheese, small jar of butter. Small fry-pan, ditto cookpot; two mugs, two plates, cutlery, two large water-bottles. I think that's it. . . ."

"I should jolly well hope so!" It sounded as if he was planning to stay out all week. "I hadn't planned on spending my whole holiday cooking!"

"I can cook as well, you know that."

True, of course; boys and girls were taught together at school, in case parents or future wives ever became sick. Tam was competent, and he had helped Nan once or twice.

We went to the barn to collect what we needed. Everything was free on this trip, of course, and after lunch each pair would be given enough perishables to last them through until midday tomorrow. We managed to get everything we needed, and I added some dried mushrooms and some fresh french beans, plus a couple of slices of gammon. I almost forgot a sharp knife for cutting and slicing.

Tam took the heaviest items in his rucksack, and slung the cooking pots on the outside. Our sleeping bags were rolled tight, to be fastened on top of our rucksacks, and the water bottles would be slung from our belts.

Lunch over—meat and potato pie, carrots and peas,

followed by summer pudding—we collected our
perishables, wrapped in cabbage leaves and tied with
string in a net, and went in search of the others.
Immediately Lally relieved us of our rucksacks and
slung them on the backs of the twins; Sven was already
heavily laden as well.

"The least we can do," she said graciously. "Seeing
what you are doing for us. . . ."

Just what we were supposed to be doing, for
heaven's sake, apart from accompanying them to
their camping site, and meeting them on the way
back?

Bill and Ben lifted the poles carefully onto their
padded shoulders and were obviously waiting for the
order to forward march! as their feet were tramping
up and down like soldiers.

Tam was looking at Sven's loaded rucksack. "Damn!
Completely forgot about lanterns; you set off—river
road—and I'll catch you up. . . ."

It didn't take him long, as we were going downhill
and it was a fairly well-worn track. At the end of
the first three-quarters of an hour we swung away
inland after a short rest, arriving about an hour later
at a pretty little wood, with a small stream running
away towards the river.

"You be all right here?" asked Tam, taking our
rucksacks from the twins. Bill and Ben had sweat
running freely down their faces but otherwise looked
happy enough.

Lally looked around, shrugged her shoulders. "It'll
do."

"Shall we help you set up camp?" I asked politely.
She shook her head vigorously. "We've not decided

where to settle just yet," she said. "Don't forget we're supposed to be with you. . . ."

"What do you mean?" I said.

"I told Sven to tell Joe and Betty we were traveling with you; you know we have to tell them our route in case of accidents."

This had always been the practice since, some years back, a couple had got themselves into difficulties, one of them breaking an ankle, and it had taken two days to find them after the others had returned.

Tam had a face like thunder. "You'd no right to do that! Suppose something happens? Who gets into trouble, you or us? I've a good mind to—to give up the whole idea!"

"Tam!" I pleaded, my hand on his arm. "Don't spoil everything!"

He calmed down, but his parting shot was directed at Lally. "You'd better be here when we get back, or there'll be trouble. . . ."

"Have a nice day!" sang out Lally as we stamped off. I didn't turn to look, but I'll bet she was pulling a face, because I could hear the twins giggling.

Tam set a blistering pace, and before long I was beginning to wish we were back with the others; at least there would have been someone to carry the rucksacks: mine was beginning to feel unbearably heavy and uncomfortable. At the end of an hour I was ready to drop, but when I suggested a break Tam shook his head. "Another few minutes . . ."

The few minutes turned into at least an hour, and it must have been five o'clock before he turned aside, searched for a moment, then slung off his rucksack by a small spring that ran from beneath a rock, to disappear into a pool some yards away. I collapsed on the ground, leant over and cupped my hands in the icy water of the pool, drinking deep. When I had finished I splashed water on my face, neck and arms and lay back with a sigh.

"That's better: I was about to drop!"

"Well, don't get too comfortable. We've only done about ten miles altogether——"

Ten miles! No wonder I was bushed. "It feels like a hundred. . . . My feet are killing me!"

"Stick 'em in the pool for a while." He rummaged in the net-bag that held the perishable food. "Here!" He tossed me a roll and a hard-boiled egg. "We'll rest for a half-hour and then press on."

"Go on? Where? I thought we were stopping here for the night!"

"No way! There are three hours at least of daylight left, and I want to put as many miles as I can between us and the village."

"Yes, but exactly where are we *going*?"

"To the End of the World and back again!" He grinned. "Come on Pretty, you're not going to give up on me yet, are you?"

Of course not, so we walked, more slowly now, until dusk made the rocky going dangerous. Tam was obviously looking for some landmark, and at last he pointed to two pines just ahead. And beyond them was a small ravine, and we slipped into it and shucked off the rucksacks.

"Two-pine stop," said Tam with satisfaction. "It's on the map."

I remembered: I also recalled it was only about five miles short of the red limit line. That meant——

camp five miles from the village, us five miles short
of the limit, twenty-five miles from village to line—

"Hey, we've walked fifteen miles! Gee, I've never
walked so far in my life!"

Without warning he took my head in his hands
and gave me a swift kiss on the forehead. "I'm proud
of you, Pretty! Now, let's eat. What's left of the
perishables?"

Cold roast chicken—well, warm roast chicken
now—four rolls, two hard-boiled eggs, half-a dozen
plums, two slices of nut-cake and some coleslaw.

"Right. Chicken, coleslaw, two rolls and the cake
tonight. Rest for breakfast. Okay with you?"

After that kiss I could have eaten my sandals without
complaint.

By the time we had eaten and shared one of the
flasks of water it was full dark, a soft breeze blowing
up from the south and early stars pricking through
the coverlet of the night sky. I rinsed our plates as
best I could with a little of the water, and wiped my
face and hands on my dampened flannel, although
I still felt itchy and sticky with sweat.

"We haven't much water left. . . ."

"River-way tomorrow. Let's get some sleep. I want
to be off early in the morning. . . ."

But not *this* early!

"It's still dark!" I protested. Not quite true, there
was a greyish light, the hint of red in the east, the
sleepy twitter of birds, a crisp feel to the air.

"Early? Must be all of five-thirty. . . ." He laughed
at my indignant expression. "Come on, I've made
us chamomile tea." And the small saucepan was

bubbling away on a tiny fire of twigs and sticks. We finished off the remains of the perishables and within a half-hour were trekking south-east. The rising sun shone in our eyes, half-blinding me, but before long I could hear again the comforting roar of the river.

"Rapids," said Tam. "We'll find that as long as the land falls away to the south. There should be a plateau further on, and the river will widen out. We can bathe, fill our bottles and, if we're lucky, fish for lunch."

"Have you any tackle?"

"Net, hooks and line in my pack. Took lessons from old Ragnald last year: thought it might come in useful."

The thought of fresh fish for lunch spurred me on, and we made rapid progress. By midday we had reached the plateau, stretching away from us for many miles, a flat scrubland. As Tam had forecast, here the river belled out, running slower on a bed of gravel. There were plenty of fish in the shallows, mostly trout keeping pace with the water, their noses always pointing upstream.

"Light us a fire, Pretty."

"I want a wash. . . ."

"Afterwards. Light us a fire, find some straight sticks and mix a couple of pancakes. Let the embers die down a bit and it's grilled trout for lunch! Go on. . . ."

Three small trout each later, char-grilled to perfection on skewers over the fire with pancakes, and all I wanted was a good dunking to feel all was right with the world. After washing the plates and fry-pan we took it in turns for a good all-over soaping and a good soak. Lying in the shallows my hair streamed away like river-weed, tiny minnows tickling my ears, nibbling my toes. When we were children we had all bathed naked, boys and girls together, but after ten years old we were segregated. While we teenagers jibbed at the rule, my Nan was firmly in favor.

"When I was a child," she said, "—yes, in the days of the dinosaurs, as you lot would say—it was considered a disgrace to bare yourself in front of the opposite sex. This was a reaction against the permissiveness of the latter half of the twentieth century. I doubt, for instance, that my father had seen me unclothed since I was a baby. My mother, God rest her soul, died when I was seven, but by then she had taught me certain rules of behavior which I have never forgotten."

"But—but when you got married, how did you . . ."

"My Padraig had been brought up much as I had, and we found out about love and sex together, and in privacy. After all, what's the point of a present you receive already unwrapped?"

A stone splashed into the water by my right ear: I realized that I had been daydreaming.

"Come on," said Tam, throwing me a towel as I knelt up in the water. "Time to be on our way . . ."

We walked for three hours or so, south by southeast, the noise of the river gradually dying away to our left. We stopped for a drink and a handful of dried fruit, then pushed on again. By now there was a knot of fear in my stomach that wouldn't be quieted. We finally made camp in a small wood, and Tam built a fire which made the growing darkness close in quickly. He put the first of the gammon steaks on to cook slowly, and shoved two of the potatoes into the edge

of the fire. "About half-an-hour, I guess," he said.
"By tomorrow we can——"

I sprang to my feet, the tension that had been
building up inside me all day finally finding its way
to the surface.

"Tomorrow? As far as I'm concerned there won't
be a tomorrow unless you tell me right now where
the hell we are going!"

CHAPTER FOURTEEN

He stared at me, genuinely puzzled. "What do you mean: where are we going? You can see which way we're going. South, as far as we can."

"Of course I can see which direction it is. I'm not daft! But you never told me before we started, and you never said we were going to have to break the law to do it!"

"Whose law? What law?"

I tried to control myself. "The line, the thin red line on the map! I recognized one of the marker boulders yesterday. I didn't say anything because I thought you wouldn't be going much further, but we must have done at least ten miles since then."

"Nearer fifteen. We've made good progress." He turned the potatoes. "If we're lucky we might make journey's end tomorrow."

I stared at him. "Didn't you hear what I said? I said we've broken the law by crossing that boundary. And where and what is 'journey's end,' anyway?"

He stood up, angry too. "Of course I heard what you said! And I asked you 'Whose law?' Who forbade us to go beyond that line?" He ignored the second part of my question.

I shrugged. "I don't know who: Mayor Gross, I suppose . . ."

"Exactly! Who always lays down the law? Who always says what we may and may not do? Who hems us in day and night with petty restrictions, silly laws, impossible standards of behavior? Who dictates every move from birth—who shall survive, who shall die—through our schooldays—what we shall be taught, what discouraged—right up to what jobs we shall do for the rest of our lives, and even down to whom we shall marry?" He paced about, his fists clenched. "I, for one, am sick of it! Where's all this 'freedom' everyone talks about? Our lives are run by a petty dictator. He may only have a little village to play with, but he's sure making a good job of playing with us, his toys!"

I had never heard him talk like this, had had no idea of the resentment building up inside him.

"What's gotten into you?"

"Nothing that wasn't there before!" He scowled. "I'm sick and tired of all this hedging in, rules, regulations! Aren't you? Remember the fuss he made when we went to the Wilderness when we were kids? What harm did that do to us? None at all!"

Remembering Lally's obsession I wasn't too sure about that.

"What was it that old poet said? 'Cabined, cribbed, confined . . .' Something like that. Well, that's exactly how I feel."

"Look, Tam: We all get fed up with rules and regulations, but why spoil our holiday griping about it? At least we're safe and secure in the village and life isn't so bad. . . ."

I might as well have been talking to the wind.

"And why can't we go beyond the red line? Has anyone ever said? What is there to fear? Have you seen any bands of savages, man-eating rabbits, space-invaders? No, and you won't. The only reason we've been told not to go any further is not because there's any danger. It's because Gross doesn't want us to find out there's another life out there, other people, other towns or villages. He wants to keep us for himself, exercise his petty tyranny, just to satisfy his overweening ego!" Then without a change of tone or expression: "The gammon's done: put the other piece on."

I collapsed, laughing. It was a welcome release from tension, and at least now I knew what had been biting him. He wasn't amused, however.

"You haven't been listening to me!"

"Oh, I have, I have indeed! And I'm not laughing at you—not really. . . ."

"Yes you are. . . ."

"Not at what you're saying, believe me. I'd never have thought of it in quite that way. No, it was just that—that you were getting a bit over the top. Rather like that man you were castigating . . ." and I grinned up at him.

He sat down, and the scowl was replaced by a grin. "Sorry, Pretty: guess you're probably right. Let's have something to eat, then we can talk some more."

Between bites I asked him what had been worrying me most. "How do you know they won't find out we went over the line?"

"Who's to know?"

I looked around at the deserted night landscape.

"Well, no one, I suppose. Unless someone sees us coming back. . . ."

"They won't. Pass the butter."

"Supposing we have an accident?"

"We won't. I wouldn't take you anywhere dangerous, you should know that."

"How do you know?"

"I've got a map. . . . No, not now. When we've finished supper."

We seemed to finish our meal with maddening slowness and after that there were the plates and pan to wipe ready for our next visit to the river. Then a lick and a promise to our hands and faces . . .

Tam lit the lantern, then rummaged in his rucksack. "I thought for a moment I'd lost it. . . ." He gave me a teasing wink. "Here it is!"

What he showed me was an old canvas-backed quarter-inch to a mile Survey map dated some seventy years ago. It was a contour map and showed an area approximately sixty miles north to south and half that east to west. It was in remarkably good condition apart from the folds, which were fragile and slightly stained. We had all seen atlas maps of what the world used to look like, but those were on a much tinier scale: a whole continent across two pages.

"Do you see anything familiar?"

I bent closer. "Why, yes! That's the village, only it had a different name! There's the river, the plantation, and they've even got the Wilderness marked! What's that sort of star in the middle of it?"

Tam consulted a list at the bottom of the map. "Site of archeological interest," he read. "That must be the ring of stones. And there, that tiny dot to the south-east of the village, is the Herb-Woman's house, if I'm not mistaken."

It was fascinating. The village had changed its shape considerably; then there had been only one street, and a chapel that had long since disappeared. Of course it didn't show the orchards, the bathing-pool, the forge or the bath-house, but on the site of what must now be the school there had been a windmill, and the fields were more or less the same shape.

"Where on earth did you get this?"

"Sheer chance. You know when your dad married Grizzle, and I took over Gabby's room when they all moved round?" I nodded. "Well, it was in a right mess and I gradually gave it a face-lift. She took her dressing-table and stool and wanted a small set of shelves in a corner to put those ghastly bits of pottery she collects on—rabbits and dogs and fish—but she couldn't shift it, so I promised to try and get it free. Well, it took some doing, because it was nailed to the wall, but when I finally got it away, I found this map jammed down the back. Must have slipped down years ago."

"Magic! Gee, the plantation goes on forever. . . . And the river gets bigger and bigger. What are these marks?"

"Rapids. Waterfalls. Look further down. . . ."

"The river: it kinks to the left—"

"West."

"West, then. It goes for quite a way and turns south then disappears off the edge of the map—"

He plonked his finger down on the map. "And we, my pretty Pretty, are right here!"

He took his finger away; if he was right, then we

were within twenty miles or so of the southern boundary of the river!

"Is that where we're going?"

"Of course! I wanted to see just how far we could get. It's all a preparation for when I leave."

"Leave where? Leave the village? But why?"

"I've told you why! All I want to do is get away from our little dictator!"

"A *little* dictator—if he is at all. I mean, he's not like those other ones we've read about, Hitler and Mussolini—"

"What's the difference? Okay, they were dealing with millions and Gross has a couple of hundred or so; but he still behaves in the same way they did! He's trying to create a master-race of his own—no deformities, no blacks, no mutants—and he enslaves our wills, our freedoms, our ambitions, our very lives! That village we live in is just like those prison camps they used to write about in Germany, Poland, Russia, Bosnia, Uganda, South Africa. All right, so he doesn't whip us, brand us, gas us, but just the same every day we die a little death—from boredom, frustration, the numbing little rules and regulations that bind us as surely as chains and fetters. . . . And it's not only that; he doesn't want us to progress any further. Remember when that fellow Watney said he could get some sort of electricity going by building special windmills? And what about when Andrews wanted to prospect downriver to see if he could find enough river-sand to make glass? *Dear* Gross said both were too dangerous!" He ran out of breath.

I began to wonder just how good I was at reading people. Here was my gentle, good natured, pliable

Tam turning into a burning revolutionary in front of my eyes. I had thought I knew everything there was to know about him, the boy I had grown up with, the lad who had practically been a brother to me— just how wrong could one be! And if I had been wrong about Tam, how much did I really know about lesser acquaintances like Sven and Lally, Rosellen and Brian? And even Nan . . .

He seized my hand. "Don't you see, Pretty? If we can get this far and prove old Gross wrong, then there must be other things he's been wrong about too! We can't be the only people left in the world. It's been fifty years, and during that time other pockets of mankind must have survived. Well, as soon as I can I'm going to look for them; the first thing I'm going to do is to follow the river down to the sea."

"The sea . . ." I had only read about it, seen pictures and photographs in the old encyclopedias. I couldn't imagine something so vast as that stretching blue-green to the horizon, the waves rolling and crashing onto the beach, the smell of salt, the cry of the sea-gulls—

He was watching my face. "Wouldn't you like to see it, too?"

"Of course! But there's no chance of that. Anyway, it's probably better in the imagination."

"It's worth a try, surely?"

"You're talking pies in the sky, Tam. How would we get there without some form of transport? How could we carry all the food we'd need? How long would it take? What dangers lie between here and there? How many obstacles—pollution, poison, hostiles—might we not come across?"

He shook his head. "I have no idea, but I intend to find out one day soon, whether you decide to come or not. It's a bit like space exploration, isn't it? No one has ever proved that there is intelligent life out there in the Universe, but with all the primitive life-forms that were found in the past it's a thousand—no, more like a million—to one that there is. And I think I'm more likely to find some reasonable human beings and signs of civilization than I am to meet some little green men from Mars!"

As I rolled myself up in my sleeping bag I was dead tired, but I couldn't sleep at once. My mind was buzzing with a thousand ideas, thoughts, questions. Some of it was too vast to contemplate—like the journey to the sea, but there were other, smaller details. He had called me "my pretty Pretty," hadn't he? And he wanted me to go with him. . . .

"Hey, Pretty: I forgot to tell you. You know that hand-drawn map we all studied? Well someone had written something over the part we're in right now. Later on it had been rubbed out, but if you stand at a particular angle you can just make out what it said."

I turned towards him. "Well?"

I heard him chuckle. " 'Here be dragons . . .' "

The next day was like the forced marches of prisoners I had read about. We rose before dawn and ate while walking, halting only for a sip of the remaining water and a brief, too brief, rest. By the middle of the afternoon my legs were numb, and I was counting a thousand steps at a time, my eyes on the ground, too tired to take any interest in our surroundings. My shoulders ached from the weight of the rucksack, my head throbbed with the heat of the sun, I was being bitten by thousands of insects and there was a roaring in my head that was getting louder and louder—

There was a shout from Tam, who had drawn farther and farther ahead. I raised my weary head and there he was a hundred yards or so away waving his arms.

"We're there! We've made it! Come *on*, Pretty!"

I took a few stumbling steps forward like one of those string puppets we used to make at school, but my head started to spin, I couldn't see for the salt sweat in my eyes, and before I knew what was happening the ground came up and hit me, hard—

CHAPTER FIFTEEN

I came to with Tam splashing cold water on my face.

"Come on, Pretty, come on!" he was muttering, and he sounded genuinely worried.

I opened my eyes. My head hurt where I had bumped it on the ground, I was momentarily seeing double, but I wasn't seriously hurt. I sat up. "Sorry: guess I was just exhausted. Can I have a drink?"

He handed me the flask. The water was bitingly cold, but I drank greedily: I hadn't realized how thirsty I was.

"Hey, that's enough!" he said snatching away the flask. "You know what they say: warm drinks in summer, cool in winter, otherwise you get stomach cramps. Here, a lick of salt, and then some honey . . ." The standard remedy for heat exhaustion.

"First time I've done this," I said struggling to my feet.

"There's a time for everything. . . ."

"And Ecclesiastes to you," I said. "Are we there? By the river?" That must have been the roaring noise I had thought was in my head, because it was still there.

"Yes, and we're lucky. The noise is a waterfall, but

just below it the water has carved out a little bay, a backwater. We can bathe, wash the clothes and the pots. D'you feel fit enough?"

Apart from a slight headache, I did, and an hour later as dusk settled round us we were clean and respectable once more, sitting by a comfortable fire, spiced sausage sizzling in the fry-pan, potatoes in the embers, a slice of corn-bread already cooked and our change of clothes spread over bushes to dry. We were in a little hollow, some distance from the river, and the sound of the water was muted. My drying hair spun in strands across my face as I bent to turn the sausage, my mouth watering with the enticing aroma. God, was I hungry!

Tam was leaning back on his elbows, the firelight ruddy on his face. "Well, we made it."

"Where are we exactly?"

"A couple of miles west of where the river kinks across. The waterfall is marked on my map."

I remembered, but that little mark had no way prepared me for the sight of water thundering down over twenty-five feet into the ravine below, throwing up spray in a rainbow of color. The falling water had carved out a deep pool beneath it, and for the first time I appreciated the power of water. I wondered if the sea had the same power.

"Where do we go tomorrow?"

"Well, I wanted to find a crossing point for the future, but there's none here. If the map is correct, the plantation is about five miles to the west, and the river curves away south just before that. I'm hoping for shallower water between here and there."

"You're not thinking of trying to cross?" I was horrified.

"No, of course not, not right now. I just want to satisfy myself that there is an escape route if I need it."

So he was still obsessed with this talk of wandering off into the unknown. Perhaps it was just talk, I comforted myself. Many young men—and some of the older ones, too—were full of what they would do, how they would behave, if only the right circumstances presented themselves. But that was all it was, talk. The best thing to do was go along with his wild ideas; tested, many of those who boasted the most, did the least. I nodded.

"You realize that this is our fourth day?" he went on. "So there is only tomorrow to explore, if we have to be back to meet Lally and Sven in five days time. Bedtime, Pretty. I'll wash the pots in the morning— no, wait. If we put a vegetable stew on tonight, we'll only have to heat it up tomorrow. I'll do it, you get some sleep. . . ."

I was only too glad to leave it to him, but as I wrapped myself up I reflected that this trip was supposed to be about loving, not roving. . . .

We were off at first light again, after a plate of stew and the remains of the corn-bread from the night before, taking cheese and dried fruit for lunch. Walking along the banks of the river, it was clear that there could be no crossing this far east. The big waterfall was succeeded by other, smaller ones, interspersed with rapids, and the land was dropping quite sharply to the west and south. On the far bank was a deciduous forest, not one of the ancient ones, that seemed to stretch away to the southern horizon. Everything looked deserted, no hint of any other humans. Perhaps the Mayor had been right and we were the only survivors.

"You're not listening, Pretty!"

No, I wasn't. " 'Course I was!"

"What did I just say then?"

I guessed, aware of the position of the sun in the sky "Time to eat." We shucked off the rucksacks loaded now only with the water bottles and lunch, and of course the precious map. Tam went to fetch some more water and came back rubbing a grazed knee.

"Seems the cliffs down to the river are getting steeper," he said ruefully, dabbing his knee with water and some leaves of Self-Heal.

"Is there any point in going on, then? Look, we can already see the beginnings of the plantation."

He studied the map. "We're about two-thirds of the way there. We'll go on for a couple of hours, then head back if we don't find anything."

So from midday on we followed the banks of the river, Tam checking now and again to see if there was any lessening in the turbulence of the river. About an hour and a half later he reported that the river had changed its course somewhat, and that there was a thin strand of sand on this side.

"Might as well see if we can climb down and see how far we can walk. . . ."

The spray from the river was cooling and pleasant, although the sand underfoot was rather gritty and full of river-pebbles. After a mile or so the river started to advance back up to the cliffs again, and we realized that if we couldn't find a way up we should have to retrace our steps. The river still ran as rapidly as ever, bubbling furiously like a pot on the boil over the shallows. Tam halted.

"Perhaps we'd better turn back. . . ." He looked and sounded tired and disappointed.

"S'pose so. Sorry, Tam. . . ."

It was then, just as we were about to give up and I was feeling really sorry for him in spite of my earlier fears, that we heard a sound. An alien sound, a noise you wouldn't expect down here in a million Sundays.

A shout, followed by another. And somebody laughing.

With one accord we ducked down like a pair of wild animals coming unawares upon the hunters. We grabbed each other's hands and listened, as though our ears were the only key to our survival. Perhaps, just perhaps, we had imagined it. . . . Please God!

But no, there it was again: not one voice, not two—half a dozen at least! Somewhere ahead of us, around the next bend in the river were other beings! But who, what? Were they real people? If so, where had they come from? Were they like us? Or creatures from another planet? I felt cold with fear, right down to my toes.

We looked at one another, looked towards the sound, and then with one accord we crept slowly forward on hands and knees. Tam slipped off his rucksack and I did the same. We moved forward as quietly as we could although the noise of the river would effectively drown any small noise we had made. Ahead of us the cliffside curved out towards the water, leaving only a narrow strip of sand, less than a foot wide. With infinite care we inched our way round, trying not to think of the rushing water beside us.

Luck was with us. The path continued past the curve, and here the river widened out and was calmer. Across from us the forest was less dense, opening out into a small bay with a grassy slope above.

And there, drawn up on the grass, were what I recognized as canoes. . . .

There was no one in sight, but we could hear voices away in the woods, happy, laughing voices, some sounding like kids or teenagers, others like adults. We crouched behind a couple of self-seeded oleanders, their pink flowers already fading. We waited for perhaps a half-hour, the voices now nearer, now farther, then just as I was beginning to get cramp in the calves of my leg, they appeared.

There were a dozen young people, between the ages of fourteen and eighteen I guessed, and two bearded men. They were all carrying wood of some sort, obviously to build a fire, all except one boy who was being towed on a sort of wooden trolley. To my horror I saw he had no arms or legs, only stumps, although he was shouting and laughing like the rest of them. Looking at the others I saw that all of them, except for the two eldest, had some sort of disability, and two of them were *black*! Some dragged their legs as they walked, one had a head too big for his body, another had a hump-back—

"Mutants!" I whispered to Tam. He nodded.

"Interesting . . ."

This was the first time I had seen these deformed and colored people that I now realized Mayor Gross had tried so hard to eradicate from our community. They were not a pretty sight, but apart from their deformities they seemed to be a happy enough bunch.

I concentrated on the coloreds, as I had never seen any before, except in the encyclopedias. Apart from the color of their skins, which was really a rich, dark brown, like chestnuts when you took the outer covering off, the shape of their faces was different. Their heads were rounder, with tightly curled hair like black lambs; they had more pronounced jaws, thicker-lipped mouths and wide, flat noses. I thought they looked quite nice. I saw they weren't there just because of their color: one of them had webbed toes and fingers, the other one leg shorter than the other. But surely all these deformed kids couldn't be as happy as they sounded? And where on earth had they come from? Now that I looked closer I could see a couple of large tents almost hidden in the trees. So, they must be camping like we were. Anyway, wherever they came from and wherever they were going to, Tam had been right: there were other people who had survived!

I can't explain quite how excited and awed we both were: it was like seeing pictures come to life, or being able to press a switch and have the light come on. It was magic, just like the moving pictures Nan had told us about.

They had all been romping about, but suddenly one of the older ones blew a whistle and they all stopped whatever they were doing and formed up into a line. One of the bearded ones brought out some bottles and poured a rosy-colored liquid into some small cups that looked so thin and squashy that they might have been made of paper. One bottle was emptied and Beard handed it to one of the younger ones who tipped it up and drained the last drop. As the sun glinted on it I realized it must be glass, precious glass that was so hard to come by. Even in the village there were only a small number of bottles left, and these were more precious than gold; Nan had two, one small and one large, and these were kept for specials, like sloe wine or double-distilled cider. Even the glass in everyone's windows had gone, utilized for the greenhouses, and we all had wooden, louvered shutters instead. So what happened next wasn't entirely unexpected.

The young boy, having enjoyed tipping back the bottle, now limped to the water's edge and threw the bottle as hard as he could into the river, where it bobbed away down the current.

At the same time Tam yelled "Don't," and in one movement he had left my side and dived into the river. I screamed and jumped to my feet.

"Tam, wait!" and a moment later I had joined him in the turbulent waters.

We were in no danger, both of us could swim like fishes, having been coached from an early age—this insisted on after six children had drowned after part of the riverbank had collapsed some ten years earlier. We had started with dog-paddle in the bathing pool, had progressed to the swimming pool and then done some tough swims in the river itself. The current was perhaps a bit stronger than we were used to, but we were in no peril. Ahead of me Tam was swimming strongly towards the bottle, bobbing ahead of him neck up, so it wouldn't sink, and I paddled

behind, ready for backup if he needed it. I glanced
across at the opposite bank, where the strangers were
standing open-mouthed on the bank; suddenly one
of the Beards shouted something and pushed one
of their canoes into the water, paddling frantically
across the current to reach us.

I waved at him and yelled: "Don't bother! We're
okay! We can manage. . . ." But he wasn't listening.
I saw that Tam had reached the bottle and snatched
it from the water, and I made ready to swim with
him back to our side, but suddenly the canoe was
between us and a frantically paddling Beard was
shouting urgently. "Grab the stern! Grab the stern!"

I glanced across at Tam, and he gave a mental shrug.
We were desperately curious about the strangers,
and wouldn't it be as good a way as any to get
acquainted? So, we allowed ourselves to be "rescued,"
and trailed behind the canoe to the far bank, where
we scrambled up the bank.

Now I began to realize how foolish we had been.
Not only had we exposed ourselves to complete
strangers, we had joined them without any thought
of our safety. What if they had weapons? What if
they bore some unknown infection? What if they
meant to capture us? In spite of their deformities
we were completely outnumbered. What if—most
terrible thought of all—what if they were *Cannibals*?

All this didn't seem to faze Tam, however. I saw
him raise his hand in the universal sign of peace
and take a step towards the group who stood
watching. One or two of them took an immediate
step backwards, and I suddenly realized that they
were as scared of us as we were of them!

Our "rescuer," Beard One, muttered something to Beard Two, then walked back to us, his hands spread wide in a gesture of being weaponless.

"Don't be afraid. We wish to be friends. We should like to talk, is all." It was a little difficult to understand him. He had a lazy drawl and seemed to swallow some of his consonants. I supposed that isolation must have changed the way many spoke, and he would have equal difficulty understanding our more clipped speech.

We nodded, and Tam said, speaking slowly: "We have no objection to talk, but perhaps we had better stay at a distance, in case of infection."

"*We* are clear of any infection," said Beard Two indignantly.

"Among yourselves and your community, yes, but we have had no contact with others for fifty years among ours, and either of us may carry bacteria inimical to the other. In the olden times the common cold was fatal to both tropical savages and northern tribes alike."

"You are learned," said Beard One, looking surprised.

Don't overdo it Tam, I thought, and said aloud: "We have been taught from books that were salvaged from the ruins."

"Very well." Beard Two gestured to his campers and slowly they sat down in a semicircle about ten yards away. The two Beards squatted down between us and them, but we remained standing.

Tam introduced us by name, then Beards One and Two did the same: Bob and Chuck. There was a silence.

"Where are you from?" asked Beard Two, Chuck.

"North," I said.

"East," said Tam.

A pity. We had spoken together, though Tam repaired the crack smoothly enough. "We come from many miles north and east of here," he said. "At first we traveled to the west, but found no signs of life. Indeed the land is barren and blasted, and as yet has not recovered enough to grow the smallest tree or blade of grass. Then we found this river and have followed it this far, but it has only been in the last twenty miles or so that we have seen any vegetation to equal this." And he gestured to the woods behind the campers. "And where do you come from?"

I wondered just what it needed to make someone a good liar. Imagination perhaps, something I had obviously not given Tam enough credit for in the past.

"Our town lies some hundred miles downriver. It is a thriving community on the western side of a great lake, some twelve miles long. This river empties into it, then goes on at the other end to the sea. Our town is called Lakeside and we raise cattle and horses, which we trade south for cottons, sugar, wool, flour and salt."

I sensed that the words "sugar" and "wool" touched a chord with Tam as his next question showed. "And these goods: do they come from far?"

"Many hundreds of miles," said Bob. "And at high cost. But of course we need them, and we get a good exchange for our beasts. May we ask about your community?"

Tam turned to me as if to say: *your* turn to make something up!

"Our small village is made up of survivors of the holocaust that overwhelmed all the cities to the east in the last days," I said. "There are less than a hundred of us left, largely because we have little ground for growing crops, living as we do in the mountains. Our goats and sheep are weak and puny with interbreeding and lack of winter feed. Our expedition was to see if living was more viable farther south. Your news has encouraged us."

"Well, I am sure you would be welcome at Lakeside," said Chuck warmly. "Especially if you have skills we have not."

"I am a woodcarver and maker of musical instruments," said Tam. "And my friend here is a scribe and teacher."

"Then you would be more than welcome! We have no one with those skills. Will you not travel back with us and see our town for yourselves?"

Tam shook his head. "I guess we have found out what we came for, and we have been away too long already. Our people will despair of our return. We must carry the good news as fast as we can. Tell me: is the river navigable all the way down to Lakeside?"

"Mostly. There are a couple of places where we have to use porterage, but the canoes are light enough."

"And do you come here every year?"

"It is part of our Youth Training Scheme. A different environment, a little hardship, toughens them up no end," said Bob. "We've been coming here for the last four years. No further because of the rapids and the waterfalls, and now you have told us what the terrain is like upriver, I shall mark our maps accordingly."

"You have maps? We have to memorize our own,"
I said, delighting in my duplicity. It was like acting
in a play you made up as you went along. "You see
we have no paper, nor any means to make it. . . ."
True.

"You haven't? Then let me give you one of ours,"
and Bob disappeared into one of the tents and came
back with one that showed the river, woods, hills
and streams. High ground was marked as such, there
was no attempt at contouring. Along the river there
were little stars, presumably marking camping-sites.

"Thank you," said Tam. He fingered the thick,
coarse paper on which the map was printed. "Do
you make your own paper?"

"We have a small paper-mill, yes," said Chuck.
Another plus I thought. "But the press is hand-driven,
and can be erratic."

"Marvelous!" said Tam. "How well you have
done. . . . And bottles, like this?" and he held up the
one we had been rescued for. Mind you I didn't blame
him jumping in the river for it; he could get at least
fifty tokens for it in Deliverance, especially as it had
some kind of fastener at the top. We could always
say we found it by the river. . . .

"Yes, we have a good supply of suitable sand, and
a small workshop for what we need. Would you like
another?"

"That would be most kind," I said, as Tam hesitated.
"We have no artifacts like that left. They have become
broken over the years." Tam looked at me as if I
were doing a Little Orphan Annie, but I didn't care.
It worked, anyway: we got two more.

Tam looked at me furiously. "We have to give you

something in return. . . ." We had been brought up to believe that exchange was the correct thing to do.

"Be easy," said Chuck. "You have given us valuable information. Will you not reconsider joining us? You would be most welcome."

For answer Tam shook his head and tugged at the pocket of his sleeveless top, producing one of his little pan-pipes. It was a bit damp, but he could play anything and he treated them to a couple of folk-tunes, and in a moment the kids were clapping their hands together in time to the music. When he had finished he handed the pipes to Bob.

"A gift," he said.

Bob took the instrument and looked at it admiringly. "We have nothing like this!"

Tam looked at me. The only thing I was wearing apart from shorts and a top and sandals was a small necklet of river-pearls he had given me two birthdays ago. I touched it and he nodded. I unfastened the toggle at the back and handed it to Chuck.

"A gift," I said. Reluctantly.

"Again, we have nothing like this. . . . I thank you both. Wait a moment," and he dived into one of the tents again, coming back with a small package. "Here is a special food we have been able to make from some exotic beans we bought from a traveling merchant. You are welcome to some. And now, we will get you back across the river, as it is getting late."

We hadn't noticed it but the sun was declining fast. I opened my mouth to say we would swim it, but one look at Tam's face and I shut up. This time we were in, instead of out of, one of the canoes, and I must say Bob made heavy weather of it, but we managed. As we got out and thanked him I knew there was another question I must ask.

I nodded across the river. "The youngsters: are they exceptional? I mean they all seem to suffer some form of—of disability. . . ." I could feel myself flushing.

Bob looked puzzled. "No, they are fairly representative. About thirty per cent of our people are mutated in some way. We call it Physically Disadvantaged. Aren't you the same?"

"No," said Tam shortly. "We have been fortunate."

Bob shrugged, then lifted his long hair away from his ears "Look: even me." His ears were mere holes in his head.

I could feel myself shrinking away from the ugliness, and knew Tam felt the same. Part of me was tremendously sorry for the mutations we had seen, another part was glad for once that Mayor Gross had kept that from us, but the third—and greatest part, I'm ashamed to say—was just a sick feeling of disgust.

"We shall be here next year if you care to join us then," said Bob, and thrust back into the current.

We watched him reach the opposite shore in safety and waved. They all waved back.

"Right," said Tam. "Race you back to camp. Hope the rest of that stew is still eatable. I'm starving!"

CHAPTER SIXTEEN

Of course we could neither talk nor think of anything else than our meeting with the strangers for the rest of the day. All the way back to the camp, eating the rest of the stew, cooking pancakes to eat with honey, washing, getting ready for bed, it was; "Do you remember . . ." "What did you think . . ." and so on.

And it had all happened so quickly! Looking back we must have been with them about an hour at least, yet in memory it seemed more like five minutes. Then there were all the things we had meant to ask if we had thought about them at the time. What sort of houses did they live in, what did they eat, did all the men wear beards, did they have the same marriage customs, what was their religion, were they lucky enough to wear cotton all the time, how did they heat their homes, what did they cook their food on—all my questions. Tam's afterthoughts were somewhat different. Did they have electricity, did they have a barter system or was it coinage, did they use any type of vehicle, were they in touch with many other communities other than those they traded with, had they any means of long-distance communication, and so on.

I kept trying to remember what they looked like, what they wore, how they spoke, but Tam was more interested in what they had said. We agreed that their speech was difficult to understand, but as they had not been in mass communication for so many years this must affect everyone who had been isolated for any length of time and we must have sounded equally strange. The news that they traded from far for their sugar and wool made Tam wonder whether it would be more economical for them to trade with us, in exchange for, perhaps, cotton, paper, salt. . . .

I looked at him in horror. "You weren't thinking of telling anyone we met them, were you? Just think what they would do to us! We've broken every rule in the book—they'd shut us up for the rest of our lives!"

Tam laughed at my expression. "Of course not, silly! Not yet, anyway."

"What do you mean: 'not yet'?"

"Just what I said. Not yet; sometime maybe, when the time is right."

"And it can't ever be right as long as Mayor Gross is in charge. So, you've had it."

"For the time being, maybe. But I still mean to go away, especially now I know I shall be welcomed by the people we met today. With the map I should be okay, though it might be difficult with the food situation. Perhaps I might 'borrow' one of the ponies. Once I'm gone, no one will have any idea where I went."

"Can't you wait until next year, when they come back?" I didn't want to lose him, I suddenly realized.

"And if I wait for a year, a whole year—" he made

it sound like a lifetime "—would you agree to come with me?"

I opened my mouth to say, that yes, perhaps I would when he answered his own question.

"No. Of course you wouldn't. You'd make some excuse, like your Nan needed you, or you wanted to wait another year, or you didn't care to trust yourself to me."

For some reason this made me blazing mad. "Yes, well, that could be it! You've not been exactly honest with me about this trip, have you? And we've still got to get back without anyone finding out where we've been. And you've dragged me at top speed each day just to satisfy your conviction that there was life after the Apocalypse! And—and you made me give away the only pretty necklace I had, just so—just so . . ." And to my utter annoyance and chagrin, I burst into tears.

There was a moment's hesitation, then he shuffled over to where I was sitting, and put his arms round me and gave me a comforting hug. Trouble was, it was the sort of brotherly hug he sometimes gave me when I got emotional at the wrong time of the month: TOM. What was worse, I could tell he was trying not to laugh. . . .

"It's not funny!" I howled.

"Never said it was. . . . Look, stop crying, wipe your eyes, and I'll tell you why I let you give them your necklace."

I sniffed myself into silence. "Well?"

"Because I knew I had another one. Here . . ." He fished in his rucksack and brought out the one he had given Joe and Betty a few tokens for, the one that had been left in exchange for stolen goods. I looked at the string of blue and white beads in disbelief, then flung them back at him.

"How dare you try and pass off that tatty rubbish on me! At least the necklace you gave me was *real*!"

He was obviously taken aback at my reaction. "What's got into you?"

"You bought that from Joe and Betty for ten, fifteen tokens, I don't recall. What I do remember is that you told them it was rubbish. So, you can keep it! Better still, find another girl who will appreciate it!"

He went white. "If you're not very careful I will!"

"You just do that! Now, can I get some sleep?" Angrily I rolled myself up in my sleeping-bag, clothes and all. From the sounds I could hear, Tam was doing the same. After a while I found I was too hot, and also thirsty. Out of the sleeping-bag, off with my clothes, on with my shift, all in the dark. Now where the hell was the water-bottle? After fumbling about in the dark, I stubbed my toe on the damned thing and let out a yelp of pain. Instantly there was a flicker of light, and on came the lantern.

"What on earth are you doing, Pretty?"

"Looking for this." I unstoppered the flask and took a good swig. Great. I took another.

"Hey, leave us a mouthful!" He scrambled out of his sleeping-bag and stripped down to his shorts. I handed him the flask. Between us we finished it off, then sat looking at each other.

"I guess I should have explained—"

"I'm sorry I blew my top—"

We had spoken together. We looked at one another in the kindness of the lantern-light.

"Look, I should have explained better about that necklace. It's not quite what you think. Sure, I told Joe and Betty it wasn't worth much, but that was because I wanted to be able to buy it for you, and I knew I couldn't afford the real price. They didn't lose out: I paid for the goods that were stolen, and that's all they wanted."

"What do you mean: the real price?"

"Take another look: here."

Leaning closer to the lantern I turned the necklet over between my fingers. The blue stones were very bright, graded from back to front in increasing size, all oblong. Each of the blue stones was alternate with a round milk-colored one, round and also graded, the whole threaded on a thin gold-colored chain.

"I must admit it looks much prettier than I thought."

"It's also more valuable: those blue stones are turquoises, the white ones cultured pearls. And the chain is gold."

"You mean—it's real?"

"Of course. My mother once had some turquoise beads which she traded with the Herb-Woman, and the gold is marked on the clasp. As for the pearls, I read up on those years ago."

I handed it back "I can't take this: it's far too valuable. River-pearls are one thing, gold and turquoises are quite another."

"I bought it for you and you will wear it if I have to force it on!" He was grinning now. "And by the way, I don't know any other girl I would want to give it to!" He rolled over and fastened the old-fashioned clasp at the front, then hitched it round to the back of my neck. "There! It really suits you!" And for the first time, he leant forward and gently, too gently, kissed me full on the lips.

During the next two days there was no time for anything except walk, walk, walking. There was scarcely time even for thought, although when I finally fell asleep, thinking of that kiss, all I could dream about were those strangers, and more specifically their horrible deformities, so that I would awake in the middle of the night, sweating and afraid.

We had four days—to be accurate, three and three-quarters—to get back to our rendezvous with Lally and Co. I don't think either of us had realized just how difficult the journey back would be. Although our rucksacks were much lighter, as the food had gone down, the weather became much hotter and all the route was, however gradually, uphill. We scarcely had time to eat—honey, dried fruit and nuts for breakfast, pemmican and fruit for lunch, and the only cooked meal at night, bacon and pancakes.

We kept by the river, for water and washing, but the land was more difficult to traverse right there. We had no time for fishing, digging for edible roots and gathering fresh fruits, all the things we were supposed to do on expeditions like this, so gradually we were eating less and less: in fact we were in danger of running out of food altogether.

To add to our troubles, on the afternoon of the second day, when we stopped for a short breather and to refill the water-bottles, including Tam's glass ones, to save us time later on, and we were still nowhere near the infamous red line, we noted that it was not only getting hotter and more breathless, but the sky was clouding over a sort of greyish yellow, and over to the west a great black cloud, like the anvil in the forge at Deliverance, was rearing up into the sky.

"There's a hell of a storm coming," said Tam. He glanced across at the plantation, at this stage some five or six miles distant. "Come on, Pretty: we're going to have to run for it!" And run we did, a hot wind puffing in our faces, the rucksacks bumping up and down on our backs, the uneven ground making us stumble and fall more than once as we raced towards the shelter of the trees and into the teeth of the storm. Already we could hear the rumble of distant thunder and every now and again the sky was lit up by an eerie yellow flash of lightning, sometimes a slash across the sky, sometimes a great blanket of light that pulsed and throbbed like a giant panting animal.

We paused for a moment to gather breath, still short of the plantation by a couple of miles, and Tam started to gather up pieces of wood, moss, twigs. We were near a small spinney. I copied him, thrusting the firewood into my near-empty rucksack realizing we needed dry wood for a fire. It only took five minutes or so before we set off again, but as it was, we were a good half-mile away from the shelter of the trees when the first drops of rain started to fall, thick, heavy and warm like great drops of fresh-shed blood.

Five minutes later we were soaked to the skin as the full force of the storm hit us. The rain was driving in our faces, cold as ice, and there was hardly any pause between the flashes of lightning and the crash of thunder. A grey veil of hail came stinging our

faces and bare legs and arms just as we reached the
dubious safety of the trees. Once this had been a
well-managed pine plantation, with orderly rows of
trees interspersed with broad rides, but fifty or sixty
years of neglect had brought down many of the trees
and left great patches of land open to the sky. Chance
seeding of the same by wind, squirrels and birds,
meant that there were scrub and deciduous trees
as well as the pines.

We didn't know which way to go, so pushed as far
into the forest as we could, hoping to find a thick
stand of pines with a dry carpet of needles. The light
had almost gone now: it was late in the day and that,
combined with the darkness of the storm had us
crashing around half-blind. Every now and again a
flash of lightning would light up the trees, whitening
the trunks until they looked like the colonnades of
some great ruined temple, the ensuing darkness
disorientating us still further.

Suddenly there was an extra bright flash of
lightning, a great thump, and a tree to our right burst
into flame, riven from crown to root. The shock threw
me to the ground, knocking the breath from my lungs.
The rain sizzled the fire out in seconds, leaving a
smell of wet iron and soot. I could feel that the hair
on my head was sticking up in feathery strands, the
way it did sometimes when I brushed it too vigorously.
Tam was also flat on his face, but he rose to his feet
and pulled me to mine, shouting in my ear: "Quick!
There looks to be some sort of shelter over there. . . ."

Another flash of lightning showed us a sort of large
teepee formed of some half-dozen fallen trees.
Crouching down we crawled into a gap at the front,

and found ourselves tumbling down some three feet into a sort of hollow. It was as dry as a bone and cozy as a nest, with pine needles cushioning the floor.

After we had got ourselves right way up and sorted out, Tam lit the lantern. It was obvious that at some time the mound had been excavated under the fallen tree to form a shelter, because the gaps in the wood had been caulked with wood and earth and moss, and behind us was a ring of blackened stones and a small pile of wood and cones.

We didn't bother to question who, how or why. We lit a fire, I made some pancakes, and we fried up the rest of the bacon. Our wet outer clothing we hung optimistically from knobbles in the branches above us and curled up in our sleeping-bags. Outside the storm gradually lessened, to return a half-hour later as storms do, but greatly subdued, and I finally fell asleep to the monotonous drip, drip, drip of the rain from the branches of the trees above our shelter. . . .

We must have been abed early, because of the storm and the darkness and our exhaustion, so my mental sleep-clock gave me the right number of hours and woke me pre-dawn, wide awake and rested. The fire was still smoldering, so I replenished it with what we had brought, put on my still-damp clothes and fished around for something to eat. Flour—I thought we had more than that left—for pancakes, with honey and some cheese for dessert. Only thing was, I couldn't find the fry-pan, the cheese or the honey. After searching both rucksacks thoroughly and having a quick scout round outside, I woke Tam.

"Hey! Where did you put the fry-pan last night?"

He was never very good first thing in the morning, and by the time he had come to and declared he had put the pan outside the shelter so the rain would part-wash it and no, he hadn't seen the honey or the cheese, the sun was poking red dawn-fingers aslant the trees and the sweet babble of siskin and piping of tits could clearly be heard.

"Well, they're missing. So is half the remaining flour."

"You're sure?"

"Positive."

"Better look through everything else then and see if there's anything else gone astray."

There was. A pair of my knickers, the ones that Nan had embroidered with pink roses. My favorite pair . . .

We looked at each other in consternation.

"Who the hell . . .?"

"How do I know! The pan was outside, the cheese, flour and honey over there—" I pointed, "—and my knickers were folded up in my rucksack."

"Could have been an animal?" Even he didn't sound the least convinced.

"Oh, yeah?"

"Squirrels could have taken the honey—"

"In the middle of the night? In a jar? And I suppose carefully measured out half the flour, dragged the fry-pan off, towing the cheese in it and are using my knickers to line their drey for the winter! No, whoever did this was human." I looked around the shelter. "Probably the same people who built this." I shivered. Whoever or whatever, they had been skilled enough to take what they wanted without waking us. "Let's get the hell out of here!"

"We must eat first. What is there?" In the end I chucked the rest of the pemmican into the stewpot with a little flour, water and the last of the salt, boiling it quickly into a kind of mush, which we spooned out of the pot, burning our tongues in the haste, and then ate the last of the nuts.

God knows what we would do for food for the day and a half remaining; all we had was some cheese, flour and dried fruit, and two flasks and half a bottle of water. We'd just have to manage. Tam doused the fire with earth and we packed up as quickly as we could.

I wanted to go back to the river, but he pointed out that would add a couple of miles at least and that it was still drizzling, so we decided to stay on the fringes of the plantation, but we hadn't gone more than a hundred yards when he dropped down on his hands and knees.

"Look here. . . ."

On a comparatively bare patch of damp earth were the distinct impression of footprints. Not one, but two or three different ones—and they were all barefoot. One looked small enough to be a child's, one was large and splayed, and the third was about my size. There seemed to be others, but these were blurred.

"They're not fresh," said Tam, but nevertheless he spoke in a whisper. "There are one or two dead pine-needles on top. . . ."

"Our thieves, d'you think?"

"Could be. Let's go!"

Luckily for us the footprints were pointing away
to the south, the way we had come, but nevertheless
fear of the unknown lent wings to our feet and by
midday Tam announced that we were probably "legal"
again, past the limit of the red line on the map. We
ate half the remaining cheese, drank some water,
and pushed on, but about three I was absolutely
whacked and begged for a rest. "We've still got twenty-
five miles to go, and we can't do that in half a day!"
said Tam.

"Please! Half an hour . . ."

"Half an hour then. I'll wake you."

But he must have slept too, for when I woke the
sun was way over to the west. Woke? No, I was woken.
Someone was treading on my foot, hard.

I sat up and blinked. We were surrounded. . . .

CHAPTER SEVENTEEN

For a moment I was paralyzed with fear and disbelief. Around us were crowded perhaps a dozen individuals, none of them really resembling one another although three were dwarfs, just like in my book of fairy tales, another two midgets, and there was one man who was extraordinarily tall and thin, rather like an elongated skeleton. They were all barefoot and only partially clad, in a weird assortment of skins, scraps of cloth and bits of fur. They were all different ages, too. The youngest was perhaps my age, the oldest a mass of wrinkles. They wore their hair long, some plaited, some loose, and all of them were lean and brown. The two youngest were naked, but wore necklaces of animal teeth, and they were all armed.

Two had spears, half-a-dozen bows and arrows, two sharp knives and the youngest slingshots.

The one who had trodden on my foot had an arrow nocked into the string of his bow, although he stepped back when he saw I was awake. None of them said a word.

Frantically I jabbed a finger into Tam's ribs.

"For God's sake *wake up!*"

For once he was instantly awake, uncoiling himself

into a sitting position. Assessing the situation at a glance he attempted to rise to his feet, to be halted by a threatening growl from those surrounding us, accompanied by a hissing intake of breath. He sat back on his haunches, spreading his hands wide in a gesture of conciliation, which had no effect whatsoever.

He tried speech. "We-are-friends," he said slowly, attempting a smile.

At least this loosened their tongues, but only among themselves, and in a language that was foreign to me, with a singing lilt to it. It seemed they were discussing their captives, but although they spoke to one another they never took their eyes from us.

"What do you want?" I asked desperately. "We are poor, we have nothing but what you see. . . ."

"Shut up, Pretty," muttered Tam. "They can't understand you."

"Then what do we do?"

"Nothing. Wait for them to make a move. Can't you see they're waiting for someone—or some-*thing*?"

I looked at them more carefully, avoiding eye contact. It seemed Tam was right. They had threatened, but they had made no move to take anything or harm us. For the first time they looked hesitant, and one of them glanced over his shoulder. The plantation held the heavy silence and heat of late afternoon: even the birds were silent. We seemed to be the only living creatures.

I was still terrified, but I reached over and squeezed Tam's hand. "They must have been the ones who pinched our things last night," I murmured. "They probably built that shelter, too."

"If they wanted our belongings, then why didn't they take them all? Why only half the flour? And if they meant us harm, why not do it while we were asleep? It just doesn't add up."

"You're right! Shall we . . .?"

He knew what I meant. Moving slowly he rose to his feet; standing, he dwarfed them all but the tall thin man. The strangers snarled again, raising their weapons, but did no more than that. He reached down and pulled me up beside him. A hiss, but nothing else.

"Good. Now, bend down and pick up your ruck-sack—slowly—and put it on. . . ." A moment later he did the same, both of us without any interference.

"What now?"

"Now we start walking."

"Walking? How can we—they'll stop us!"

"I don't think so, especially if we walk towards the open. This is obviously their territory, the trees, and we're the intruders. I don't think they'll be so keen on being caught in the open. Hold my hand. Now, if we walk slowly towards that gap in the trees . . ."

I hadn't been willing to believe it, but as we walked towards the strangers, looking straight over the tops of their heads, they parted to let us through. I felt a sudden surge of relief, but to my horror they closed in behind us and kept pace on the right hand side, as if heading us away from the edge of the plantation.

"Don't look back!" hissed Tam. "Just keep going. Speed it up a bit, those short-arses'll have a job keeping up."

Theoretically, yes, but even the dwarfs, although they made two steps to our one, had no difficulty keeping pace. We came to a junction in the rides, the right hand path leading to the open. The path was straight and true, obscured only by a thick bush halfway along.

"Right," said Tam under his breath: "When I say run, run! I'll go to the left of that shrub, you go to the right. And just keep on running, whatever happens! Right: *run!*"

Fear lent me temporary wings and I was just ahead of Tam, the rucksack bouncing uncomfortably on my back, the strangers gradually falling back, a stitch in my side but blessed open land ahead of me when it happened—

The bush in front of me burst open!

It split into two halves, I twisted my foot under me and fell heavily with all the breath knocked out of me. As I whooped for breath Tam came to a halt beside me.

"God help us: what is *that*?"

"*That*" was difficult to describe. Between the two halves of the now obviously human-constructed bush stood a creature out of fantasy. It was male, as my stolen knickers outlined unmistakably. It was about my height, as brown as a chestnut and probably about my age, too. A shock of fox-red hair stood up in a tangle about its head, framing a round face with sparkling dark eyes and surprisingly white teeth filed to points in front. It had distinctly pointy ears and was wearing a big smile.

Tam was gasping at my side. "You—you okay?"

" 'Course you is! Both is! Good surprise, yes?" The creature was laughing wholeheartedly. "Took surprise out of you . . ." and he capered around us, genuinely happy, rattling the bone necklaces and bracelets he wore, his only clothing apart from the stolen knickers. "Loken's people herded you well din' they?" He clapped his hands, addressed a few words in that lilting language to his followers, who sat down in a circle behind us, grinning just as he was, but now relaxed, their weapons laid down by their sides.

Had we been persuaded to take this route? That was the only explanation for the trap, for trap it had been.

"At least you speak our tongue," said Tam, still breathing hard. "What's the meaning of this, anyway? Who are you? Where do you come from? And who are these—these followers of yours? What do you want with us? Isn't it enough that you stole our food and our belongings?" He gestured towards my knickers, already looking well worn.

The boy grinned, waved his hands. "Good take, that." He pointed to the two midgets. "Tiss and Siss do that. You snore."

"That was stealing. . . ."

For the first time the boy frowned. "Not steal! Your Wise Woman say barter. You take our shelter, we get wet all night, we take food. Barter, *not* steal! Loken steal, yes, but not from friends. *Barter*." He spoke as if we were the foreigners, learning a strange language.

Was the Wise Woman our Herb-Woman?

"That still doesn't explain who you are, and what you are doing here on our land," said Tam.

"Your land? *Our* land! This has always been ours!" He frowned again. "You go 'way. You not belong here! Go, not come back!"

"Nothing would please us more," said Tam between his teeth. "But that still doesn't tell us who you are, where you came from and why we have never seen you before—unless you are the ones who have been—been bartering from the village before?"

"Both sit down. I tell."

I couldn't have got up unless dragged, my twisted ankle hurt too much, but Tam strode forward aggressively, his fists clenched. "Look here, we're not taking any orders from you! Either you tell us what we want, or—"

On the word "orders" the boy put two fingers in his mouth and whistled, and by the time Tam had got to "want" we were joined by three of the strangest and most hideous dogs I had ever seen, who ranged themselves in front of the boy, ears back, teeth bared.

One was a huge bristly creature, black with two teeth protruding from the bottom jaw like a boar, the second was grey, tall and slim with a woolly coat, and the third was short and long, with, I swear, six legs. He spoke to them softly and they fawned around his feet, tongues lolling.

"Found them as pups, no food, men throw stones, try to kill. They now Loken's children. . . ." He looked up at us, tapped each dog in turn. "Meet Biter—" (the black one with teeth) "—Tracker—" (the thin one) "—and Digger." The one with six legs.

Tam put a foot forward, and immediately all changed: the dogs were on the alert, coats bristling. He moved back, but still he persisted with his questioning of our captor. If it had been left to me I should have been a screaming jelly.

"You still want to know? Sit down, as I say, and

we will eat. We eat, and I tell." He snapped his fingers and his tribe disappeared into the plantation.

Tam tried to emphasize the importance of our rendezvous.

"You meet friends? No worry, you get there. Loken help."

I tried to stand—I wanted to go to the bathroom— but my damaged foot crumpled under me, and I sat down again.

"You hurt? Loken's fault. Let Loken see. . . ." His fingers were surprisingly gentle: he smelt of wood-smoke, sweat and the open air. "Wait here: get herbs."

While he was away Tam helped me behind one of the trees to relieve myself. The dogs didn't move. Perhaps they knew we weren't going anywhere.

Some half-hour later we were seated in front of a blazing fire, my ankle bandaged in cooling herbs, and eating from our fry-pan with our fingers. Meat, roots, herbs, leaves—they were all delicious. When I learned afterwards that the meat included squirrel, I nearly threw up, but it seemed a waste, so I didn't. We finished with toasted pine-nuts.

As we ate, Loken—as he called himself—told us a bit about himself. Apparently at the time of the Apocalypse his people had been circus performers— the language they spoke among themselves was a sort of bastardized Italian, the language of all circus folk. Those who escaped the initial destruction sheltered in deep caves, their normal winter quarters, but over the years disease and the chronic lack of food had decimated them. Eventually the older folk had died and Loken had been sent out as a babe in arms—"With them," he said proudly, pointing to the oldest of the dwarfs—who had apparently cared for him until he was old enough to take charge of the remaining group.

"I lead them where is best pickings," he said. "We steal, okay? But no other way we can live. Two, three of my people they settle. Now I have few left. We steal, but not here. Here we barter, like Wise Woman say. Time now for all my people to find place to live. Summer travel, winter dig-in. Down there—" he pointed south "we steal. Up here, we barter."

"And what do you trade in?" I asked.

He laughed, flung his arms wide. "Anything! Nothing! What people want. Your Wise Woman, she give us clothes, blankets, flour in—barter—for salt, herbs, seeds, curios. Two times a year I come. Sow-time and Gather-time. I bring her what I steal, what is different, she give me good barter." He pointed at me. "You wear one of my steals round neck." He was looking at my necklace. "Got from way west. You like?"

"Very much," I said. "Very pretty. . . ."

"Like you name!" He laughed delightedly; we had introduced ourselves earlier. "Find more next year. Pretty for the Pretty, yes?"

Tam shot me a glance which meant: don't encourage him. I smiled to myself.

Tam rose to his feet and made a courteous little speech of thanks. "And now we really must go—"

Loken pointed to the sky where the first stars were pricking through, and then leant forward to touch my bandaged ankle. "Sleep now, travel later."

We tried to explain again about our rendezvous the following afternoon; he listened, his head on one side, then he turned away as if he were considering. We waited. At last he turned round and called his tribe towards him, obviously ordering them to do something. They nodded and scattered into the trees. Loken turned to us.

"Pretty ankle hurt 'cos I make too big surprise. So will get you to friends in time. Promise." He produced a small bottle from the debris of our meal. "We drink to being friends. I think you no tell about Loken and his people. Right?"

We nodded. Telling about any of the things that had happened to us spelt trouble. He poured a small amount of the liquid into our mugs and topped it up with water.

"Is cordial: very good. Wise Woman say: 'Your health'" He drank from his own mug—I reckoned an earlier steal. The cordial tasted like bubbly water, with a hint of the bitterness of dandelion leaves and a sort of musty aftertaste. It wasn't until I had emptied the mug and started to feel the numbness and tingling in my toes and fingers, and the veil of darkness began to creep in from all sides that I realized with horror that we must have been poisoned!

I tried to get up, but the numbness was creeping all over—

"Tam!" I croaked, but glancing over I saw him topple over on his side, a silly grin on his face. Well, if this was poison, then it didn't hurt. The last thing I remember was a voice in my ear whispering: "Sleep, my pretty one, sleep. . . ."

Someone was trying to shake me awake, but it was such a long way to travel and I was so sleepy. . . .

Just let me stay here wherever it was a little bit longer, surely it wasn't time to get up for school—

"Pretty. Pretty, wake up! It's time to go—"

"Go 'way . . ."

"Wake *up*!"

I opened my eyes reluctantly and saw Tam's anxious face bent over mine, "Thank God! I thought for a moment . . . You feeling okay?"

"I feel terrible! Give me a drink, my mouth tastes awful!" I drank gratefully, and Tam handed me what looked like two large biscuits.

"Breakfast: sorry there's no more, but they don't taste too bad."

I struggled out of my sleeping-bag. We were once more in the open, under the shade of a large beech tree. "Where are we? How did we get here?"

"Good question! I'm not sure, but I think Loken gave us some sort of sleeping-draught and they carried us here in litters. I seem to remember being jolted up and down, but then I passed out again. My back is killing me. . . ." He rubbed it, wincing. "I'll say one thing for them: they must have traveled! It's just after midday, but we're less than a mile from the rendezvous. How's your ankle?"

I tested it gingerly. "Not bad; a bit twingy, but much better. Whatever Loken put on it, it certainly worked!" I shook my head. "Who would have thought we would meet two sets of people so unlike! Who would have thought we would have met anyone at all, come to that. . . ."

"Which reminds me," said Tam with a grin, "I think I've worked out a way to explain the loss of the frypan and your—er, underwear. You sprained your ankle on the river-bank, your rucksack tipped up and we lost—what we bartered. What do you say?"

"I say I can't wait till we catch up with the others: just hope they've got some food left—I'm *starving!*"

But when we made our slow way to the rendezvous an hour later, there was nobody there. . . .

CHAPTER EIGHTEEN

Tam pivoted on his heels, staring in every direction. "Right place, right day, right time," he said. "And neither hide nor hair of them."

"Lally never was very punctual," I said, shucking off my pack with a sigh of relief, to nurse my injured ankle which was beginning to throb.

"Sven usually is."

"Not when he's with her."

"She sure knows how to pick 'em." He grinned, his pack following mine. "I don't know about you, but I'm not only starving I'm bone dry as well. The river's only about a quarter mile away; think you can make it? You could bathe that ankle of yours—"

"And you could have a bath! Have you any idea how grubby you look? 'Sides, you don't exactly smell of roses. . . ." There were leaves in his wildly tangled hair, his shorts were torn and filthy and one toe poked out from his laced boots.

"Seen yourself? You look as if you'd been dragged through not one but two hedges backwards!"

"Right," I said. "It's the river. Give me a hand. . . ." I rose to my feet reluctantly, and fished in my rucksack for what was left of my clean clothes, a towel and comb, noticing as I did the briar scratches on my arms and legs. I could smell my own sweat, and could only imagine what my hair looked like. "What happens if they turn up while we're gone?"

"Leave 'em a marker—the 'Back Soon' one."

"Better leave a 'This Way' as well, just in case."

Because of the shortage of paper and writing materials all messages in the village were either in pokerwork or carved; "Not at Home," "Call Again," "Don't Disturb," "Back in Five Minutes" and "Help!" were favorites, left hanging on the front door. Of course in the open we had to make do with sticks and stones: a combination of a circle plus an arrow for direction was enough in this case. Other recognized markers were formed of squares, triangles, angles, crosses or straight lines, used in combination if necessary, and understood by us all.

I suppose we were at the riverside for about an hour, washing, drying off, changing, drinking our fill and filling the flasks, but when we arrived back at the rendezvous the others had still not arrived. I began to worry. We sat down to wait, but privately I had decided that if they didn't arrive in the next hour or so we would make our way back to camp. We had no food, although I rummaged about in both rucksacks, just in case. We could leave another marker, if necessary, and go back for them in the morning. Tam found a handful of rather furry nuts in one of his pockets and we made them last out as long as we could, but it only made us hungrier.

For a while we talked of our experience with Loken and his tribe.

"Let's face it," said Tam. "He and his people needed

those things, the food and all, more than we did.
Remember how thin they all were?"

"No excuse for thieving."

"Barter."

"Yes; I reckon the Herb-Woman is the one they've
been dealing with. Perhaps we should have a word . . ."

"No complaints though: Loken and his people
might be useful. He knows the way of the woods,
and when and if I decide to strike out on my
own—"

"Oh, you're not on that again!"

"The more I think about it, the more I'm convinced
it's the right thing to do. Don't you see—"

But he was interrupted. There was a shout from
the slope above us and looking up, we could see one
of the twins waving his arms like a cockerel with
the staggers.

"It's Bill! Or Ben . . ."

"Something's wrong!" said Tam. "Wait there, I'll
go and fetch him down."

It was Ben, but it was difficult to make out what
he was saying, except that there was something wrong
with Lally.

"Won't wake up! Won't wake up!" he kept saying,
and: "Beeping Sleauty!" over and over again. He kept
pointing to the north and in the end we shouldered
our packs again and followed his lead, my ankle
holding up pretty well after its soak in the icy
riverwater earlier.

About a half-mile further on we found the others.
Bill was dancing round like a disjointed puppet, and
Sven was kneeling at the side of a recumbent Lally.
White as death, she was tossing her head from side

to side, her eyelids fluttering, while every now and again she gave a soft moan.

I dropped down and took her head in my lap, noticing that she had a greenish slime trickling from the corner of her mouth.

"What have you done to her? Lally, Lally, wake up!" She was icy cold. I cuddled her up close and glared at Sven.

His face was red, his hair tousled. "We—we've had to carry her. I don't know what's the matter, wish to hell I did! She's never been this way before. Always been all right after . . ." He trailed off.

"Well, she's not all right now!" I snapped, rubbing her cold hands. "We'd better get her back to camp, pronto!"

"I'll go," said Tam. "There are a couple of stretchers in the barn for emergencies, but I'll get Joe to bring the cart, so you both can ride. Be as quick as I can!" And he was away.

It would be a good hour and a half before he could be back, so I made Lally as comfortable as I could, wrapping her up in our sleeping bags, Sven's jacket under her head. The twins were still weeping and wailing so I sent them off to gather wood to make a fire; not that it was cold, but I wanted them out of the way while I had a word with Sven.

"Right," I said. "You asked us to cover for you on this trip, didn't you? That's why we went off together and were supposed to meet up here to go back to camp as though we had been with you the whole ten days? True?"

He nodded, reluctantly. "Something like that. . . . But she wasn't meant to get ill like this. We—we just wanted a little time on our own, to—to do our own thing, without other people poking and prying."

"Time on your own?" I said incredulously. "With the twins hanging round your necks? Oh, come on! Pull the other one!"

He went redder still, if that were possible. "We needed them. To—to carry stuff, fetch wood, clear up . . . You know."

"No, I *don't* know. Where exactly did you go that needed all that toting of stuff? And what in the world made Lally so sick?"

"Look, I'll explain it all later, I promise. When she's better. When—when Tam comes back, all you have to say is that she ate something that disagreed with her. . . ."

"Such as? Is that what really happened? And if so, just what could make her so sick? She looks as if she's been poisoned—"

"Don't say that!" From being red faced, he now went almost as white as Lalage. "They wouldn't do that!"

"Who wouldn't?"

A voice behind us said "Pillar-cats."

"Green cows," said another. Bill and Ben were back.

"Beeping Sleauty don't like their milk," said one of them. "Taste ba-a-ad!"

I rounded on them. "Just tell me, right now, exactly where you've been. And no lies, mind, or it'll be smacks all round!"

"Din' go there!" bellowed Bill (or Ben).

"Where didn't you go?"

"Oh, stop it!" shouted Sven, suddenly. "Don't pick on them. Lally told them not to tell. Okay, okay, so we went to the Wilderness. It was her idea, she's always been crazy about the place. We knew if we told you, you wouldn't cover for us."

Remembering the last time I had been there, I couldn't understand the fascination it still held for Lally. For me it had lost its earlier charm and had changed from my childhood memories. Then it had been a place of faery, difficult of true recall perhaps, but still full of memories of light and shade, flowers and fruit, a sun that shone all day long and dreams of elves and fairies taking part in theatricals. The last time I had visited it had been at night, and the ambiance had been totally different—for me at least, although Lally had apparently seen it still with the eyes of a bewitched child. To me the gloom, the unpleasant smell and the churned-up mud, together with the impression that things had shrunk, gave the whole place a sinister aspect.

I remembered, too, the warnings the Herb-Woman had relayed through her daughter: that there were dark and powerful forces hidden in the Wilderness, ones it would be wise not to wake. For me the only evidence of anything unusual had come from those unexplained deep sleeps, the illusion of others around us and the strange vibrations I had when touching the ring of ancient stones. Was it because the others had been—literally—stung, and Tam and I never had?

Full of foreboding I rolled up first one and then the other of Lally's sleeves, but there were only a couple of yellowing bruises around wrists and upper arms, as though someone had gripped her too tight. As a matter of course I looked at her legs also, finding

the same discoloration about her ankles and above
her knees, and they now assumed the aspect of some
kind of binding or restriction—but who would do
such a thing? Surely not Sven or the twins either,
unless it was some strange form of bondage I could
only guess at.

Time passed with agonizing slowness, while Lally
still lay there in a stupor, the twins moaned quietly
in the background and Sven kept asking if she was
any better, but at last I heard a shout from the
direction of the river path and Tam came running
with Joe close behind, carrying a stretcher. After that
it didn't take long to load Lally and me onto the wagon
with all the gear, and transport us back to camp. Betty
took a close look at Lally and ordered Joe to return
her to the village immediately, together with Sven
and explanations.

She looked at my ankle and told me "cold compresses
and keep off it for a couple of days," then disappeared
to dish up supper, which did more for our well-being
and morale than anything in the last week, or so it
seemed. Baked potatoes with butter and chopped
chives, slices of gammon with parsley sauce and green
beans, followed by fruit bread and chamomile tea or
goat's milk, and we were fit to burst.

Afterwards we sat around the campfire and
exchanged news and gossip; everyone had a story to
tell, some lurid, some commonplace, but they were
all so busy with their own adventures to notice that
Tam and I were, for us, remarkably silent. Obviously
most couples had paired off happily; I looked across
the fire at Tam—yes, across, not next to me as if he
considered us as a fixture—and wondered just exactly

how he thought of me. Okay, so it hadn't been exactly a classic holiday, where all that mattered was that a boy and girl go off to find out what it's all about— after all, which of the others had discovered two different types of human tribes? Who else had walked their feet off and gone into forbidden territory? Who else had friends who had spent their week secretly in the Wilderness, from where at least one of them had returned seriously ill? And all of this a deadly secret . . .

So, Tam and I weren't Romeo and Juliet, Rochester and Jane or Cupid and Psyche, but I had thought there was a special kind of fondness between us. In my own way I loved him, and I had believed he felt the same way. I felt strangely angry, deprived of something I couldn't name; at the same time I had one of those strange yearnings that my Nan called my "growing pains."

That night, with the lamp swinging crazily from the tent-pole and the flaps tightly closed against mosquitoes and suicidal moths, we talked quietly of what had happened on our journey, conscious that the twins were next to us—we had taken the tent next to them in order to keep an eye on them, seeing that neither Sven nor Lally were here.

I decided to change the subject. "Tam . . ."

"Yes?" He yawned, a jaw-cracker.

"I was thinking . . ."

"About?"

I hesitated. "Us." There, I'd said it.

He yawned again. "And?" He was lying on his side, facing away from me.

"I guess this is difficult for me to say . . ."

"Then don't say it. Things have a way of sorting themselves out, Pretty."

"I don't think this will. Not unless we talk about it." At least he knew what I was on about. "When we get back we have to answer that questionnaire— you know the one that asks how we got on, whether we intend to—oh, heck! You know what I'm trying to say! Why do you have to make it so difficult. . . ."

"I haven't changed my mind: have you?"

"Of course not! But . . . we don't seem to be exactly committed, do we?"

"Perhaps it's a bit early for all that. Look, you and I grew up together didn't we? Your Nan treated me like I was one of the family, and you were a special sort of pal." He turned over to face me. "Then we both started to grow up. You know from school what happens to our bodies, our hormones. I started to look at other girls, you at other boys—don't deny it— but as it turned out we were both more comfortable with each other."

"Then why—"

"Will you shut up and listen? Comfortable, yes, but neither of us was head-over-heels in love, were we? I suppose most girls—"

"I'm not 'most girls'!"

"No you're not!" At last there was a grin on his face. "You're a one-off. I've never disputed that. Well, one-off girl, I thought you would be willing to accept my point of view without me having to explain."

"And that point of view is . . .?"

"I need my freedom, at least for a while, especially as I now plan to do a bit of traveling. How would you feel if I married you, then suddenly took off for parts unknown and left you with a brace of kids?"

"Don't be silly!" I was smiling now. "Besides, you asked me to go with you, remember?"

"And I also told you why you wouldn't. I need space, Pretty. I want to find out what this world is made of; I don't want to be stuck forever in the prison-camp of Deliverance! Can't you see that?"

The trouble was, I could. After all we had seen and experienced and done in the last few days, if I had been a boy nothing would have pleased me more than to join him. But I wasn't, and I couldn't. So, being what I was, I fell back on stupid anger and resentment.

"You know what they'll say, don't you?"

"What?"

"That you're queer. . . ." Immediately I said it I could have bitten out my tongue. I half-expected him to reach across and slap me on the face.

"And if I were?" Not the answer I had been expecting.

"Don't be so bloody stupid! If you even hint at such a thing you know what will happen! Remember that couple they told us about?"

This had happened many years ago, before we were born. Two young men had fallen in love with each other; they were gentle and handsome, according to my Nan, and never threatened harm to anyone. When their relationship had been discovered by Mayor Gross, they had been sentenced by the Council to the ultimate punishment: banishing to the Barren Lands across the river. According to tradition, they were being swung across the river but the rope had broken and flung them into the raging torrent beneath.

Since then no one had professed any interest in their own sex. . . .

"Don't worry, I'm not going to chuck my life away."

"Then what do we say when they face us with that bloody questionnaire? We've got to persuade them that we've had a super time together, that we suit each other, that we—we intend a firm future relationship. . . ." Then I laughed, for he was clutching his heart with an expression of acute indigestion, his eyes rolled back into his head. "Oh, come on, idiot! If you really are set on going off on an expedition, don't you see this would stop them suspecting anything? Remember what they ask us?" I ticked the items off on my fingers; they were familiar to us both, having heard from others just how it went. "How long have you been going out together; are you serious in your relationship; are you sexually compatible; are there any physical problems; does your family approve; what are your ambitions for the future; do you think you are ready for a stable relationship; how many children do you plan on having; are you prepared to teach your children to respect and observe the rules that bind our life here; and—"

"And when do you plan to marry. . . . Let's give them the works, then! Yes to everything that matters—"

"Except the sex bit—" I knew I was blushing.

"Okay: We believe in the sanctity of marriage and aren't going to anticipate it—"

"How many children?"

"Four?"

"Ten!" I was entering into the spirit of the thing.

"Oh, Pretty! They'd know we were conning them!"

"Right, then: no plans, just what the Lord provides. . . . How's that?"

"Perfect. And we are not planning to get married for a couple more years: we feel we need time to mature, to know we will both be responsible parents and useful members of the community."

"And that should give you time to plan your escape. . . ." So, what was there in it for me, I thought miserably.

He leant over and took my hand, squeezing it hard. "Don't call it that!" I tried to draw my hand away, but he held it tighter. "Listen to me; I'm only going to say this once. I know of no one else I had rather spend my life with than you, but I'm not ready for any commitment. But this I promise: wherever I go and however long I am gone, I will come back one day if I can. Then, perhaps, we will both be ready to talk about this again. . . ."

He released my hand and blew out the lantern, leaving me to the darkness of my thoughts.

CHAPTER NINETEEN

We had all thought that Lally's illness would be only a temporary thing once she got back home, but we were wrong. Put to bed with the doctor and his trainee-assistant in constant attendance, they nevertheless declared themselves confounded by her continued unconsciousness and the greenish froth that dribbled from her mouth. She was clammy and cold also, in spite of the blankets and hot bricks she was surrounded with. They tried everything: plunging her first into hot water, then cold; tried to make her drink broth and/or sugared water through a feeding-cup; dosed her with purgatives and emetics; rubbed her with oil, scrubbed her with salt—all to no avail.

Eventually she was removed to the little Infirmary, for round-the-clock nursing, but every day she grew paler and thinner. In the end her distraught parents did what we all thought they should have done in the first place: they summoned the help of the Herb-Woman.

After a thorough examination she called on our families to "borrow" us as she called it, and that very night we—Tam and I, Bill and Ben and Sven—gathered by Lally's bedside, together with the Herb-Woman and her daughter. The nurse had been sent

away, and we gathered round the narrow cot on which
Lally lay unconscious and scarcely breathing.

"Right," said the Herb-Woman, her shadow huge
on the wall behind her. "This child is gravely ill and
there's nothing I know of that will cure her. In a few
days she will die unless I can find out how to treat
her, and that is why I have asked you all here. The
clue to her well-being lies with you all. I am going
to ask you some questions and I want the truth. Any
lies, evasions or half-truths can damn this child's
chance of recovery. We'll start with you, Tamerlane
and Prettiance. . . ." She was the only person, apart
from our teachers, who ever gave me my full name.

She asked little of us, except how, why and when,
but in the telling of how we found Lally, we unwillingly
revealed how we had conspired with her to pretend
we had all been together for the trip. She was gentle
with the twins, but her questions were clever enough
to get them to admit they had spent their time in
the Wilderness, and it didn't need a glance at Sven's
guilty expression to confirm what they said. In fact
it didn't need a single question for him to be
immediately on the defensive.

"All right, all right! So we shouldn't have gone there!
But she insisted. And—and before, it wasn't like
this. . . ."

"How many times have you been there?"

"Since we were forbidden? I don't know really; it
has always been difficult to remember afterwards.
Perhaps twice or three times a year. . . ."

"Why did she want to go there?"

"She—sees things I don't. It's like a game to her.
She really sees herself as a Princess, and acts out

her fancies just as if they were real." He suddenly
pointed at me "It's all your fault! All those stories
you told us. . . ."

I was shocked by the accusation, but it was Tam
who came to my defense.

"Rubbish! There were lots of us heard those tales,
and it didn't affect us. It was only Lally who took it
seriously. She was always the star of the show, and I
guess she couldn't bear to lose that when she grew
older. She has always wanted to be the center of
attention, and this was one way of being it."

I was surprised—and pleased—by his defense, but
the Herb-Woman slowly shook her head.

"You are right and wrong, boy. Right to defend
Prettiance, but wrong about the stories. The trouble
was, all you children were in the wrong place at the
wrong time when that book of stories first gotten
opened. Others were awake too. Powers who both
looked and listened, and saw how you paid Lalage
the homage due to a real Princess."

"You mean . . . someone thinks she's a real Princess?"
Sven sounded baffled.

"That could be one explanation. But there are
others. . . . You told me Sven, son of Torvald, grandson
of Arne the Tall, that Lalage 'saw' things that you
didn't; what sort of things?"

He shrugged. "Like the things we thought we saw
when we were kids. Fairies, elves, gnomes, castles,
witches, kings and queens, lambs with ribbons round
their necks, cats walking on their hind legs . . ."

"Just like the illustrations in Prettiance's book?"

He nodded.

"And did *you* see any of these things? The truth,

boy!" For he had started to deny it, but she must have seen something in his eyes, for he stammered and fell silent. "Look it's the girl you love we are trying to save and we have no chance unless I know all the facts. Remember she may die if I can't help her. In case you are worried that whatever you say may be repeated outside, I think I can promise you that nothing you reveal will go beyond these four walls. Am I right?"

We all nodded.

"I must know just how much of this affected you, too. Don't you understand that I can only help if I understand the Powers that are ranged against us? Now, did you see anything at all that she said she saw?"

"Yes. Sometimes. At least I thought I did. But it might have been that I wanted to see what she did. . . ." He waved his arms helplessly, caught in his own incoherence. "It was—I told myself I must be dreaming. But it could be—seemed sometimes— to be real. To me, too. I was sometimes—I thought I was—dressed as a Prince, Lally's Prince. But it couldn't be. I was Sven the shepherd. . . . But I did see things—dreamt them. Not always good. There were things that frightened me. Things that looked like one thing, then turned into another."

"Such as?"

"The castle. There was a castle, with a bed on which Lally slept, the Sleeping Beauty. Then it wasn't—a castle or a bed, I mean. It was an operating theater and Lally was unconscious and They—They were doing things to her. . . ."

"They? Who were They? And what were they doing?"

But he shook his head. "I don't remember."

"Let's leave that for a moment. Was there anything else that looked like one thing and turned into another?" She was remarkably calm and matter-of-fact, while the rest of us were listening with increasing alarm and mystification.

"Yes, lots of things. I particularly remember the sheep. They were picture sheep, not real ones like we have. They were woolly toys—'Baa-baa Black Sheep' and 'Mary had a Little Lamb'—you know? Well sometimes they were like that, and sometimes, when they were cropping the grass—they—they were different. . . ."

"Pillar-cats," interrupted Bill (or Ben).

"Nasty," added the other. "Slimy."

She turned to them at once. "Did you see any fairies? Or a castle?"

They shook their heads.

"A room with a big bed in it?"

"Big room. Little bed. Shiny . . ."

"Was your Lally on the bed?"

They nodded.

"Was she asleep?" Another joint nod. "Were there other—things—near to your Lally?" More nods. "Were they doing things to Lally?"

This time there wasn't a spoken answer; instead they turned to each other and buried their heads on each others' shoulders. She changed her tack. "Good boys: you remember very well." She went over and touched their heads. "It's all right: we are going to make Lally well. Your words will help. What did Lally eat?"

The answer didn't make sense. "Pillar-cat juice."

Knowing the twins as we did, "pillar-cats" were caterpillars. What on earth did caterpillars have to do with it?

"What color were the pillar-cats?"

The twins glanced at each other. I knew they weren't good at colors. They could see them, but the words associated with them didn't seem to make sense. They tended to describe a color in context with a well-known object; thus blue was "like sky."

"Like grass."

"So Lally, your Sleeping Beauty, drank some juice from the green-as-grass caterpillars? Is that it? Big caterpillars?"

They nodded. "*They* made her!" It was Ben.

"Asleep. Put it in mouth." Bill.

"Make her sick . . ."

"Not wake up."

The Herb-Woman patted them. "Just what I wanted to know. *Good* boys!" And from some pocket or other she produced a couple of bon-bons and popped them into their mouths. They chewed contentedly.

"Right!" The Herb-Woman rubbed her hands together briskly. "Now I know what we must do. Sven, Tamerlane: wrap Lalage up tightly in blankets, and fetch a stretcher out of that cupboard. Perdita, go down and make sure the nurse is asleep: my cowslip wine should have done the trick. Prettiance: light the other lantern and open the door at the back: here's the key. Make sure the coast is clear. Bill, Ben: you are going to carry your Lally to where we can make her better!" She clapped her hands. "Come along, come along: what are you all hanging about for?"

Now was not the time to question or wonder. She

was like the sternest of school-teachers, and we
scuttled away to do her bidding as if we had been
threatened with the cane, or were a parcel of kids
on their first day in school. Less than five minutes
later we found ourselves in Greek Street, behind the
Infirmary and facing onto the allotments, Lally a dark
bundle on a stretcher between the twins, the Herb-
Woman holding one lantern, Perdita the other.

The Herb-Woman stepped forward. "I will lead
the way. Sven and Tamerlane will walk on either side
of the stretcher to keep it steady and take over from
the twins if necessary. Perdita, you spy out ahead;
Prettiance bring up the rear with the other lantern,
and make sure we're not followed. Are you all ready?"

"But where are we going?" asked Tam. "To your
place?"

For answer she put her finger to her lips. "Hush!
Just follow me. . . ."

We turned left, towards the river: so it wasn't going
to be the Herb-Woman's cottage, nor the church,
which I had half-suspected. Instead we crept past
the backs of houses, windows open in the warm late-
summer night air, the occupants going about their
business oblivious to our procession outside. We met
no one, and even the dogs on guard outside the
warehouses didn't bark.

At the river we turned left again. The Herb-Woman
took the shade from her lantern.

"Quicker by way of the fields, but we have to keep
the stretcher steady. Best foot forward now, and mind
the stones on the path."

Now I knew where we were going: to the Wilderness!

All at once the night air turned darker, took on a

sudden chill, or so it seemed to me. Tam, his face pale by starlight, turned to look at me: so he realized as well. It didn't seem to have dawned on Bill and Ben, however: they were still stumping along happily with the stretcher between them, refusing any help.

I opened my mouth to protest, shut it again. If the Herb-Woman thought this was the only way to help Lally, then that was that. However there was no place on earth, known or unknown, that I was less willing to visit at night, any night.

We made good progress as there were gates to the highest pasture now, but it was only when we opened these that the twins realized where we were headed. They began to shake, so the semiconscious Lally started to moan. The Herb-Woman spoke to them reassuringly, then indicated that Tam and Sven should take over.

"Their reaction is interesting," she observed in her normal voice, as we were far enough from the village to have no fear of being either observed or overheard. "For sometimes the young and innocent see things that we lose when we are adults. . . ."

I remembered how, even at the start of things, their dreams had been disturbing, and I wondered how much their personal devotion to Lally had made them overcome their fears: if we had listened to them more closely at the beginning, would Lally have been so close to death? Now they were really showing their fear, with no Lally to talk them out of it. I had never seen them so upset; I had heard of people's teeth chattering, as mine had done once or twice when caught out in the cold, but on a warm summer's night?

But the Herb-Woman was equal to it. "Now then,

my brave boys, time you had a rest. Perdita will take
the lantern and lead the way, and you will take my
hands and help me over the difficult bits. Then we
can face whatever dragons there are together."

"Pillar-cats."

"*Them.*"

"Whoever and Whatever. All of them. You know
I'm invincible, don't you? That means nothing can
harm me. Now, we're going to tell those baddies that
they must make your Lally well at once, aren't we?
Then we can take her home. Come on then," and
come on they did, as meek as lambs. She was a tall
woman, but even so they towered over her, shambling
along on either side.

We crossed the top pasture at a good pace and,
too soon for me, reached the thick, near-impenetrable
hedge that had once enclosed enchantment but was
now a place of threat. We found the old tunnel easily
enough, and as Sven, Lally and the twins had passed
through several times during the camping holiday,
we squeezed through easily enough: and even the
Herb-Woman with her voluminous skirt managed
it, by stooping, and the stretcher went through
comfortably as well. Once through she stood up,
dusted herself down and remarked "Years since I
was here, but the Force Field seems to be weaker."

She was speaking to her daughter, who nodded.
"It seems Their minds are on something else. I noticed
it the last time I was here."

I wanted to ask what on earth the Force Field was,
but they had moved away. Had it anything to do with
the way the hedge always seemed to resist any entry
but the tunnel? If so, who had put the resistance

there? And why? If it was to keep us out, why had we rather been encouraged to return?

But there was no time to ponder over this because we were on the move. We made our way through the trees and along the path I knew so well, the moon now casting its pale light on our progress. As we came nearer to the center once again I could smell that unpleasant odor we had come across before, and I noticed that Perdita had her fingers to her nose. We halted at the entrance to the glade.

It had been bad enough the last time we had been here, Tam and I, when we had followed Sven and Lally and found her dancing in the churned-up mud where once had been a pleasant stretch of greensward. Now it looked like a disaster area, some two or three times its previous circumference, extending into the fringes of the wood, and all around the trees and bushes had been stripped of their leaves and bark as if a whole herd of starving deer had rampaged for half a month. The stench was terrible and the stumps of stone that marked the circle were half-buried in filth.

The Herb-Woman held up her hand. "This is as far as you go. Put down the stretcher. I shall manage on my own."

"But—but what are you going to do?" cried Sven.

"That is my business. Do as you are told." Suddenly she seemed as tall as a tree. "Go now, to the entrance tunnel. When there, join hands and empty your minds of everything except the well-being of Lalage. You will see nothing, hear nothing else. Stay there until I come. . . ." She stooped down and lifted Lally from the stretcher as easily as she would carry a child.

"But what if it doesn't work?" Sven was distracted, wringing his hands, tears running down his cheeks.

"You had better pray it does. Now *go!*"

I was the last one to run back along the path, and I turned once, just in time to see the Herb-Woman stride into the stone circle, Lally close in her arms. . . .

CHAPTER TWENTY

"But what exactly *happened*?"

It was the first time Tam and I had had truly to ourselves in the five days since Lalage's miraculous recovery. Now we were in the orchard, ostensibly volunteers to collect the small windfalls brought down by a thunderstorm the previous night, and destined for the pigs. He had filled one pannier, I half another before we dared take a breather behind the rhubarb bins, but even so he kept bobbing up and down to see we weren't overheard.

"I don't know: I just don't remember. Truly . . ."

"You do recall us going to the Wilderness?" I asked.

"Of course. If we did, that is."

"What do you mean '*if* we did'? We were all there."

"How do you know? Have you asked the others?"

"Of course not! Lally would know nothing about it, it's useless talking to Bill and Ben, Sven has been shut up with Lally and her parents and I haven't seen Perdita or her mother. What makes you think we weren't there, if we both remember it?"

"Do you recall the trip back? Or who carried the stretcher? Or how we got her back to bed?"

I shook my head. "N-no. Don't you?"

"No, I don't." He plucked a stem of sweet-grass

and chewed the soft base. "I'm pretty convinced, like you, that we carried her up to the Wilderness and that the Herb-Woman carried her off and told us to go away and pray, or something like that. But as for the rest . . . It could all have been a dream. When we woke up, we were back in the Infirmary. So, if we went on an expedition, how the hell did we get back, and how come we don't remember that?"

He was right: it didn't make sense. I was sure I had seen the Herb-Woman carry Lally into the stone circle, but the next thing I remember is the day-nurse at the Infirmary coming to open the shutters in Lally's room. I had rubbed my eyes and stretched, creaky as a flight of old stairs, to find I had been sleeping on the floor, together with the rest of us, except the Herb-Woman who was sitting on the chair by Lally's head. Everyone stared at everyone else, trying madly to discover how we had got where we were, but before we had time to say anything the blinds had gone up and a bar of sunlight struck right across Lally's face. As we rose to our feet, fearing the worst, she slowly opened her blue eyes, stretched her arms above her head, yawned, and sat up.

"Goodness me! Wherever am I? Tell you what, I'm so hungry, and *so* thirsty. . . ." Her cheeks were rosy, her lips full of color, and there seemed no restriction in her movements. The day nurse gave a yell, crossed herself, then bounded out and down Main Street, shouting at the top of her voice that "The Vigil" had been successful and Miss Lally was miraculously cured.

It appeared afterwards that when the Herb-Woman had "borrowed" us, she had explained that

it was a last-hope all-night vigil that was to be held
to try and cure the patient. At the same time the
priest was to do the same in the church, with Lally's
parents. However it was, within twenty-four hours
of observation Lally was back home again, enjoying
all the fuss and attention. Opinion in the village was
sharply divided as to the efficacy or otherwise of
the two different methods of healing, and Mayor
Gross underlined his dislike of the Herb-Woman
and her "cures," by ordering a service of thanksgiving
in the church. Most people, however, didn't really
care which method had worked the miracle, were
just happy to see the attractive girl out and about
again.

Tam broke into my thoughts.

"We'll have to go and see her, you know."

"Lally?"

"No, idiot: the Herb-Woman."

"She's not going to tell us—"

"Not about that, though we could ask her, I
suppose. . . . No, I meant we must see her about
Loken, I'm sure she knows him."

With all the complications since our return I had
completely forgotten the thieving, wild forest-boy,
but Tam was right. "When?"

"Next Sunday after church, if we don't get roped
in for harvesting."

"That'll be a week or two yet. I'll try and get hold
of Perdita and ask for an appointment."

"Please. I'll do the same if I see her first."

But when we finally reached her cottage, the Herb-
Woman neatly anticipated any questions we might

have about Lally's recovery. She took one look at our faces, nodded to herself as if to say "I thought as much," then led us over to a table laid in the shade of a venerable oak, whose branches scarcely cleared the ground.

"Sit yourselves down," she said. "You'll take a bite to eat?" and a moment later Perdita appeared with a large platter of salad, tiny tomatoes, chopped hard-boiled duck eggs, cubes of goat's-milk cheese, sliced onion, cucumber and radish on a bed of lettuce, dandelion, nasturtium and sorrel leaves, dressed with a herby oil. The Herb-Woman plonked down a large jug and sliced corn-bread. "Eat first, questions—and some answers—later."

We discovered just how hungry and thirsty we had been when the salad platter was empty, nothing but crumbs were left of the bread and the jug of elderflower champagne had been refilled. By now we were replete and completely disarmed, so it was no surprise when our hostess chose exactly which way the conversation should go.

"Let's get your obvious questions out of the way first. You want to know just how Lally was cured and why you don't remember much of what happened. Firstly I'm not sure Who or What finally removed the poison she was infected with, and that's the truth. I merely took her to where the harm had come from, invoked what powers of communication I had, and asked that she be cured. Then I left it to Them—and before you interrupt, Prettiance, no, I'm not sure who They are, although I have my suspicions. But don't forget that I warned you all, through Perdita, to leave well alone. All this wouldn't have happened if that poor girl Lalage hadn't been so susceptible. I am feared that this has disturbed that which should be best left alone. . . ." She closed her eyes for a moment, leant her forehead on a finger on her right hand which bore a thin, almost transparent ring. "Time will tell," she muttered.

"Perdita goes there," I said.

She answered for herself. "Only on the fringes, never towards the center. That night was the first time." She shivered. "It was horrible—that smell. . . . I'm glad I didn't go there before."

"What would have happened if someone had seen us?" asked Tam. "And by the way, how did we all get back: fly?"

"If we had been seen carrying the girl on the stretcher I would have said that I suspected an obstruction in her throat and thought a good shaking-up would dislodge it. As to how you returned to the Infirmary, why, you got there on your own two feet. And you are about to ask me why you don't remember it? Well, that remains my secret. Anything else, before we talk about your meeting with my friend Loken?"

"How did you—?" Tam grinned. "Silly question, I guess."

"But a simple answer: he told me."

"Was he still wearing my—my underwear?" I asked, in spite of myself.

"Almost. He wasn't impressed with their staying-power."

"We shall have to make him some leather breeks," murmured Perdita, a little smile on her lips.

"He's a thief!" I said angrily.

"Thief? Well of course he is," said our hostess. "How

else do you think he and his tribe have survived? I have high hopes of that lad."

"But you can't condone crime," I said. "However necessary they think it is."

"Of course I don't condone it!" she said sharply. "Quite the reverse. Since we became acquainted I have tried to instill into him the value of barter. It doesn't work all the time, I admit, but I keep trying. Remember a few years ago when your Mayor believed wolves had broken into the ice-house and stolen a side of beef?" She chuckled. "That was Loken's first steal. Since then he and I have seen each other about twice a year, and we exchange goods to our mutual benefit. He travels far and wide, he and his people."

"How long will he be here?" asked Tam.

"Who knows? Usually he's around till the end of October. South for the winter, then back here in the spring."

"Why don't he and his people settle down somewhere?" I asked.

"What skills have they to offer? They are ex-circus performers, at least their parents and grandparents were. They are not farmers, artisans, carpenters or builders. Their only skills lie in the quickness of an eye, speed, balance and adaptability. Some of them have settled in other communities, but the ones still with Loken prefer their traveling life. Just like the Romanys," she added with a smile. "Though even some of us settle down eventually."

Did that mean she was a gypsy? Tam, however, had seized on another part of her conversation.

"Other communities? Then there really are other villages, towns, cities then?"

"Did you seriously think we were the only survivors? Surely you had more sense than that!"

"You know what Mayor Gross teaches us," I said. I looked at her, at Perdita, sure they could be trusted. "Tell them who we met, Tam. . . ."

The Herb-Woman listened with quiet attention, nodding sometimes as if in confirmation of something she already knew, at other times widening her eyes in surprise. When Tam had finished she smiled, shaking her head at the same time.

"Well, well, well! You did have an adventurous time. A lot of what you told me I had already managed to untangle from Loken's rather garbled accounts. These would not have seemed worth a mention by the boy as his people are 'different' as well, but I didn't know about the mutations. You have fleshed out his stories for me. I knew about the town by the lake, and there are also other settlements further south, I believe. You said you kept the location of Deliverance a secret?"

"You know how Mayor Gross is. . . . We've all been safe here. . . . What about strangers bringing in disease or infection?" I gabbled, while Tam was silent.

"You don't agree with her, boy?"

"To some extent, yes, ma'am. The Mayor has done a lot for the village, I don't deny that. It's a well-provisioned, thriving community with a good social order, and I can see that strangers could well upset the balance, but—" He paused.

"But?" she prompted.

"But it's just so boring! If we keep on like this, in another fifty years we shall still be a cozy, dull, medieval village, with nothing to show for our isolation: no new technology, no new ideas, no contribution to the world outside."

"You want to travel, then?"

"You bet! I'm young, fit and curious. There must be something beyond this village, and I want to see for myself!"

"And so you should!" She clapped her hands. "Life is for living, not for rotting away in a backwater."

"But I don't want him to go!" I burst out. "It could be dangerous, especially on his own."

"Then why don't you go with him? Besides, what is life without the spice of adventure! Stew without herbs, that's what. . . ."

I was silent for a moment. "I couldn't go because my Nan needs me, she's not getting any younger."

I saw the Herb-Woman and her daughter exchange glances, but couldn't interpret them.

"Then perhaps you shouldn't go, but there is no reason for you to discourage others," she said gently enough, but it still hurt. Shortly afterwards we broke up, and although we had eaten well I felt sort of empty inside, as though the food had been siphoned out of my stomach. As soon as I reached home I made a point of persuading Nan to take a stroll with me, and later that evening I was happy to let her beat me at chess. . . .

I didn't see a great deal of Tam that autumn. We were both working, he in the woodworking shop and with his recorder classes, and I in the Town Hall, already taking notes at the council meetings and writing them up afterwards, together with the responsibility of dusting and polishing the council chamber and running the small village library.

Our questionnaire on the success of our camping holiday was accepted without comment; apart from Lally's mysterious illness and even more mysterious recovery, the only other interest stemming from the holiday was the marriage of Rosellen and Alex in November; apparently they had become reconciled quite early in the expedition, because their first baby arrived at the end of March.

Christmas came and went much as usual, but Spring was late this year, and Sven and his father lost more lambs than usual, in spite of their care. Sowing also took place later, and early blossom in the orchards was blackened by late frosts, so it looked like being a lean year.

Tam celebrated his eighteenth birthday in the middle of March. To mark his official coming-of-age his presents were more substantial than usual. His parents gave him a pair of stout new boots, his sisters a collarless woolen shirt, my father and Griselda a leather waistcoat and Nan and I one of the strong leather belts with an old-fashioned buckle, a purse on the left side and a loop for his sheath-knife on the right.

Now I was earning I had a few extra tokens laid by, and I wanted to buy something extra for Tam that was just from myself, and was also a surprise. Surprises were nice, especially as one grew older; Nan had always managed it with me: a silver ribbon, a carved wooden box, mug with my name on it, cuddly toy.

The idea was great, but the imagination wasn't equal to it. Just as I was despairing, at the Saturday market

before his birthday there was a clear-out from one
of the houses that was to be taken over by a newly-
married couple, the previous occupant having died
at ninety-seven, and there was just what I wanted.

Inside a battered leather case was something I had
only seen once before: a compass. It was obviously
well over the hundred-year mark, something left over
from the original inhabitants of the village; the brass
was tarnished, the leather smelt of mold, but it looked
to work okay. It seemed the ideal gift for the young
man who had everything, but I wasn't prepared for
the ecstatic reception Tam gave it.

"Pretty! You *darling*!" and he swept me off my feet
and gave me the biggest, most uninhibited and most
enthusiastic hug I had ever had. "Just what I need!
Wherever did you find it?"

I felt like saying "at the end of the rainbow, where
else?" but resisted the temptation, instead giving him
the right explanation.

"How did you know I'd have given my all just to
have one of these?"

I didn't, and still couldn't see why he needed it,
but wasn't going to admit it. "Women's intuition," I
said.

While we were talking he was checking it, apparently
to his complete satisfaction. "Perfect, just perfect! They
made these things to last in those days. Icing on the
cake, that's what it is!" And he gave me another hug.
"What can I do to show how much I appreciate this?"

I could have told him. . . .

"I know," he continued. "There's a hop at the
Church Hall in a fortnight's time—the April Fool's
Day one. Care to get trodden on?"

"But you don't like dancing!" I couldn't remember the last time he had attended one.

"But this will be an exception—to celebrate my birthday and your wonderful gift. A special thank-you."

"You're sure?"

"Sure. Got something to wear?"

"I'll find something." Nan had made me a skirt and top for Easter which I hadn't yet worn.

"Good. Let them all see us together. . . ."

My heart leapt: was he changing his mind about our relationship? I was even more optimistic when he called for me on the night of the dance bearing a bunch of yellow and white daisies to pin to my dress, and then proceeded to dance nearly every dance with me. From the glances exchanged by the older generation clustered round the walls, it seemed we had their full approval. Our contemporaries seemed to think our behavior of intent also, because even Lally came up to me in one of the intervals and congratulated me.

"Caught him at last, then? When's the wedding? I *insist* on being a bridesmaid. . . ."

I wanted to tell her that it wasn't like that at all, that we hadn't discussed our future, that I didn't even know whether I wanted to get married, but instead brushed aside her question with one of my own.

"Surely you'll be on your way to the altar first? After all, it was settled years ago, wasn't it?"

"You'd be surprised," she said, turning away with a toss of her lovely head.

That night when Tam walked me home, the stars were bright in the sky and up in the pastures the ewes were calling their lost lambs, a sad, an uneasy sound.

Tam bent his head and kissed my forehead, my eyes, my nose, my mouth: gently, too gently.

"Thank you for a wonderful evening, Pretty: I'll never forget it. Take care of yourself always, my one-off girl. . . ."

And the next day he was gone.

CHAPTER TWENTY-ONE

I was having the devil's own job keeping awake. A sudden draft sent the candles flickering; even with the new reflectors it was difficult to write. I leant forward to trim them, and then looked again at my hastily scribbled notes. What was left? Proposal to erect a maypole for May first, Labor Day: defeated six votes to two. Proposal to till a few more acres south of the village: carried unanimously.

It had been a long, boring Council Meeting. Now that I was Chief (and only) Clerk, my predecessor's eyes having finally failed him, I was not only in charge of taking and writing up the Minutes, I had to prepare Mayor Gross's diary, play housemaid with dusting and polishing the Council Chamber, the Mayor's office and the entrance hall; I also had my duties as Chief Librarian in the village library. And of course any free time I might have left was fully utilized during sowing, planting and harvest.

It had been another hard winter and late spring, the second in succession, and the previous year's harvest had been poor. Now in the run-up to Easter everyone was trying to put the cold, dark days behind them and welcome the warmer weather with new clothes and extra celebrations. I had no heart for dressing up, and if it hadn't been for Nan doing over my wardrobe single-handed and coming up with a long red, white and green skirt to team with my green jacket, I should probably have been the shabbiest girl in the village.

Not that I would have cared. After Tam had left, nothing had seemed to matter much. He had been gone nearly a year now, and never a word.

He had left two letters, one to his parents, the other to Mayor Gross, the latter of which I had had to copy into the town records with a heart as heavy as lead. His letters had been formal in the extreme, merely saying that he had decided to go adventuring, would sometime return if he could and emphasizing that he had not shared his plans with anyone else. In spite of this disclaimer I had been the object of much speculation after he went, some believing I knew more than I would tell, but the majority seemed to commiserate on the loss of my boyfriend, their voices full of sympathy, their eyes greedily searching my face and figure to guess just what had made Tam run away from what they considered his commitment to me.

I had gone straight to the Herb-Woman, reckoning if anyone knew where he had gone, she would. She confirmed that he had been to see her, asking when she expected to see Loken, but had said nothing of his intentions. She guessed they had gone south together.

For six months I had moped, avoiding everyone, burying myself in my work, then in the autumn Perdita sought me out as I was walking home one night.

"Loken came," she said. "He reports that he took Tam south with him. Loken believes he meant to continue towards the sea. He said Tam has a magic arrow with him which will show him the way. . . ."

The compass? No wonder he was so pleased to get it. "Any message for me?"

She shook her head, so I thanked her, telling myself I should be glad he was apparently safe and well, but inwardly hurt that he had not thought to send a message, a token, anything. . . .

That night Nan grew quite cross with me. We were playing checkers, as my father and Griselda, and of course the boys (three of them now) were all safely upstairs.

"Do pay attention, child!" she scolded, neatly removing three of my pieces. "And stop sighing like that: you'll blow out the candles."

I burst into tears. Then it all had to come out. Not only Loken and his band, but also the boys and girls we met by the river. She listened to my garbled tale in silence, first closing the door to the stairs so there would be no chance of being overheard. I finished, of course with my meeting with Perdita.

"And he didn't even have the decency to send a message!" I sobbed.

Nan looked at me in silence for a moment, then got up, fished out the precious sloe-wine, poured me a glassful, then advised me to "stop sniveling like a baby!"

I mopped my eyes, took a gulp of the wine, and immediately felt better. "I'm not sniveling; surely you of all people should understand how I feel!"

She sat down, folded her arms and stared at me.

"Sure I understand how you feel. After all I near as dammit had the bringing up of you. It must be all of—oh, twelve years, give or take, that time when you first went to school and found you weren't the center of attention—that you had your first attack of pique!"

"*Pique?*" I couldn't believe what I was hearing. "What do you mean, pique?"

She shrugged. "Pique, wounded pride, call it what you will. It's all the same. You've built up an idea of how things should be in a perfect world and when you find out that those you have depended on to behave in a particular way turn out to have ideas of their own, then you stamp your foot and protest that it isn't fair."

"But I love Tam—"

"No you don't. Not yet, anyway. You are fond of him, you depend on him he's always been there to boost your ego, but as for love, real love, you don't know the first thing about it!"

How on earth had my usually kind, sweet Nan suddenly turned so nasty?

"What do you know about what I feel? What do you know about love? You're old, you can't possibly remember—" I stopped, appalled. How on earth could I have said anything so hurtful?

But it seemed she had taken no offense. She just smiled. "I do have a good memory," she said gently. "And I do remember what it felt like to be really in love. I loved your grandfather more than I loved myself. And that is why I know you don't really love Tam. If you did you would not now be weeping and wailing and complaining that he hasn't had the time

or the forethought to sit down and write a love-letter!
What you should be doing is to thank the good Lord
that he is safe and is doing what he wants to do,
instead of languishing at home at your beck and call.
You should be proud of him, rather than regretting
his absence. At least he has had the courage to do
what many of us would have liked to do. . . ."

"Such as?"

"Escape."

"Escape from what? Whom?"

"Mayor Gross's little kingdom for one thing, escape
from boredom, from the stifling of any initiative.
Escape into adventure, exploration, new ideas, a
different way of life. Maybe better, maybe worse,
but at least a comparison, a choice."

I gazed at her in amazement. "You approve?"

"Of course I do. When I was young there was still
enough to do here, building a safe haven for everyone,
but gradually even Padraig began to wish for
something else. He wanted, like many others still
do, to find if anyone else survived, and if so to
exchange ideas, thoughts, experience. He wanted
to share what we had that was good, and maybe find
other things that were better." She sighed. "But he
died before he could put his ideas into action."

"We were told at school there *was* nothing else,
that if anyone else had survived, they would be so
far away and in such small numbers it would be useless
trying to contact them."

"Well, you've proved them wrong, haven't you?"
She leant forward and gave me a kiss. "Now, enough
of this moaning and groaning about a boy who I am
sure will be back before long, if only to ask you to

join him in his adventures." She tapped my arm. "Your move, darling. . . ."

I gathered the subject was closed. I also lost the game.

I awoke with a start. Somewhere a door had slammed, and for a moment I was at a loss to remember where I was. I was in the dark, except for a faint light in the hall. I realized I had dropped off over the notes for the Council Meeting. Never mind, I should just have to find time tomorrow morning before I opened up the library.

My candles had burned down, guttered and gone out, and I could tell by the hardening coolness of the wax that this must have been some time ago. As if to echo this, outside in the square the church clock struck a wheezy nine. I must have slept for three-quarters of an hour. Too late now to seek fresh candles. By feel I closed the big ledger and put it away on the shelf, capped the ink, put the pens back in their box, shuffled my notes together and put them away in the long drawer of the desk.

Rubbing the back of my neck, where I had developed a crick, I moved towards the door, wondering who had left candles burning on the table by the models of old and new Deliverance. Peering across the hall I saw that the door to Mayor Gross's study was slightly ajar, and there were both lights and the murmur of voices. Unwilling to disturb what must be on-going discussions about the plan to cultivate land south of the village, I tiptoed quietly across the marble floor towards the great double doors that led to Church Square. I was halfway there when

I heard something that stopped me dead in my tracks.

"There is only one answer, and you all know it. We must cull those that are useless to the community to give the rest of us a better chance." Although in his late seventies or early eighties, no one knew for sure, Mayor Gross still had a strong resonant voice. "After all, we have always practiced this method with the new-born, animal or human, and beasts of no further value are also culled, so why not humans as well?"

"But what about the . . ." A much softer voice, and I couldn't hear the rest.

"You don't think I shall shout it from the rooftops, do you? That's one of the reasons I called you all back here this evening, knowing we wouldn't be disturbed."

"Have you considered . . ." The second voice again: I thought I recognized the Mayor's eldest son.

"I think we have several options, but we shall have to consider them all very carefully before taking action."

Whatever in the world were they talking about? Normally I should have dismissed it as none of my business and carried on going, but the one word "cull" had me guessing: one culled animals, sure, when they became old or unproductive, but hadn't he said something about humans, too? Nan would have called me nosy, but a cold prickle of alarm was running up and down my spine, compelling me to hear more. Circling round the hall and missing some of the conversation, I approached the study from the back, so I could peer through the jamb.

Around the embers of the fire were seated four

men: the Mayor's two eldest sons and the men we all referred to as his lieutenants. One of them, a big burly fellow, was the son of one of the original settlers, the other was the Mayor's first wife's brother. There was a decanter of some white spirit, together with five glasses, a legacy from the former inhabitants of the village. Mayor Gross was on his feet, the branched candles sending his shadows rearing and dwindling on the walls as he paced back and forth.

"Are you saying then," asked his brother-in-law, "that age should be the criterion?"

"Of course not!" said Gross irritably. "One's age has little to do with one's ability, mentally at any rate. No, I am talking about those who are infirm, a burden both to themselves, their relatives and certainly to the community. There are drones in every hive, and we have our fair share. I could name you off the top of my head at least twenty who have never pulled their weight, or have the wrong or disruptive attitude to what I have been trying to build all these years. Look at Silas Edge, Joan Toogood, Jan Schmidt, Nelly Stevens, Jacob Wise, William and—"

"Yes, yes," interrupted his second son. "I'm sure we could all find plenty of candidates for culling, but are we absolutely certain it is necessary?"

"We-are-not-going-to-be-able-to-feed-them-all," said the Mayor very deliberately. "How many times do I have to tell you? We have had two bad years, and our stocks are running low. It is what was called in the old days a Catch 22 situation. We breed more stock, but where do we get their feed? We cultivate more land farther from the village, then spend all our time traveling to till, sow, weed and harvest. . . ."

"It's possible," said the burly one, Frank Ordy.

"But not practical. The answer is, and always has been, to keep the population within reasonable limits, so we can exist on the bounty around us and not seek it farther afield."

"We should have to be very careful," said the eldest son, Claus. "There mustn't be the slightest suspicion. . . ."

"There won't be," said his father. "This is just between the five of us in this room, no one else. We shall meet again in a fortnight's time here, same time." He stopped pacing. "And now, gentlemen, if you will join me in a drink?"

I heard the creak of chairs, the shuffle of feet and found I was backing away across the hall, terrified of discovery. My heart was pounding like the big bass drum of the village band till I was frightened it would burst out of my chest. I was trembling all over, but I mustn't stop to think about what I had heard, I must just get away before they found out I had been listening. I must reach the front doors, open them, get out, and then run home as fast as I could.

Somehow I reached the double doors, somehow my shaking hands turned the handle, somehow I swung the door wide enough to slip through undetected, somehow I managed to shut it again silently—

And then I ran as if the Devil himself was at my heels.

Nan had left me a message on the kitchen slate, but my shaking hands made the letters dance in front of my eyes, and my brain could make no sense of

the message. It looked like "Go NE to . . ." My troubled
mind stupidly equated this with the instructions I
had been given on treasure-hunts as children: but
why go north-east? I thrust the slate violently aside,
remembering just in time how precious they were.
Every slate in the village, including those used in
school, had been utilized from those rescued from
a derelict building, then framed in wood and
cushioned in felt, to protect them from breakage.
Few roofs had had needed repair since the early days
because of the synthetic materials used, but if they
had we used the old-fashioned pottery tiles, dating
back to Roman times.

I tried to force myself to behave normally, although
my mind was still churning with what I had heard.
Come on, girl: What would I normally do? Eat my
supper. I wandered over to the stove, and there was
a pot of stew, gently simmering. I had never felt less
like eating anything, but knew what would happen
if I neglected to feed myself: questions, interrogations.

Filling a bowl, I damped down the flues and left
the pan to soak. The bread was already cut, curling
a bit at the edges with being left out. Sitting down I
shoved the food into my mouth, expecting it to taste
like cardboard, but was surprised to find that I was
absolutely ravenous, so much so that I went into the
larder to cut some cheese for dessert.

The room was warm, my hands had stopped
shaking, and at last I could sit back and think upon
what I had heard. It was incredible, unbelievable!
Mayor Gross was proposing a plan whereby those
he considered superfluous were to be eliminated,
and those others had agreed with him! I just couldn't

believe what I had heard! Those names he had quoted were people I knew: Silas, who had broken both legs in an accident two years back, but who had adapted so well to his wheelchair; Joan, a bit do-lally perhaps; Nell didn't know what day it was, but she sang like an angel in church. And the last names he had mentioned: "William and" Had he been referring to poor Bill and Ben?

How could anyone even think of killing these people? It was barbaric, evil, unthinkable. And how did I know that his plans didn't include people like my Nan? For the first time I was glad she hadn't been up when I arrived back home. I realized I would have blurted it all out without thinking, risking alarming her without, perhaps, reason. No, I must find someone who would listen to me, be objective, and give me the best advice possible: who else to tell, what to do to stop this horrendous plot! And there was only one person I could think of. . . .

I looked again at the note Nan had left for me, and almost laughed at my earlier interpretation. No "north-east" about it at all!

"Gone to bed early with a bit of a headache," it read. "Your supper on the stove."

The Herb-Woman heard me out in silence, her fingers busy with her knitting, never a stitch faltering. When I had finished she continued to the end of the row she was on, before setting down wool and needles. We were sitting in her cottage at the table, the door open to the bleating of a kid and birdsong. Sunday afternoon, my free time. Had Tam not left, had I never heard Mayor Gross's vile plans, then on such an April day Tam and I would have been wandering the lanes together to gather a posy of primroses or an armful of yellow iris from the river. . . .

"You are sure that is exactly what you heard? You haven't added any interpretations of your own? You haven't forgotten anything?"

"I don't think so." I shook my head.

"Then, in that case, we are in trouble. Deep trouble." She drummed her fingers restlessly on the table. "I shall need time and space to think this one out. And we could do with other heads to share this with; not anyone who might be threatened. We need old heads on young shoulders with a still tongue in their heads." She rose to her feet abruptly. "Leave it to me. And don't worry!" She brushed her right hand across my forehead and I felt the nudge of the ring she wore. "Come back here on Wednesday after work; tell your family you are eating out with a friend."

I did feel a little easier in my mind, though I found it difficult to behave in the Town Hall as if nothing had happened, especially when dealing with Mayor Gross. Luckily I came across him seldom, at least face to face, and I knew nothing really bad could happen before their next meeting.

When I reached the cottage on Wednesday the grass was sparkling with the remnants of a fickle April shower, but the westering sun was now shining again, a gentle breeze disturbed my hair, and bees buzzed happily around the rosemary and thyme. I entered the cottage to find a lantern lit and delicious smells coming from the stove.

"Come, child; we'll eat first."

Perdita served us with a clear vegetable soup and

bread, a cheese fondue spiced with ale and mustard seeds and an apple crumble made with dried apple rings, with a topping of crushed hazel-nuts, then set a glass of blackberry wine in front of us to finish. The Herb-Woman asked after Nan, pleased that her potion had relieved her headaches, and enquired after my father, Griselda and the babes, and seemed content with the answers.

"So you see, things sorted themselves out after all. Remember how unhappy you were a few years back when you were dreading the advent of a stepmother?"

"But you changed all that!"

"Your faith did." She chuckled. "So did hers. . . . Now, to business."

We settled around the table, the dark outside now bringing the brightness of the lantern to bear. An errant moth fluttered round the light, and the blackberry wine was warm in my stomach.

But we never got started. There was a crashing noise outside, as though someone had tripped over a bucket, followed by a muffled curse. We jumped to our feet just as a stranger appeared in the doorway. He stepped forward, cracked his head against the low lintel and sat down abruptly.

"Hell and Damnation!" said a familiar voice. "I always forget how low that cursed thing is. . . ."

CHAPTER TWENTY-TWO

"Tam!"

I shrieked out his name even as I leapt from the table and ran to hug him, half-smothering him in the process. He was rescued by the Herb-Woman and Perdita however, and seated at the table with a pad of witch-hazel clamped to the bruise on his forehead and a glass of spirit in his hand.

"Drink it!" said the Herb-Woman sternly, then: "Have you eaten?"

"Not since last night—but I'm okay, don't bother. . . ."

They bothered. A bowl of thick vegetable broth, a hunk of cheese, masses of bread and a mug or two of milk appeared as if by magic.

"Now, eat first, talk afterwards. No questions, Prettiance: let the lad pull himself together."

As he ate and drank his fill I had a chance to study the boy I hadn't seen for a year. No, not a boy: he had become a man. He was taller, thinner, and dressed in a ragbag of clothes that just about covered his nakedness, but no more. His face was drawn, the cheekbones prominent, his eyes sunken. There were new lines on his face, running down from the corners of his mouth, and crinkling at the corners of his eyes. He was tanned, although it was still early spring, which argued he had spent a great deal of his time out of doors. But the biggest change of all to me was that he had a thin line of moustache and the beginnings of a beard. . . .

I watched in silence as he wolfed down the food and drink, and accepted a glass of toddy, leaning back in his chair with a great sigh and patting his stomach.

"God! That was good. Thank you both."

"You look as if you had a hard journey," I ventured. "Welcome back!"

He smiled at me. "Hi there, one-off girl! Well, Loken and his lot don't hang about, you know! Hey, listen: d'you know I got as far as the sea? You wouldn't believe how beautiful it is, and how *huge*! It looks like it goes on forever, and—"

"How long ago did you get my message?" interrupted the Herb-Woman.

"A week ago. Loken sent the two youngest, Dai and Lew, and they caught me just as I arrived by the lake. They said it was urgent, so we came part of the way by the river, and Loken has a couple of ponies now—proper bartering I promise you!—so the last part didn't take too long. What's it all about, anyway?"

She smiled. "He didn't make it sound as urgent as all that, did he? You could have taken it a bit easier; I'm sorry, but Loken isn't the best communicator in the world."

"I've been trying to teach him to read and write, but it's still a bit of a struggle. . . . You did say it was important though? He got that bit right?"

"Yes, he did. And it's not good listening. Well now we're all here, if Prettiance wouldn't mind telling her story again? I have already told Perdita. . . ."

So I told him all I had overheard. He listened without comment, only the widening of his eyes, the pursing of his lips and an occasional frown the punctuation of my narrative. When I had finished he leant back in his chair as if digesting what I had said.

"So," he said at last. "Involuntary euthanasia."

Put like that it had an even colder, more scientific sound to it than the simple word "cull."

"Other dictators have tried to do the same," he said, his eyes seeing beyond us, the room, "but their motives were racial, religious, tribal, political, not just a campaign to limit the population just to suit the megalomaniacal obsession of a man who finds he has too many dolls for his model village! But to kill off all the old and useless just because they can't help being what they are—it's obscene! He hasn't even the excuse of those other dictators: he is still a child, playing with his toys. . . . And how on earth did he get the others to agree with him? *And* keep quiet about it?"

"I think I can answer that," said the Herb-Woman. "His two eldest sons are just like him, his brother-in-law is part of the family also, and owes him a favor—don't ask how I know this, because I won't tell you, but I did have dealings with Gross's first wife before she so—so providentially died. As for number four, he is deeply in the Mayor's debt. Does that help?"

"How many people know about this?"

"Just us around this table, Tamerlane," she answered. "I told Prettiance that we needed the help and counsel of old heads on young shoulders before we decided what to do. At all costs we must prevent Mayor Gross from knowing what Prettiance overheard, otherwise she will be in danger also. I sent you a message because you were once a part of all this and if I'm not mistaken will still want to be a part of it in spite of the fact that you have chosen to leave the village behind. Now, of course, you can view this with the detachment of one who has seen a part of the world we have not and may be able to give us valuable advice."

Tam ran his fingers through his hair, a habit he had had as a child when perplexed. "I don't know what to say. . . . Sure, I've seen other towns and settlements; not all of them perfect, by any means, and many of them could learn a lot from Deliverance: organization, division of labor, intensive agriculture and so on. I suppose the greatest difference is that there is no discrimination against the old, mutants, cripples: they reckon they all have a part to play. Of course there are rogue bands, like Loken and his tribe, but even these are getting fewer apparently, as towns expand and welcome all newcomers as having something to contribute." He considered. "There is another difference, of course. All these other communities trade with one another, so no-one goes short. If Deliverance did the same, instead of trying to shut itself away from the world, there would be enough for all. Our sugar, wool, corn and pottery, for cotton, wheat, glass, salt and dried fish."

"An excellent idea, which should have been put into operation years ago," said the Herb-Woman. "But that doesn't solve the present problem. You can't just walk into Mayor Gross's office and demand that we open up Deliverance to the rest of the world. You'd never get out of the door again. Neither, before you suggest it, can you either post leaflets round the town, or call a general meeting to expose his plans. You wouldn't survive them either, and it would put Prettiance in jeopardy."

"Then what do we do?" I asked. "We can't just leave it!"

"How do you think he plans to get rid of all those people?" asked Perdita. "He can't start killing them off without someone noticing."

"He said it would have to be planned very carefully," I said. I looked around at their expectant faces. "And before you suggest it, Tam, I am *not* going to hide myself away and spy on their next meeting. It's too dangerous."

"I wasn't going to—"

"Now, now, children! I don't believe for a moment he will do anything drastic until after the harvest— after all, it might be better than he thought, in which case he could postpone everything. As to the method . . . It could be a slow poison, administered in a medicine, then blamed on one of my herbal potions—"

"That would mean the cooperation of the doctor or his assistant," said Perdita. "And I don't see that happening."

"What about a Retirement Home?" suggested Tam. "Many families would be glad to have the responsibility of grandparents taken from them. A death or two there would be expected."

"But he wants to get rid of a lot at one go," I said. "I'm sure of it. Like chucking his toys away at one fell swoop."

"We could put leaflets and posters out," said Tam slowly. "If you would agree to come with me, Pretty. That way you wouldn't be there to blame."

"And what about Nan? They'd say she knew, and my father and your sister, too. Gross could easily deny everything."

"They'd believe you when the first target died. . . ."

"And that would be one life lost!"

"Well, you think of something then!"

"That'll do, children," admonished our hostess. "This sort of squabbling is getting us nowhere. We need more time to think about this in a constructive manner." She rose to her feet. "Tamerlane, it's dark enough for you to walk Prettiance part of the way home. Don't get caught. We shall arrange another meeting. In the meantime I must see Loken, and provide you with some decent clothing. . . ."

Although the night was chilly for early April, Tam didn't seem to notice the cold, and obviously found it difficult to adapt his longer stride to mine.

"Sorry, Pretty: I've got used to trying to keep up with Loken."

"Does he still steal everything?"

"No, the Herb-Woman has apparently taught him the value of trading and barter pretty well. And he does see the advantage of not being treated as a criminal. But, don't forget, moral scruples were never part of his education. It's a whole new ballgame. He's good company, however, full of stories and superstitions. Remember that ring of stones up in the Wilderness?" I nodded: how could I forget? "Well, he has shown me others on our travels, and he also swears they are places of Power. He says there are roads running below that his people called Ley-Lines that form a network of Power with these stone circles—like an irrigation system—and if ever the Power is needed in one place more than another then it rushes along these channels in a surge of strength to help out where it is most needed."

"But what does this 'Power' look like? What does it do?"

"Loken wasn't much help there. He says you can't see it, only feel its results. He says sometimes you can hear it, like a sort of agitated humming, or feel it like a tingle under your feet." Was that what I had felt in the Wilderness? "Loken says that now there are fewer people in the world these powers are becoming stronger; They don't like people, they tend to interfere with the natural order of things. He told me of a village in Romania, where the people of a nearby village had used some of the Standing Stones to build their houses. At first the Power was respectful of their ignorance and let them be, but once they started to build within the circle itself, They took action. First it was the odd warning, a stone toppling over for no reason, crushing whoever was passing by. Then all the cattle were taken with a madness and dashed themselves at the remaining stones until their surface was darkened with blood like a sacrifice."

I shivered. "Did they heed the warnings?"

"Apparently not. They still persisted in vandalizing the site, aided by some fanatical preacher who encouraged them, saying that all the disturbance was just pagan mumbo-jumbo. Eventually the stones struck back."

"How?"

"There was to be a great Festival of Light to be held in the village on Midsummer's Eve, and everyone in the surrounding villages was invited. But when the guests arrived they found the village deserted. Every man, woman and child had vanished, although food and drink were left out in the village square for the visitors. And none of the villagers was ever seen again. . . ."

"No one?"

"No one. But they say the stones were splashed with fresh blood!"

I glanced up at his face. "You're making it up!"

"I'm not! That's how it was told to me. Only a folk-tale, perhaps, but these things always hold some truth. Remember the tales of the stones in old Deliverance?"

Of course I did; how the villagers had been forced to return the stones to the ring in the Wilderness. I shivered again, and abruptly changed the subject.

"Tell me more of what you've seen, where you've been."

He had stopped to sniff at the early apple-blossom, but of course there was no scent at night. "Another time, Pretty: we're nearly back at the village."

"Just something," I begged. "Something for me to remember when you're gone. Tell me more about the sea. . . ."

He leant back against the apple tree, causing the frail blossoms to fall onto his shoulders, looking like giant snowflakes in the light from my lantern.

"It's so difficult to describe. . . . Well, at my first glimpse I didn't know what it was. It was a misty morning and as we topped a hill I saw what I thought was just another faraway plain, made bluey-grey by distance. Then we descended into a valley and I lost sight of it. During the morning the sun came out, and when next I looked I couldn't believe my eyes! Even at that distance the sun was sparkling on the crawl of waves and it stretched from horizon to horizon—why I could even see the curve of the earth! But it wasn't until we got real near that I could appreciate it fully." Even in the dark I could sense his whole being alight with enthusiasm. "Once we were on the beach the first thing you noticed was the strange, salty smell. Then the noise, as regular as the tick of the church clock, a splashing, sucking noise as the waves ran up the beach and then back again. I ran into the water, just as I was, clothes and all, and at once I felt the swirl and tug of the waves. This was in winter, but even then the water was warm. I even tasted it: salty and gritty!"

"Oh, how I wish I'd been there!" And I really meant it, my imagination filled with longing.

He gripped my arm. "Then why don't you leave all this and come with me? Now's your chance. Leave all this corruption behind. We can do so much together. There's a whole big world out there, just waiting to be recolonized, reawoken, revitalized!"

At first I was fired with his enthusiasm, and for two pins would have walked away with him there and then, but gradually commonsense reasserted itself. Life wasn't meant to be full of easy choices; there were obligations and affections one couldn't ignore.

"I can't, you know I can't." Gently I freed myself from his grasp. "I couldn't possibly abandon Nan, for a start—"

"Bring her too!"

"How can I? She wouldn't come, anyway."

"How do you know? Have you asked her?"

"Of course not!" Even so, I couldn't help remembering the talk we had had, how she and Padraig, all that long time ago, had thought of leaving.

"Well, why don't you try? Do you think she would object to you going, for starters?"

I shook my head. "No. I suppose not."

"Well, then?"

"I would be asking her to give up all she knows. Besides, she's not a young woman any more; that's part of the reason I'm so worried about what Mayor Gross has in mind."

"She's what—sixty-five? That means she was ten years old when she walked all the way here. I'm sure she's still capable of walking with us to Lakeside. There she would be safe and comfortable for the rest of her life. Think about it."

"I don't think she'd do it," and all the while wondering whether she would. I couldn't tell her Mayor Gross's plans, because that was still secret. If I did manage to persuade her, then as Tam said, she would be safe, but what about all those others who were threatened? We couldn't play Pied Piper to all the old and unwanted in Deliverance. "Besides, there would be no need if we can foil Mayor Gross's plans."

"And we haven't the slightest idea how to do that."

"Not yet. But we'll think of something, I'm sure. Will you be here long?" Please, pretty pretty please, I thought.

"At least until Loken's finished trading with the

Herb-Woman and I get some new clothes. See you tomorrow at her place?"

I nodded. "I'll try." Meaning I would, come hell or high water. "Anything I can get you from the village?"

He shook his head. "Nothing I can think of . . . Oh—maybe some candy? That's one thing I've really missed!"

After all my hopes though, I only managed to get to see him four times before he was off again, and each time it was in company—the Herb-Woman, Perdita and even Loken. The latter had grown another couple of inches and now he was as tall as me, over-topping Perdita by a couple of inches. He had also had his hair cut, which was an improvement. I grew quite jealous of these others who had shared, or been told of, Tam's travels, for while I was there the conversation was mainly of how we could beat Gross at his own game. Loken was part of the secret now, and he suggested kidnapping the Mayor and abandoning him in some wilderness miles from the village. He was quite serious about it, too, but we managed to keep straight faces even while we discounted it.

My farewells to Tam were said in company, so there was no opportunity to say anything special. I reached up and kissed his cheek, awkwardly, blushing as I did so, trying to make it look casual. He looked embarrassed too, but his face brightened when I gave him a bag of the special hard, minty candy he liked best. It had cost me all my spare tokens.

"Hey, this'll last me for weeks! A real kind thought, One-off! I'll be back in the autumn: in the meantime don't worry too much, but remember what I asked

you. I haven't regretted my decision, and I'm sure
you wouldn't either. . . ."

As the Herb-Woman had predicted, there was no
sign that Gross's plans had gone any further forward
during spring and early summer, and there had been
no more clandestine meetings after the one that had
been planned—unless the Mayor washed his own
glasses and put away his own decanter, which I
doubted, this being my job.

That was a busy season, even busier than I remembered. Sowing, planting, pruning, weeding—what
weeds there were that year! especially ragwort,
ground-elder and thistles—tending lambs, calves and
chicks, gathering in the first crop of hay; watering
and irrigating the lower levels, pollinating; renewing
window-frames and shutters with winter-seasoned
wood, gathering rushes for baskets and panniers, and
hazel and willow for the little coracles we used on
the lower reaches of the river; repairing the nets;
dredging the fish-pool, cleaning out the swimming
and bathing pools.

Not that there wasn't more than enough to do in
every home. Changing winter wear for summer;
gathering moth-repellent herbs, sweeping, dusting,
polishing throughout, sun-bleaching any linens and
cottons that still held together, renewing the feathers
in pillows and duvets, together with cleaning the faded
velvets that still hung in places like the Town Hall.
Then there were the rush-bottomed chairs to repair,
leather seats to mend or renew and fresh baskets
for food and stores to be woven.

As far as village business was concerned, after the

next Committee Meeting Gross declared business
suspended until the end of July, unless an emergency
arose, thus giving this year's "volunteers" time to give
the Town Hall its annual once-over, with which I
wasn't involved, thank goodness.

At the beginning of July, a month after my eighteenth
birthday, the Herb-Woman invited me to supper. After
we had eaten, and dusk was shading the day's brightness, we went outside to enjoy the last of the warmth.
She sat on a stool, Perdita and I at her feet. Around
us in her herb-garden the bees were still busy with
the five blues; thyme, rosemary, basil, lavender and
sage, while overhead the last of the swallows competed
with the first of the bats for the fat July insects, and
a mother hedgehog with three young were rootling
happily in the undergrowth. The Herb-Woman
brought out a clay pipe from one of her pockets, a
packet of herb-tobacco from another, tamped it down,
lit it and blew the fragrant and intoxicating smoke in
a blue-grey cloud above our heads.

"No holiday camp for you this year?" she asked.
Perdita, of course, had never been asked.

"They suggested it this year and last," I said. "But
I refused. I told them I was quite happy as I was."

"Next year they may insist."

"Not while Gross is trying to cut back on the
population."

"True. . . . Now, my dears, I have brought you here
together to tell you an old, old story, but one you
should know before you are a year older. Last month
you both came of age: an important time in your
lives. Now pay attention . . ."

"Once upon a time," she said, and we settled down

comfortably, for this was the way all good stories should begin. "There was a pretty woman who was expecting her first child. It so happened that one day, when the rest of the village was busy with the first hay-harvest, and only her mother was with her in the house, that she experienced her first birth-pangs. Her mother went for the doctor, but he was attending someone up in the fields who had badly gashed his leg on a scythe, and the official midwife was attending someone who had complications after an earlier birth. So the mother did what she could and soon was born a beautiful baby girl.

"But no sooner had the young wife put it to her breast, after counting all its fingers and toes, which all mothers seem to do, when she felt some more pains coming. This time her mother ran to someone she knew was skilled in healing, and together they delivered a second girl, smaller than the first. The new mother stretched out her arms to nurse the second baby, pulled away the wrappings for the routine examination, expecting the same perfection she had found in her first-born. But suddenly she thrust the second baby away from her with an expression of horror.

" 'Look, look! She is accursed!' she cried. Her mother and the other bent over the baby, and sure enough, on the left hand was a rudimentary sixth finger. 'He will have her killed,' sobbed the mother. 'He will destroy my baby! In the name of God, please take her, hide her!' and she thrust the baby towards she who had helped at the birth. . . ."

I saw a startled look on Perdita's face: she sat up suddenly, clasping her left hand in her right.

The Herb-Woman took no notice, but continued with her tale. "In vain both women pleaded with the young mother, saying it would take but a small operation to remove the tiny excrescence, but she would have none of it, pointing out that the doctor, who was bound to examine them, would know at once and report the malformation. . . ."

She was silent for a moment, then resumed. "So the helper took pity on both babe and mother, allowing the latter to hold the baby for a while. She kissed it, blessed it and handed it over, turning her face away so she would not see it go. The helper took the child back to her own house safe from prying eyes, and brought it up as her own, aware that no one in the village she lived in would dare to question her, or any deformity in the child. . . ." The tobacco was finished: she tapped out the ash on the heel of her shoe.

"And so they lived happily ever after," I said, clapping my hands.

"So far, so good."

"But didn't the sisters ever discover each other? You can't just end it there," I objected. "There must be a happy ending."

"Why are you telling us this?" asked Perdita, one hand still clasped in the other, her face strangely pale.

"Because it is time it was told. Prettiance, first-born, meet your twin sister, Perdita. Perdita, second-born, meet your twin sister, Prettiance. . . ."

CHAPTER TWENTY-THREE

I felt that nothing would ever surprise me again, and to judge from her expression, Perdita felt exactly the same. We stared at one another, back to the Herb-Woman, then at each other again. We spoke together.

"I don't believe it!" Me.

"How can it be?" Perdita.

"I assure you, my dears, it's the truth, and nothing can alter it. You, Perdita, always knew you were adopted—"

"But I've always thought of you as my mother! Nothing can change that!" And judging from her expression she didn't want a sudden sister to change all that. "Besides, we don't even resemble each other. How can we possibly be twins?"

"Just what I was going to ask," I said.

She looked at us both. "Twins aren't always identical; you were obviously conceived at different times, even different months: it does happen. That would explain the difference in size. And isn't it a mercy you *don't* look like each other! Can you imagine if you had grown up looking exactly identical the whole place would have been gossiping, and in five minutes Gross would have been investigating.

"As it is, I now see before me two lovely healthy

309

girls, same age, same mother and father, but so different you are a delight! Let's look at you . . . My Perdita is not as tall as you, Prettiance, and she has long, straight, dark brown hair and hazel eyes, and her complexion is more swarthy, all characteristics inherited from her father. You, Prettiance, have your mother's coloring and hair, wavy with golden glints, and her greeny-grey eyes. On the other hand, you have your father's nose, Perdita her mother's."

Perdy's nose was slim and aquiline, mine frankly a bit snubby.

"The one thing you should both be glad about is that you have your mother's generous mouth and her sweet temper. Now I will leave you two to make friends. . . ."

For a moment we gazed at one another; I was hideously embarrassed, and I thought she was about to cry, for she suddenly screwed up her face and turned away, her shoulders shaking. Oh, dear God! Why was it all so difficult! How awful it would be if she regretted it, didn't want me as her sister. . . . I was going to get up and creep away, when she suddenly turned, her face bright with laughter.

At once she started to giggle helplessly, and so did I, more with relief than anything else. Funny was better than tragic.

"Would you believe it, Pretty!"

"No, I wouldn't. But I always wanted a sister. . . ." True.

"So have I! Sometimes it's been awfully lonely. And all this time—"

"We were living only half-a-mile apart—"

"And never knew it!"

I shook my head. "It's the sort of thing that happens in a novel, not in real life."

"But I do have that extra little finger: look!" And she unclasped her left hand to show the tiny baby finger curled into her palm. "See? I can wiggle it, but it isn't as strong as the others. . . . Just think! That ol' Mayor would have had me disposed of just for this."

"Is that why you wear mittens when you come to market?"

"Sure."

"Well I think it's neat. I should have one on my right hand, just to match yours. But I have got something: I'll show you. Nobody looking? Right." Hoisting my skirt, I pulled down my knickers and turned my back on her. "See anything?"

"No-o-o. Yes. A red mark on your right cheek, like a little raised heart."

"That's it." I adjusted my clothes. "That would have been enough to condemn me too, if it hadn't been hidden by my diaper—so you see, we're both marked for life!"

We giggled again, like kids half our age, and then suddenly we were hugging and kissing each other, tears of laughter, thankfulness and joy mingling with our embraces.

Perdita wiped her eyes and took my hand. "D'you know what my name means? The lost one. But I'm lost no longer. What about yours?"

"Nobody seems to know for sure. My Nan—gosh! your Nan too, I guess—said my—our—mother read it someplace. Another version has it that it's a combination of 'pretty,' which came from my—sorry, our Dad—and Nance, which was our mother's name. Short for Nancy. I wish I'd managed to ask her, but she died when I was still a toddler."

"So, we were both brought up by surrogate mothers, me by Ma'am, as I call her, and you by your—our—grandmother. Hey, you're right: it's difficult to remember who's who and what's what!"

"And that is one thing you must do your best to forget, for the time being at least," said the deep voice of the Herb-Woman behind us. "For everyone's sake. Let's get rid of Gross first, then you can acknowledge your sisterhood to everyone. But, until then, mouths shut. . . ."

My various jobs kept me away from most of my ex-school friends, and with many of them married, or at least betrothed, I became further distanced. The only time we seemed to see each other was during the gleaning or between rows of apples or late peas. To further occupy any spare time I might have, as autumn approached there were the days at home with Nan, stoning, drying, preserving and bottling, and the reluctant overhauling of our cold-weather clothes, and with three small children underfoot and Griselda pregnant again, this meant concentrate or else.

I did come across Bill and Ben from time to time, wandering restlessly from one end of the village to the other, or haunting the gift shop where Lally and her parents lived. They seemed sadly changed since that time, two years back, when we were all on holiday together. Gone were the jolly, carefree lads I remembered; in their place were two drawn, haggard young men, who appeared to have lost their faith in others. They seemed to avoid us all, except of course Sven and Lally, and as the former was busier than ever with the sheep and the latter was increasingly hidden away in her parents' shop, the twins were thrown back on each other's company.

Lally herself looked pale and distracted, and she was always "in the back" or "resting" according to her parents, if ever I had occasion to go into the shop, so we had little conversation, except for a word or two after church, and even then she had scarcely anything to say and was barely civil sometimes.

Rumors about her were still rife since her unfortunate illness two years ago. Whilst most people accepted that she had been poisoned by eating some unknown plant, there was still a core of hardened gossips who had her a) consumptive through being caught out in the wet, b) cancerous, c) had become pregnant and taken some abortifacient that had caused internal bleeding she could not staunch.

Apart from all this, Perdita and I became closer, the few times we managed to be together. I had told Nan, of course, what the Herb-Woman had revealed, and she, too, had made an effort to visit Perdita and assure of her love, and it delighted me to see them grow closer.

Once the Council Meetings recommenced I kept a sharp ear open for any indication that Gross was going ahead with his evil schemes, but there seemed to be nothing suspicious. During this time, however, I made my own investigations, trying to find out whether his pessimism as to our resources was justified. At first I did it all the wrong way, balancing population and housing against the tally of produce, but suddenly realized that all I had to do was check on the harvest records for the last five years, plus the head of stock. The first three years showed a slight increase, but the last two were quite different. There was a dramatic fall in arable goods, except for sugar, and a corresponding drop in the head of stock. It didn't take a mental graph to show we were losing, and although this year's figures weren't fully complete, it was obvious that it had been another bad year. Each year about this time there was also an accounting of stocks before the harvest; other years had shown a healthy surplus: this year we were right down on everything.

Knowing what I did, it was obvious we would either have to start another settlement farther south and/ or begin trading with other settlements, or go under. But of course Mayor Gross would deny the existence of other survivors, and would be afraid of a rival village not under his control so, to him, the only logical solution to our present problems must be a drastic reduction in our present population. Biased as I was, I could still see with a horrified fascination just how justified—to him—his idea of a "cull" would be.

How I longed for Tam's return! October was already wasting towards November, and there was still no sign of either him or Loken, although the Herb-Woman kept assuring me that Loken wouldn't return until he was sure the best of the weather was over, and it was true that we had had a late and warm Fall, swifts and swallows delaying their journeys south, with an abundance of insects still to be found.

I was taking notes at the October 25th Committee

Meeting, when I got the first inkling that Gross hadn't abandoned his plans. To an innocent bystander it would have seemed just another of his beneficent schemes for the well-being of everyone, but I noted his increased excitement and the gleam in his eye when he proposed extra-special celebrations this year for Hallowe'en. "To put behind us a poor year, and give us heart for the winter to come," was the way he put it.

His proposal was that every section of the community should have their own special treat. A party for the pre-schools in the afternoon, with a beetle-drive/bingo-call/chess-championship for the parents at the same time. In the evening the usual Trick or Treat for the youngsters, followed by a Fancy-Dress dance for those from teens to twenties. The older folk were not to be neglected either: they were to have their own concert at the same time, at a different venue, the Church Hall not being large enough to accommodate everyone.

There was no immediate opposition to his idea, how could there be? But my suspicions were immediately aroused when the first hands raised in assent were those who had been at the meeting I had eavesdropped on earlier in the year. Each party was voted on separately, all unanimous until it came to the last, the old folks Nostalgia Night, as it was to be called. The other venues were passed unanimously, as was to be expected, but the one for the old folks caused some opposition.

Gross suggested the old covered market, at the other end of the village. This was a rackety, ramshackle wooden building, and for years there had been talk

of pulling it down and erecting a brick building in
its place, but somehow other projects had taken
precedence. At the moment it was only used for the
Saturday market if it was raining, and even then there
were notices plastered to the walls warning about
the risk of fire. There was only one entrance or exit,
double doors maybe, but supposing there was a fire
and these became jammed?

A horrible suspicion rose in my mind: was this the
cover for Gross's determination to wipe out a portion
of the population at one go? I was about to rise to
my feet and question his decision, which would have
been entirely against all precedent and would have
got me into real trouble, but luckily for me another
member of the Council, Harry Ross, commonly
known as " 'Onest 'Arry," rose to his feet.

"Forgive me, Mayor Gross, but I be a master
carpenter, as you well know, and I reckons as that
place be a dire fire risk. The wood be old, and well-
wormed, and it only needs a spark or two to set it
off. We ain't never used that place at night before,
and I'd hate to think as there'd be any risk to my
parents, who is well into their eighties—"

"A few lanterns here and there are not going to
cause a conflagration," interrupted Mayor Gross
smoothly. He chuckled indulgently, baring his long
yellow teeth and dry-rubbing his hands together. "I
think you underestimate the carefulness of our
Golden Oldies. I just want them to have a good time
with the rest of us."

"It could be held on another night," said Zachary
Trevor, the general barber and hairdresser.

"Hallowe'en only comes one day a year, like

Christmas," said Gross's eldest son. "I think it's an excellent idea. What do you say?" He turned to his brother.

"Fine, just fine. Shall we put it to the vote?"

And of course it was carried unanimously, apart from Harry Ross abstaining. I duly noted down the formal proposal and the result, my heart full of dread for something I couldn't yet put into words.

"Now, seeing you had reservations about the safety of the building, I think the best person to organize Nostalgia Night and ensure everyone's safety would be you, Harry Ross," said the Mayor. "You may co-opt anyone else to help you at your discretion. Purely voluntary, of course. The cost of decorations, food and small prizes will be borne from the General Nuisance Fund. I suggest you hold a 'best mask' competition in conjunction with the concert. . . ."

The fund he mentioned was one that attracted small fines for minor transgressions: spitting in the street, swearing in public, blocking the drains, fighting, making too much noise for the neighbors, depositing rubbish anywhere except in the official dump, refusing community work, not turning up for work without sufficient cause, committing a public nuisance, being drunk and disorderly, sexual harassment etc. etc.— in fact any excuse for gathering a few tokens here and there.

The official list of punishable offenses, kept at the Town Hall, grew year by year. And in fact several recent offenders had not even known that their transgressions were punishable. Sometimes I wondered whether Gross sat up late at night devising new offenses. . . . Tam had been caught once as a child, an ill-judged ball shattering a neighbor's shutters. He had only been ten at the time, so his parents had not only to pay the fine, but also for the repair of the shutter. That had resulted in one of his more severe beatings.

Tam, Tam, Tam! How I wish he were here! I just knew something terrible was about to happen, and I didn't see any way to stop it. The worst part was that I didn't know the how, just supposed the when.

After the meeting I took a lantern and hurried down to the Herb-Woman's but everything was tight-shuttered. Obviously she and Perdita were out on one of their herb-gathering-under-the-moon jaunts, and in fact I thought I saw the light of a lantern bobbing away towards the plantation. Damn them! Why couldn't they be there when I needed them!

I returned home to supper and my old childish habit of nibbling at my nails, while trying to concentrate on a game of checkers with Nan. All at once she leant over the board and slapped my hand away from my mouth.

"Come on now: what's the matter? You've been like a pan of popcorn with a badly fitting lid all summer! Can't you tell me?"

"It's nothing," I said. How could I possibly explain? She would probably be going to that Nostalgia Night herself.

"You're not still worrying about that boy?"

"Tam? Of course not."

She leaned forward and cleared the board in a couple of quick sweeps. "And what makes me think you are being a trifle economical with the truth when you keep insisting nothing is the matter? You can't keep still for two seconds flat, you keep sighing loud enough to blow out all the candles, you've quite gone off your food, and you toss and turn all night."

I stood up and went to the window, staring unseeing into the night outside. I must say something. "It's— it's this place. It's getting me down."

"Then why don't you leave?" She said it in a perfectly matter-of-fact way, and I turned to see her putting away the checker pieces in their box, just as if we had been discussing the weather.

"Wouldn't you mind?"

"If you mean wouldn't I miss you, then yes of course I would." She put the game away in the cupboard. "Even now, I miss you when you go to work. I would miss you still more if you got married and went to live with your husband. More so, if you left the village and went adventuring." She paused. "But get this straight. All my grief at losing you would be more than balanced by the fact that you were finding your way in the world, doing what you really wanted to do, fulfilling a destiny I believe you deserve."

I hesitated. "Would you come with me?"

"What—me? An old woman like me would only hold you up. There is always a time to let go, to push the fledgling out of the nest. I love you very much, you know that, but—"

"Supposing I said—I said your life might be in danger if you stayed here?" The last words came out in a rush.

She looked at me. "What are you not telling me?"

I shook my head. "I didn't mean to say that. It's nothing. Just that . . ."

"Well? Come on, Pretty: what's the threat? Who's going to harm an old woman like me?"

"Don't keep saying 'old' like that! You're not old. You still work hard, do all the cooking, babysit the kids, help out at the crèche. . . ."

"You didn't answer my question!"

"No one in particular, of course not. It's just that— that . . . well, some of the *really* old people, the ones that can't work anymore, or who are crippled . . . Some people might think they were, well sort of— you know . . ."

"No, I don't."

"Superfluous. The population is growing all the time, and it's getting to the stage when there isn't going to be enough food to go round. Don't you see? Before long someone is going to suggest that the really old have had their day. That life is for the young. . . ."

"I see . . ." She was silent for a moment. "Mayor Gross, I suppose."

"I didn't say anyone had actually said anything. . . ." I was panicking now.

"You don't have to. So that's what you've been worrying about!" Now she looked as upset as I felt. I wished I hadn't opened my mouth. She saw my face and motioned me to sit down. "I'll make us a cup of chamomile tea, and then you can tell me all about it. Lucky the others won't be back till later. What did you hear, or overhear? Just exactly what do you suspect? You can trust me. . . ."

So I told her everything, all except the suspicions of Nostalgia Night. She looked stricken.

"How could he even consider such a thing. . . ." I

knew who she meant, and also knew she wasn't just thinking of herself, but of the other elders she had known since she was a child. "Have you told the Herb-Woman? She's the wisest person I know."

I explained that we had been puzzling over the whole thing all summer and had got nowhere. I thought I had got a further clue this evening but when I had gone to see her they were out.

"We didn't want to worry anyone until we were sure. . . ."

"Well you'll be worrying more than yourselves if you don't do something about that crook sharpish," she said briskly. "Go seek her out tomorrow night. The others are out again, and I'll cover for you."

The following night was overcast, the air thick and too warm for late October. A screech-owl over to my left made me jump and nearly drop my lantern. At last I could see light peeking through the cottage shutters and breathed a sigh of relief: they were home. Now I was so near my goal I blew out the lantern and stepped forward confidently. A moment later a hand was clamped over my mouth, my arms were pinioned at my side and I nearly fainted from shock. Then I realized I recognized that individual body-scent I had known for so long—Tam was back!

CHAPTER TWENTY-FOUR

He released me almost at once and I turned and flung my arms around his neck, plonking an enthusiastic kiss in the general direction of his mouth, telling myself how glad I was to see him, grateful that now he might be able to solve all our problems—convincing myself, by the by, that it wasn't just that I wanted to kiss him. As of course I did.

All that happened was that I knocked my mouth against his bristly chin, although he did hold me close for a moment before pushing me gently away.

"Still the same old impulsive Pretty! Come on, let's go see the others, then you can tell me what's been happening to you."

Although I was dying to find out how he was—better than he looked last time, summer having tanned him almost as dark as the Herb-Woman, and he seemed taller than ever—where he had been, what he had done and seen, I knew that what I had to tell them was more urgent, so I rushed through my suspicions as quickly and concisely as I could.

The Herb-Woman looked grave. "It certainly looks as though he plans something drastic," she said slowly. "As I remember in that old barn of a place there is only one exit?"

"Double doors, with a bolt on the outside," said Perdita. "So if something happened inside, the door happened to be locked and there was no one around to hear . . ."

"He couldn't do it!" burst out Tam. "No one could be that *evil*!"

"Hush a moment," said our hostess. "Is there any access from the roof? Skylight, window, anything like that?"

I could see the way her mind was working, but once again it was my sister who answered. "A couple of skylights, yes. When there is a market in there they open them, to let in more light."

Tam spelled it out for us. "So, you get their concert going, give them something to eat and drink, then while they're all enjoying themselves the door is quietly bolted from the outside, and someone who is waiting on the roof opens the skylights, if they aren't already open, and pours down some inflammable material and follows it with a torch or two. . . . And there is no one around to hear, the other jollifications being held at the other end of the village and parents at home with the children. I can't believe it!"

"You'd better!" said the Herb-Woman. "Perdita, get out the glasses and that bottle labeled 17. Plenty of water with it, mind. . . ."

Even diluted liberally, the fiery liquid burned down my throat and kicked my stomach like a bolt of lightning. Tam sniffed before he drank, then a slow smile, the first of the evening, spread across his face. "Where the hell did you get this?" He sipped appreciatively.

"Where I got all the rest of my treasures." One

by one the Herb-Woman flung open her cupboards, holding a candle high to show the contents. I saw reams of paper, dozens of pencils, towels and sheets and pillowcases, glass bottles, phials, tumblers and jars, flatware, bolts of cloth and other bottles I couldn't identify, except that they were all neatly numbered.

"When the original inhabitants fled," said our hostess, "I realized that they wouldn't be back. I also guessed that others would take their place, sooner or later. So, I did a Loken." She smiled at me. "I stole. I went through every house in the village—it wasn't difficult to break in—and I took whatever I thought might be useful to me in the years to come. I knew it would be years before we had any communication with others, so I not only took what you see here, but seeds, preserves, pans, any dried or tinned food left, wool, thread, needles, medicines and feeding-bottles, safety pins, bandages, scissors, plastic bags, a magnifying glass, a telescope, a couple of mattresses, blankets, and a good supply of sugar, flour, yeast, a culture of vinegar and all the wines and spirits I could find. Oh, and I replenished my stock with the best of the goats and chickens. I also helped myself from the orchards and allotments."

"But since then you've given back to the villagers a hundred-fold," said Perdita loyally. "Advice, potions, herbs, treatment; besides, when the others came they would have drunk all the whisky in five minutes flat and been none the better for it, and you did leave them loads of baked beans, you told me so. . . ."

"Only because they disagreed with me; your Nan

enjoyed them, though." She smiled at me again. "She says she's never forgotten that first meal."

"You must have been awfully young," I said.

"Young? Not really."

"But it was fifty-five years ago. Nan was only ten, and you and she look about the same age."

"How nice of you! How old do you think I am? No, don't disappoint me by guessing, I'll tell you. Your Mayor and I probably share a year, if nothing else. I am over eighty."

"You don't look anywhere near that!" My amazement was genuine. "But—but—"

"If I am as old as that how could they possibly think I was Perdita's mother?" she finished for me. "Simple. I have a secret charm that not only helps me in all I do, it also has the gift of keeping me both looking and feeling younger than I am. Look!" And she held out her right hand; on the middle finger was a curled sliver of horn, fitting snugly against her brown skin. "This is a magic twist of horn from a fabled unicorn, found by my gypsy grandmother many years ago, who passed it to me when I was your ages, children."

"No such thing as unicorns," said Tam.

"If you truly believe that, then I am sorry for you," she said. "A little magic is needed every now and again."

For no reason I suddenly recalled those fairy stories I had read to my friends when we were children, and how they seemed to come alive for us all in the Wilderness. Prince and princess, king and queen, courtiers—if that was magic, as I had thought at the time, then I wanted no part of it now. And yet . . . I glanced across at Tam, and I thought I saw an answering flicker of memory in his eyes. For a moment we were back there in the glade, part of a story that came true before our eyes; I could see now those splendid dresses, the cruel spindle that pricked Lally's finger, the bower where she lay. . . .

"Hey, Pretty!" said Tam. "You're away with the fairies!"

I came to with a sudden jerk. "Sorry: I was miles away." To cover my embarrassment I turned once more to the Herb-Woman. "Is it really magic? Your ring, I mean?"

She stretched out her hand. "What do you think?"

I had an overwhelming desire to touch the pretty thing, now glowing and sparkling like the multi-colored opals I had seen in the encyclopedias we read as children. I touched it, and all at once sprang back, my whole hand tingling.

Her eyes widened. "What's the matter?"

"It—it bit me!" I laughed uneasily. "You know when you brush your hair so that it crackles? Or when you're real hot and touch a piece of metal? Static electricity I think they call it—well, it was like that, only different. It sort of pushed me and pulled me at the same time. A static-electricity-magnet if you like. . . ."

I thought I had been singularly unclear, but what I hadn't expected was our hostess's reaction.

She leant forward, gripping my wrist, her eyes boring into mine. "You're sure? That's what you felt? Drawn and repelled at the same time, a tingling shock?"

I nodded.

"What color is it? No, wait, Tam—?"

"I can't even see it properly—"

"Perdita?"

"Transparent."

"Prettiance?" There was urgency in her voice. I leant forward.

"Sort of a pearly color." I fingered the necklace Tam had given me, which I wore all the time. "But with a sort of—sort of—"

"Yes?"

"A silvery sheen, with little specks of color in it. Red, blue, green. Why?"

She didn't answer but stood up almost roughly, then went over to the door, opened it and went outside, letting in a blast of colder air. I looked at Tam, who was obviously bewildered by the turn things had taken, and at Perdy, who, I was surprised to see, had tears in her eyes.

I spread my hands helplessly. "What did I do? What did I say?"

Tam shrugged. "Search me."

Perdita leant forward and patted my hand. "You didn't do anything wrong," she said. "Don't worry, Pretty. I'm glad it's you."

"What's me?" I was totally fazed.

"I can't tell you right now. She will, sometime. Believe me, it's something she's been waiting for for years. That's what's important. It's a sort of happy-sad moment for her. She'll be okay in a minute. . . ."

It was longer than that, perhaps ten, but suddenly she breezed in again, a big smile on her face, and ordered Perdita to pour out a little more of the whisky, as Tam christened it, with plenty of water, of course.

"I think I have an idea how to beat old Gross at

his own game. Drink up, sit down and listen!"

She outlined her plan, and for a half-hour or so
we argued the pros and cons, but agreed on the
principle of the thing.

"Great!" said Tam. "I'm sure Loken and his people
will cooperate. We'll need lots of paper and pencils,
though: give us a hand, Perdita?"

"Of course. I'm coming too." She glanced at the
Herb-Woman. "You know we're sisters?"

Tam nodded. "She told me last night. So, I inherit
you both!" He grinned. "What a pair . . ."

I turned to the Herb-Woman. "You're sure you
can persuade Nan to come too?"

"I'll see her tomorrow. Our whole plan depends
on you both disappearing. We don't want you getting
into trouble. Tam, walk her back part of the way and
then come back here and we'll discuss what you shall
write. Come back tomorrow, Prettiance: by then we
will have decided how and when."

Tam didn't say much on the way back, and all my
questions as to what he had done, where he had been,
he parried with the remark that there would be plenty
of time when we were all on our way. But when I
asked him if he had any regrets, he shook his head.

"None, none at all. I should have left years age."

"How would you have managed at thirteen or
fourteen? Besides, you hadn't met Loken then, and
he must have been a real help."

"I was lucky to meet him when I did, but without
him I would have left sooner or later."

"It sounds idyllic," I said wistfully.

"Don't you believe it!" He was serious. "It's nowhere
near perfect. It's hard work, frustration, even danger

sometimes. The world outside the cozy comfort of Deliverance is hard, strange, different, above all challenging. It's new, exciting, and never boring. But I haven't regretted an instant."

It was a comfort to know I would share the experience with Nan and my sister.

And Tam. . . .

I told Nan what we had discussed, and she thought the Herb-Woman's solution a good one.

"So you're really going this time," she said, but it wasn't a question.

"Yes, and so are you!" I gave her a quick hug. "So get packing: I don't know how long we've got. We're discussing that tomorrow."

The discussion didn't take long. The best time to leave, we all agreed, was on Saturday night, Hallowe'en itself, while everyone would either be indoors with the children, or at the dance. We were to bring our belongings—one rucksack, plenty of warm clothes—down to the cottage the evening before. On the night, Nan would make an excuse to visit a friend overnight, so would I. I was to attend the dance for an hour or so, just so I was seen, then slip away to be at the cottage for ten o'clock latest. We would have a light meal and be away by eleven, ready to travel through the night. If we were lucky, no one would miss us till the following lunch-time.

If the discussion hadn't taken long, the decisions as to what to take and what to leave took ages. It was a good job nobody else came up to the attic Nan and I shared, because it shortly resembled a rummage sale after the first rush. We were also to provide some of the provisions, so we pooled our resources—after

all we wouldn't need tokens any more—and bought
flour, sugar, oil and dried fruit; Perdita was responsible
for apples, potatoes and cheese. It would take us a
week at best to reach Lakeside, there wouldn't be
time for foraging, and we would be a party of ten,
counting Loken and his friends.

Just to be on the safe side Nan "borrowed" the
largest cooking pot and frying pan, the ones used
only rarely for parties, also a large ladle. I doubted
whether Griselda would even notice they were gone.
In a way I felt sorry for her: she would have to learn
so much in so short a time, besides having three little
ones plus a fourth on the way. But my father loved
her, and he would probably forgive a few burnt
offerings, and she could always co-opt her unmarried
sisters to help out.

I had mixed feelings about leaving my father. I
knew I should have loved him more, but then the
reverse had been true as well. Even now he was
awkward with me, and I guess that to him I was still
an intruder, the one who had weakened my mother
by being born. Of course he didn't know about
Perdita, which was just as well, otherwise there would
have been two of us to blame.

It sounds silly, but I was far more obsessed with
my packing than I was with the thought of the
tremendous step I was taking, leaving all I had ever
known for the great, big outside world. Perhaps it
was nature's own way of concentrating my mind on
trivia to save it from worrying too much on what
the future held—I don't know. All I did know was
that one rucksack was far too small to hold all the
things I wanted to take, and that I packed and

repacked the wretched thing, both mentally and physically, for the next three days.

Sleeping bags we had been told to bring, so that would be rolled on top, together with my waterproof cape. Warm underwear, at least two changes, a jumper or two, my warm sleeveless sheepskin jacket, trews, socks, a change of footgear. Then there were washing things, a towel, brush and comb, soap. Plus the clothing I would be wearing when I left. But what about my sewing and mending kit, a small mirror, knitted cap, gloves? At the moment it was still too warm for these last, but I could stuff them in the pockets of the leather jacket Nan had given me at Christmas.

What about personal possessions? From a child I had collected little mementos and presents and though I loved my wooden doll, collection of shells, copy of *Jane Eyre*, carved animals and other bits and pieces, did I really need them? I decided, regretfully, not. But there was one thing I couldn't leave behind, however much the extra weight might burden me, and that was my precious book of fairy tales.

The last thing to do was to write a farewell note, the sort that could be read by anyone.

"Dear Father and Griselda," I wrote. "This is to tell you I am leaving Deliverance. I am going with Tamerlane, whom I have been in touch with recently. He tells me of another settlement to the south where there are people willing to take us in, and apparently there are other towns farther away which we may travel to. I am sorry not to have told you of my plans, nor anyone else, but I believe you can see why it was essential to keep it secret. Love to you all, and my friends. Prettiance."

I asked Nan whether I should include her in my note, but she told me she was quite capable of making her own farewells, thank you very much. . . .

Suddenly it was Saturday, and before I knew it I was laying out my dress for the dance. It was my favorite, with a green-striped skirt and a green bolero top. Well, this would be the last time I should wear it. A wave of nostalgia temporarily submerged me as I laid out the green slippers and ribbon to go with it. I guessed this was what people felt like just before they left their homes to get married. Sort of, can I have just twenty-four more hours being single? Am I really doing the right thing? Have I forgotten anything? Oh gee: I never said goodbye to so-and-so, I never took a sentimental journey through the place where I was born and grew up. . . . Is it too late to change my mind?

Nan came into the room behind me. "All ready? Good. Your dance doesn't start till eight, does it? Give me plenty of time to go down the other end and watch their faces when they see the notice!"

This notice had been the Herb-Woman's bright idea. She reckoned that if it didn't rain for the Saturday morning market, 'Onest 'Arry and his helpers would get ready the wooden hall in the morning, putting out chairs and tables, decorating with pine and fir branches. They would also set up the tables with flatware, ready for the goodies to be brought in at the last moment. One of the two pianos, now on their last legs, had been put on the improvised platform, ready for "Fingers" Fred Mulloney to pound out the old favorites.

The "Nostalgia Night" festivities were not scheduled to start until eight-thirty, half an hour after our dance began. When the Golden Oldies arrived all dolled up in their best, they would be faced with a barred door—not only barred, but padlocked—and the following notice:

SORRY FOLKS! WE HAVE HAD TO CANCEL TONIGHT'S FESTIVITIES AS THE HALL HAS BEEN DECLARED A FIRE RISK. ALL ENQUIRIES TO MAYOR GROSS.

Underneath was the Mayoral seal, and a fair copy of his name—one of the reasons I had to get out, fast.

That should set the cat among the pigeons! Not only would there be an immediate trek to the Mayor's house, poor Harry would be under siege, and as neither would know anything about it, and Nan would be there to whip up the indignation, it should be something to witness. Nobody likes to be done out of a treat, and our elders were as vociferous as any.

The notice would be put up at the last minute by Loken, after it was dark, and in case anyone thought to open up the hall and proceed willy-nilly, two of his band would have climbed down through the skylights earlier and "rearranged" the furniture so that a concert would be impossible. To add to the confusion, all the tallow lamps in the streets would be extinguished at a given moment, leaving everyone in the dark, both physically and mentally.

As I entered the Church Hall, where "The Ramblers" were already warming up, I suddenly realized what I would miss most about Deliverance: my friends. These I had grown up with; we had played and quarreled, gone to school together, shared good times and bad, worked with in the fields and orchards, ran against, swum against; all the traumas of growing up were there, plus the memories we shared. "Do you remember when . . ." was one of our favorite starters.

They were all there: Rosellen (she must have got a baby-sitter), Alex, Neil, Brian, Alice, Nigel, Bessie, Sandra, Peter, Louise, Jocelyn, Carl, Ellen, Sue, Hans—

And Lally and Sven. He was dressed conservatively in dark-blue trews and a loose grey shirt, but she was a picture, a picture I recognized from a long, long time ago. . . .

My mind flashed back to the little tableaux we used to do for our parents at the end of each school year. At one, I remembered the Firsts had mimed small excerpts from Shakespeare, while the Seconds had recited the verse from the side of the stage. In order to get as many involved as possible there had been excerpts from "Midsummer Night's Dream." Rosellen had been a red-haired Titania, Alex a skinny Bottom; the delicate Alice had been Ariel to my Caliban (all the boys had refused the part) and Sven had been a cardboard-sword-brandishing Henry V, with all the younger boys eager to play his soldiers.

But this was not the picture Lally's appearance had revived. It had been a short excerpt from "Hamlet," where the chorus had recited the madness and death of Ophelia. Our enterprising teachers had dressed her in a long white robe, like a bride, had loosened her hair so that it hung down her back, twining it with flowers of the field: poppies, marguerites, scabious, milkweed, yarrow, daisy and ragged robin, and a wealth of bindweed and ivy. I remembered how she had danced her madness before casting herself into a painted stream, danced as though all sense had gone, except the consciousness of her own wild beauty. . . .

Now, at this dance she wore a similar white dress, and her hair, her glorious fair hair hung down loose to her waist. She wore a wreath like Ophelia, only this time it was of those flowers and berries to be found in late October: Old Man's Beard, hips and haws, a late rose or two, and in her hair leaves of red and gold, yellow and brown. Round her neck she wore a discarded snakeskin, studded with tiny shells. Her cheeks bore a hectic flush, her eyes a giddy sparkle, and although she had lost still more weight since the last time I saw her, she was still the most beautiful girl I had ever seen.

Poor Sven looked a miserable shadow of himself, stumbling through the steps, his face red with embarrassment, but Lally looked every inch the princess from some fairy tale. I danced a couple of dances myself, then sat down at the side near the door, determined not to waste any more energy. I listened to the chimes of the church clock next door: at least another half hour before I could leave. Time had run away before, now it was crawling.

I watched the other dancers; Lally seemed to dance every dance, her color heightened, her energy apparently inexhaustible, dragging Sven around like a toy on a string, like those wooden toys on wheels my little half-siblings played with.

There was an interval, and we were joined by several of those who had expected their Nostalgia Night and had (thank God) been robbed of it by our notice. Predictably they were full of their grievances. "A scandal! . . . No one will take the blame . . . That carpenter fellow didn't know anything, and the Mayor went spare . . ."

I'll bet he did. I wondered whether he'd got his special letter yet, or whether it would be waiting for him at the Town Hall in the morning. . . .

There was a tap on my shoulder, a rustle of skirts. "Hi there, Pretty!" and there was Lally, her wreath slightly askew, her breath smelling of mint. "Long time no see. . . . I just wanted to say 'thank you' for everything: the stories, our playlets, your help when I was so ill. Guess we shan't be seeing each other in the future, so I'd better say goodbye right now," and she bent and kissed my cheek. "Good luck with your Tam!" and she was gone.

How on earth did she know about our plans? My heart beating unpleasantly fast, I looked around to see if anyone could have overheard our conversation. No, it seemed not, but I had to get out of here, even if it wasn't quite time yet. The interval over, someone asked me to dance, but I made an excuse about going to the bathroom, and made my way outside.

The air struck cold on my flushed cheeks, and the full moon rode high in a sky sprinkled with stars. I took a deep breath: now it was all beginning.

I stumbled once or twice on my way to the cottage, because the bright moon made the shadows deep and dark across my path, but I had scarcely reached halfway when I thought I heard footsteps behind me. I nearly died there and then. Oh, God, I was discovered! Mayor Gross had sent his sons after me because he knew I had forged his name—

"Pretty! Pretty! Stop, stop . . ."

Those voices I recognized: no need to be feared of Bill and Ben. But what on earth did they want at this time of night? I didn't remember seeing them at the dance. . . .

I turned and faced them. "What on earth do you want?"

"Beeping Sleauty, she fly away with Beasts. . . ."

"Stop her, or she die. . . ."

"What on earth are you talking about?" I almost stamped in my impatience to be gone. More than anything I didn't want them to know where I was going, so I was perhaps shorter with them than I should have been. "What beasts? And how can she fly?"

They must have got some weird tease all muddled up in their minds, but obviously it had had a bad effect on them, for their faces were covered in what looked like sweat, and they were trembling violently.

I repeated my questions, and added another. "Why come looking for me?"

"You her friend, you tell her stories," said one of them.

"You help her get well again," said the other.

"No more than most, and far less than some. Off you go, boys, and find someone else. Go and find Sven."

"He go, too."

"Well, she'll be all right then. Now, if you'll excuse me? I have an appointment to keep. . . ."

I tried to move away, but to my amazement they grabbed at my arms, so hard it hurt. Glancing up at their faces I could see that what I had taken for sweat was in fact tears and snot, running freely down their cheeks. Perhaps there really was something wrong.

"You come!"

"You come now!"

I thought rapidly. Better waste five minutes now and see if I could make sense of this, rather than run away and have them follow. After all, it was probably some silly Hallowe'en game Lally was playing, getting away with Sven to play private games: trying to conjure up future partners with apple peel and mirrors, or gathering bat's bones and beeswings, bryony and bathwater to boil up into a potion to soak their toes in at midnight—or whatever was the latest harmless Samain trick to summon up the spirits. I tried to explain this to the twins, but they shook their heads. "Go with beasts! Go with beasts!" they chanted.

I took a deep breath. "Tell me—slowly—and one at a time, exactly what is going on. . . ."

It took time and patience, but it appeared that when Lally had said goodbye to me she really had meant that *she* was going away, she wasn't referring to *my* escapade. I found it difficult to believe, but when I remembered her words and her farewell kiss, there was a chill in my stomach. All the time I was trying to work out what could possibly persuade the comfort-loving Lally to abandon everything for the sort of life I was anticipating. Apparently it was only Sven she was leaving with, which made the whole thing even more mysterious. And no, they weren't taking either food or transport.

"But where is she going?" I asked for at least the fifth time.

"New kingdom."

"In stars."

"Beeping Sleauty . . ."

Oh, not *that* again!

I sighed. "And how will she get to the stars?"

"With beasts. Fly."

"Why is she going with beasts? Why would she want to do that?"

"We see them, she don't."

"What do they look like, then?"

But they shook their heads, twisted their hands in agony, and one of them wet his pants: I could see the dark trickle creep down his leg.

"Where is she now?"

"Gone. There . . ."

"And where's there?"

They looked at me in surprise as though I should have known the answer.

"To her flying palace."

"Where beasts wait . . ."

"*Where?*" I was getting desperate.

"Wilderness, of course!"

CHAPTER TWENTY-FIVE

My heart skipped a beat. She wasn't still risking her life and her sanity going to that place, surely?

I began to say something, then broke off when I saw a lantern bobbing down the path towards us. In a moment the Herb-Woman appeared.

"I had a feeling . . ." she began, then saw Bill and Ben. "They have brought bad news?"

Quickly I explained what they had said about Lally. She asked her own questions and received more or less the same answers. She looked at me.

"You have decided?"

I nodded, miserably. "I'll have to go. I don't want to, but . . ." I couldn't explain that, although Lally had never been a close friend, I still felt that my life was wrapped up in hers, ever since those early days when we had acted out the fairy stories. Whatever she was thinking of doing now had something to do with all that, I was certain.

"Well then, go with my blessing. I will send Tamerlane and Perdita after you. Go quickly: we shall wait for your return." She turned away, but suddenly seemed to change her mind. "Here, child: you would have got this sooner or later, but I guess the time is now. It will help to protect you from any harm." She

seemed to fumble for a moment, her lantern swinging
wildly, then grabbed hold of my right hand. For a
moment I felt the heat of the lantern almost scorch
my hand, then she was gone again down the path to
the cottage, and my hand felt pleasantly cool again.

"We go," said one of the twins.

"Now," said the other, and they both grabbed my
hands and hurried up the path back to the village.
I remembered the story of that girl Alice, which
my Nan had told me when I was small, and like
her I felt my feet scarcely touch the ground as we
went on that mad chase. Up into Church Square,
where I could hear the music of the dance, then
down Main Street, where we stumbled a little
because all the street lights were out—another of
Loken's ploys—and right into a group of Golden
Oldies, still bemoaning the loss of their Hallowe'en
entertainment. One of them, Goody Gummer, the
biggest gossip in the village, forced us to a halt, her
arms akimbo.

"Here, you, Pretty! You work in that there Town
Hall. Did you know anything about all this?"

My brain was still working. "It was Mayor Gross's
idea to hold this concert in the Market Hall," I said,
as smoothly as I could for trying to catch my breath.
"He was supported by his sons, but there was
considerable opposition from other members of the
Council, particularly from 'Onest 'Arry, who said this
place could go up like a tinder box. I reckon you've
been saved from a very nasty experience."

" 'Arry says as he don't know nothing about it. . . ."

"Well he would, wouldn't he? Everyone's frightened
of crossing the Mayor. I reckon it's time he took his

retirement, and you voted someone more caring into his place," I added recklessly, conscious that I wasn't going to be around to get blamed for my speech. "Must go now: see you!" And the twins and I were off again, helter-skelter towards the river path, easier to travel in the bright moonlight than the stumbly path across the fields.

The moon was near its zenith, throwing our shadows towards the river bank like broken toys. I ran less easily now, and all at once doubled up as a sudden stitch in my side stabbed like a knife. The boys were at my side in an instant, not waiting for me to recover: they laced their hands into a classic carrying hold and I found myself jogging up the path, my arms across their shoulders. After five minutes I begged down: I was becoming sick with the uneven movement.

Luckily we heard hooves on the path behind us, and a moment or two later Tam and Perdita came in sight, riding two of the village wagon-ponies.

Tam threw himself off, tossed me onto the bare back of his pony and handed me the halter.

"Thought they were worth borrowing: get going! We'll keep up!" And he gave my pony a slap on its rump, sending it off careering after Perdita's, almost throwing me off. After that, though, the going was much quicker, and before long we could see the bulk of the Wilderness looming up on our left, a dark blot on the high pastures, seeming to absorb the brightness of the moon. A great black mouth, I thought, sucking nourishment from the night. . . .

Ahead of me Perdita tugged her pony to a halt and slid from its back, and I did the same, tucking up the halters, pointing our mounts in the right direction for home and giving them a slap that set them trotting back. Tam and the twins came panting up, and we opened the gate to the high pastures.

I thought I could see a flash of white and the glow of a lantern some way ahead, and Tam confirmed it. "It's them all right, and they're not so far ahead. Come on!"

It was more difficult walking in the pasture, although the sheep were grazing away to the west. We kept close to the drystone walling for the first part of the journey, our moon-shadows padding along beside us like a frieze on an uneven surface. We had lost sight of Lally and Sven by now, as they had disappeared behind a curve in the hedge, but at last we reached the tunnel, the only way in, and smelt the pungent odor of crushed grasses and leaves, which meant they had come this way very recently. Until the last moment I had hoped they had gone somewhere else: I didn't want to enter the Wilderness again, ever, not after the last time.

Once through the tunnel we brushed the dirt and leaves from our clothes and listened. At first there was nothing, except an intense stillness: no birds, no insects, no small scurryings in the undergrowth. The place was abandoned of life, but that horrible smell I had noticed last time was still here, and it was worse than ever. Okay, it was autumn, when everything smelt of the quiet decay of leaves and plants as they sank back into the soil to give it next year's sustenance; a pungent, sad, but not unpleasant odor. This, though, was different. It was a dead, acrid smell, with a sharp, metallic undertone, and although the moon still shone bright above us the air had a thick, dusty quality.

Suddenly we heard Lally's voice: she was singing. It was an incongruous choice for that ominous place: "My love is like a red, red rose . . ." Her voice came clear and distinct. She had a very pretty voice, and I remembered she had sung the same ballad at one of our school concerts. But even as we listened she broke off in mid-verse, paused for a moment, and then started again. "Bye, Baby Bunting, Daddy's gone a-hunting . . ." What in the world was the matter with her? Had she and Sven come all this way at night just to sing snatches of song? She stopped and started again. "Early one morning, just as the sun was rising . . ."

Enough was enough. It sounded as if she was having a one-girl party, not a young woman threatened by beasts. We pushed forward along the path, our progress helped by a sort of greenish glow that seemed to come from the center of the wood. The glow increased as we progressed, a sickly emerald in color and we grew more confident, careless of snapped twigs or the clatter of stones.

The singing stopped ("Here we go round the Mulberry bush . . ."), as though she had heard our noisy approach.

"Lally?" I called out. "Lally, are you all right?"

Instantly the light went out, like a lantern doused by a sudden wind, and we came to a sudden halt, momentarily disorientated.

"Lally? Sven? Hey, are you two okay?" My voice cracked, I was suddenly frightened. "Answer me!"

A moment's pause, then the light came on again,

but this time it was a different color. It was a warm, rosy glow, just like the first flush of dawn, and with it came Lally's voice.

"Of course I'm here! Where else could I be? Come on in, you're just in time for the celebrations!" and she appeared on the path ahead of us, her hands held out in welcome. "How nice of you to come, Pretty! You too, Tam: long time no see. . . . I can't exactly remember who I invited, but you're very welcome." She peered over our shoulders. "I'm sure I didn't invite the gypsy girl though, and who's that lurking behind? I might have guessed it! I told you two to stay at home, didn't I? I don't want you here spoiling all the fun. Just go home boys, right now!"

There was something distinctly odd about all this: I felt as though I had suddenly slipped into someone else's dream. I could sense that Tam was as bewildered as I was. Better play along.

"Don't worry about them," I said lightly. "I invited them along to keep us company, and you know they won't be any trouble, will you boys?"

They shook their heads mutely. They were holding hands, I noticed, and their eyes were wide with apprehension.

Lally shrugged, as though she had suddenly lost interest. "Oh well, I suppose they can stay," she said indifferently. She took my left hand—hers was cold and clammy, I noticed, although her face was flushed as though she had a fever—and led me into the glade, the others following.

I stared about me in astonishment. She had mentioned a party, but this looked more like a fancy-dress ball. The turfed glade seemed full of people of all shapes and sizes, young and old, women and children and even some folks disguised as animals. The whole area was bathed in that pinky-silvery glow I had noticed before, and colored lanterns swung from the branches of the trees, splashing kaleidoscopes of red, blue and yellow onto the grass and the guests.

I thought I recognized many of the costumes that thronged the glade. There was a girl in a red cloak with a covered basket on her arm—Red Riding Hood? And surely that was Goldilocks, talking animatedly to a child dressed convincingly as a small, brown bear. The boy with the slanty eyes carrying a lamp must be Aladdin and the girl with one glass slipper, Cinderella. A mermaid was sitting on a rock, combing her hair, and a tabby cat with a pair of red boots was copying her as he smoothed his whiskers with his claws.

Of course! These people were all dressed like the folk in the fairy-tales I had read aloud when we were young, and they were all attired exactly like the illustrations in the book.

Exactly.

So exactly that I saw with a thrill of horror that the wolf with Red Riding Hood was only half an animal, the front half. Just as it had been in the book: the other half of the wolf had been cut off the page; I could recognize the picture quite clearly.

"You must come and meet everyone," said Lally, still holding my hand, but instead of making formal introductions she led me among her "guests," if that's what they were, nodding and smiling to one and all as they bowed in return, just like a bunch of well-trained courtiers. "Aren't they just great?" she said happily. "So nice of them to be giving me this farewell party."

"Farewell?" I echoed, trying to listen and watch at the same time, for at the very edge of my vision it seemed that the guests had less substance, but if I turned my head sharply they were still there, in all their bright book-illustration colors. I wondered if I was hallucinating, or being threatened with my first migraine headache. "Farewell?" I said again "Why, where are you going, Lally? And where is Sven?"

"Sven? Oh, he's somewhere around. Resting, I guess. He's coming too."

"*Where?* Where are you both going? Are you running away?"

"Running? Oh, no, not *running*!" She giggled. "*Flying*, rather!" She giggled again. "Do you realize it will be the first time any of us have flown? I do wish you and Tam could come too, but we've been specially picked and trained for this trip. Perhaps next time. . . ." And she twirled me round with surprising strength till I felt dizzier than ever. "Come on Pretty, live up to your name—don't look so jealous!"

Jealous? Of what, exactly! "Stand still a minute, Lally, and tell me just what's going on!"

"We haven't *time*! Dearest Pretty, questions can wait for another day. I shan't be gone forever, you know. Just a little trip to the moon and back or something like that. . . ." She laughed hysterically. "I'll give you a wave on the way up! They're going to show me all sorts of wonderful things and there's a marvelous reception waiting; after all They said it wouldn't be every day They had the chance to welcome a real Princess!"

What was she *talking* about? Had all those acted-out fairy-tales turned her mind at last?

"But Lally—you aren't a *real* Princess. . . ."

She put her finger to her lips. "Shhh . . . They don't know that. It's a secret! I assure you they truly believe I am a Princess and Sven is a Prince. That's why we're getting all this special treatment: you don't think I'm going to pass all this up just because it isn't *quite* true, do you? And you're to *promise* not to tell, either!" and she gripped my hand tighter than ever, then just as suddenly released it. "It's time! I must go find Sven," and she ran off.

I walked back to Tam and Perdy who were standing where we'd left them.

"What did she say?" asked Tam.

I told them. "She was behaving in a very irrational way," I added. "Where are Bill and Ben?"

"Hiding back down the path. They seem terrified," said Perdy. "I don't blame them: this charade is pretty confusing."

"They keep talking about beasts," said Tam worriedly. " 'B-a-a-ad.' " It was a good imitation.

"Well there's a little bear, a cat in boots and half a wolf over there," I said. "But no beasts, as such."

"How the hell do we know?" Tam waved his hands helplessly at the "guests" who were still circling aimlessly around the glade. "We can't be seeing what we think we're seeing! These are pictures from that blasted book of yours, Pretty! I mean, just look at them! But they can't be real. We're adults now, and what we're seeing must be just a dream, a living illusion."

"Not our dream," said Perdita suddenly. "Hers. They are giving her the dream *she* wants, just to persuade her They mean her no harm, and as part of all this we are being given the same treatment. We weren't meant to be here—remember how the color of the light changed when we arrived?—but now we are here They hope to persuade us too that They are harmless. My adoptive mother—the Herb-Woman—had a dream last night in which she saw Lalage and the twins in terrible danger!"

"The twins? But they aren't scheduled to go anywhere," I said. "Lally warned them away. She said it was Sven she was taking with her—wherever."

"And that's another thing I don't understand," said Tam. "All this talk about flying to the moon: is that going to be a sort of simulated flight, like this must be a simulated ball?"

I shrugged. "How the hell do I know?"

"But you *do*!" cried Perdy. She seized my right wrist. "Have you asked the ring to help?"

"What ring?"

"The ring on your finger; the ring she said would protect you!" She was angry, I could see that, just like she had been that night when I had said the ring the Herb-Woman wore had been like a tingling magnet. I looked down at my right hand, and there, on the middle finger, was the self-same ring, glowing softly. I remembered now how she had fumbled with my hand just before I left with the twins.

"But what does it do?"

"With you wearing it? I don't know. Try it: twist it round your finger, rub it, blow on it! Ask its help to find out what the hell is happening!"

The first thing I tried to do was pull it off, but it wouldn't budge. It twisted round quite easily, but nothing else happened. I glanced back over my shoulder: everything was just as it had been before. Right: I believed I was going to sound like a real twit, but I also believed the Herb-Woman had given me her "magic" ring for a purpose. I stroked it gently.

"Hey, there, ring," I murmured, hoping I was speaking so softly that Tam and Perdy couldn't hear my ridiculous mumblings. I turned away just to make sure. "I believe you can help me. We need to know just what is happening here, and who are these people or beasts or whatever Lally is convinced she's flying away with." Strangely enough, as I started speaking I seemed to gain confidence that what I was doing was just right. "I know you helped your previous wearer, so I hope you will help me, too. She said you were from the horn of a unicorn, and I believe her. . . ." The ring felt warm, hotter than my skin, and now I began to sense a faint throbbing, as though it was constricting the blood-flow in my finger, but it wasn't tight. "And please help us to do what is right. Whatever that is," I added hurriedly.

Then I looked up. "Oh, my *God!*"

They weren't there, they weren't real. Those fairy-tale figures, so substantial a few moments ago, were crumbling before my eyes. They were just a series of fake images, breaking up before my eyes into a series of fragmented pieces: a boot, a sleeve, half a face, struggling to present a whole, but shivering and dissolving before my eyes. I tried to move my feet, but found they were ankle-deep in a filthy sludge. And the smell, that terrible smell, was back again. The only living creatures I could see were a bedraggled Lally, trying to rouse Sven from sleep on the other side of the glade, and Tam and Perdita.

I turned to the others. "Did you see that? I wouldn't have believed it!"

"See what?"

"Tam—didn't you see them all disappear? Look down and tell me what you're standing in. . . ."

"I'm standing on the grass. Everyone's still there."

I turned to Perdy. "You?"

"I know they're not real, I know we're standing in the most disgusting filth, but my eyes tell me something quite different."

"But why can't you see? I don't understand it!" I was almost frantic. The queer greeny-yellow light was back, so was the sickening stench, the "guests" had all disappeared and a disheveled and dirty Lally was slipping and sliding in the mud as she tried to lead a half-asleep Sven towards us—and they couldn't see it!

"You are the only one who can see the truth of what is happening because you wear the ring!" hissed Perdita.

"Well, you wear it then!" I struggled to remove it from my finger, but it was stuck fast. "Damn! It won't budge. . . ."

"Because it belongs to *you* now: you can't remove it unless that is what *it* wants. It's chosen you, and there's nothing you can do about it!"

The ring was getting warmer, throbbing harder, getting quite uncomfortable in fact. It seemed it had a power of its own There was also an unpleasant buzzing and humming in my ears, and a strange clicking noise. How could I get the others to see and hear what I was? Without conscious thought I turned to Perdy and touched the ring to her eyes, nose, ears and mouth, then brushed it across her fingers.

She jumped as if stung, blinked rapidly, then put her fingers to pinch her nose. "Dear Lord!" She clutched my hand. "Do the same to Tam, quick!"

But he had moved away from us, going to help Lally who was still struggling with a sleepy Sven. I tried to run towards him, but stumbled and slipped in the stinking mud so that I almost fell, and Perdita was doing no better. The buzzing and clicking became louder, more urgent, and Lally suddenly dropped Sven's hand, stood for a moment as if listening, then called out. "I'm coming! I'm coming . . ." and stumbled away towards the trees at the back of the glade.

"Where's she going?" I had nearly reached Tam and Sven.

Tam shrugged. "No idea."

"I know," said Sven, seeming to wake up properly at last. "And I must go as well. It must be nearly midnight." And with that he was gone, following Lally far faster than I would have thought possible.

We three looked at each other; now would have been my chance to touch Tam with the ring but, shame to say, I entirely forgot what I was supposed to do. Instead we began to follow the other two, conscious that most of our questions as to what was going on were still unanswered. Perdy and I slutched uncomfortably through the mud, and Tam was still convinced he was walking through grass, judging by the way he was moving his feet.

Lally and Sven had disappeared behind a screen of dead and dying trees, their skeleton branches hung with a greenish moss and browning ivy, and when we reached the spot where they had disappeared a completely alien sight met our eyes.

I rubbed my eyes, I rubbed my ring, but the scene remained the same. In that case what we were seeing was real. . . .

It couldn't be!

A short silvery ramp led up from the forest floor into what looked like a metal chamber, circular, with a low ceiling of the same material. The whole was lit by some kind of subdued lighting, the source of which seemed to be a tube of swirling matter in the center that appeared to reach from floor to ceiling.

There was no sign of Lally or Sven.

We looked at each other again then, slowly and carefully, as though urged against our will by some inner compulsion, we walked up the ramp and into the chamber and the unknown.

CHAPTER TWENTY-SIX

We stood at the top of the ramp. Just inside, but no further. To our left were what seemed like a series of low cages. There was slight movement from one of these and, leaning forward, I suddenly realized what the twins had meant when they kept talking about "pillarcats"; inside those cages were what looked like huge, smooth green caterpillars with wide gashes for mouths but apparently no eyes—

"So that's where they keep the lambs," said Tam. "Pretty little things, aren't they?"

Perdita's eyes were wide with fear. "They're cattle!" she whispered. "Fed on the grass outside, then sucked for their juices. Look!" She pointed to what looked like a series of holes along the side of one of them. "I bet that's what poisoned Lally. . . ." Her hand crept out and clasped mine. "Let's get out at here!"

"Just a minute." I whispered back. "What in hell are those?" I pointed to what looked like a small glass tank of clear liquid, fastened to the wall just above the cages, and divided into small compartments with some things floating inside. "They look like unborn baby rats. . . ."

"Fish . . ." said Tam dreamily. "An aquarium."

"Those are human embryos," said Perdy grimly.

"Or part human, anyway. What have they been *doing* here? Experimenting with Lally and Sven? What is this place, anyway?"

Tam turned and smiled at us. "Why, it's the Sleeping Beauty's palace, that's what it is. Why, what did you think it was?"

I stared at him in amazement, suddenly remembering his mutterings about lambs and fish: he hadn't been trying to make light of things or being sarcastic, he just hadn't seen things as they truly were! Of course: he needed the power of the Ring to see straight. Rapidly I gave him the same treatment I had Perdy earlier: eyes, nose, ears, mouth, hands.

For a moment he stood as if waking from a dream, then as he took in what we had already seen he started back in horror. "I don't believe it!" His face was as white as bleached linen and he was trembling. "We've got to get out of here!"

"We can't without Lally and Sven!" I cried.

"Then where are they?"

"Here we are!" came a happy voice, and Lally and Sven stepped out from the back of the cabin, and stood in front of a large panel of padded and buttoned material, like a large fancy headboard. "How do you like our costumes?" She twirled about, her hair flying about her head. "Different, aren't they"

They certainly were. Both she and Sven were as naked as the day they were born. It was obvious they were as unaware of this as the Emperor with his new clothes: it was also obvious it would be useless to tell them, even though Lally was stroking the folds of her imaginary dress with admiring fingers and Sven was adjusting his nonexistent collar. How could they be so deluded?

But until I got the Ring, hadn't we all been deluded too?

It was time to get both them and ourselves away from all this, but there was one more question.

"What is this place?"

She looked puzzled. "What does it look like! It's my flying palace, of course. All the comforts of home." She giggled. "They've even got our beds ready for us. Look!" And she pointed to one side where stood two of what looked to me exactly as I imagined Snow White's glass coffin. "Anyway, it's time we were off. Our friends say you should stand well clear when we take off so you don't get hurt."

"It's not time to go anywhere but home, Lally," said Tam quietly. "You must forget all this foolishness, and come back with your friends." He entered the chamber and walked purposefully towards the pair and took Lally's arm, apparently unfazed by her nakedness. "You too, Sven. Give us a hand, Pretty, Perdy. . . ."

I flashed a look at Perdita: she nodded, and together we strode over to Lally. Tam relinquished his hold and turned to Sven, as Perdy and I tried to drag the naked girl towards the ramp. For a moment she froze, then became a person possessed, struggling like a madwoman, twisting and turning in our grasp, even trying to fasten her teeth in our hands.

We managed to drag her as far as the top of the ramp as Tam wrestled with the reluctant Sven, then she threw back her head and screamed. Instantly the lights behind us grew brighter and brighter until, glancing back, I was almost blinded.

"Help me!" Lally cried. "They're trying to steal me away! I want to be with you . . . I'm your Princess, remember?"

And then They came.

The Beasts.

Since then time has blessedly blunted the worst of the horror I felt when I first saw those alien creatures, but even now I have only to close my eyes to see them piling out of that central twisting pillar, like a nestful of disturbed ants. Only these weren't ants. They were like nothing I had ever seen or imagined before. I couldn't even compare their makeup with anything I knew.

They could walk upright, but some did, some didn't. They had arms and legs, although they weren't limbs as we knew them. They had heads, but not like any heads I had ever seen, and their language was that strange clicking and hissing I had heard before. I suppose they resembled insects, with their thin, attenuated "limbs," but then their trunks looked semi-transparent, with a sort of coil inside, like a bed-spring, which meant they could grow taller or shrink down as needed, Their "faces" were black, triangular, fringed by what looked like gills, their "eyes" large and slanted upward, their "mouths" a thin grey proboscis, with what looked like a sucker at the end—

Perdy and I were so startled we released our hold on Lally involuntarily and she scrambled back into the chamber, her face innocent of any fear or distaste as she rushed into their embrace.

"I'm here! Take me away, now!"

At the same time it suddenly felt freezing cold, Tam came skidding out of the chamber to land on his face beside us, and I felt the ramp beneath us shudder and start to move upwards. I looked back into the chamber, to see that the creatures had lifted Lally off the ground and were carrying her over to one of the coffin-like beds, lowering her down till she lay comfortably, her hands folded on her chest.

Beside me Tam rose to his feet. "We can't let her go like that!" He tried to move forward, but again came that blast of cold air that seemed to freeze our joints so that we couldn't move.

"Lally! Lally! Sven! For God's sake come out of there before it's too late. . . ." I didn't recognize my own voice. Beside me Perdy was weeping and Tam was praying. Frantically I rubbed my ring: "Please, please, please make them see what danger they're in!"

Under our feet the ramp was still juddering upwards, an inch or two at a time, our weight obviously keeping it from rising faster, and for no reason I remembered the tingly feeling under my feet and the shocks I had had when touching the stones in the circle behind us, now almost drowned in the sea of slutch created by the grazing of those hideous creatures, the "pillarcats" that Bill and Ben had seen so clearly.

Was it the twins' innocence that had made them see things so clearly all this time? If so, it could only be their devotion that had kept them following Lally's delusion all these years, braving the terrible creatures that had surrounded her just to be near her. They say that love is blind: in their case they had seen only too clearly.

Like Perdy I was now weeping, like Tam I was praying, for through my tears I could see a kind of gossamer thread was creeping up from Lally's feet to bind her in an obscene cocoon, and that the creatures had hold of Sven and were leading him towards the other coffin. I grabbed Tam by one hand, Perdita by the other, and one last time we tried to rush the creatures and enter the chamber, and once more we were repelled by that chill blast. Backing off we found the ramp was almost level and we fell to our knees, still holding hands. I called out once more, the ring on my finger almost burning through the skin.

"Lally! Sven! Open your eyes! See what's really there! Tell them who you really are. . . ."

Suddenly I saw Lally's eyes open; she tried to sit up, her eyes full of bewilderment. "Where am I?" One of the creatures bent down to restrain her. Her eyes showed a growing terror and recognition. She stretched out her hand to Sven. "Help me!" I saw that he, too, now saw things as they really were. He struggled free of his captors and stood for a moment irresolute. Lally called out to him again. "If you love me . . ."

He took one step towards her and then stopped, as his captors closed in again. I shall never forget the anguish on his face as he took one last look at her beseeching face then turned away, bursting through the creatures trying to restrain him and rushing blindly down the ramp past us, his arms flailing as though he was trying to brush away a crowd of wasps, his face streaming with tears.

"No, no, *no*! I can't! Forgive me!" He stumbled

off the end of the ramp, fell to his knees, regained his bare feet, and pounded away naked through the forest, still calling out wildly. As his cries died away I looked back at Lally, and it seemed as though at last she saw us too, for she made one last effort to tear herself out of the gossamer mesh that was gradually immobilizing her.

"Tam! Pretty! Please take me away from here. . . ." She was hysterical, and my guts twisted with terror and pity as I realized there was nothing we could do, that we were condemned to watch her agony as she was taken from us. "Tam! Pretty! Bill! Ben!" she called out our names once more, half-strangled now by her restraints.

But somebody heard.

Just as the throbbing and vibration increased, the ramp started to rise once more and Lally screamed one last, terrified scream that sliced through my heart like a knife, there was a sudden thump at the far end of the ramp and two figures came rushing up behind us, hand in hand, yelling like banshees and literally trampling over us as they burst through whatever barrier had held us back.

In a moment Bill and Ben had reached Lally and were trying to lift her from her coffin, at the same time fighting off the creatures that surrounded her. Others of the beasts were clustered round what had looked like a padded headboard but in fact must have been an instrument panel, for at their touches the light increased and there was a blast of heat from beneath the ramp making it impossible to stay where we were without cooking. One by one we dropped over the side of the ramp to the ground beneath;

my last desperate glance showed me that Lally had
her eyes closed, cushioned between the battling twins,
whose bellows of rage rose above the whirring,
clicking and humming in the machine.

I hope by then she was unconscious, I hope she
never knew what happened next. I hope she saw the
twins coming to her rescue, believed she was safe
and fainted with relief. I shall never cease hoping it
was so.

As Tam, Perdy and I scrambled to our feet we saw
the ramp snap shut against the hull of what we now
recognized must be some sort of spaceship. Now
we could hear nothing except that humming, which
increased in volume and was now accompanied by
a high-pitched whine, like that of a mosquito just
before it stings, but much, much louder.

I was standing there, stunned by what had
happened, deafened by the noise, when Tam
suddenly grabbed my arm and started to drag me
away, Perdy at his side. He put his mouth to my
ear.

"Taking off . . . not safe!" was all I could make out,
but I allowed him to half lead, half pull me away,
but we were only about fifty yards away when there
was a roar behind us and a blast of hot air that had
us tumbling head over heels like chaff. As I rolled
across the ground I tried to scrabble with hands and
toes to find something to hang onto, and at last,
bruised and shaken, I ended up with a thump against
a hard object that knocked the breath from my body.
The blast of air was still charging across the space
between us and the machine, so I wrapped my arms
around what I discovered was one of the stones that

stood in a ring about the glade where we had played
as children. I saw that Tam and Perdy were safe,
sheltering also as I was.

I was trembling with frustration, fear and anger
as we watched the alien craft take off from our world
for the unknown. At first it seemed it was rising
unaided, then I saw its initial rise was from three
legs that increased telescopically until the craft was
some twenty feet in the air. There was another blast
of power that singed my hair and then the legs
withdrew into the main body, and the craft hung
suspended for a moment by its own power.

The moon shone down, bright and impassive, and
once the craft was clear of the few stunted trees that
had surrounded it, I could see it looked like a silvery,
inverted soup-bowl, with a girdle of winking lights,
which now started to spin around until they blurred
into one streaming band. As I watched, the craft
started to rise still further, till it loomed over us like
some threatening symmetrical cloud. And the worst
of it was, it was carrying away our friends, a beautiful
girl with no more sense than the reflection in her
mirror, and two good-hearted innocents whose love
was stronger than their fear—

It wasn't fair, it wasn't fair! In my rage I slammed
my fist again and again into the stone I was sheltering
behind, only finding later that I had drawn blood that
had trickled onto the stone. All at once I remembered
what night it was: Hallowe'en, All Saints Eve, Samain:
the night when all God-fearing folk in the past had
stayed within doors, closing all doors and windows
and building great fires in the home-hearths to keep
out the evil spirits that roamed after midnight—

Damn them all to hell and back! What right had these aliens to steal what rightly belonged back here on earth? I thumped the stone still harder and yelled out: "Why doesn't somebody, something *do* anything! You can't let them get away with desecrating this place and stealing what doesn't belong to them! In the name of all the gods, bring them *back*. . . ."

There was a sudden silence; the machine hanging above seemed to have cut back on its engines and was hovering, neither gaining height nor losing it, and faintly in the distance I heard an unfamiliar sound: the church bells in the village were ringing an alarm. This had happened only once in my lifetime, when wolves had got among the sheep, but I had never forgotten the discordant clamor that set one's teeth on edge. Why were they ringing now? There hadn't been time for the naked Sven to reach the village and raise the alarm: probably it was Loken's scheme for torching the old wooden Market Hall to get rid of the potential danger once and for all. If so they would all be scurrying around like ants, their only weapons buckets and the nearest water, in this case the swimming pool.

There was a sudden burst of sound from the machine above us and it started to edge higher and higher. At the same time I felt the ground beneath me start to shake and tremble, as if the craft was sending great waves of energy back down to us— but this was originating from beneath our feet. I had never experienced an earth tremor before, but this must be it. I hung onto the stone for grim life as the shaking and rocking continued, getting more violent by the moment.

Then suddenly I felt a great blow to my body and I was hurled back from the shelter of the stone to land with a crash at the fringes of the forest, Tam and Perdy close by. As we struggled to our feet the ground beneath us was moving like an underground terrier shaking itself free of a soaking, and we were forced to hang onto the nearest tree to stay upright. There was another roar of sound from the craft above us and it rose several feet higher, swaying slightly from side to side as though seeking to dodge an obstruction.

Then something happened that I still find difficult to believe.

The stones in the circle suddenly reared up and shook themselves free of the mud and slime they had lain in and thrust upwards towards the space craft like snapping teeth. And they started to sing! Not music as we would know it, but a dissonant creaking and groaning, as though they were intoning a sort of war-music of their own. For some reason this terrified me more than anything that had gone before.

I knew that what we were witnessing was a battle between two great Powers that we should probably never see the like of again. Not only were they each great in their own way, they were also devoid of emotion as we humans knew it. It was just one Power against another, as mechanical and unfeeling as two magnets playing for a handful of iron filings.

No. I was wrong. There was emotion here: from the ground beneath arose a terrible anger, an anger against the violation of Their sacred place, a desire to overcome and destroy the invader.

Around us the trees were tossed back and forth as if by a subterranean tempest, and even as I watched the earth spewed up shrubs and saplings as if the roots had no longer anything firm to cling to. Against this we three were as powerless and puny as ants in a sandstorm; gradually we crept together till we were concentrated in a cowering heap. The air was thick with earth, twigs, small stones, whirling and twirling around us.

Above us the alien craft was yawing from side to side in increasing desperation, trying to escape the relentless pull from below, but it was no use. It made one last thrust towards freedom and for a moment I thought it had made it as it gained increased height, but then the maelstrom of Power around us grew until we were tossed into the air ourselves like broken toys, and we saw the spacecraft begin a descending spiral towards the earth below. Whether the next thing that happened was triggered in the machine itself or the result of the Powers below, we will never know, but suddenly there was a tremendous explosion, leaving all three of us temporarily deaf as the spaceship imploded. It just disappeared, folding in upon itself like a suddenly clenched fist. Slivers of fire streamed away into the darkness beside us, setting fire to trees and shrubs and grass.

I stood there stunned, stricken, as the pieces of the craft that were left tumbled into the circle formed by the stones. Then the earth opened up and swallowed them up as though they had never been, opening up like a great maw to suck the shattered remains deep into the earth, with the sound of a giant baby sucking on an empty bottle. . . .

The tears were streaming down my face as the others pulled me away. The whole of the Wilderness was on fire now, and sparks caught at our clothing and smoke choked us as we raced for the tunnel and safety. Beside us a tree suddenly plumed in flame and tendrils of fire fought to outrace us through the sere grasses. We were only just in time: as we squeezed through the tunnel the hedge flared up on either side of us.

As we raced down through the pastures the sky was lit before and behind: down below the old Market Hall was blazing, behind the Wilderness was consuming itself in a fury-driven inferno.

Then the heavens opened and it started to rain like I'd never known. We saw the blaze in the village quickly extinguished, but the forest behind us continued to burn as though fueled by the water, the flames shooting ever higher and higher. . . .

They were waiting for us with towels, soup, sympathy, two loaded ponies and Loken and his people. Half an hour after we arrived we were ready to go again, rain or no.

I turned to Nan. "Why aren't you ready?"

"Because I'm not coming, child. No, don't argue. The time for escape was a long time ago. Since then I've become accustomed to this way of life. My place is here, with she you call the Herb-Woman. I shall keep her company now that she no longer has Perdita. Together we shall help to make Deliverance a better place, now that I believe that we have persuaded Mayor Gross to give up his post. After all, I was here when it all started, and it is up to me to see it through.

No, don't say anything: my mind is made up. Off you go, and God be with you all!"

More tears, but just as we were starting off, Perdita and I riding on the already loaded ponies, the Herb-Woman came running after us, a covered basket in her hands, which she thrust into my lap.

"Here, something I promised you many moons ago. . . ." and she disappeared into the darkness.

Tentatively I lifted the lid a little way. Inside the basket was curled a small, perfectly black kitten. Yellowy brown eyes looked up at me.

"Hi, there!" It said, perfectly clearly. "My name's Bungee. When do we eat?"

EPILOGUE

I have been here at Lakeside for three years. I teach language and calligraphy in the junior school, and have a small adobe house—living room, bedroom, bathroom and kitchenette—on the outskirts of town.

From the living room there is a view of the Blue Mountains to the east, from the bedroom just the seemingly endless prairie. In the summer it is a sea of wheat, in the winter they bring up the horses and cattle to graze on the stubble.

The town itself is still growing: to date there are about six or seven thousand inhabitants, of all races, colors and creeds, one of the things I found difficult to come to terms with at first. When one has been brought up to one creed, one color and a belief in ethnic purity, it takes a bit of getting used to seeing all the black, brown and yellow faces in class and streets and to pass not only a tiny mosque but also a synagogue on the way home. But I'm learning, and they are all friendly.

Another thing to adjust to was the diet. Brought up as I was with corn providing the only flour, I still find wheat insipid. However it makes beautiful meat pies, and I love the beef, a Christmas treat in Deliverance, a daily standard here. I do miss goat's milk and cheese, and they eat far less fruit than we did, as the ground and the weather—much hotter in summer, much colder in winter—doesn't favor the orchards I was used to. No cider, of course, only wine imported from further south. It's expensive— they have the same kind of token system we did— but imports and exports are on a barter basis. They export cattle, hides and horses, import cottons, salt, rice and metals. The thing I missed most at first was sugar: the only sweetener they had came from hives, and was strictly rationed, much as our salt used to be.

The journey here was a trip I prefer to forget. Once the weather broke it rained all the time, the river paths were flooded and we had to detour, and a journey that should have taken a week took twice that. Many times I wished myself back in front of the kitchen fire or tucked up snug in bed with the rain outside, not in. Even with all Loken's expertise we couldn't keep a fire going longer than for a quick fry-up, and indeed we were running short of food by the time we reached the town.

We were immediately put into the Rest-House, a sort of rendezvous for all travelers, where we were dried out, fed and rested. Tam had been this way before of course, and he intended to travel farther south with Loken to over-winter, but once they learnt that Perdita and I intended to stay we were housed where I live now. The furniture was spartan: two beds and a curtained recess for clothes in the bedroom, the bare minimum of pans, crockery and cutlery, a small table with two stools and a couple of fireside chairs for the living room. By the time we had used a few tokens we had the materials for a large and small rag-rug and enough feathers for a couple of thick duvets. Perdita gathered rushes for mats and shopping bags.

I was immediately put to work in school, at first as a substitute teacher but after Christmas full-time, and Perdy sold her herbs and simples in the market, soon finding out they were more in demand for drawer-sweeteners and flavorings rather than cures, so by spring she was ready to go south as well. During the winter we had spent many hours on the rug in front of the fire, just catching up on all we had missed together as kids.

I couldn't blame her for going, and missed her sorely at first, but we kept in touch by letter, brought in by the frequent traders. At the moment she is doing well in a small fishing village by the sea and sees Loken more often as the seasons pass. One night she told me why she was so upset that the Herb-Woman had given me the ring: she believed it might shorten her life, but judging by Nan's letters they are both thriving. Until recently I only heard from them twice a year, but now that Rosellen's brother Brian has had the enterprise to open up a regular trade between Deliverance and Lakeside, I only have to wait a month or two for news. Brian heard from my letters how short we were of sweeteners, so he loaded up a couple of ponies with sugar, knitted goods and a barrel of cider and got Loken to guide him here. His goods were an instant success, and he returned with salt, salted beef and cotton drawers, and firm orders for more from Deliverance. Since that time the trading has been regular, to the benefit of all, and there is even talk of a common currency.

And why is all this exchange of goods, ideas, and even people possible?

Because the rule of Mayor Gross is over. The letter I had Tam write for me, signed "Anonymous," told him that an intruder had been seen in the Town Hall on the night they had discussed their plans for Nostalgia Night, and that unless he resigned immediately, all would be revealed. . . . And it worked! I would have signed it, but I didn't want to get any of my family into trouble. As it is, my father is now on the Council, and Harry Ross the carpenter is the new Mayor. They are building a new village to the south, on the old camping site, mainly to supply fodder and grow more vegetables, plus the dyeing and treating of wool. The place is called—what else?—New Deliverance.

They say that Gross has gone quietly mad. He is never seen in public, and rumor has it that he plays all day with boxes of bricks. Generally people are sympathetic, because of course they don't know the truth behind it all. They blame his "indisposition" on the traumatic events of that fatal Hallowe'en night: the burning of the Market Hall, the naked Sven's breakdown (nobody believed his story about the spaceship, because no one had had the time to look up and see it and of course all the remains were swallowed up), a picnic gone wrong, and the tragic deaths of Lally and the twins, trying to put out a fire in the Wilderness which left only the Standing Stones.

That is what is generally believed. Once Sven had recovered from his coma he remembered nothing, but his grief for Lalage has not stopped him from getting betrothed to a nice, quiet, sensible girl who designs knitting patterns. As for my other friends, Rosellen is moving here with Alex next spring, once the youngest (number four) is ready to travel, and Neil and Alice are already at New Deliverance. It seems that Perdy's palm-reading is all coming true, although Alex hasn't written his book yet, and I have yet to become the Journeyer she promised.

But I will be, I'm determined on that. Once Alex comes he can have my school job, and I shall ask Tam to take me with him on his next journey south, pointing out that he once promised to take me to see the sea. We only see each other twice a year, and gradually the different life he leads is taking him away from me. He is still warm, considerate, affectionate, but now I want more than that. The passing of the years have only made me surer how much I need him, and I believe the only way to make him realize that he needs me too—and he does: sometimes women see these things more clearly— is to share his travels with him.

In the meantime, even without Tam and Perdy, I'm not exactly lonely. No way! Perhaps the greatest gift of the Ring I now wear is to allow me to communicate with the animal world, and *my* animal world is filled with just one object: Bungee.

He's a full-grown black tom now, is the greatest companion anyone could ask for and has only three things on his mind: food, sleep and sex, but I come a good fourth. He has taught me to read some of his body language, interpret his "talk" and even thought-read. It's much easier than you would think.

I prepare something special for his supper, send out a clear "Where-are-you? It's-all-ready . . ." all the time looking at his dish, and after a moment will come *his* picture: a nearby street from cat's eye view as he plods home.

Here he is now. "Hi there! What's to eat, then?"

The events of that terrible night of Hallowe'en will be with me always, but mercifully my nightmares are decreasing. I miss Nan very much, and all that was good of Deliverance. I realize, too, just how many lessons I have learned, especially about Power. Not only the power that old megalomaniac imposed on us with his dream village, nor the high-tech mechanical powers of the aliens, not even the hidden powers that this earth still holds in its ancient stones and customs, but one more important than all the rest: the power of love.

The love that made a mother give up a baby so that it would survive, the love of a grandmother for her granddaughter and vice versa, the love and gratitude that turned a lazy and feckless Griselda into a good wife and mother, and, most of all, the love and devotion that turned two simple-minded young men into willing sacrifices to the image of their Princess. . . .

I have buried the book of fairy tales. After what happened I found I never wanted to turn the pages again. I wrapped it safe from decay and went out one morning with Bungee to find a spot where it would be safe until perhaps someone who didn't know its sad history would find and read it with the delight I once did, without the same associations it now has for me.

I have told Bungee what I intend to do, and he says he's quite happy to travel too. By the way, he lives up to his name, the name the Herb-Woman gave him: he has the most prodigious leap in the world, a fact I soon found out after putting some food "safely" on the highest shelf. He is also a thief, and I love him. That's another kind of love.

But there is another. With the spring will come a cessation to the whining wind that sears the winter prairie; the air will soften, the flowers will bloom, the young cattle will fill the air with their calls. I will cast off the thick duvet and woolen wear, the birds will sing all day in my tiny garden and the sun will rise earlier and earlier. . . .

And with the spring will come Tam.

My love.